An ALA Best Fiction for Young Adults

Bram Stoker Award short list

Winner of the Cybils Award,
Young Adult Fantasy & Science Fiction category

★ "In turns mythic and down-to-earth, this intense novel combines adventure and philosophy to tell a truly memorable zombie story, one that forces readers to consider them not just as flesh-eating monsters or things to be splattered, but as people."
—*PUBLISHERS WEEKLY*, STARRED REVIEW

"This is anything but another zombie novel."—CHARLAINE HARRIS, AUTHOR OF THE SOOKIE STACKHOUSE SOUTHERN VAMPIRE SERIES

"Thrilling, enticing, and surprisingly touching. *Rot & Ruin* will grip readers from beginning to end, and make them question who the real monsters are. It had me hooked from page one."
—HEATHER BREWER, AUTHOR OF
THE CHRONICLES OF VLADIMIR TOD SERIES

"This is a romping, stomping adventure. And while most zombie novels are all about the brains, this one has a heart as well. . . . Anyone with a pulse will enjoy this novel, and anyone with a brain will find plenty of food for thought inside."
—MICHAEL NORTHROP, AUTHOR OF *GENTLEMEN*

"George Romero meets *The Catcher in the Rye* in this poignant and moving coming of age novel set during zombie times."
—NANCY HOLDER, *NEW YORK TIMES* BESTSELLING AUTHOR OF
THE WICKED SERIES AND *POSSESSIONS*

"This is no ordinary zombie novel. Maberry has given it a soul in the form of two brothers who captured my heart from the first page and refused to let go."
—MARIA V. SNYDER,
NEW YORK TIMES BESTSELLING AUTHOR OF *INSIDE OUT*

Praise for

Rot & Ruin

"This is a romping, stomping adventure. And while most zombie novels are all about the brains, this one has a heart as well. With the dead prowling all around, fifteen-year-old Benny Imura learns the bittersweet lessons of life, love, and family in the great Rot and Ruin. Anyone with a pulse will enjoy this novel, and anyone with a brain will find plenty of food for thought inside."
—MICHAEL NORTHROP, AUTHOR OF *GENTLEMEN*

"George Romero meets *The Catcher in the Rye* in this poignant and moving coming-of-age novel set during zombie times. I welled up at the end, then smiled through my tears when I realized there was going to be a sequel. Bravo, Jonathan Maberry. Can't wait to read more."
—NANCY HOLDER, *NEW YORK TIMES* BESTSELLING AUTHOR OF THE WICKED SERIES AND *POSSESSIONS*

"An action-packed, thought-provoking look at life—and death—as readers determine the true enemy."
—*KIRKUS REVIEWS*

Also by Jonathan Maberry

Dust & Decay

ROT & RUIN

ROT &

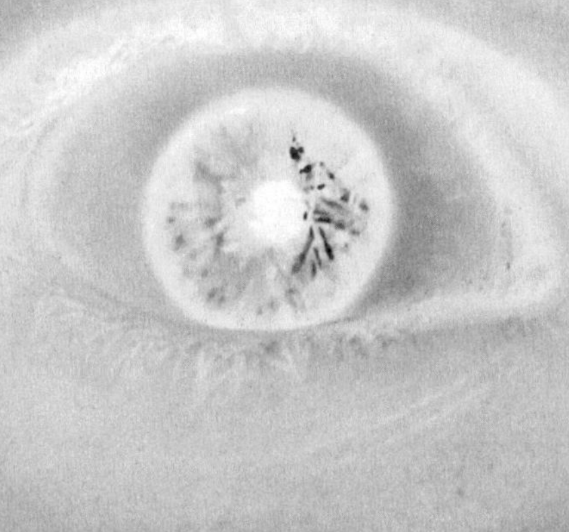

RUIN

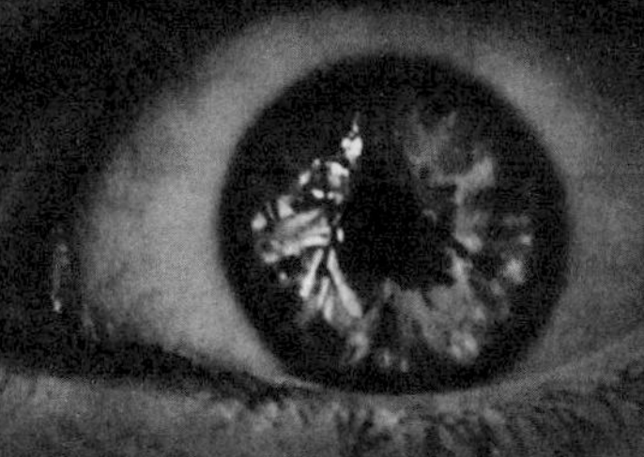

Jonathan Maberry

SIMON & SCHUSTER BFYR
NEW YORK LONDON TORONTO SYDNEY

ACKNOWLEDGMENTS

Special thanks to some real-world people who were willing to enter the world of Benny and Tom Imura. I believe that if the world ends, you'll still be there. My agents, Sara Crowe and Harvey Klinger; David Gale and Navah Wolfe at Simon & Schuster; Nancy Keim-Comley, Tiffany Schmidt, Greg Schauer, Rob and Andrea Sacchetto, Randy and Fran Kirsch, Jason Miller, Sam West-Mensch, Keith Strunk, Charlie and Gina Miller, Arthur Mensch; and the Philly Liars Club: Gregory Frost, Don Lafferty, L. A. Banks, Jon McGoran, Solomon Jones, Ed Pettit, Merry Jones, Maria Lambra, Sara Shepherd, Kelly Simmons, Keith Strunk, and Dennis Tafoya.

Excerpt from *The Onion Girl* by Charles De Lint used by permission of the author.

Richard Pryor's comment used by permission of Jennifer Lee Pryor.

SIMON & SCHUSTER BFYR

An imprint of Simon & Schuster Children's Publishing Division
1230 Avenue of the Americas, New York, New York 10020

Also available in a SIMON & SCHUSTER BFYR hardcover edition
Book design by Laurent Linn
Zombie Card art by Rob Sacchetto
The text for this book is set in Augustal.
Manufactured in the United States of America
First SIMON & SCHUSTER BFYR paperback edition May 2011
2 4 6 8 10 9 7 5 3 1
The Library of Congress has cataloged the hardcover edition as follows:
Maberry, Jonathan.
Rot & Ruin / Jonathan Maberry. — 1st ed.
p. cm.
Summary: In a post-apocalyptic world where fences and border patrols guard the few people left from the zombies that have overtaken civilization, fifteen-year-old Benny Imura is finally convinced that he must follow in his older brother's footsteps and become a bounty hunter.
ISBN 978-1-4424-0232-4 (hardcover)
[1. Zombies—Fiction. 2. Survival—Fiction. 3. Bounty hunters—Fiction. 4. Brothers—Fiction.] I. Title. II. Title: Rot and Ruin.
PZ7.M11164Ro 2010 [Fic]—dc22 2009046041
ISBN 978-1-4424-0233-1 (pbk)
ISBN 978-1-4424-0234-8 (eBook)

For the young writers in my Experimental Writing for Teens class: Rachel Tafoya, Clint Johnston, Brandon Strauss, Brianna Whiteman, Jessica Price, Tara Tosten, Jennifer Carr, Kellie Hollingsworth, Nathanial Gage, Maggie Brennan, Kris Dugas, Evan Stahl, and Jackson Toone. You always amaze and inspire me.

And, as always, for Sara Jo.

PART ONE
Family Business

"I don't know what's waiting for us when we die—
something better, something worse.
I only know I'm not ready to find out yet."

—Charles De Lint, *The Onion Girl*

1

Benny Imura couldn't hold a job, so he took to killing.

It was the family business. He barely liked his family—and by family he meant his older brother, Tom—and he definitely didn't like the idea of "business." Or work. The only part of the deal that sounded like it might be fun was the actual killing.

He'd never done it before. Sure, he'd gone through a hundred simulations in gym class and in the Scouts, but they never let kids do any real killing. Not before they hit fifteen.

"Why not?" he asked his Scoutmaster, a fat guy named Feeney who used to be a TV weatherman back in the day. Benny was eleven at the time and obsessed with zombie hunting. "How come you don't let us whack some real zoms?"

"Because killing's the sort of thing you should learn from your folks," said Feeney.

"I don't have any folks," Benny countered. "My mom and dad died on First Night."

"Ouch. Sorry, Benny—I forgot. Point is, you *got* family of some kind, right?"

"I guess. I got 'I'm Mr. Freaking Perfect Tom Imura' for a brother, and I don't want to learn *anything* from him."

Feeney had stared at him. "Wow. I didn't know you were

related to him. He's your brother, huh? Well, there's your answer, kid. Nobody better to teach you the art of killing than a professional killer like Tom Imura." Feeney paused and licked his lips nervously. "I guess being his brother and all, you've seen him take down a lot of zoms."

"No," Benny said with huge annoyance. "He never lets me watch."

"Really? That's odd. Well, ask him when you turn thirteen."

Benny had asked on his thirteenth birthday, and Tom had said no. Again. It wasn't a discussion. Just "No."

That was more than two years ago, and now Benny was six weeks past his fifteenth birthday. He had four more weeks grace to find a paying job before town ordinance cut his rations by half. Benny hated being in that position, and if one more person gave him the "fifteen and free" speech, he was going to scream. He hated that as much as when people saw someone doing hard work and they said crap like, "Holy smokes, he's going at that like he's fifteen and out of food."

Like it was something to be happy about. Something to be proud of. Working your butt off for the rest of your life. Benny didn't see where the fun was in that. Okay, maybe it was marginally okay because it meant only half days of school from then on, but it still sucked.

His buddy Lou Chong said it was a sign of the growing cultural oppression that was driving postapocalyptic humanity toward acceptance of a new slave state. Benny had no freaking idea what Chong meant or if there was even meaning in anything he said. But he nodded agreement because the look on Chong's face always made it seem like he knew exactly what was what.

At home, before he even finished eating his dessert, Tom had said, "If I want to talk about you joining the family business, are you going to chew my head off? Again?"

Benny stared venomous death at Tom and said, very clearly and distinctly, "I. Don't. Want. To. Work. In. The. Family. Business."

"I'll take that as a 'no,' then."

"Don't you think it's a little late now to try and get me all excited about it? I asked you a zillion times to—"

"You asked me to take you out on kills."

"Right! And every time I did you—"

Tom cut him off. "There's a lot more to what I do, Benny."

"Yeah, there probably is, and maybe I would have thought the rest was something I could deal with, but you never let me see the cool stuff."

"There's nothing 'cool' about killing," Tom said sharply.

"There is when you're talking about killing zoms!" Benny fired back.

That stalled the conversation. Tom stalked out of the room and banged around the kitchen for a while, and Benny threw himself down on the couch.

Tom and Benny never talked about zombies. They had every reason to, but they never did. Benny couldn't understand it. He hated zoms. Everyone hated them, though with Benny it was a white-hot consuming hatred that went back to his very first memory. Because it *was* his first memory—a nightmare image that was there every night when he closed his eyes. It was an image that was seared into him, even though it was something he had seen as a tiny child.

Dad and Mom.

Mom screaming, running toward Tom, shoving a squirming Benny—all of eighteen months—into Tom's arms. Screaming and screaming. Telling him to run.

While the *thing* that had been Dad pushed its way through the bedroom door that Mom had tried to block with a chair and lamps and anything else she could find.

Benny remembered Mom screaming words, but the memory was so old and he had been so young that he didn't remember what any of them were. Maybe there were no words. Maybe it was just her screaming.

Benny remembered the wet heat on his face as Tom's tears fell on him as they climbed out of the bedroom window. They had lived in a ranch-style house. One story. The window emptied out into a yard that was pulsing with red and blue police lights. There were more shouts and screams. The neighbors. The cops. Maybe the army. Thinking back, Benny figured it was probably the army. And the constant popping of gunfire, near and far away.

But of all of it, Benny remembered a single last image. As Tom clutched him to his chest, Benny looked over his brother's shoulder at the bedroom window. Mom leaned out of the window, screaming at them as Dad's pale hands reached out of the shadows of the room and dragged her back out of sight.

That was Benny's oldest memory. If there had been older memories, then that image had burned them away. Because he had been so young the whole thing was little more than a collage of pictures and noises, but over the years Benny had burned his brain to reclaim each fragment, to assign meaning and sense to every scrap of what he could recall. Benny remembered the hammering sound vibrating against his chest that was Tom's panicked heartbeat, and the long wail that was his own inarticulate cry for his mom and his dad.

He hated Tom for running away. He hated that Tom hadn't stayed and helped Mom. He hated what their dad had become on that First Night all those years ago. Just as he hated what Dad had turned Mom into.

In his mind they were no longer Mom and Dad. They were the *things* that had killed them. Zoms. And he hated them with an intensity that made the sun feel cold and small.

"Dude, what is it with you and zoms?" Chong once asked him. "You act like the zoms have a personal grudge against you."

"What, I'm supposed to have fuzzy bunny feelings for them?" Benny had snapped back.

"No," Chong had conceded, "but a little perspective would be nice. I mean . . . everybody hates zoms."

"You don't."

Chong had shrugged his bony shoulders and his dark eyes had darted away. "Everybody hates zoms."

The way Benny saw it, when your first memory was of zombies killing your parents, then you had a license to hate them as much as you wanted. He tried to explain that to Chong, but his friend wouldn't be drawn back into the conversation.

A few years ago, when Benny found out that Tom was a zombie hunter, he hadn't been proud of his brother. As far as he was concerned, if Tom really had what it took to be a zombie hunter, he'd have had the guts to help Mom. Instead, Tom had run away and left Mom to die. To become one of *them*.

Tom came back into the living room, looked at the

remains of the dessert on the table, then looked at Benny on the couch.

"The offer still stands," he said. "If you want to do what I do, then I'll take you on as an apprentice. I'll sign the papers so you can still get full rations."

Benny gave him a long, withering stare.

"I'd rather be eaten by zoms than have you as my boss," Benny said.

Tom sighed, turned, and trudged upstairs. After that they didn't talk to each other for days.

2

The following weekend Benny and Chong had picked up the Saturday edition of the *Town Pump*, because it had the biggest help wanted section. All of the easy jobs, like working in stores, had been long-since snapped up. They didn't want to work on the farms, because that meant getting up every morning at the crack of "no way, José." Besides, it meant dropping out of school completely. They didn't love school, but it wasn't too bad, and school had softball, free lunches, and girls. The ideal fix was a part-time job that paid pretty good and got the ration board off their backs, so over the next several weeks, they applied for anything that sounded easy.

Benny and Chong clipped out a bunch of want ads and tackled them one at a time, having first categorized them by "most possible money," "coolness," and "I don't know what it is, but it sounds okay." They passed on anything that sounded bad right from the get-go.

The first on their list was for a locksmith apprentice.

That sounded okay, but it turned out to be humping a couple of heavy toolboxes from house to house at the crack of frigging dawn while an old German guy who could barely speak English repaired fence locks and installed dial combinations on both sides of bedroom doors, as well as installing bars and wire grilles.

It was kind of funny watching the old guy explain to his customers how to use the combination locks. Benny and Chong began making bets on how many times per conversation a customer would say "what," "could you repeat that," or "beg pardon."

The work was important, though. Everyone had to lock themselves in their rooms at night and then use a combination to get out. Or a key; some people still locked with keys. That way, if they died in their sleep and reanimated as a zom, they wouldn't be able to get out of the room and attack the rest of the family. There had been whole settlements wiped out because someone's grandfather popped off in the middle of the night and then started chowing down on the kids and grandkids.

"I don't get this," Benny confided to Chong when they were alone for a minute. "Zoms can't work a combination lock any more than they can turn a doorknob. They can't work keys, either. Why do people even *buy* this stuff?"

Chong shrugged. "My dad says that locks are traditional. People understand that locked doors keep bad things out, so people want locks for their doors."

"That's stupid. Closed doors will keep zoms out. Zoms are brain-dead. Hamsters are smarter."

Chong spread his hands in a "hey, that's people for you" gesture.

The German guy installed double-sided locks, so that the door could be opened from the other side in a real, nonzombie emergency; or if the town security guys had to come in and do a cleanup on a new zom.

Somehow, Benny and Chong had gotten it into their heads that locksmiths got to see this stuff, but the old guy said that he hadn't ever seen a single living dead that was in any way connected to his job. Boring.

To make it worse, the German guy paid them a little more than pocket lint and said that it would take three years to learn the actual trade. That meant that Benny wouldn't even pick up a screwdriver for six months and wouldn't do anything but carry stuff for a year. Screw that.

"I thought you didn't want to actually work," said Chong as they walked away from the German with no intention of returning in the morning.

"I don't. But I don't want to be bored out of my freaking mind either."

Next on their list was for a fence tester.

That was a little more interesting, because there were actual zoms on the other side of the fence that kept the town of Mountainside separate from the great Rot and Ruin. Most of the zoms were far away, standing in the field or wandering clumsily toward any movement. There were rows of poles with brightly colored streamers set far out in the field, and with every breeze the fluttering of the streamers attracted the zoms, constantly drawing them away from the fence. When the wind calmed, the creatures began lumbering in the direction of any movement on the town side of the fence. Benny wanted to get close to a zom. He'd never been closer than a hundred yards from an active zom before. The older kids said that if you looked into a zom's eyes, your reflection would show you how you'd look as one of the living dead. That sounded very cool, but there was a guy with a shotgun dogging Benny all through the shift, and that made him totally paranoid. He spent more time looking over his shoulder than trying to find meaning in dead men's eyes.

The shotgun guy got to ride a horse. Benny and Chong had to walk the fence line and stop every six or ten feet, grip the chain links, and shake it to make sure there were no breaks or rusted weak spots. That was okay for the first mile, but afterward the noise attracted the zoms, and by the middle of the third mile, Benny had to grab, shake, and release pretty fast to keep his fingers from getting bit. He wanted a close-up look, but he didn't want to lose a finger over it. If he got bit, the shotgun guy would blast him on the spot. Depending on its size, a zom bite could turn someone from healthy to living dead in anything from a few hours to a few minutes, and in orientation, they told everyone that there was a zero-tolerance policy on infections.

"If the gun bulls even *think* you got nipped, they'll blow you all to hell and gone," said the trainer, "so be careful!"

By late morning Benny got his first chance to test the theory about seeing his zombified reflection in the eyes of one of the living dead. The zom was a squat man in the rags of what had once been a mail carrier's uniform. Benny stood as close to the safe side of the fence as he dared, and the zom lumbered toward him, mouth working as if chewing, face as pale as dirty snow. Benny thought the zom must have been Hispanic. Or was still Hispanic. He wasn't sure how that worked with the living dead. Most of the zoms still retained enough of their original skin color for Benny to tell one race from another, but as the sun continued to bake them year after year, the whole mass of them seemed to be heading toward a uniform grayness as if "the Living Dead" was a new ethnic category.

Benny looked right into the creature's eyes, but all he saw were dust and emptiness. No reflections of any kind. No hunger or hate or malice either. There was nothing. A doll's eyes had more life.

He felt something twist inside of him. The dead mail carrier was not as scary as he had expected. He was just *there.* Benny tried to get a read on him, to connect with whatever it was that drove the monster, but it was like looking into empty holes. Nothing looked back.

Then the zom lunged at him and tried to bite its way through the chain links. The movement was so sudden that it felt much faster than it actually was. There was no tension, no twitch of facial muscles, none of the signs Benny had been taught to look for in opponents in basketball or wrestling. The zom moved without hesitation or warning.

Benny yelped and backpedaled away from the fence. Then he stepped in a steaming pile of horse crap and fell hard on his butt.

All of the guards burst out laughing.

Benny and Chong quit at lunch.

The next morning Benny and Chong went to the far side of town and applied as fence technicians.

The fence ran for hundreds of miles and encircled the town and its harvested fields, so this meant a lot of walking while carrying yet another grumpy old guy's toolbox. In the first three hours they got chased by a zom who had squeezed through a break in the fence.

"Why don't they just shoot all the zoms who come up to the fence?" Benny asked their supervisor.

"'Cause folks would get upset," said the man, a scruffy-looking guy with bushy eyebrows and a tic at the corner of his mouth. "Some of them zoms are relatives of folks in town, and those folks have rights regarding their kin. Been all sorts of trouble about it, so we keep the fence in good shape, and every once in a while one of the townsfolk will suck up enough intestinal fortitude to grant permission for the fence guards to do what's necessary."

"That's stupid," said Benny.

"That's people," said the supervisor.

That afternoon Benny and Chong walked what they were sure were a million miles, had been peed on by a horse, stalked by a horde of zoms—Benny couldn't see anything at all in their dusty eyes—and yelled at by nearly everyone.

At the end of the day, as they shambled home on aching feet, Chong said, "That was about as much fun as getting beaten up." He thought about it for a moment. "No . . . getting beaten up is more fun."

Benny didn't have the energy to argue.

There was only one opening for the next job—"carpet coat salesman"—which was okay because Chong wanted to stay home and rest his feet. Chong hated walking. So Benny showed up, neatly dressed in his best jeans and a clean T-shirt, and with his hair as combed as it would ever get without glue.

There wasn't much danger in selling carpet coats, but Benny wasn't slick enough to get the patter down. Benny was surprised they'd be hard to sell, because everybody had a carpet coat or two. Best thing in the world to have on if some zoms were around and feeling bitey. What he discovered, though, was that everyone who could thread a needle was selling them, so the competition was fierce, and sales were few and far between. The door-to-door guys worked on straight commission, too.

The lead salesman, a greasy joker named Chick, would have Benny wear a long-sleeved carpet coat—low knap for summer, shag for winter—and then use a device on him that was supposed to simulate the full-strength bite of an adult male zom. This metal "biter" couldn't break the skin through the coat—and here Chick rolled into his spiel about human bite strength, throwing around terms like PSI, avulsion, and postdecay dental-ligament strength—but it pinched really hard, and the coat was so hot, the sweat ran down under Benny's clothes. When he went home that night, he weighed himself to see how many pounds he'd sweated off. Just one, but Benny didn't have a lot of pounds to spare.

"This one looks good," said Chong over breakfast the next morning.

Benny read out loud from the paper. "'Pit Thrower.' What's that?"

"I don't know," Chong said with a mouth full of toast. "I think it has something to do with barbecuing."

It didn't. Pit throwers worked in teams, dragging dead

zoms off the backs of carts and tossing them into the constant blaze at the bottom of Brinkers Quarry. Most of the zoms on the carts were in pieces. The woman who ran orientation kept talking about "parts," and went on and on about the risk of secondary infection; then she pasted on the fakest smile Benny had ever seen and tried to sell the applicants on the physical fitness benefits that came from constant lifting, turning, and throwing. She even pulled up her sleeve and flexed her biceps. She had pale skin with freckles as dark as liver spots, and the sudden pop of her biceps looked like a swollen tumor.

Chong faked vomiting into his lunch bag.

The other jobs offered by the quarry included ash soaker—"because we don't want zom smoke drifting over the town, now, do we?" asked the freckly muscle freak. And pit raker, which was exactly what it sounded like.

Benny and Chong didn't make it through orientation. They snuck out during the slide show of smiling pit throwers handling gray limbs and heads.

One job that was neither disgusting nor physically demanding was crank generator repairman. Ever since the lights went out in the weeks following First Night, the only source of electrical power was hand-cranked portable generators. There were maybe fifty in all of Mountainside, and Chong said that they were left over from the mining days of the early twentieth century. Town ordinance forbade the building of any other kind of generator. Electronics and complex machines were no longer allowed in town, because of a strong religious movement that associated that kind of power with the "Godless behavior" that had brought about "the end." Benny heard about it all the time, and even some of his friends' parents talked that way.

It made no sense to Benny. It wasn't electric lights and computers and automobiles that had made the dead rise. Or, if it was, then Benny had never heard anyone make a logical or sane connection between the two. When he asked Tom about it, his brother looked pained and frustrated. "People need something to blame," Tom said. "If they can't find something rational to blame, then they'll very happily blame something irrational. Back when people didn't know about viruses and bacteria, they blamed plagues on witches and vampires. But don't ask me how *exactly* the people in town came to equate electricity and other forms of energy with the living dead."

"That doesn't make even a little bit of sense."

"I know. But what I think is the real reason is that if we start using electricity again, and building back up again, then things will kind of go back the way they were. And that this whole cycle will start over again. I guess to their way of thinking—if they even consciously *thought* about it—it would be like a person with a badly broken heart deciding to risk falling in love again. All they can remember is how bad the heartbreak and grief felt, and they can't imagine going through that again."

"That's stupid, though," Benny insisted. "It's cowardly."

"Welcome to the real world, kiddo."

The town's only professional electrician, Vic Santorini, had long since taken to drinking his way through the rest of his life.

When Benny and Chong showed up for the interview at

the house of the guy who owned the repair shop, he sat them down in the shade of an airy porch and gave them glasses of iced tea and mint cookies. Benny was thinking that he would take this job no matter what it was.

"Do you know why we only use hand-cranked generators in town, boys?" the man asked. His name was Mr. Merkle.

"Sure," said Chong. "The army dropped nukes on the zoms, and the EMPs blew out all of the electronics."

"Plus Mr. Santorini's always sauced," said Benny. He was about to add something biting about the bizarre religious intolerance to electricity when Mr. Merkle's face creased into a weird smile. Benny shut his mouth.

Mr. Merkle smiled at them for a long time. A full minute. Then the man shook his head. "No, that's not quite right, boys," Merkle said. "It's because hand-cranked machines are simple, and those other machines are ostentatious." He pronounced each syllable as if it was a separate word.

Benny and Chong glanced at each other.

"You see, boys," said Mr. Merkle, "God loves simplicity. It's the devil who loves ostentation. It's the devil who loves arrogance and grandiosity."

Uh-oh, Benny thought.

"Mr. Santorini spent the first part of his life installing electrical appliances into people's homes," said Mr. Merkle. "That was the devil's work, and now he's sought the oblivion of demon rum to try and hide from the fact that he's facing a long time in hell for helping to incur the wrath of the Almighty. If it wasn't for Godless men like him, the Almighty would not have opened the gates of hell and sent the legions of the damned to overthrow the vain kingdoms of mankind."

Out of the corner of his eye, Benny could see Chong's fingers turning bone white as he gripped the arms of his chair.

"I can see a little doubt in your eyes, boys, and that's fair enough," said Merkle, his mouth twisted into a smile that was so tight, it looked painful. "But there are a lot of people who have embraced the righteous path. There are more of us who *believe* than don't." He sniffed. "Even if all of them don't yet have the courage of their faith to say so."

He leaned forward, and Benny could almost feel the heat from the man's intense stare.

"The school, the hospital—even the town hall—run on electricity from hand-cranked generators, and as long as right-minded people draw breath under God's own heaven, there won't be any ostentatious machinery in *our* town."

There was a whole pitcher of iced tea on the table, as well as quite a pile of cookies, and Benny realized that Mr. Merkle probably had a lot to say on the subject and wanted his audience comfortable for the whole ride. Benny endured it for as long as he could and then asked if he could use the bathroom. Mr. Merkle, who had now shifted from simple electricity to the soul-crushing blasphemy that was hydroelectric power, was only mildly thrown off his game, and told Benny where to go inside the house. Benny went inside and all the way through and out the back door. He waved to Chong as he vaulted the wooden fence.

Two hours later Chong caught up with him outside of Lafferty's, the local general store. He gave Benny a long and evil look.

"You're such a good friend, Benny, I'll really miss you when you're dead."

"Dude, I gave you an out. When I didn't come back, didn't he go looking for me?"

"No. He saw you go over the fence, but he kept smiling that smile of his and said, 'Your little friend is going to burn in hell, do you know that? But *you* wouldn't spit in God's eye like that, would you?'"

"And you *stayed*?"

"What could I do? I was afraid he'd point at me and say 'Him!,' and then lightning bolts would hit me or something."

"Scratch that job off the list?"

"You think?"

Spotter was the next job, and that proved to be a good choice, but only for one of them. Benny's eyesight was too poor to spot zoms at the right distance. Chong was like an eagle, and they offered him a job as soon as he finished reading the smallest numbers off a chart. Benny couldn't even tell they were numbers.

Chong took the job, and Benny walked away alone, throwing dispirited looks back at his friend sitting next to his trainer in a high tower.

Later, Chong told Benny that he loved the job. He sat there all day, staring out over the valleys, into the Rot and Ruin that stretched from California, all the way to the Atlantic. Chong said that he could see twenty miles on a clear day, especially if there were no winds coming his way from the quarry. Just him up there, alone with his thoughts. Benny missed his friend, but privately he thought that the job sounded more boring than words could express.

■ ■ ■

Benny liked the sound of bottler, because he figured it for a factory job of filling soda bottles. Benny loved soda, but it was sometimes hard to come by. Some pop was old stuff brought in by traders, but that was too expensive. A bottle of Dr Pepper cost ten ration dollars. The local stuff came in all sorts of recycled bottles—from jelly jars to bottles that had actually once been filled with Coke or Mountain Dew. Benny could see himself manning the hand-cranked generator that ran the conveyor belt or tapping corks into the bottlenecks with a rubber mallet. He was positive they would let him drink all the soda he wanted. But as he walked up the road, he met an older teenager—his pal Morgie Mitchell's cousin Bert—who worked at the plant. When Benny fell into step with Bert, he almost gagged. Bert smelled awful, like something found dead behind the baseboards. Worse. He smelled like a zom.

Bert caught his look and shrugged. "Well . . . what do you expect me to smell like? I bottle this stuff eight hours a day."

"What stuff?"

"Cadaverine. What, you think I work making soda pop? I wish! Nah, I work a press to get the oils from the rotting meat."

Benny's heart sank. Cadaverine was a nasty-smelling molecule produced by protein hydrolysis during putrefaction of animal tissue. Benny remembered that from science class, but he didn't know that it was made from actual rotting flesh. Hunters and trackers dabbed it on their clothes to keep the zoms from coming after them, because the dead were not attracted to rotting flesh.

Benny asked Bert what *kind* of flesh was used to produce the product, but Bert hemmed and hawed and finally changed the subject. Just as Bert was reaching for the door to the plant, Benny spun around and walked back to town.

There was one job Benny already knew about: erosion artist. He'd seen erosion portraits tacked on every wall of the town's fence outposts and on the walls of the buildings that lined the Red Zone, the stretch of open land that separated the town from the fence.

This job had some promise, because Benny was a pretty fair artist. People wanted to know what their relatives might look like if they were zoms, so erosion artists took family photos and zombified them. Benny had seen dozens of these portraits in Tom's office. A couple of times he wondered if he should take the picture of his parents to an artist and have them redrawn. He'd never actually done it, though. Thinking about his parents as zoms made him sick and angry.

But Sacchetto, the supervising artist, told him to try a picture of a relative first. He said it provided better insight into what the clients would be feeling. So, as part of his audition, Benny took the picture of his folks out of his wallet and tried it.

Sacchetto frowned and shook his head. "You're making them look too mean and scary."

He tried it again with several photos of strangers the artist had on file.

"Still mean and scary," said Sacchetto with pursed lips and a disapproving shake of his head.

"They *are* mean and scary," Benny insisted.

"Not to customers they're not," said Sacchetto.

Benny almost argued with him about it, saying that if he could accept that his own folks were flesh-eating zombies—

and that there was nothing warm and fuzzy about it—then why can't everyone else get it through their heads?

"How old were you when your parents passed?" Sacchetto asked.

"Eighteen months."

"So, you never really knew them."

Benny hesitated, and that old image flashed in his head once more. Mom screaming. The pale and inhuman face that should have been Dad's smiling face. And then the darkness as Tom carried him away.

"No," he said bitterly. "But I know what they look like. I know *about* them. I know that they're zoms. Or maybe they're dead now, but, I mean—zoms are zoms. Right?"

"Are they?" the artist asked.

"Yes!" Benny snapped, answering his own question. "And they should all rot."

The artist folded his arms across his chest and leaned against a paint-spattered wall, head cocked as he assessed Benny. "Tell me something, kid," he said. "Everyone lost family and friends to the zoms. Everyone's pretty torn up about it. You didn't even really know the people you lost—you were too young—but you got this red-hot hate going on. I've only known you half an hour, and I can see it coming out of your pores. What's that all about? We're safe here in town. Have a life and let go of the stuff you can't change."

"Maybe I'm too smart to just forgive and forget."

"No," said Sacchetto, "that ain't it."

After the audition, he hadn't been offered the job.

3

"It was a 1967 Pontiac LeMans ragtop. Bloodred and so souped-up that she'd outrun any damn thing on the road. And I do mean *damned* thing."

That's how Charlie Matthias always described his car. Then he'd give a big braying horselaugh, because no matter how many times he said it, he thought it was the funniest joke ever. People tended to laugh *with* him rather than *at* the actual joke, because Charlie had a seventy-inch chest and twenty-four-inch biceps, and his sweat was a soup of testosterone, anabolic steroids, and Jack Daniels. You don't laugh, he gets mad and starts to think you're messing with him. Something ugly usually followed Charlie becoming offended.

Benny always laughed. Not because he was afraid of what Charlie would do to him if he didn't, but because Benny thought Charlie was hilarious. And cool. He thought there was no one cooler on planet Earth.

It didn't matter to Benny that the car Charlie always talked about had run out of gas thirteen years ago and was a rusted piece of scrap metal somewhere out in the Rot and Ruin. Nor did it matter that the fact the car could even drive was at odds with history; not after the EMPs. In Charlie's stories, that car had lived through the bombs and the ghouls and a thousand adventures, and could never be forgotten. Charlie said he'd been a real road warrior in the LeMans, cruising the blacktop and bashing zoms.

Everyone else at Lafferty's General Store laughed too, though Benny was sure a couple of them might have been faking it. About the only person who didn't laugh at the joke was Marion Hammer, known to everyone as the Motor City Hammer. He wasn't as big as Charlie, but he was bulldog ugly and had pistol butts sticking out of every pocket, as well as a length of black pipe that hung like a club from his belt. The Hammer didn't laugh much, but when he was in a mood, his eyes would twinkle like a merry pig, and one corner of his mouth would turn up in what could have been a smile but probably wasn't.

Benny thought the Hammer was insanely cool too. . . . Just not as insanely cool as Charlie. Of course, no one was as cool as Charlie Matthias. Charlie was a six-foot, six-inch albino with one blue eye and one pink one that was milky and blind. There was a rumor that when Charlie closed his blue eye, he could see into the realm of ghosts with his dead eye. Benny thought that was wicked, too . . . even if he privately wasn't so sure it was true.

The pair of them—Charlie and the Hammer—were the toughest bounty hunters in the entire Rot and Ruin. Everyone said so. Except for a few weirdoes, like Mayor Kirsch, who said that Tom Imura was tougher. Benny thought that was a load of crap, because Charlie said Tom was "a bit too easy on zoms," and he said it in a way that suggested Tom was either shy of a real fight or didn't have the raw nerve necessary to be a first-class zombie-hunting, badlands badass. Besides, Tom wasn't half as big as Charlie or as mean-looking as the Hammer. No, Tom was a coward. Benny knew that firsthand.

Working as a bounty hunter was a tough and dangerous business. None tougher, as far as Benny knew. Most of the hunters were paid by the town to clear zoms out of the areas around the trade route that linked Mountainside to the handful of other towns strung out along the mountain range. Others worked in packs as mercenary armies to clear out towns, old shopping malls, warehouses, and even a few small cities, so that the traders could raid them for supplies. According to Charlie the life expectancy of a typical bounty hunter was six months. Most of the young men who tried that job gave it a month or two and then quit, discovering that actually killing zoms was a lot different from what they learned from family members who had survived First Night, and a whole lot different from the stuff they were taught in school or the Scouts. Charlie and the Hammer had been the first of the hunters—again, according to Charlie—and they'd been at it since the beginning, making their first paid kills eight months after First Night.

"We kilt more zoms than the whole army, navy, air force, and marines put together," the Hammer bragged at least once a month. "And that includes the pansy-ass National Guard."

For all their bluster and bad odors and violent tendencies, Charlie and the Hammer were popular all around town, partly because they looked too tough and ugly to be scared of anything. Maybe even too ugly to kill. If even half of their reputation was to be believed, then they'd been in more close-combat tussles with the living dead than anyone, and certainly more than any of the other bounty hunters working this part of the Ruin. They were even tougher than legendary hunters, like Houston John, Wild Bill Fairchild, J-Dog and Dr. Skillz, or the Mekong brothers. Then again, Benny had to measure reputation against reality with only guesswork to go on, and in the end it probably didn't matter who'd done the most killing or taken the most heads. According to Don Lafferty, owner of the general store, Charlie and the Hammer had bagged and tagged one hundred and sixty-three named heads and maybe two thousand nameless dead. Every single kill had been a paid job, too.

Charlie and the Hammer also did closure jobs—locating a zombified family member or friend for a client and putting them to final rest. Mayor Kirsch said they had as high a closure rate as Tom did, though Benny doubted it. No way Tom's rate could be *anywhere* near Charlie's tally. Tom never had extra ration dollars to spare, and Charlie was always buying beer, pop, and fried chicken wings for the crowd who gathered around to listen to his stories.

"When you gonna retire?" asked Wrigley Sputters, the mail carrier, as he poured Charlie another cup of iced tea. "You boys have to be rich as Midas by now."

"Midas?" asked the Hammer. "Who's he?"

"I think he sold mufflers," offered Norbert, one of the traders who used armored horses to pull wagons of scavenged goods from town to town, "and then bought a kingdom."

"Yeah," said Charlie, nodding as if he knew that to be the truth. "King Midas. Definitely from Detroit. Made a fortune outta car parts and such."

And everyone agreed with him, because that was the smart

thing to do. Benny nodded, even though he had no clue what a muffler was. Lou Chong and Morgie Mitchell nodded too.

"Well, boys," said Charlie with a wink. "I ain't saying I'm as rich as a king, but me and the Hammer got us a whole pot of gold. The Ruin's been good to us."

"Yeah, it has," agreed the Hammer, his purple lips pursed knowingly. "We kilt us a mess o' zoms."

"My uncle Nick said you killed the four Mengler brothers last month," said Morgie from the back of the crowd.

Charlie and the Hammer burst out laughing. "Hell yes! We killed them deader'n dead. The Hammer snucked up on their place, half-past sunrise, and tossed a Molotov onto the roof. All four of them dead suckers come staggering out into the morning light. Streaked with old blood and horse crap and who knows what. Skinny and rotten, smelled worse than sweaty pigs, and we were fifty feet away."

"Whatcha do?" asked Benny, his eyes ablaze.

The Hammer snorted. "We played some."

Charlie snickered at that. "Yeah. We wanted to have some fun. This business is getting so's killing these critters is way too easy. Am I right or am I right?"

A few people chuckled or nodded vaguely, but nobody said anything specific. It was one of those times when it wasn't clear what the right answer would be.

Charlie plowed ahead. "So me and the Hammer decide to make this a bit more fair."

"Fair," agreed the Hammer.

"We laid down our weapons."

"All of 'em?" Chong gasped.

"Every last one. Guns, knives, the Hammer's favorite pipe, numchucks, even them ninja throwing stars that the Hammer took off that dead zom who used to run that karate school on the other side of the valley. We stripped down to our jeans and beaters and just went in, mano a mano."

"Went in *whut*?" asked Morgie.

"It means 'hand to hand,'" Chong said.

"It means 'man to man,'" Charlie snapped.

Even Benny knew Charlie was wrong, but he didn't say so. Not right to Charlie's face, anyway. No one was that dumb.

Charlie threw Chong a quick, ugly look and plunged back into his story. "Anyways, we came up on them with just our knuckles and nerves, and we fair beat them zoms so bad, they died surprised, woke up, and died of shame all over again."

Everyone burst out laughing.

Someone cleared his throat, and they all looked up to see Randy Kirsch, the town mayor, standing there, his arms folded, bald head cocked to one side as he looked from Benny to Chong to Morgie. "I thought you boys were supposed to be out job hunting."

"I got a job," Chong said quickly.

"I'm fourteen," said Morgie.

"We just stopped in for a cold bottle of pop," Benny said.

"And you've had it, Benjamin Imura," said Mayor Kirsch. "Now you three run along."

Benny thought Charlie was going to object, but the bounty hunter simply shrugged. "Yeah . . . you boys got to earn your rations just like grown folks. Skedaddle."

Benny and the others got up and slouched past the

mayor. Before they even reached the door Charlie was in full stride again, telling another of his stories, and everyone was laughing. The mayor followed the boys outside.

"Benny," he said quietly, the hot sun glinting off the polished crown of his shaved head. "Does Tom know you've been hanging out here?"

"I don't know," Benny said evasively. He knew darn well that Tom had no idea that he spent a part of every afternoon listening to Charlie and the Hammer tell their stories.

"I don't think he'd like it," said Mayor Kirsch.

Benny met his stare. "I guess I really don't care much what Tom likes and doesn't like," he said, then added "sir" to the end of it, as if that word could somehow improve the tone of voice he'd just used.

Mayor Kirsch scratched at his thick black beard. He opened his mouth to say something and then closed it again. Whatever he wanted to say, he kept to himself. That was fine with Benny, who wasn't in the mood for a lecture.

"You boys run along now," Kirsch said eventually. He stood on the porch of the general store for a while, but when Benny was all the way down the street and looked back, he saw the mayor go back into the store.

The mayor and his family lived next door to Benny, and he and Tom were friends. Mayor Kirsch was always talking about how tough Tom was and what a good hunter Tom was and what a fine example Tom set for all bounty hunters. Blah, blah, blah. It made Benny want to hurl. If Tom set such a fine example as a bounty hunter, then why didn't the *other* bounty hunters ever tell stories about him? None of them bragged about how they'd seen Tom single-handedly kick the butts of four zombies at once. Even Tom didn't talk about it. Not once had he ever told Benny about what he did out there in the Ruin. How boring was that? Benny thought the Mayor had a screw loose. Tom was no kind of role model to anyone.

Chong said he had to get ready for work. He was scheduled for a six-hour shift in his tower, and looked pleased about it. Benny and Morgie found their friend Nix Riley, a redheaded girl with more freckles than anyone could count, sitting on a rock down by the creek, writing in her leather-bound notebook. She had her shoes off and her feet in the water. The red nail polish on her toes looked like rubies under the rippling water.

"Hello, Benny," said Nix with a smile, peering at him from under her wild red-gold curls. "How's the job hunting going?"

Benny grunted and kicked off his shoes. The cold water was like a happy party on his hot feet. Morgie slouched around and sat on Nix's other side, and began untying his clunky work boots.

They told Nix about Charlie and the Hammer, and about the mayor rousting them.

"My mom won't let me anywhere near those guys," said Nix. She and her mother lived alone in a tiny house by the west wall, over in the poorest part of town. Up until this past winter, Nix had always been a skinny, gangly kid who was more one of the guys than a girl. Like Chong, Nix was a bookworm and always had several books in her satchel, but unlike Chong, Nix wanted to write books of her own. She was always scribbling poems and short stories in her journal. Of all of them she'd always been the real geek, but that had changed over the last ten months. Now Nix wasn't a stick figure anymore, and Benny found it weird being around her. Especially on hot days when she wore a tight T-shirt and shorts. He kept wanting to look at her—especially at what she was doing to that T-shirt—but it made him feel really awkward. Nix had always been like Morgie and Chong. Now she was a *girl*. There was no way to ignore that fact anymore.

What made it worse was that Benny was pretty sure Nix had a crush on him. He liked her, too, though he'd rather have an arm cut off than say so. Even to Chong. Dating a friend was an old taboo among his crew. He and Chong had sworn a blood oath on it when they were nine or ten. Nix was really cute, and he liked looking at her, but dating her would be like dating Chong. Besides, with a girl who he'd known since they were just out of diapers, there was no chance at all that she'd think he was mysterious and interesting. Sure, she already liked him, but what would happen if they started dating and she tried to discover his secrets, only to find out that he didn't have any? Or, worse, what would happen if he asked her out and found out that Nix really didn't have a thing for him? Benny couldn't imagine dealing with rejection from someone who knew everything about him and who he'd be seeing all the time. The whole thing made Benny want to bang his head against a wall.

"How come?" asked Morgie. The question brought Benny back to the conversation.

"It's complicated," Nix said, looking down at the sunlight on the rippling water. "And Mom won't tell me all of it, but I think she and Charlie had some kind of fight or something.

She *really* doesn't like him. I'm not allowed to be around him unless Mom's there. Or Mayor Kirsch or Tom."

She nudged Benny with her foot while she talked.

Benny pretended not to notice the nudge. He asked, "Why Tom?"

"Mom likes Tom."

"Likes? You mean likes him like she likes your dog, Pirate, or *likes* likes?"

"Likes likes." She cut him a sideways look. "Tom's hot."

"That's sick," Benny said.

"You look a lot alike, you know," said Nix.

"Please kill me now," Benny asked the heavens.

"Why can't you be around Charlie without your mom or Tom?" Morgie asked. Unlike Benny, Morgie had become infatuated with Nix. And with more than her new figure. He actually *liked* her. Morgie had never made that oath about never dating friends, and Benny couldn't quite grasp how he was able to fixate on Nix without feeling weird about it.

"She says that he doesn't treat girls the right way sometimes."

"What's that supposed to mean?" asked Benny, his voice sharper than intended.

Nix gave him a long considering stare. "You can be so naive sometimes."

"I repeat, what's that supposed to mean?"

"It means that guys like Charlie seem to think that anything they put their hands on belongs to them. Mom's afraid to be alone with either of them, and I wouldn't want to be caught in a dark alley with them either."

"You're nuts."

"You're not a girl," Nix said. "Or let me put it another way: You're a boy, so therefore you're probably incapable of understanding."

"I understand," said Morgie, but Nix and Benny both ignored him.

"Is your mom just saying this stuff or did something actually happen?" asked Benny. His voice was heavy with skepticism, and Nix simply shook her head and turned away. She kept staring off at the distant fence line.

"Well, *I* think Charlie and them are really cool," said Benny.

The moment stretched too thin to support any more conversation, at least on that topic, so they let it go and said nothing. After a while a cool breeze came along, and they all laid back and closed their eyes. The breeze blew the tension away like fine grains of sand.

Without looking at Benny, Nix said, "Did you get a job yet?"

"Nah." He told them about all the jobs he'd applied for and how each one had turned out.

Nix and Morgie were not yet fifteen. They hated the thought of getting jobs nearly as much as Benny hated the process of finding one, but at least they had a couple of months before they had to go looking.

"What are you going to do?" Nix asked, propping herself up on her elbows. The sunlight on the water flickered like flecks of gold in her green eyes, and when Benny realized he was thinking that, he made himself look away.

"I don't know."

"Why don't you ask your brother for a job?" she said.

"I'd rather be tied down over an anthill."

"What is it with you two?"

"Why does everyone ask me that?" Benny snapped. "Tom's a loser, okay? He walks around like he's Mr. High and Mighty, but I know what he really is."

"What?" asked Morgie.

Benny almost said it, almost called his brother a coward to his friends. But that was a line he hadn't ever crossed. On some level he felt that if he called Tom a coward, then it might make people wonder if he was one too. They were only half brothers, but they were still related, and Benny didn't know if cowardice was something that could be passed on through blood.

"Just leave it alone" was all he said. He sat up and fished on the bank for stones that he could throw. He found a few, but none of them were flat enough to skip, so he plunked them far out into the stream. Morgie heard the noise, sat up, and joined him.

Nix grabbed her notebook and wrote for a while. Benny tried very hard not to look at her. He mostly succeeded, but it took effort.

"Well," said Nix sometime later, "summer's almost over, and if you don't get a job by the start of school, they'll cut—"

"My rations," he barked. "I know, I know. Geez."

Nix fell silent. Morgie pretended to kick her foot, but she kicked him back for real, and they got into a loud argument. Benny, disgusted with them and with everything, got up and stalked away, hands in his pockets, shoulders hunched under the August heat.

SEPTEMBER WAS TEN DAYS AWAY, AND BENNY STILL HADN'T FOUND A JOB. He wasn't good enough with a rifle to be a fence guard; he wasn't old enough to join the town watch; he wasn't patient enough for farming; and he wasn't strong enough to work as a hitter or a cutter—not that smashing in zombie heads with a sledgehammer or cutting them up for the quarry wagons was much of a draw for him, even with his strong hatred for the monsters. Yes, it was killing, but it also looked like hard work, and Benny wasn't all that interested in something described in the papers as "demanding physical labor." Was that supposed to attract applicants?

So, after soul-searching for a week, during which Chong lectured him pretty endlessly about detaching himself from preconceived notions and allowing himself to become part of the cocreative process of the universe (or something like that), Benny went and asked Tom to take him on as an apprentice.

At first Tom studied him with narrow-eyed suspicion.

Then his eyes widened in shock when he realized Benny wasn't playing a joke.

As the reality sank in, Tom looked like he wanted to cry.

He tried to hug Benny, but that wasn't going to happen in this lifetime, so they shook hands on it.

Benny left a smiling Tom and went upstairs to take a nap before dinner. He sat down and stared out the window, as if he could see tomorrow and the tomorrow after that and the one after that. Just him and Tom.

"This is really going to suck," he said.

5

That evening Tom and Benny sat on the front steps and watched the sun set over the mountains. Benny was depressed. He looked at the sunset as if it was a window into the future, and all he saw was forced closeness with Tom and the problems that went with it. He also didn't understand Tom. He knew Tom had run away and yet he now made his living killing zoms. Tom never talked about it at home. He never bragged about his kills, didn't hang out with the other bounty hunters, didn't do anything to show how tough he was.

On one hand, zoms were not supposed to be hard to kill in a one-on-one situation—not against a smart and well-armed person. On the other hand, there was no room for mistakes with them. They were always hungry, always dangerous. No matter how he tried to work it out in his head, Benny could not see Tom as the kind of person who could or would hunt the living dead. It was like a henhouse chicken hunting foxes.

Over the last couple of years Benny had almost asked Tom about this, but each time, he'd left his questions unspoken. Maybe the answers would somehow show more of Tom's weakness. Maybe Tom was lying and really doing something else. Benny had worked out a number of bizarre and unlikely scenarios to try and explain chickenshit Tom as a zombie killer. None of them held water. Now, with the reality of what they were going to do tomorrow morning as clear and real as the setting sun, Benny finally put the question out there.

"Why do you do this stuff?"

Tom cut a quick look at him, but he continued to sip his coffee and was a long time answering. "Tell me, kiddo, what is it you think I do?"

"Duh! You kill zoms."

"Really?"

"That's what you say," Benny said, then grudgingly added, "That's what everyone says. Tom Imura, the great zombie killer."

Tom nodded, as if Benny had said something interesting. "So, far as you see it, that's all I do? I just walk up to any zombie I see and *pow*!"

"Uh . . . *yeah*."

"Uh . . . *no*." Tom shook his head. "How can you live in this house and not know what I do, what my job involves?"

"What's it matter? Everybody I know has a brother, sister, father, mother, or haggy old grandmother who's killed zoms. What's the big?" He wanted to say that he thought Tom probably used a high-powered rifle with a scope and killed them from a safe distance; not like Charlie and Hammer, who had the stones to do it mano a mano.

"Killing the living dead is a part of what I do, Benny. But do you know why I do it? And for whom?"

"For fun?" Benny suggested, hoping Tom would be at least *that* cool.

"Try again."

"Okay . . . then for money . . . and for whoever's gonna pay you."

"Are you pretending to be a dope or do you really not understand?"

"What, you think I don't know you're a bounty hunter? Everybody knows that. Zak Matthias's uncle Charlie is one too. I heard him tell stories about going deep into the Ruin to hunt zoms."

Tom paused with his coffee cup halfway to his lips. "Charlie—? You know Charlie Pink-eye?"

"He gets mad if people call him that."

"Charlie Pink-eye shouldn't be *around* people."

"Why not?" demanded Benny. "He tells the best stories. He's funny."

"He's a killer."

"So are you."

Tom's smile was gone. "God, I'm an idiot. I have to be the worst brother in the history of the world if I let you think that I'm the same as Charlie Pink-eye."

"Well . . . you're not exactly like Charlie."

"Oh . . . that's something then . . ."

"Charlie's the *man*."

"Charlie's the man," echoed Tom. He sat back and rubbed his eyes. "Good God. What could you possibly find interesting about a thug like Charlie?"

"Because he tells it like it is," Benny said. "I mean, it's kind of weird that we're surrounded by, like, a zillion zoms, we learn about First Night and zombies in school, but they just talk around it for the most part. They don't tell us *about* it. It's crazy. We have all those salvaged textbooks from before First Night that tell us about the world—politics and cars and all that—but you know what we have for First Night? A pamphlet. Does that make any sense? I can tell you the make and model of every car that ever rolled out of Detroit, but I can't tell you about how Detroit fell during First Night. I know about cell phones and computers and all that *before* stuff. . . . But I don't know anything about what's on the other side of the fence. . . . Except what I learn from Charlie. Twice a month we practice zombie killing in gym class by hitting straw targets with sticks, and we do some of that kind of crap in the Scouts, but nobody—I mean *nobody*—except Charlie and the Hammer ever really *talks* about zoms. Our teachers must think we're all learning about zombies from our folks, but none of my friends have heard squat at home. You're even worse because killing zoms is your job, and you never talk about it. Never. Yeah, you'll help me with math and history and all that stuff, but when it comes to zoms . . . I learn more off the back of Zombie Cards than I ever do from you. Everyone over twenty years old in this stupid town acts like we're living on Mars. I mean, how many people even go to the Red Zone let alone all the way to the fence? Even the fence guards don't talk about the zoms. They talk about softball and what they had for dinner last night, but they all pretend the zoms aren't even there."

"People do go to the Red Zone, Benny. They go there to post erosion portraits for the bounty hunters."

"Oh, yeah? Well, I know for a fact that most people pay kids to post the portraits for them. How do I know? Because I've put up about a hundred of them."

"You—?"

"Zombie Cards don't buy themselves, Tom. And when people ask kids to put the pictures up, they don't even say what they are. I mean, we're standing there, both looking at an erosion portrait, and no one ever mentions the word 'zom.' Most people just say, 'Hey, kid, want to hang this for me?' They never say where. They know that we know, but they can't actually come out and say it. It's freaking weird, man."

"People are scared, Benny. They're in denial. You're only fifteen, so you and your friends don't really understand what it was like during First Night."

"No joke, Mr. Wizard. That's my whole point! We *want* to know."

Tom pursed his lips. "I guess . . . people probably want to shelter you from it."

Benny wanted to throw something at Tom. He eyed a heavy book; that might wake him up. "How the heck can anyone shelter us? We live behind fences, surrounded by the Rot and Ruin. Maybe you've heard of it? Big place, used to be called America? Filled with zoms? It's not fair that people don't tell us the truth."

"Benny, I—"

"It's our world too," Benny snapped. His words hit Tom like a slap. Then into the silence Benny dropped another bomb. "Don't get on my case for listening to Charlie if he's the only one who thinks we ought to know truth."

Tom stared at him for a long time as different emotions flowed like water over his face. Finally he threw the last of his coffee into the bushes beside the porch, and stood up.

"Tell you what, Benny . . . Tomorrow we're going to start early and head out into the Rot and Ruin. We'll go deep, like Charlie does. I want you to see firsthand what he does and what I do, and then you can make your own decisions."

"Decisions about what?"

"About a lot of things, kiddo."

And with that Tom went inside and to bed.

Tom and Benny left at dawn and headed down to the southeastern gate. The gatekeeper had Tom sign the usual waiver that absolved the town and the gatekeeping staff of all liability if anything untoward happened once they crossed into the Ruin. A vendor sold Tom a dozen bottles of cadaverine, which they sprinkled on their clothing, and a jar of peppermint goo that they dabbed on their upper lips, to kill their own sense of smell.

"Will this stuff stop the zoms?"

"Nothing stops them," said Tom. "But this slows them down, makes most of them hesitate before biting. Even drives some away. It gives you an edge and a little breathing room, but don't think you can stroll through a crowd of them with no risk."

"That's encouraging," Benny said under his breath.

They were dressed for a long hike. Tom had instructed Benny to wear good walking shoes, jeans, a durable shirt, and a hat to keep the sun from boiling his brains.

"If it's not already too late," Tom said.

Benny made a rude gesture when Tom wasn't looking.

Despite the heat, Tom wore a lightweight jacket with lots of pockets. He had an old army gun belt around his narrow waist, with a pistol snugged into a worn leather holster. Benny wasn't allowed to have a gun yet.

"Eventually," Tom said, then added, "Maybe."

"I learned gun safety in school," Benny protested.

"You didn't learn it from me," Tom said with finality.

The last thing Tom strapped on was a sword. Benny watched with interest as Tom slung a long strap diagonally across his body, from left shoulder to right hip, with the hilt standing above his shoulder so that he could reach up and over for a fast right-handed draw.

The sword was a *katana*, a Japanese long sword that Benny had seen Tom practice with every day for as long as he could remember. That sword was the only thing about his brother that Benny thought was cool. Benny's mom, who was Tom's adopted mother, was Irish, but their father had been Japanese. Tom once told Benny that the Imura family went all the way back to the samurai days of ancient Japan. He showed Benny picture books of fierce-looking Japanese men in armor. Samurai warriors.

"Are you a samurai?" Benny had asked when he was nine.

"There are no samurai anymore," Tom said, but even back then Benny thought that Tom had a funny look on his face when he said that. Like maybe there was more to say on the subject, but he didn't want to say it right then. When Benny brought the subject up a couple of times since, the answer was always the same.

Even so, Tom was pretty damn good with the sword. He

could draw fast as lightning, and Benny had seen him do a trick once when Tom thought no one else was looking. He threw a handful of grapes into the air, then drew his sword and cut five of them in half before they fell to the grass. The blade was a blur. Later, after Tom had gone off to a store, Benny counted the grapes. Tom had thrown six into the air. He'd only missed one. That was sweet.

Of course, Benny would sooner eat broken glass than tell Tom how impressive he thought it was.

"Why are you bringing that?" he asked as Tom adjusted the lay of the strap.

"It's quiet," Tom said.

Benny understood that. Noise attracted zoms. A sword was quieter than a gun, but it also meant getting closer. Benny didn't think that was a very smart idea. He said as much, and Tom just shrugged.

"Then why bring the gun?" Benny persisted.

"'Cause sometimes quiet doesn't matter." Tom patted his pockets to do a quick inventory to make sure he had everything he needed. "Okay," he said, "let's go. We're burning daylight."

Tom tipped a couple of fence runners to bang on drums six hundred yards north, and as soon as that drew away the wandering zoms, Tom and Benny slipped out into the great Rot and Ruin and headed for the tree line.

Chong waved to them from the corner tower.

"We need to move fast for the first half mile," cautioned Tom, and he broke into a jog-trot that was fast enough to get them out of scent range but slow enough for Benny to match.

A few of the zombies staggered after them, but the fence runners banged on the drums again, and the zombies, incapable of holding on to more than one reaction at a time, turned back toward the noise. The Imura brothers vanished into the shadows under the trees.

When they finally slowed to a walk, Benny was sweating. It was a hot start to what would be a scorcher of a day. The air was thick with mosquitoes and flies, and the trees were alive with the sound of chattering birds. Far above them the sun was a white hole in the sky.

"We're not being followed," Tom said.

"Who said we were?"

"Well . . . ever since we left you keep looking back toward the fence line."

"No, I don't."

"Or are you looking to see if any of your friends came to see you off? Other than Chong, I mean. Maybe a certain red-haired girl?"

Benny stared at him. "You are completely delusional."

"You're going to tell me that you don't have a thing for Nix Riley?"

"A world of no."

"How come I found a sheet of paper with her name written on it maybe a million times?"

"Must have been Morgie's."

"It was your handwriting."

"Then I guess I was practicing my penmanship. What is it with you? I told you, I don't have a thing for Nix. Let it go."

Tom turned away without another word, but Benny caught his smile. He cursed under his breath for the next mile.

"How far are we going?" Benny asked.

"Far. But don't worry, there are way stations where we can crash if we don't make it back tonight."

Benny looked at him as if he'd just suggested they set themselves on fire and go swimming in gasoline. "Wait—You're saying we could be out all *night*?"

"Sure. You know I'm out there for days at a time. You're going to have to do what I do. Besides, except for some wanderers, most of the dead in this area have long since been cleaned out. Every week I have to go farther away."

"Don't they just come to you?"

Tom shook his head. "There are wanderers—what the fence guards call 'noms,' short for 'nomadic zombies'—but most don't travel. You'll see."

The forest was old but surprisingly lush in the late August heat. Tom found fruit trees, and they ate their fill of sweet pears as they walked. Benny began filling his pockets with them, but Tom shook his head.

"They're heavy and they'll slow you. Besides, I picked a route that'll take us through what used to be farm country. Lots of fruit growing wild. Some vegetables, too. Wild beans and such."

Benny looked at the fruit in his hand, sighed, and let them fall.

"How come nobody comes out here to farm this stuff?" he asked.

"People are scared."

"Why? There's got to be forty guys working the fence."

"No, it's not the dead that scare them. People in town don't trust anything out here. They think there's a disease infesting everything. Food, the livestock that have run wild over the last fourteen years—everything."

"Yeah . . . ," Benny said diffidently. He'd heard that talk. "So . . . it's not true?"

"You ate those pears without a thought."

"You handed them to me."

Tom smiled. "Oh, so you trust me now?"

"You're a dork, but I don't think you want to turn me into a zom."

"Wouldn't have to get on you about cleaning your room, so let's not rule it out."

"You're so funny, I almost peed my pants," Benny said without expression, then said, "Wait, I don't get it. Traders bring in food all the time, and all the cows and chickens and stuff. . . . They were brought to town by travelers and hunters and people like that, right? So . . ."

"So, why do people think it's safe to eat that stuff and not the food growing wild out here?"

"Yeah."

"Good question."

"Well, what's the answer?"

"The people in town trust what's inside the fence. *Currently* inside the fence. If it came from outside, they remark on it. Like, on the second Wednesday of every month, folks will say, ''Bout time for the wagons, ain't it?,' but they don't really acknowledge where the wagons come from or why the wagons are covered in sheet metal and the horses wrapped in carpet and chain mail. They know, but they don't know. Or don't want to know."

"That doesn't make any sense."

Tom walked a bit before he said, "There's town and then there's the Rot and Ruin. Most of the time they aren't in the same world, you know?"

Benny nodded. "I guess I do."

He stopped and stared ahead with narrowed eyes. Benny couldn't see anything, but then Tom grabbed his arm and pulled him quickly off the road and led him in a wide circle through the groves of trees. Benny peered between the hundreds of tree trunks and finally caught a glimpse of three zoms, shuffling slowly along the road. One was whole; the other two had ragged flesh where other zoms had feasted on them while they were still alive.

Benny opened his mouth and almost asked Tom how he knew they were there, but Tom made a shushing gesture and continued on, moving soundlessly through the soft summer grass.

When they were well clear, Tom took them back up to the road.

"I didn't even see them!" Benny gasped, turning to look back.

"Neither did I."

"Then how . . . ?"

"You get a feel for this sort of thing."

Benny held his ground, still looking back. "I don't get it. There were only three of them. Couldn't you have . . . you know . . ."

"What?"

"Killed them," said Benny flatly. "Charlie Matthias said he'll go out of his way to chop a zom or two. He doesn't run from anything."

"Is that what he says?" Tom murmured, then continued down the road.

Benny shrugged, then followed.

7

TWICE MORE TOM PULLED BENNY OFF THE ROAD SO THEY COULD CIRCLE around wandering zombies. After the second time, once they were clear of the creatures' olfactory range, Benny grabbed Tom's arm and demanded, "Whyn't you just pop a cap in them?"

Tom gently pulled his arm free. He shook his head and didn't answer.

"What, are you afraid of them?" Benny yelled.

"Keep your voice down."

"Why? You afraid a zom will come after you? Big, tough zombie killer who's afraid to kill a zombie."

"Benny," said Tom with thin patience, "sometimes you say some truly stupid things."

"Whatever," Benny said, and pushed past him.

"Do you know where you're going?" Tom said when Benny was a dozen paces along the road.

"This way."

"I'm not," said Tom, and he began climbing the slope of a hill that rose gently from the left-hand side of the road. Benny stood in the middle of the road and seethed for a full minute.

He was muttering the worst words he knew all the while he climbed up the hill after Tom.

There was a narrower road at the top of the hill, and they followed that in silence. By ten o'clock they'd entered a series of steeper hills and valleys that were shaded by massive oak trees with cool green leaves. Tom cautioned Benny to be quiet as they climbed to the top of a ridge that overlooked a small country lane. At the curve of the road was a small cottage with a fenced yard and an elm tree so gnarled and ancient that it looked like the world had grown up around it. Two figures stood in the yard, but they were too small to see. Tom flattened out at the top of the ridge and motioned for Benny to join him.

Tom pulled his field glasses from a belt holster and studied the figures for a long minute.

"What do you think they are?" He handed the binoculars to Benny, who snatched them with more force than was necessary. Benny peered through the lenses in the direction Tom pointed.

"They're zoms," Benny said.

"No kidding, boy genius. But what *are* they?"

"Dead people."

"Ah."

"Ah . . . *what*?"

"You just said it. They're dead *people*. They were once living people."

"So what? Everybody dies."

"True," admitted Tom. "How many dead people have you seen?"

"What kind of dead? Living dead, like them, or dead dead, like Aunt Cathy?"

"Either. Both."

"I don't know. The zombies at the fence . . . and a couple of people in town, I guess. Aunt Cathy was the first person I ever knew who died. I was, like, six when she died. I remember the funeral and all." Benny continued to watch the zombies. One was a tall man, the other a young woman or teenage girl. "And . . . Morgie Mitchell's dad died after that scaffolding collapsed. I went to his funeral too."

"Did you see either of them quieted?"

"Quieted" was the acceptable term for the necessary act of inserting a metal spike, called a "sliver," into the base of the skull to sever the brain stem. Since First Night, anyone who died would reanimate as a zombie. Bites made it happen too, but really any recently deceased person would come back. Every adult in town carried at least one sliver, though Benny had never seen one used.

"No," he said. "You wouldn't let me stay in the room when Aunt Cathy died. And I wasn't there when Morgie's dad died. I just went to the funerals."

"What were the funerals like? For you, I mean."

"I dunno. Kind of quick. Kind of sad. And then everyone went to a party at someone's house and ate a lot of food. Morgie's mom got totally shitfaced—"

"Language."

"Morgie's mom got drunk," Benny said in way that suggested having his language corrected was as difficult as having his teeth pulled. "Morgie's uncle sat in the corner singing Irish songs and crying with the guys from the farm."

"That was a year, year and a half ago, right? First spring planting?"

"Yeah. They were building a corn silo, and Mr. Mitchell was using the rope hoist to send some tools up to the crew working on the silo roof. One of the scaffolding pipes broke, and a whole bunch of stuff came crashing down on him."

"It was an accident."

"Well, yeah, sure."

"How'd Morgie take it?"

"How do you think he took it? He was fu—I mean, he was screwed up." Benny handed back the glasses. "He's still a little screwed up."

"How's he screwed up?"

"I don't know. He misses his dad. They used to hang out a lot. Mr. Mitchell was pretty cool, I guess."

"Do you miss Aunt Cathy?"

"Sure, but I was little. I don't remember that much. I remember she smiled a lot. She was pretty. I remember she used to sneak me extra ice cream from the store where she worked. Half an extra ration."

Tom nodded. "Do you remember what she looked like?"

"Like Mom," said Benny. "She looked a lot like Mom."

"You were too little to remember Mom."

"I remember her," Benny said with an edge in his voice. He took out his wallet and showed Tom the image behind the glassine cover. "Maybe I don't remember her really well, but I think about her. All the time. Dad, too. I can even remember what she wore on First Night. A white dress with red sleeves. I remember the sleeves."

Tom closed his eyes and sighed, and his lips moved. Benny

thought he echoed the words "red sleeves." Tom opened his eyes. "I didn't know you carried this." His smile was small and sad. "I remember Mom. She's was more of a mother to me than my mom ever was. I was so happy when Dad married her. I can remember every line on her face. The color of her hair. Her smile. Cathy was a year younger, but they could have been twins."

Benny sat up and wrapped his arms around his knees. His brain felt twisted around. There were so many emotions wired into memories, old and new. He glanced at his brother. "You were older than I am now when, y'know, *it* happened."

"I turned twenty a few days before First Night. I was in the police academy. Dad married your mom when I was sixteen."

"You got to know them. I never did. I wish I . . ." He left the rest unsaid.

Tom nodded. "Me too, kiddo."

They sat in the shade of their private memories.

"Tell me something, Benny," said Tom. "What would you have done if one of your friends—say, Chong or Morgie—had come to Aunt Cathy's funeral and took a leak in her coffin?"

Benny was so startled by the question that his answer was unguarded. "I'd have jacked them up. I mean, *jacked* them up."

Tom nodded.

Benny stared at him. "What kind of question is that, though?"

"Indulge me. Why would you have freaked out on your friends?"

"Because they dissed Aunt Cathy, why do you think?"

"But she's dead."

"What the hell does that matter? Pissing in her coffin? I would *so* kick their asses."

"But why? Aunt Cathy was beyond caring."

"This is her funeral! Maybe she's still, I don't know, *there* in some way. Like Pastor Kellogg always says."

"What does he say?"

"That the spirits of those we love are always with us."

"Okay. What if you didn't believe that? What if you believed that Aunt Cathy was only a body in a box? And your friends peed on her?"

"What do you think?" Benny snapped. "I'd still kick their asses."

"I believe you. But why?"

"Because," Benny began, but then hesitated, unsure of how to express what he was feeling. "Because Aunt Cathy was mine, you know? She's my aunt. My family. They don't have any right to disrespect my family."

"No more than you'd go take a crap on Morgie Mitchell's father's grave. Or dig him up and pour garbage on his bones. You wouldn't do anything like that?"

Benny was appalled. "What's your damage, man? Where do you come up with this crap? Of course I wouldn't do anything sick like that! God, who do you think I am?"

"Shhh . . . keep your voice down," cautioned Tom. "So . . . you wouldn't disrespect Morgie's dad . . . alive or dead?"

"Hell, no."

"Language."

Benny said it slower and with more emphasis. "Hell. No."

"Glad to hear it." Tom held out the field glasses. "Take a look at the two dead people down there. Tell me what you see."

"So we're back to business now?" Benny gave him a look. "You're deeply weird, man."

"Just look."

Benny sighed and grabbed the binoculars out of Tom's hand, put them to his eyes. Stared. Sighed.

"Yep. Two zoms. Same two zoms."

"Be specific."

"Okay. Okay, two zoms. One man, one woman. Standing in the same place as before. Big yawn."

Tom said, "Those dead people . . ."

"What about them?"

"They used to be somebody's family," said Tom quietly. "The male looks old enough to have been someone's granddad. He had a family, friends. A name. He was somebody."

Benny lowered the glasses and started to speak.

"No," said Tom. "Keep looking. Look at the woman. She was, what? Eighteen years old when she died. Might have been pretty. Those rags she's wearing might have been a waitress's uniform once. She could have worked at a diner right next to Aunt Cathy. She had people at home who loved her. . . ."

"C'mon, man, don't—"

"People who worried when she was late getting home. People who wanted her to grow up happy. People—a mom and a dad. Maybe brothers and sisters. Grandparents. People who believed that girl had a life in front of her. That old man might be her granddad."

"But she's one of *them*, man. She's dead," Benny said defensively.

"Sure. Almost everyone who ever lived is dead. More than

six billion people are dead. And every last one of them had family once. Every last one of them *were* family once. At one time there was someone like you who would have kicked the crap out of anyone—stranger or best friend—who harmed or disrespected that girl. Or the old man."

Benny was shaking his head. "No, no, no. It's not the same. These are zoms, man. They kill people. They eat people."

"They used to *be* people."

"But they died!"

"Sure. Like Aunt Cathy and Mr. Mitchell."

"No . . . Aunt Cathy got cancer. Mr. Mitchell died in an accident."

"Sure, but if someone in town hadn't quieted them, they'd have become living dead, too. Don't even pretend you don't know that. Don't pretend you haven't thought about that happening to Aunt Cathy." He nodded down the hill. "Those two down there caught a disease."

Benny said nothing. He'd learned about it in school, though no one knew for sure what had actually happened. Some sources said it was a virus that was mutated by radiation from a returning space probe. Others said it was a new type of flu that came over from China. Chong believed it was something that got out of a lab somewhere. The only thing everyone agreed on was that it was a disease of some kind.

"That guy down there was probably a farmer," Tom said. "The girl was a waitress. I'm pretty sure neither of them was involved in the space program. Or worked in some lab where they researched viruses. What happened to them was an accident. They got sick, Benny, and they died."

Benny said nothing.

"How do you think Mom and Dad died?"

No answer.

"Benny—? How do you think?"

"They died on First Night," Benny said irritably.

"They did. But how?"

Benny said nothing.

"How?"

"You let them die!" Benny said in a savage whisper. Words tumbled out of him in a disjointed sputter. "Dad got sick and . . . and . . . then Mom tried to . . . and you . . . you just ran away!"

Tom said nothing, but sadness darkened his eyes, and he shook head slowly.

"I remember it," Benny growled. "I remember you running away."

"You were a baby."

"I remember it."

"You should have told me, Benny."

"Why? So you could make up a lie about why you just ran away and left my mom like that?"

The words "*my* mom" hung in the air between them. Tom winced.

"You think I just ran away?" he said.

"I don't *think* it, Tom. I remember it."

"Do you remember why I ran?"

"Yeah, 'cause you're a freaking coward is why!"

"Jesus," Tom whispered. He adjusted the strap that held the sword in place, and sighed again. "Benny, this isn't the time or place for this, but sometime soon we're going to have a serious talk about the way things were back then and the way things are now."

"There's nothing you can say that's going to change the truth."

"No. The truth is the truth. What changes is what we know about it and what we're willing to believe."

"Yeah, yeah, whatever."

"If you ever want to know my side of things," said Tom, "I'll tell you. There's a lot you were too young to know then, and maybe you're still too young now."

Silence washed back and forth between them.

"For right now, Benny, I want you to understand that when Mom and Dad died, it was from the same thing that killed those two down there."

Benny said nothing.

Tom plucked a stalk of sweet grass and put it between his teeth. "You didn't really know Mom and Dad, but let me ask you this: If someone was to piss on them or abuse them—even now, even considering what they had to have become during First Night—would it be okay with you?"

"Screw you."

"Tell me."

"No. Okay? No, it wouldn't freaking be okay with me. You happy now?"

"Why not, Benny?"

"Because."

"Why not? They're only zoms."

Benny abruptly got up and walked down the hill, away from the farm and away from Tom. He stood looking back along the road they'd traveled, as if he could still see the fence line. Tom waited a long time before he got up and joined him.

"I know this is hard, kiddo," he said gently, "but we live in a pretty hard world. We struggle to live. We're always on our guard, and we have to toughen ourselves just to get through each day. And each night."

"I hate you."

"Maybe. I doubt it, but it doesn't matter right now." He gestured toward the path that led back home. "Everybody west of here has lost someone. Maybe someone close or maybe a distant cousin three times removed. But everybody lost someone."

Benny said nothing.

"I don't believe that you would disrespect anyone in our town or in the whole west. I also don't believe—I don't want to believe—that you'd disrespect the mothers and fathers, sons and daughters, sisters and brothers who live out here in the great Rot and Ruin."

He put his hands on Benny's shoulders and turned him around. Benny resisted, but Tom Imura was strong. When they were both facing east, Tom said, "Every dead person out there deserves respect. Even in death. Even when we fear them. Even when we have to kill them. They aren't 'just zoms,' Benny. That's a side effect of a disease or from some kind of radiation or something else that we don't understand. I'm no scientist, Benny. I'm a simple man doing a job."

"Yeah? You're trying to sound all noble, but you *kill* them." Benny had tears in his eyes.

"Yes," Tom said softly, "I do. I've killed hundreds of them. If I'm smart and careful—and lucky—I'll kill hundreds more."

Benny shoved him with both hands. It only pushed Tom back a half step. "I don't understand!"

"No, you don't. I hope you will, though."

"You talk about respect for the dead and yet you kill them."

"This isn't about the killing. It isn't, and never should be, about the killing."

"Then what?" Benny sneered. "The money?"

"Are we rich?"

"No."

"Then it's obviously not about the money."

"Then *what*?"

"It's about the *why* of the killing. For the living . . . for the dead," Tom said. "It's about closure."

Benny shook his head.

"Come with me, kiddo. It's time you understood how the world works. It's time you learned what the family business is all about."

THEY WALKED FOR MILES UNDER THE HOT SUN. THE PEPPERMINT GEL RAN off with their sweat, and had to be reapplied hourly. Benny was quiet for most of the trip, but as his feet got sore and his stomach started to rumble, he turned cranky.

"Are we there yet?"

"No."

"How far is it?"

"A bit."

"I'm hungry."

"We'll stop soon."

"What's for lunch?"

"Beans and jerky."

"I hate jerky."

"You bring anything else?" Tom asked.

"No."

"Jerky it is, then."

The roads Tom picked were narrow and often turned from asphalt to gravel to dirt.

"We haven't seen a zom in a couple of hours," Benny said. "How come?"

"Unless they hear or smell something that draws them, they tend to stick close to home."

"Home?"

"Well . . . to the places they used to live or work."

"Why?"

Tom took a couple of minutes on that. "There are lots of theories, but that's all we have—just theories. Some folks say that the dead lack the intelligence to think that there's anywhere other than where they're standing. If nothing attracts them or draws them, they'll just stay right where they are."

"But they need to hunt, don't they?"

"'Need' is a tricky word. Most experts agree that the dead will attack and kill, but it's not been established that they actually hunt. Hunting implies need, and we don't know that the dead *need* to do anything."

"I don't understand."

They crested a hill and looked down a dirt road to where an old gas station sat beneath a weeping willow.

"Have you ever heard of one of them just wasting away and dying of hunger?" Tom asked.

"No, but—"

"The people in town think that the dead survive by eating the living, right?"

"Well, sure, but—"

"What 'living' do you think they're eating?"

"Huh?"

"Think about it. There're more than three hundred million living dead in America alone. Throw in another thirty-odd million in Canada and a hundred ten million in Mexico, and you have something like four hundred and fifty million living dead. The Fall happened fourteen years ago. So—what are they eating to stay alive?"

Benny thought about it. "Mr. Feeney says they eat each other."

"They don't," said Tom. "Once a body has started to cool, they stop feeding on it. That's why there are so many partially eaten living dead. They won't attack or eat one another even if you locked them in the same house for years on end. People have done it."

"What happens to them?"

"The trapped ones? Nothing."

"Nothing? They don't rot away and die?"

"They're already dead, Benny." A shadow passed over the valley and momentarily darkened Tom's face. "But that's one of the mysteries. They don't rot. Not completely. They decay to a certain point, and then they just stop rotting. No one knows why."

"What do you mean? How can something just stop rotting? That's stupid."

"It's not stupid, kiddo. It's a mystery. It's as much a mystery as why the dead rise in the first place. Why they attack humans. Why they don't attack one another. All mysteries."

"Maybe they eat, like, cows and stuff."

Tom shrugged. "Some do, if they can catch them. A lot of people don't know that, by the way, but it's true. . . . They'll eat anything alive that they can catch. Dogs, cats, birds—even bugs."

"Well, then, that explains—"

"No," Tom interrupted. "Most animals are too fast. Ever

try to catch a cat who doesn't want to be caught? Now imagine doing that if you're only able to shuffle along slowly and can't strategize. If a bunch of the dead came upon cows in a pen or fenced field, they might be able to kill them and eat. But all the penned animals have either long-since escaped or they died off in the first few months. No . . . the dead don't *need* to feed at all. They just exist."

"Morgie says that out here wild animals turn into zoms."

"Nope. As far as anyone's been able to tell, only humans turn into the living dead. We don't have the science to try and figure out why, and I don't know if it's true everywhere, but we know it to be true here. Otherwise every time you bit into a chili dog, it'd bite back."

They reached the gas station. Tom stopped by the old pump and knocked on the metal casing three times, then twice, and then four more times.

"What are you doing?"

"Saying hello."

"Hello to . . . ?"

There was a low moan, and Benny turned to see a gray-skinned man shuffling slowly around the corner of the building. He wore ancient coveralls that were stained with dark blotches and, incongruously, a garland of fresh flowers around his neck. Marigolds and honeysuckle. The man's face was shaded for a few steps, but then he crossed into the sunlight, and Benny nearly screamed. The man's eyes were missing, and the sockets gaped emptily. The moaning mouth was toothless, the lips and cheeks sunken in. Worst of all, as the zombie raised its hands toward them, Benny saw that all of its fingers had been clipped off at the primary knuckles.

Benny gagged and stepped back, his muscles tensed to turn and run, but Tom put a hand on his shoulder and gave him a reassuring squeeze.

"Wait," said Tom.

A moment later the door to the gas station opened, and a pair of sleepy-eyed young women came outside, followed by a slightly older man with a long, brown beard. They were all thin and dressed in tunics that looked like they had been made from old bed sheets. Each wore a thick garland of flowers. The trio looked at Benny and Tom and then at the zombie.

"Leave him be!" cried the youngest, a black girl in her late teens, as she ran across the dirt to the dead man and stood between him and the Imura brothers, her feet planted, her arms spread to shield the zombie.

Tom raised a hand and took his hat off so they could see his face.

"Peace, little sister," he said. "No one's here to do harm."

The bearded man fished eyeglasses from a pocket beneath his tunic, and squinted through dirty lenses.

"Tom . . . ?" he said. "Tom Imura?"

"Hey, Brother David." He put his hand on Benny's shoulder. "This is my brother, Benjamin."

"What are you doing here?"

"Passing through," said Tom. "But I wanted to pay my respects. And to teach Benny the ways of *this* world. He's never been outside of the fence before."

Benny caught the way Tom put emphasis on the word "this."

Brother David walked over, scratching his beard. Up close he was older than he looked. Maybe forty, with deep brown eyes and a few missing teeth. His clothing was clean but threadbare. He smelled of flowers, garlic, and mint. The man studied Benny for a long moment, during which Tom did nothing and Benny fidgeted.

"He's not a believer," said Brother David.

"Belief is tough to come by in these times," said Tom.

"You believe."

"Seeing is believing."

Benny thought that their exchange had the cadence of a church litany, as if it was something the two of them had said before and would say again.

Brother David bent toward Benny. "Tell me, young brother, do you come here bringing hurt and harm to the Children of God?"

"Um . . . no?"

"Do you bring hurt and harm to the Children of Lazarus?"

"I don't know who they are, mister. I'm just here with my brother."

Brother David turned toward the women, who were using gentle pushes to steer the zombie back around the far side of the building. "Old Roger there is one of Lazarus's Children."

"What? You mean he's not a zom—"

Tom made a noise to stop him.

A tolerant smile flickered over Brother David's face. "We don't use that word, little brother."

Benny didn't know how to answer that, so Tom came to his rescue.

"The name comes from Lazarus of Bethany, a man who was raised from the dead by Jesus."

"Yeah, I remember hearing about that in church."

The mention of church brightened Brother David's smile. "You believe in God?" he asked hopefully.

"I guess. . . ."

"In these times," said Brother David, "that's better than most." He threw a covert wink at Tom.

Benny looked past Brother David to where the girls had taken the zombie. "I'm, like, totally confused here. That guy was a . . . you know. He's dead, right?"

"Living dead," corrected Brother David.

"Right. Why wasn't he trying to . . . you know." He mimed grabbing and biting.

"He doesn't have teeth," said Tom. "And you saw his hands."

Benny nodded. "Did you guys do that?" he asked Brother David.

"No, little brother," Brother David said with a grimace. "No, other people did that to Old Roger."

"Who?" demanded Benny.

"Don't you mean 'why?'"

"No . . . *who*. Who'd do something like that?"

Brother David said, "Old Roger is only one of the Children who have been tortured like that. You can see them all over this county. Men and women with their eyes cut out, their teeth pulled, or jaws shot away. Most of them missing fingers or whole hands. And I won't talk about some of the other things I've seen done. Stuff you're too young to know about, little brother."

"I'm fifteen," said Benny.

"You're too young. I can remember when being fifteen meant you were still a child." Brother David turned and watched the two young women return without the old zombie.

"He's in the shed," said the black girl.

"But he's agitated," said the other, a pale-skinned redhead in her mid-twenties.

"He'll quiet down after a spell," said Brother David.

The women stood by the gas pump and eyed Tom, although Tom seemed to suddenly find something fascinating about the movement of the clouds. Benny's usual inclination was to make a joke at Tom's expense, but he didn't feel like it. He turned back to the bearded man.

"Who's doing all this stuff you're talking about? To that old man. To those . . . others you mentioned. What kind of dirtbags are out here doing that stuff?"

"Bounty hunters," said the redhead.

"Killers," said the black girl.

"Why?"

"If I had an answer to that," said Brother David, "I'd be a saint instead of a way-station monk."

Benny turned to Tom. "I don't get it. . . . *You're* a bounty hunter."

"I guess to some people that's what I am."

"Do you do this kind of stuff?"

"What do you think?" Tom asked, but Benny was already shaking his head. Tom queried, "What do you even know about bounty hunters?"

"They kill zombies," Benny said, then flinched as he saw the looks of distaste on the faces of Brother David and the two women. "Well . . . they do! That's what bounty hunters are there for. They go out here into the Rot and Ruin, and they hunt the, um, you know . . . the living dead."

"Why?" asked Tom.

"For money."

"Who pays them?" asked Brother David.

"People in town. People in other towns," said Benny. "I heard the government pays them sometimes. Mostly for clearing out zoms on trade routes and stuff life that."

"Who'd you hear that from?" asked Tom.

"Charlie Matthias."

Brother David turned a questioning face to Tom, who said, "Charlie Pink-eye."

The faces of the monk and the two women fell into sickness. Brother David closed his eyes and shook his head slowly from side to side.

"What's wrong?" asked Benny.

"You can stay to dinner," Brother David said stiffly, eyes still closed. "God requires mercy and sharing from all of His children. But . . . once you've eaten, I'd like you to leave."

Tom put his hand on the monk's shoulder. "We're moving on now."

The redhead stepped toward Tom. "It was a lovely day until you came."

"You should get out of here," said the younger woman.

"No," said Brother David sharply, then repeated it more gently. "No, Sarah," he said to the redhead. "No, Shanti," he said to the black teenager. "Tom's our friend, and we're being rude." He opened his eyes, and Benny thought that the man now looked seventy. "I'm sorry, Tom. Please forgive the sisters, and please forgive me for—"

"No," said Tom. "It's okay. Sarah's right. It was a lovely day, and saying that man's name here was wrong of me. I apologize to you, to her, to Sister Shanti, and to Old Roger. This is Benny's first time out here in the Ruin. He met . . . that man . . . and had heard a lot of stories. Stories of hunting out here. He's a boy, and he doesn't understand. I brought him out here to let him know how things are. How things fall out." He paused. "I haven't taken him to Sunset Hollow yet. You understand?"

The three Children of God studied him for a while, and then one by one they nodded.

"What's Sunset Hollow?" Benny asked, but Tom didn't answer.

"And I thank you for your offer of a meal," said Tom, "but we've got miles to go, and I think Benny's going to have a lot of questions to ask. Some of them are better asked elsewhere."

Sister Sarah reached up and touched Tom's face. "I'm sorry for my words."

Sister Shanti touched his chest. "Me too."

"You've got nothing to be sorry about," Tom said.

The women smiled at him and caressed his cheek. Shanti turned and placed her hands on either side of Benny's face. "May God protect your heart out here in the world." With that she kissed him on the forehead and walked away. Sister Sarah smiled at the brothers and followed Shanti.

Benny turned to Tom. "Did I miss something?"

"Probably," said Tom. "Come on, kiddo. Let's roll."

Brother David shifted to stand in Tom's path. "Brother," he said. "I'll ask once and then be done with it."

"Ask away."

"Are you sure about what you're doing?"

"Sure? No. But I'm set on doing it." He fished in his pocket and brought out three vials of cadaverine. "Here, Brother. May it help you in your work."

Brother David nodded his thanks. "God go with you and before you and within you."

They shook hands, and Tom stepped back onto the dirt road. Benny, however, lingered for a moment longer.

"Look . . . mister," he began slowly, "I don't know what I said or did that was wrong, but I'm sorry, you know? Tom brought me out here, and he's a bit crazy, and I don't know what . . ." He trailed off. There was no road map in his head to guide him through this conversation.

Brother David offered his hand and gave him the same blessing he bestowed upon Tom.

"Yeah," said Benny. "You too. Okay?"

He hurried to catch up to Tom, who was fifty yards down the road. When he looked back the monk was standing by the rusting gas pump. Brother David lifted his hand, but whether it was some kind of blessing or a gesture of farewell, Benny didn't know. Either way it creeped him out.

When they were far down the road, Benny asked, "What was that all about? Why'd that guy get so jacked about me mentioning Charlie?"

"Not everyone thinks Charlie's 'the man,' kiddo."

"You jealous?"

Tom laughed. "God! The day I'm jealous of someone like Charlie Pink-eye is the day I'll cover myself in steak sauce and walk out into a crowd of the living dead."

"Hilarious," said Benny sourly. "What's with all that Children of God, Children of Lazarus stuff? What are they doing out here?"

"Brother David and his group are all over the Ruin. I've met travelers who've seen them as far east as Pennsylvania. Even all the way down to Mexico City. I first saw them about a year after the Fall. A whole bunch of them heading across the country in an old school bus pulled by horses, with Scripture passages painted all over it. Not sure how they got started or who chose the name. Even Brother David doesn't know. To him it's like they always were."

"Is he nuts?"

"I think the expression used to be 'touched by God.'"

"So that would be a yes."

"If he's nuts, then at least his heart's in the right place. The Children don't believe in violence of any kind."

"But they're okay with you, even though you kill zoms?"

Tom shook his head. "No, they don't like what I do. But they accept my explanation for why I do it, and Brother David and a few others have seen *how* I do it. They don't approve, but they don't condemn me for it. They think I'm misguided but well-intentioned."

"And Charlie? What do they think of him? Can't be anything good."

"They believe Charlie Pink-eye to be an evil man. Him and his jackass buddy, the Motor City Hammer. Bunch of others. Most of the bounty hunters, in fact, and I can't fault the Children for those beliefs."

Benny said nothing. He still thought Charlie Matthias was cool as all hell.

"So . . . these Children, what do they actually *do*?"

"They tend to the dead. If they find a town, they'll go through the houses and look for photos of the people who lived there, and then they try and round them up if they're still wandering around the town. They put them in their houses, seal doors, write some prayers on the walls, and then move on. Most of them keep moving. Brother David's been here for a year or so, but I expect he'll move on too."

"Charlie said that he rounds up zoms, too. He told us about a place in the mountains where he has a couple hundred of them staked out. He said it was one of the ways he and the Hammer were making the Ruin a safer place."

"Uh-huh," Tom said sourly. "The traders call it the Hungry

Forest. I think Charlie cooked up that name. Very dramatic. But it's not the same as what the Children do. Charlie rounds up zoms and ties them to trees, so that he can find them more easily when he gets a bounty job."

"That sounds smart."

"I never said Charlie wasn't smart. He's very smart, but he's also very twisted and dangerous, and his motives are not exactly admirable. He also does a lot of bulk work—cleaning out small towns and such for the traders. That doesn't make the people in town happy, because it confuses the issue of identification when you wipe out a whole town of zoms, but salvaging for stuff is more important. We've become an agricultural society. No one's made much of an effort to restart industry, and people seem to think that we can salvage forever for almost everything we need. It's like in the old days, when people drilled for oil for cars and factories without making much of an effort to find renewable sources for energy. It's a pillage-and-plunder mentality, and it makes us scavengers. That's not the best place to be on the food chain. Charlie's happy with it, though, because a cleanup job is big money." He looked back over his shoulder in the direction they'd come. "The Children, on the other hand . . . They may be crazy and they may be misguided, but they do what they believe is the right thing."

"How do they round up zoms? Especially in a town full of them?"

"They wear carpet coats, and they know the tricks of moving quietly and using cadaverine to mask their living smells. Sometimes one or another of the Children will come to town to buy some, but more often guys like me bring some out to them."

"Don't they ever get attacked?"

Tom nodded. "All the time, sad to say. I know of at least fifty dead in this part of the country who used to be Children. I'd quiet them, but Brother David won't let me. And I've even heard stories that some of the Children give themselves to the dead."

Benny stared at him. "*Why?*"

"Brother David says that some of the Children believe that the dead are the meek who were meant to inherit the earth, and that all things under heaven are there to sustain them. They think that allowing the dead to feed on them is fulfilling God's will."

"That's stupid," Benny said.

"It is what it is. I think a lot of the Children are people who didn't survive the Fall. Oh, sure, their bodies did, but I think some fundamental part of them was broken by what happened. I was there, I can relate."

"You're not crazy."

"I have my moments, kiddo, believe me."

Benny gave him a strange look. Then he smiled. "I think that redheaded woman, Sister Sarah, has the hots for you. As disgusting a concept as that seems."

Tom shook his head. "Too young for me. Though . . . I thought she looked a bit like Nix. What do you think?"

"I think you should shove that right up your—"

And that's when they heard the gunshots.

WHEN THE FIRST SHOT CRACKED THROUGH THE AIR, BENNY DROPPED to a crouch, but Tom stood straight and looked away to the northeast. When Tom heard the second shot, he turned his head slightly more to the north.

"Handgun," he said. "Heavy caliber. Three miles."

Benny looked up at him through the arms he'd wrapped over his head. "Bullets can go three miles, can't they?"

"Not usually," said Tom. "Even so, they aren't shooting at us."

Benny straightened cautiously. "You can tell? How?"

"Echoes," he said. "Those bullets didn't travel far. They're shooting at something close and hitting it."

"Um . . . it's cool that you know that. A little freaky, but cool."

"Yeah, this whole thing is about me showing you how cool I am."

"Oh. Sarcasm," said Benny dryly. "I get it."

"Shut up," replied Tom with a grin.

"No, you shut up."

They smiled at each other for the first time all day.

"C'mon," said Tom, "let's go see what they're shooting at." He set off in the direction of the gunshot echoes.

Benny stood watching him for a moment. "Wait . . . we're going *toward* the shooting?"

Benny shook his head and followed as quickly as he could. Tom picked up the pace, and Benny, his stomach full of beans and the hated jerky, kept up. They followed a stream down to the lowlands, but Benny noticed that Tom never went closer than a thousand yards to the running water of Coldwater Creek. He asked Tom about this.

Tom asked, "Can you hear the water?"

Benny strained to hear. "No."

"There's your answer. Flowing water is constant noise. It masks other sounds, which means it isn't safe unless you're traveling on it in a fast canoe, and this water isn't deep enough for that. We'll only go near it to cross it or to fill our canteens. Otherwise, quiet is better for listening. Always remember that if we can hear something, then it can probably hear us. And if we can't hear something, then it might still be able to hear us, and we won't know about it until it's too late."

However, as they followed the gunshot echoes, their path angled toward the stream. Tom stopped for a moment and then shook his head in disapproval. "Not bright," he said, but didn't explain his comment. They ran on.

As they moved, Benny practiced being quiet. It was harder than he thought, and for a while it sounded—to his ears—as if he was making a terrible racket. Twigs broke like firecrackers under his feet, his breath sounded like a wheezing dragon, the legs of his jeans whisked together like a crosscut saw. Tom told him to focus on quieting one thing at a time.

"Don't try to learn too many skills at once. Take a new skill and learn it by using it. Go from there."

By the time they were close to where they thought the gunshots were being fired, Benny was moving more quietly and found that he enjoyed the challenge. It was like playing ghost tag with Chong and Morgie.

Tom stopped and cocked his head to listen. He put a finger to his lips and gestured for Benny to remain still. They were in a field of tall grass, which led to a dense stand of birch trees. From beyond the trees they could hear the sound of men laughing and shouting, and the occasional hollow crack of a pistol shot.

"Stay here," Tom whispered, and then he moved as quick and quiet as a sudden breeze, vanishing into the tall grass. Benny lost track of him almost at once. More gunshots popped in the dry air.

A full minute passed, and Benny felt a burning constriction in his chest and realized that he was holding his breath. He let it out and gulped in another.

Where was Tom?

Another minute. More laughter and shouts. A few scattered gunshots. A third minute. A fourth.

Then something large and dark moved quickly toward him through the tall grass.

"Tom!" Benny almost screamed the name, but Tom shushed him. His brother stepped close and bent to whisper.

"Benny, listen to me. On the other side of those trees is something you need to see. If you're going to understand how things really are, you need to see."

"What is it?"

"Bounty hunters. Three of them. I've seen these three before, but never this close to town. I want you to come with me. Very quietly. I want you to watch, but don't say or do anything."

"But—"

"This will be ugly. Are you ready?"

"I—"

"Yes or no? We can head northeast and continue on our way. Or we can go home."

Benny shook his head. "No . . . I'm ready."

Tom smiled and squeezed his arm. "If things get serious, I want you to run and hide. Understand?"

"Yes," Benny said, but the word was like a thorn caught in his throat. Running and hiding. Was that the only strategy Tom knew?

"Promise?"

"I promise."

"Good. Now, follow me. When I move, you move. When I stop, you stop. Step only where I step. Got it? Good."

Tom led the way through the tall grass, moving slowly, shifting his position in time with the fluctuations of the wind. When Benny realized this, it became easier to match his brother's movement, step for step. They entered the trees, and Benny could more easily hear the laughter of the three men. They sounded drunk. Then he heard the whinny of a horse.

A horse?

The trees thinned, and Tom hunkered down and pulled Benny down with him. The scene before them was something out of a nightmare. Even as Benny took it in, a part of his mind was whispering to him that he would never forget what he was seeing. He could feel every detail being burned into his brain.

Beyond the trees was a clearing bordered on two sides by switchbacks of the deep stream. The stream vanished around a sheer sandstone cliff that rose thirty feet above the treeline and reappeared on the opposite side of the clearing. Only a narrow dirt path led from the trees in which the Imura brothers crouched to the spit of land framed by stream and cliff. It was a natural clearing that gave the men a clear view of the approaches on all sides. A wagon with two big horses stood in the shade thrown by the birch trees. The back of the wagon was piled high with zombies that squirmed and writhed in a hopeless attempt to flee or attack. Hopeless, because beside the wagon was a growing pile of severed arms and legs. The zombies in the wagon were limbless cripples.

A dozen other zombies milled by the sandstone wall of the cliff, and every time one of them would lumber after one of the men, it was driven back by a vicious kick. It was clear to Benny that two of the men knew some kind of martial art, because they used elaborate jumping and spinning kicks. The more dynamic the kick, the more the others laughed and applauded. As Benny listened, he realized that as one stepped up to confront a zombie, the other two men would name a kick. The men shouted bets to one another and then rated the kicks for points. The two kick fighters took turns while the third man kept score by drawing numbers in the dirt with a stick.

The zombies had little hope of any effective attack. They were clustered on a narrow and almost water-locked section of the clearing. Far worse than that, each and every one of them was blind. Their eye sockets were oozing masses of torn flesh and almost colorless blood. Benny looked at the zombies on the wagon and saw that they were all blind as well.

He gagged, but clamped a hand to his mouth to keep the sound from escaping.

The standing zombies were all battered hulks, barely able to stay on their feet, and it was clear that this game had been going on for a while. Benny knew the zombies were already dead, that they couldn't feel pain or know humiliation, but what he saw seared a mark on his soul.

"That one's 'bout totally messed up!" yelled a dark-skinned man with an eye patch. "Load him up."

The man who apparently didn't know the fancy kicks picked up a sword with a heavy, curved blade. Benny had seen pictures of one in the book *The Arabian Nights*. A scimitar.

"Okay," said the swordsman, "what're the numbers?"

"Denny did his in four cuts in three point one seconds," said Eye-patch.

"Oh, hell . . . I got that beat. Time me."

Eye-patch dug a stopwatch out of his pocket. "Ready . . . Steady . . . *Go!*"

The swordsman rushed toward the closest zombie—a teenage boy who looked like he'd been about Benny's age when he died. The blade swept upward in a glittering line that sheared through the zombie's right arm at the shoulder, and then he checked his swing and sliced down to take the other arm. Instantly he pivoted and swung the sword laterally and chopped through both legs, an inch below the groin. The zombie toppled to the ground, and one leg, against all odds, remained upright.

The three men burst out laughing.

"Time!" yelled Eye-patch, and read the stopwatch. "Holy crap, Stosh. That's two point nine-nine seconds!"

"And three cuts!" shouted Stosh. "I did it in three cuts!"

They howled with laughter, and the third man, Denny, squatted down, wrapped his burly arms around the limbless zombie's torso, picked it up with a grunt, and carried it over to the wagon. Eye-patch tossed him the limbs—one-two-three-four—and Denny added them to the pile.

The kicking game started up again. Stosh drew a pistol and shot one of the remaining zombies in the chest. The bullet did no harm, but the creature turned toward the impact and began lumbering in that direction. Denny yelled, "Jump-spinning back kick!"

And Eye-patch leaped into the air, twisted, and drove a savage kick into the zombie's stomach, knocking it backward into the others. They all fell, and the men laughed and handed around a bottle while the zombies clambered awkwardly to their feet.

Tom leaned close to Benny and whispered, "Time to go."

He moved away, but Benny caught up to him and grabbed his sleeve. "What the hell are you doing? Where are you going?"

"Away from these clowns," said Tom.

"You have to *do* something!"

Tom turned to face him. "What is it you expect me to do?"

"Stop them!" Benny said in an urgent whisper.

"Why?"

"Because they're . . . because . . . ," Benny sputtered.

"You want me to save the zombies, Benny? Is that it?"

Benny, caught in the fires of his own frustration, glared at him.

"They're bounty hunters, Benny," said Tom. "They get a bounty on every zombie they kill. Want to know why they don't just cut the heads off? Because they have to prove that it was they who killed the zombies and that they didn't just collect heads from someone else's kill. So they bring the torsos back to town and do the killing in front of a bounty judge, who then pays them a half day's rations for every kill. Looks like they have enough there for each of them to get almost five full days' rations."

"I don't believe you."

"Keep your voice down," Tom hissed. "And, yes, you do believe me. I can see it in your eyes. The game these guys are playing—that's ugly, right? It got you so upset that you wanted me to step in and do something. Am I right?"

Benny said nothing. His fists were balled into knuckly knots at his sides.

"Well, as bad as that is . . . I've seen worse. A whole lot worse. I'm talking pit fights where they put some dumb-ass kid—maybe someone your age—in a hole dug in the ground and then push in a zom. If the kid's lucky, maybe they'll give him a knife or a sharpened stick or a baseball bat. Sometimes the kid wins, sometimes he doesn't, but the oddsmakers haul in a fortune either way. And where do the kids come from? They *volunteer* for it."

"That's bull. . . ."

"No, it's not. If I wasn't around, and you lived with Aunt Cathy when she was sick with the cancer, what would you have done? How much would you have risked to make sure she got enough food and medicine?"

Benny shook his head, but Tom's face was stone.

"Are you going to tell me that you wouldn't take a shot at winning maybe a month's worth of rations—or a whole box of meds—for ninety seconds in a zom pit?"

"That doesn't happen."

"No?"

"I've never heard about anything like that."

Tom snorted. "If you did something like that . . . would you tell anyone? Would you even tell Chong and Morgie?"

Benny didn't answer.

Tom pointed. "I can go back there and maybe stop those guys. Maybe even do it without killing them or getting killed myself, but what good would it do? You think they're the only ones doing this sort of thing? This is the great Rot and Ruin, Benny. There's no law out here, not since First Night. Killing zoms is what people do out here."

"That's not killing them! It's sick. . . ."

"Yes, it is," Tom said softly. "Yes, it is, and I can't tell you how relieved and happy I am to hear you say it. To know that you believe it."

There were more shouts and laughter from behind them. And another gunshot.

"I can stop them if you want me to. But it won't stop what's happening out here."

Tears burned in Benny's eyes, and he punched Tom hard in the chest. "But *you* do this stuff! You kill zombies."

Tom grabbed Benny and pulled him close. Benny struggled, but Tom pulled his brother to his chest and held him. "No," he whispered. "No. Come on. . . . I'll show you what I do."

He released Benny, placed a gentle hand on his brother's back, and guided him back through the trees to the tall grass.

They didn't speak for several miles. Benny kept looking back, but even he didn't know if he was checking to see if they were being followed or looking with regret that they'd done nothing about what was happening. His jaw ached from clenching.

They reached the crest of the hill that separated the field of tall grass from an upslope that wound around the base of a huge mountain. There was a road there, a two-lane blacktop that was cracked and choked with weeds. The road spun off toward a chain of mountains that marched into the distance and vanished into heat haze far to the southeast. There were old bones among the weeds, and Benny kept stopping to look at them.

"I don't want to do this anymore," said Benny.

Tom kept walking.

"I don't want to do what you do. Not if it means doing . . . that sort of stuff."

"I already told you. I don't do that sort of stuff."

"But you're around it. You see it. It's part of your life." Benny kicked a rock and sent it skittering off the road and into the grass. Crows scolded him as they leaped into the air, leaving behind a rabbit carcass on which they'd been feeding.

Tom stopped and looked back. "If we turn back now, you'll only know part of the truth."

"I don't care about the truth."

"Too late for that now, Benny. You've seen some of it. If you don't see the rest, it'll leave you—"

"Leave me what? *Unbalanced*? You can stick that Zen crap up your—"

"Language."

Benny bent and snatched up a shinbone that had been polished white by scavengers and weather. He threw it at Tom, who sidestepped to let it pass.

"Screw you and your truth and all of this stuff!" screamed Benny. "You're just like those guys back there! You come out here, all noble and wise and with all that bull, but you're no different. You're a killer. Everyone in town says so!"

Tom stalked over to him and grabbed a fistful of Benny's shirt and lifted him to his toes. "Shut up!" he said with a snarl. "You just shut your damn mouth!"

Benny was shocked into silence.

"You don't know who I am or what I am." Tom shook Benny hard enough to rattle his teeth. "You don't know what I've done. You don't know the things I've had to do to keep you safe. To keep us safe. You don't know what I—"

He broke off and flung Benny away from him. Benny staggered backward and fell hard on his butt, legs splayed among the weeds and old bones. His eyes bugged with shock, and Tom stood above him, different expressions warring on his face. Anger, shock at his own actions, burning frustration. Even love.

"Benny . . ."

Benny got to his feet and dusted off his pants. Once more he looked back the way they'd come and then stepped up to Tom, staring up at his big brother with an expression that was equally mixed and conflicted.

"I'm sorry," they both said.

They stared at each other.

Benny smiled.

Tom's smile was slower in coming.

"You're a total pain in my butt, little brother."

"You're a world-class jerk."

The hot breeze blew past them. Tom said, "If you want to go back, then we'll go back."

Benny shook his head. "No."

"Why not?"

"Do I have to have an answer?"

"Right now? No. Eventually? Probably."

"Yeah," said Benny. "That's okay, I guess. Just tell me one thing. I know you said it already, but I really need to know. Really, Tom."

Tom nodded.

"You're *not* like them. Right? Swear on something." He pulled out his wallet and held up the picture. "Swear on Mom and Dad."

Tom nodded. "Okay, Benny. I swear."

"On Mom and Dad."

"On Mom and Dad." Tom touched the picture and nodded.

"Okay," said Benny. "Then let's go."

The afternoon burned on, and they followed the two-lane road around the base of the mountain. Neither spoke for almost an hour and then Tom said, "This isn't just a walk we're taking, kiddo. I'm out here on a job."

Benny shot him a look. "You're here to kill a zom?"

Tom shrugged. "It's not the way I like to phrase it, but . . . yes, that's the bottom line."

They walked another half mile.

"How does this work? The . . . job, I mean."

"You saw part of it when you applied to that erosion artist," said Tom. He dug into a jacket pocket and removed an envelope, opened it, and took out a piece of paper that he unfolded and handed to Benny. There was a small color photograph clipped to one corner that showed a smiling man of about thirty, with sandy hair and a sparse beard. The paper it was clipped to was a large portrait of the same man as he might be now if he was a zombie. The name "Harold" was handwritten in one corner.

"This is why erosion portraits are so useful. People have pictures done of wives, husbands, children . . . anyone they loved. Someone they lost. Sometimes they can even remember what a person was wearing on First Night, and that makes it easier for me, because as I said, the dead seldom move far from where they lived. Or worked. Guys like me find them."

"And kill them?"

Tom answered that with a shrug. They rounded a bend in the road and saw the first few houses of a small town built onto the side of the mountain. Even from a quarter mile away Benny could see zombies standing in yards or on the sidewalks. One stood in the middle of the road with his face tilted toward the sun.

Nothing moved.

Tom folded the erosion portrait and put it in his pocket, then took out the vial of cadaverine and sprinkled some on his clothes. He handed it to Benny, then dabbed some mint gel on his upper lip and passed the jar to his brother.

"You ready?"

"Not even a little bit," said Benny.

Tom loosened his sword in its scabbard, and led the way. Benny shook his head, unsure of how exactly the day had brought him to this moment, and then followed.

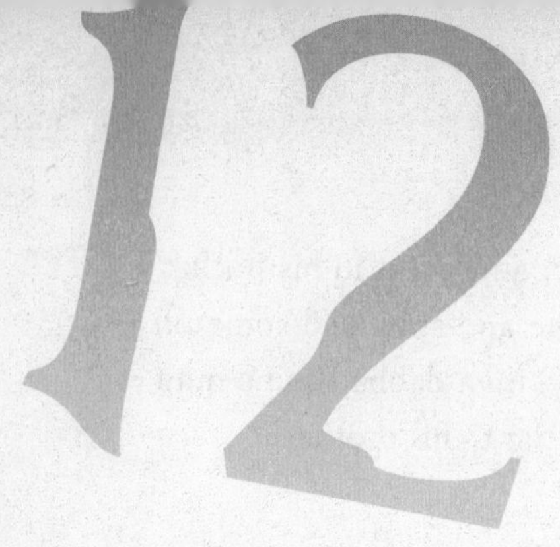

"WON'T THEY ATTACK US?" BENNY WHISPERED.

"Not if we're smart and careful. The trick is to move slowly. They respond to quick movements. Smell, too, but we have that covered."

"Can't they hear us?"

"Yes, they can," Tom said. "So once we're in the town, don't talk unless I do, and even then—less is more, and quieter is better than loud. I found that speaking slowly helps. A lot of the dead moan . . . so they're used to slow, quiet sounds."

"This is like the Scouts," Benny said. "Mr. Feeney told us that when we're in nature we should act like we're part of nature."

"For better or worse, Benny . . . this is part of nature too."

"That doesn't make me feel good, Tom."

"This is the Rot and Ruin, kiddo. . . . Nobody feels good out here. Now hush and keep your eyes open."

They slowed their pace as they neared the first houses. Tom stopped and spent a few minutes studying the town. The main street ran upward to where they stood, so they had a good view of everything. Moving very slowly, Tom removed the envelope from his pocket and unfolded the erosion portrait.

"My client said that it was the sixth house along the main street," Tom murmured. "Red front door and white fence. See it? There, past the old mail truck."

"Uh-huh," Benny said without moving his lips. He was terrified of the zombies that stood in their yards not more than twenty paces away.

"We're looking for a man named Harold Simmons. There's nobody in the yard, so we may have to go inside."

"Inside?" Benny asked, his voice quavering.

"Come on." Tom began moving slowly, barely lifting his feet. He did not exactly imitate the slow, shuffling gait of the zombies, but his movements were unobtrusive. Benny did his best to mimic everything Tom did. They passed two houses in which zombies stood in the yard. The first house, on their left, had three zombies on the other side of a hip-high chain-link fence. Two little girls and an older woman. Their clothes were tatters that blew like holiday streamers in the hot breeze. As Tom and Benny passed by them, the old woman turned in their direction. Tom stopped and waited, his hand touching the handle of his sword, but the woman's dead eyes swept past them without lingering. A few paces along, they passed a yard on their right in which a man in a bathrobe stood, staring at the corner of the house as if he expected something to happen. He stood among wild weeds and creeper vines that had wrapped themselves around his calves. It looked like he had stood there for years, and with a sinking feeling of horror, Benny realized that he probably had.

Benny wanted to turn and run. His mouth was as dry as

sand, and sweat ran down his back and into his underwear.

They moved steadily down the street, always slow. The sun was heading toward the western part of the sky, and it would be dark in four or five hours. Benny knew they could never make it home by nightfall. He wondered if Tom would take them back to the gas station . . . or if he was crazy enough to claim an empty house in this ghost town for the night. If he had to sleep in a zombie's house, even if there was no zombie there, then Benny was sure he'd go completely mad-cow crazy.

"There he is," murmured Tom, and Benny looked toward the house with the red door. A man stood inside, looking out of the big bay window. He once had sandy hair and a sparse beard, but now the hair and beard were nearly gone, and the skin of his face had shriveled to a leathery tightness.

Tom stopped outside of the paint-peeling white picket fence. He looked from the erosion portrait to the man in the window and then back again.

"Benny?" he said under his breath. "You think that's him?"

"Mm-hm," Benny said with a low squeak.

The zombie in the window seemed to be looking at them. Benny was sure of it. The withered face and the dead pale eyes were pointed directly at the fence, as if it had been waiting there all these years for a visitor to come to the garden gate.

Tom nudged the gate with his toe. It was locked.

Moving very slowly, Tom leaned over and undid the latch. The process took more than two minutes. Nervous sweat ran down Benny's face, and he couldn't take his eyes off the zombie.

Tom pushed on the gate with his knee, and it opened.

"Very, very slowly," he said. "Red light, green light—all the way to the door."

Benny knew the game, though, in truth, he had never seen a working stoplight. They entered the yard. The old woman in the first garden suddenly turned toward them. So did the zombie in the bathrobe.

"Stop," Tom hissed. "If we have to make a run for it, head into the house. We can lock ourselves in and wait until they calm down."

The old lady and the man in the bathrobe faced them, but did not advance.

The tableau held for a minute that seemed an hour long.

"I'm scared," said Benny.

"It's okay to be scared," said Tom. "Scared means you're smart. Just don't panic. That'll get you killed."

Benny almost nodded, but caught himself.

Tom took a slow step. Then a second. It was uneven, his body swaying, as if his knees were stiff. The bathrobe zombie turned away and looked at the shadow of a cloud moving up the valley, but the old lady still watched. Her mouth opened and closed, as if she was slowly chewing on something.

But then she too turned away to watch the moving shadow.

Tom took another step and then another. Benny eventually followed. The process was excruciatingly slow, but to Benny it felt as if they were moving too fast. No matter how deliberately they went, he thought it was all wrong, that the zombies—all of them up, and down the street—would suddenly turn toward them and moan with their dry and dusty voices, and that a great mass of the hungry dead would surround them.

Tom reached the door and turned the handle.

The knob turned in his hand, and the lock clicked open. Tom gently pushed open the door and stepped into the gloom of the house. Benny cast a quick look at the window to make sure the zombie was still there.

Only he wasn't.

"Tom!" Benny cried. "Look out!"

A dark shape lunged at Tom out of the shadows of the entrance hallway. It clawed for him with wax-white fingers and moaned with an unspeakable hunger. Benny screamed.

Then something happened that Benny could not understand. Tom was there and then he wasn't. His brother's body became a blur of movement as he pivoted to the outside of the zombie's right arm, ducked low, grabbed the zombie's shins from behind, and drove his shoulder into the former Harold Simmons's back. The zombie instantly fell forward onto its face, knocking clouds of dust from the carpet. Tom leaped onto the zombie's back and used his knees to pin both shoulders to the floor.

"Close the door!" Tom barked as he pulled a spool of thin silk cord from his jacket pocket. He whipped the cord around the zombie's wrists and shimmied down to bring both its hands together to tie behind the creature's back. He looked up. "The door, Benny—*now!*"

Benny came out of his daze and realized there was movement in his peripheral vision. He turned to see the old lady, the two little girls, and the zombie in his bathrobe, lumbering up the garden path. Benny slammed the door and shot the bolt, then leaned against it, panting, as if he had been the one to wrestle a zombie to the ground and hog-tie it. With a sinking feeling he realized that it had probably been his own shouted warning that had attracted the other zombies.

Tom flicked out a spring-bladed knife and cut the silk cord. He kept his weight on the struggling zombie while he fashioned a large loop, like a noose. The zombie kept trying to turn its head to bite, but Tom didn't seem to care. Maybe he knew that the zom couldn't reach him, but Benny was still terrified of those gray rotted teeth.

With a deft twist of the wrist, Tom looped the noose over the zombie's head, catching it below the chin, and then he jerked the slack, so the closing loop forced the creature's jaws shut with a *clack*. Tom wound more silk cord around the zombie's head, so that the line passed under the jaw and over the crown. When he had three full turns in place, he tied the cord tightly. He shimmied down the zombie's body and pinned its legs and then tied its ankles together.

Then Tom stood up, stuffed the rest of the cord into his pocket, and closed his knife. He slapped dust from his clothes as he turned back to Benny.

"Thanks for the warning, kiddo, but I had it."

"Um . . . holy sh—!"

"Language," Tom interrupted quietly.

Tom went to the window and looked out. "Eight of 'em out there."

"Do . . . do we . . . I mean, shouldn't we board up the windows?"

Tom laughed. "You listen to too many campfire tales. If

we started hammering nails into boards, the sound would call every living dead in the whole town. We'd be under siege."

"But we're trapped."

Tom looked at him. "'Trapped' is a relative term," he said. "We can't go out the front. I expect there's a back door. We'll finish our business here and then we'll sneak out nice and quiet, and head on our way."

Benny stared at him and then at the struggling zombie that was thrashing and moaning.

"You . . . you just . . ."

"Practice, Benny. I've done this before. C'mon, help me get him up."

They knelt on opposite sides of the zombie, but Benny didn't want to touch it. He'd never touched a corpse of any kind before, and he didn't want to start with one that had just tried to bite his brother.

"Benny," Tom said, "he can't hurt you now. He's helpless."

The word "helpless" hit Benny hard. It brought back the image of Old Roger—with no eyes, no teeth, and no fingers—and the two young women who tended to him. And the limbless torsos in the wagon.

"Helpless," he murmured. "God . . ."

"Come on," Tom said gently.

Together they lifted the zombie. It was light—far lighter than Benny had expected—and they half-carried, half-dragged it into the dining room, away from the living room window. Sunlight fell in dusty slants through the moth-eaten curtains. The ruins of a meal had long since decayed to dust on the table. They put it in a chair, and Tom produced the spool of cord and bound it in place. The zombie continued to struggle, but Benny understood. The zombie was actually helpless.

Helpless.

The word hung in the air. Ugly and full of dreadful new meaning.

"What do we do with him?" Benny asked. "I mean . . . *after*?"

"Nothing. We leave him here."

"Shouldn't we bury him?"

"Why? This was his home. The whole world is a graveyard. If it was you, would you rather be in a little wooden box under the cold ground or in the place where you lived? A place where you were happy and loved."

Neither thought was appealing to Benny. He shivered even though the room was stiflingly hot.

Tom removed the envelope from his pocket. Apart from the folded erosion portrait, there was also a piece of cream stationery on which were several handwritten lines. Tom read through it silently, sighed, and then turned to his brother.

"Restraining the dead is difficult, Benny, but it isn't the hardest part." He held out the letter. "This is."

Benny took the letter.

"My clients—the people who hire me to come out here—they usually want something said. Things they would like to say themselves but can't. Things they need said, so they can have closure. Do you understand?"

Benny read the letter. His breath caught unexpectedly in his throat, and he nodded as the first tears fell down his cheeks.

His brother took the letter back. "I need to read it aloud, Benny. You understand?"

Benny nodded again.

Tom angled the letter into the dusty light, and read:

My dear Harold. I love you and miss you. I've missed you so desperately for all these years. I still dream about you every night, and each morning I pray that you've found peace. I forgive you for what you tried to do to me. I forgive you for what you did to the children. I hated you for a long time, but I understand now that it wasn't you. It was this thing that happened. I want you to know that I took care of our children when they turned. They are at peace, and I put flowers on their graves every Sunday. I know you would like that. I have asked Tom Imura to find you. He's a good man, and I know that he will be gentle with you. I love you, Harold. May God grant you His peace. I know that when my time comes, you will be waiting for me. Waiting with Bethy and little Stephen, and we will all be together again in a better world. Please forgive me for not having the courage to help you sooner. I will always love you.

Yours forever,
Claire

Benny was weeping when Tom finished. He turned away and covered his face with his hands, and sobbed. Tom went over and hugged him and kissed his head.

Then Tom stepped away, took a breath, and pulled a

second knife from his boot. This one, Benny knew, was Tom's favorite: a double-edge, black dagger with a ribbed handle and a six-and-a-half-inch-long blade. Benny didn't think he would be able to watch, but he raised his head and saw Tom as he placed the letter on the table in front of Harold Simmons and smoothed it out. Then he moved behind the zombie and gently pushed its head forward, so that he could place the tip of his knife against the hollow at the base of the skull.

"You can look away if you want to, Benny," he said.

Benny did not want to look, but he didn't turn away.

Tom nodded. He took another breath and then thrust the blade into the back of the zombie's neck. The blade slid in with almost no effort into the gap between spine and skull, and the razor-sharp edge sliced completely through the brain stem.

Harold Simmons stopped struggling. His body didn't twitch; there was no death spasm. He just sagged forward against the silken cords and was still. Whatever force had been active in him, whatever pathogen or radiation or whatever had taken the man away and left behind a zombie, was gone.

Tom cut the cords that held Simmons's arms and raised each hand, placing it on the table, so that the dead man's palms held the letter in place.

"Be at peace, brother," said Tom.

He wiped his knife and stepped back. He looked at Benny, who was openly sobbing.

"This is what I do, Benny."

PART TWO

Zombie Cards (Collect the Whole Set!)

"Everyone carries around his own monsters."

—Richard Pryor

13

For five days after they got back, Benny did nothing. In the mornings he sat in the backyard, invisible in the cool shade of the house as the sun rose in the east. When the sun was overhead, Benny went inside and sat in his room and stared out the window. As the sun set he'd go downstairs and sit on the top step of the porch. He didn't say more than a dozen words. Tom cooked meals and laid them out, and sometimes Benny ate and sometimes he didn't.

Tom did not try to force a conversation. Each night he gave Benny a hug and said, "We can talk tomorrow if you want to."

Nix came over on the third day. When Benny saw her standing on the other side of the garden gate, he just gave her a single small nod. She came in and sat down next to him.

"I didn't know you were back," she said.

Benny said nothing.

"Are you okay?"

Benny shrugged, but kept silent.

Nix sat with him for five hours and then went home.

Chong and Morgie came by with gloves and a ball, but Tom met them at the garden gate.

"What's up with Benny?" Chong asked.

Tom sipped from a cup of water and squinted at sun-drowsy honeybees, hovering over the hedge. "He needs a little time, is all."

"For what?" asked Morgie.

Tom didn't answer. The three of them looked across to where Benny sat staring at the grass that curled around the edges of his sneakers.

"He just needs some time," Tom repeated.

They went away.

Nix came again the next day. And the next.

On the sixth morning she brought a straw basket filled with blueberry muffins that were still hot from the oven. Benny accepted one, sniffed it, and ate it without comment.

A pair of crows landed on the fence, and Benny and Nix watched them for almost an hour.

Benny said, "I hate them."

Nix nodded, knowing that the comment wasn't about the crows or anything else they could see. She didn't know who Benny meant, but she understood hate. Her mother was crippled by it. Nix could not remember a single day when her mother didn't find some reason to curse Charlie Pink-eye or damn him to hell.

Benny bent and picked up a stone, and for a moment he looked at the crows, as if he was going to throw the rock at them, the way he and Morgie always did. Not to hurt the birds, but to scare a noise from them. Benny weighed the stone in his palm, then opened his fingers to let it tumble to the grass.

"What happened out there?" Nix said, asking the question that had hung burning in the air for a week.

It took Benny ten minutes to tell her about the Rot and Ruin. But Benny didn't just talk about zoms. Instead he talked about three bounty hunters on a rocky cleft by a stream in the mountains. He spoke without emotion, almost monotone, but long before he was finished, Nix was crying. Benny's eyes were hard and dry, as if all of his tears had been burned away by what he'd seen. Nix put her hand on Benny's, and they sat like that for more than an hour after he was done, watching as the day grew older.

As they sat Nix waited for Benny to turn his hand, to take hers in his, to curl his fingers or thread them through hers. She had never felt closer to him, never believed in the possibility of *them* more than she did then. But the hour burned away and turned to ash, and Benny did not return her grip. He merely allowed it.

When the evening crickets began singing, Nix got up and went out through the garden gate. Benny had not said another word since he'd finished telling his tale. Nix really wasn't sure that he knew she'd held his hand. Or that she'd left.

She cried all the way home. Quietly, to herself, without drama. Not because she had lost Benny, but because she now knew that she had never had him. She wept for the hurt that he owned, a hurt she could never hope to remove.

Benny sat outside until it was fully dark. Twice he looked at the garden gate, at the memory of Nix carefully opening it and closing it behind her. He ached. Not for her, but because she ached for him—and he could feel it now. He'd always known it was there, but now—somehow, for some indefinable reason—he could *feel* it. And he knew he wanted her. He wanted to break his oath with Chong and forget that they were just friends and . . .

He wanted a lot of things. But the world had changed, and when he had the chance to take her hand, he hadn't.

Why not?

He knew that it had nothing to do with the oath. Or with friendship. He knew that much, but the rest of his mind was draped in weird shadows that blinded his inward eye. Nothing made sense anymore.

He could feel the heat of her touch on his hand even though she was now out of sight.

"Nix," he said. But she was gone, and he had let her go.

He got up and slapped dirt from his jeans, then looked up at the yellow August moon that hung in the sky beyond the garden fence. It was the same moon, but it looked different now. He knew it always would.

THE FOLLOWING MORNING WAS COOL FOR THE FIRST DAY OF SEPTEMBER. Benny lay in bed and stared out the window at the dense white clouds stacked tall above the mountains. The air was moist with the promise of rain.

Benny was awake for more than an hour before he realized that he felt better. Not completely. Maybe not even a lot. Just . . . better.

It was the last week of summer break. School started next Monday, although with his new job, that would only be half days. He lay there, listening to the birds singing in the trees. Tom once told him that birds sing differently before and after a storm. Benny didn't know if that was true, but he could understand why they would.

He got up, washed, dressed, and went downstairs for breakfast. Tom set out a plate of eggs for him, and Benny ate them all and then scavenged the frying pan for leftovers. They ate in silence almost to the last bite before Benny said, "Tom . . . the way you do it . . . Does anyone else do it that way? Closure, I mean."

Tom sipped his coffee. "A few. Not many. There's a husband-and-wife team up north in Haven. And there's a guy named Church who does it in Freeland. No one else here in Mountainside."

"Why not?"

Tom hesitated, then shrugged. "It takes longer."

"No," Benny said. "Don't do that."

"Do what?"

"Sugarcoat it. If this is the way it is, if I'm going to have to be a part of it, don't jerk me around. Don't lie to me."

Tom set down his cup of coffee and then nodded. "Okay. Most don't do it this way, because it hurts too much. It's too . . ." He fished for a word.

"Real?" Benny suggested.

"I guess so," said Tom. He tasted the word. "'Real.' Yeah . . . that about says it."

Benny nodded and ate the last piece of toast.

After a while Tom said, "If you're going to do this with me—"

"I didn't say I was. I said 'if.'"

"So did I. *If* you're going to do this with me, then you have to learn how to handle yourself. That means getting in better shape and learning how to fight."

"Guns?"

"Hand to hand first," Tom said. "And swords. Wooden swords in the beginning. We'll start right after school."

"Okay," Benny said.

"Okay . . . what?"

"Okay."

They didn't speak again that morning.

▪ ▪ ▪

When Benny got to the garden gate, he stood looking at it, as if it was a dividing line between who he had been before Tom had taken him out into the Ruin and who he was going to be from now on. For a week he had been unable to open that gate, and even now, his hand trembled a little as he reached for the latch.

It opened without a crash of drums or ominous lightning forking through the clouds. Benny grinned ruefully, then headed down the lane toward Chong's house.

"THE ZOMBIES ARE COMING!"

Morgie Mitchell yelled that at the top of his voice, and everyone ran. Morgie ran side-by-side with Benny and Chong, the three of them blocking the pavement to keep the other kids from getting there first. It was a disaster, though. Zak Matthias deliberately tripped Morgie, who went flying and whose flailing fingers caught the back of Moby's pants and accidentally pulled them down to his knees.

Moby wore stained drawers, and with his pants around his knees, he couldn't manage the next step, and he went down. So did Morgie. The crowd of kids hit the pair, who were already on the ground, but they were in motion, and everyone knew there was no hope. They all went down.

Only Benny, Chong, and Zak were still running. Zak was halfway down the block. Benny looked back, hesitated, grabbed Chong by the sleeve, mentally said *Screw it*, and ran even faster.

In the direction of the zombies.

They were at Lafferty's General Store. The Zombie Cards had arrived.

• • •

"Too bad about Morgie," said Chong.

"Yeah," agreed Benny. "Nice kid. He'll be missed."

They sat on the top step of the wooden porch in front of Lafferty's. A shadow fell across them.

"You guys are a couple of total jerks," said Morgie.

"Eek!" said Chong dryly. "It's a zom. Quick, run for your life."

Benny sipped from a bottle of pop and burped eloquently.

Morgie kicked Chong's foot, hard, and sat on the wooden step between his two friends. He looked at the stack of cards that lay on the step between Chong's sneakered feet. There was a similar stack—two packs still unopened—in front of Benny. Waxed-paper wrappers were crumpled on the top step.

"The guy said they're sold out already," he complained grumpily.

"Yeah. Those darn kids, huh?" murmured Benny.

"He said you two monkey-bangers bought the last couple of packs."

"Guy's lying," said Benny.

Morgie brightened. "What? He has some—?"

"We bought the last *twelve* packs," said Chong.

"I kinda hate you guys."

"He's going to start crying," Chong said to Benny in a stage whisper.

"He's going to embarrass himself," agreed Benny.

"What he's going to do," said Morgie, "is start kicking your asses."

"Eek," said Chong through a yawn.

Benny pretended to scratch his ankle, but then he moved his sneaker, and there were four packs of Zombie Cards in a neat stack, the waxed-paper wrappers still sealed. Morgie made a grab for them, ignoring the grins on his friends' faces.

"I still hate you," he said as he tore open the first pack.

"And yet," said Chong, "we'll find a way to pick up the pieces of our shattered lives and struggle on."

Morgie made a very rude gesture as he sorted through the cards.

Zombie Cards were one of the few luxuries the boys could afford. In the next town—forty miles away, along the line of mountains—two brothers had set up a printing business. All hand-crank stuff, because no one trusted electricity anymore, even when they could get it to work.

The printers did it old school. Offset printing in four colors, and they did a quality job. The Zombie Cards were printed on heavy card stock, ten cards to a pack. On the front of each card was a portrait of famous bounty hunters, like J-Dog, Dr. Skillz, Sally Two-knives, or the Mekong brothers; heroes of First Night, like Big Mike Sweeney, Billy Christmas, or Captain Ledger; someone from the zombie war, like the Historian or the Helicopter Pilot; famous zoms, like Machete-head, the Bride of Coldwater Spring, or the Monk; or random cards of famous people who had become zoms. On the back of each card was a short bio and the name of the artist. Benny's favorite card was of Ben, a tall African American man who was painted in a heroic pose, swinging a torch at a swarm of zoms who were trying to get past him to attack a blond woman who cowered behind him. The bio said that the image was based on "an eyewitness account of a valiant but tragically futile struggle against zoms in Pennsylvania." The artist had captured the nobility of the man with the torch and had made the zoms look particularly menacing, an effect enhanced by the stark shadows and light from the torch's flaring flame. It was one of the rarest cards, and Benny was the only one of his friends who had it. He also had a complete set of the bounty hunters, including Charlie Matthias and the Motor City Hammer. He still liked Charlie and the Hammer, but as much as he denied it to himself, reserve bubbled inside him when he looked at their cards. He'd already sorted through his collection, looking for the three bounty hunters he'd seen in the Ruin, but they weren't there. It reinforced Benny's belief that their actions were not in any way typical of the bounty hunters Benny knew personally. Tom had to be wrong about that.

He said nothing to his friends about what Tom had said, but he shot a quick glance at Zak, who sat on the store's porch, fanning through the dozen packs of cards he'd bought. Zak saw him watching and gave him a strange smile, then bent over his cards.

Benny shrugged, absorbed in his memories of the Ruin. So far he'd only told Nix, and he hadn't seen her since she'd left the garden the day before. Her absence was like an empty hole in his gut, but he refused to think about it.

Chong had the largest collection of Zombie Cards, mostly because he had two cousins who collected them, and they traded doubles. Morgie and Benny had a good-size set. Nix only had a few. She was poor and wouldn't take handouts, although if Benny gave her his doubles, she always accepted.

"Are you going to save any for Nix?" Chong asked as Morgie tore open his second pack.

"Why?" Morgie asked absently as he peered at the writing on the back of a card that showed a police officer in San Antonio, firing at zoms as he crashed his patrol car through a knot of them. The figures were tiny on the card, but the action was explosive, and Morgie was totally absorbed by it.

Chong and Benny exchanged a look over his bowed head, then shrugged. Morgie could be as dense as a mud wall sometimes.

They opened all of their packs of cards and sat in the shade of the porch, organizing them and reading the backs, swapping doubles with one another, bragging about cards they had and that the others didn't. Benny smiled and joked and chatted with the others, but as he sorted through the cards, he could feel how false and fragile his smile was. He wanted to feel the way he used to feel, and hated that he had to fake it.

"Hey, you even listening?" Morgie asked, and Benny turned to him, hearing the question as if it were an echo but not remembering what he was asked.

"What?"

"Joe Attentive," murmured Chong.

"I asked, what's with you and Nix?"

"Nix?" Benny tensed. "What about me and Nix?"

"She was over your house every day this week, and now she's not hanging around with us. She hasn't missed a card day all summer. What's up?" Morgie wore a smile, but it went about a millimeter deep.

Benny forced his shoulders to give a nonchalant shrug. "No, it's cool. She was just being a friend."

"What kind of friend?"

"Just a friend, Morgie." But Benny could see that answer wasn't going to cut it. He sighed. "Look, we all know Nix has a thing for me and you have a thing for Nix. Big news flash. I *don't* have a thing for Nix, and the reason you haven't seen her around the last two days is that I think she knows it, and her feelings are hurt. I'm sorry, but there it is. So, if you want to make your move, now would be a pretty good time."

"No, it wouldn't," said Chong without looking up from a card he was reading. The others looked at him. "Nix is probably feeling like total crap right about now. She could use a friend, but what she doesn't need is someone breathing down her neck or following her like a horny dog."

"What are you saying?" said Morgie, eyes narrowed.

Chong turned to him. "What part of that was unclear?"

"I don't just horndog after her. I *like* Nix. A lot."

Chong merely grunted and continued to read his card.

Morgie punched Benny's shoulder.

"Ow! What the hell was that for?" Benny demanded.

"For screwing with Nix's head!" Morgie shouted. "Now she's going to be all moody and girly, crying in her room and writing in that stupid diary of hers."

"Good God," said Benny, appealing to Chong, and the universe, for help. Chong tried to hide a smile as he pretended to read the Zombie Cards.

They sat in silence for five minutes, each of them absorbed with the cards to varying degrees, each thinking about Nix but pretending not to.

Chong tapped him with an elbow, and when he turned, his friend held out a card, so he could see the picture. "You're almost famous," he said.

The picture was that of a young man, standing with his back to a bullet-scarred wall, but instead of a gun, he held a *katana* in his hands.

Tom.

"Oh, man, don't do this to me," Benny said.

Chong smiled. "I thought you and Tom kissed and made up. I thought you were best buds now."

"Yeah, and pigs can tap dance," muttered Benny, taking the card. He flipped it over and read the back aloud. "'Card number 113: Tom Imura. Tom, a resident of Mountainside, is a first-class bounty hunter who prefers to be called a "closure specialist." He's known throughout the Rot and Ruin for his quiet manner and lightning fast sword.'"

Benny handed the card back. "I think I'm going to throw up," he said.

Chong pretended to read off the back of the card. "'Tom's brother, Benny, is known throughout the world for his noxious farts and lack of personality.' Man, they got your number."

"Get stuffed," Benny suggested.

Morgie took the card and tried to riff off Chong's remark, but beyond a few disjointed vulgarities, could come up with nothing biting.

"I am so going to bust Tom on this," said Benny. "On a Zombie Card for God's sake. Who does he think he is?"

Chong slid the card into his thick pack. "What's with you? You're supposed to be working with him. Didn't you guys go on some kind of vision-quest thing out into the Ruin? You came back all moody and introspective. What happened?"

"I got over it," said Benny.

"No, I mean, what happened out there?"

Benny just shook his head.

"Come on, dude," said Morgie. "Give us all the gory details."

It was the wrong choice of words, and Benny felt his stomach turn, and his brain started flashing overlapping images of Harold Simmons, the blind eyes of Old Roger, and the squirming torsos of the dismembered zoms in the wagon. Chong caught his change of expression, and before Morgie could say anything, he handed the last unopened pack to Benny.

"Do the honors. Maybe this one will have your own ugly face on it."

Benny faked a smile and tore open the wax paper. The first few cards were doubles they all had. There was one new one—a celebrity zom that the bio said was Larry King, but Benny couldn't tell the difference between the before and after pictures. He turned over the last card. It wasn't a bounty hunter or a famous person who'd gone zom and been bagged and tagged. No, this was one of the elusive Chase Cards—one of only six special cards that showed up so rarely that Benny, Chong, Morgie, and Nix had only two between them.

"What is it?" Morgie asked as he tried to lean closer, but Benny moved the card away. It was a weird reflex action, and even as he did it, Benny suddenly felt as if he stepped out of this moment, this place, and stood somewhere else. Someplace where the wind blew hot and dry, and the birds did not sing in the dying trees; where bones lay bright white on the ground, and the sky was as hard and dark as the bluing on a gun barrel.

Benny stared at the card. Not at the words, but at the

image. It was a girl about his own age, maybe a year older. She wore the rags of old blue jeans and roughly made leather moccasins. Her blouse was torn and patched and too small for her, and the pattern had once been bright with wildflowers, but now was so faded that it looked like flowers seen through mist. She had hair that was so thoroughly sun-bleached, it looked snow-white, and her skin was tanned to a honey brown. The girl wore a man's leather gun belt, which held a small pistol below her left hip and a knife in a weather-stained sheath on her right. She carried a spear, crudely made from a long piece of quarter-inch black pipe wrapped in leather and topped with the blade from a Marine Corps bayonet. Behind her was a heap of dead zombies. The painting was incredibly lifelike—more like a photo than a painting, but there hadn't been a working camera for years.

What held Benny's attention—what riveted him—was her expression. The artist must have known her, because he caught her with a blend of emotions on her beautiful face. Anger, or perhaps defiance, tightened her full lips into an inflexible line. Pride lifted her chin. But her hazel eyes held such a deep and ancient sadness that Benny's breath caught in his throat. He *knew* that sadness. It haunted his brother's eyes every day, and since returning from the small village on the mountainside, that sadness darkened the eyes that looked back at him from the bathroom mirror, morning and night.

This girl knew. This girl must have seen some of the things he'd seen. Maybe worse. She'd seen them with eyes that could never see things the way the bounty hunters did. This girl knew, and Benny *knew* that she knew. She knew in ways that Nix couldn't.

There was no name in the caption bar at the bottom of the card. Just these words: "The Lost Girl."

Chong leaned over. He started to make a joke, but he caught Benny's expression and kept his words to himself.

Morgie was a few steps slower to the plate than Chong. He snatched the card out of Benny's hand. "Mmm, nice rack. Almost as big as Nix's."

Benny's hand moved so fast that it surprised everyone. One second his fingers were open and empty, and the next they were knotted in the front of Morgie's shirt.

"Give it back," Benny said in a voice that was more like Tom's. Older, uncompromising. Hard.

Morgie wore half a smile for half a second, then he saw the look in Benny's eyes and surprise—tinged with fear and a spoonful of hurt—blossomed in his eyes.

"I . . . I mean . . . sure, man," he said, tripping over the words. "Sure . . . I was just . . ."

Benny took the card from between Morgie's fingers. It was bent but not creased, and Benny smoothed it on his thigh.

"I'm sorry," Morgie said, completely confused by what had just happened. Benny looked at him without seeing him, then leaned over to peer at the card. Morgie started to say something else, but Chong—out of Benny's line of sight—gave a tiny shake of his head.

A shadow fell over them, and they looked up to see Zak standing on the top step, staring down at the card. He grunted once, mumbled something unintelligible as he shoved his own cards into his pocket, then clumped down the stairs and headed home.

They ignored him. To Benny, Chong said, "Who is she?"

Benny just shook his head.

"Read the back."

Benny turned it over and slowly read the small block of printed text.

"'Chase Card number 3: The Lost Girl. Legends persist about a beautiful girl living wild and alone in the Rot and Ruin. Many have tried to find her, but none have. And some never returned. Who is . . . the Lost Girl?'"

"Doesn't tell you much," said Chong.

Morgie grunted. "Charlie Matthias said she's just a myth."

Benny's head whipped around. "You've *heard* of her?"

"Sure. Everyone's heard of her."

"I haven't," said Benny.

"I haven't," said Chong.

"Do you guys even *live* in the same town as me?" said Morgie with exasperation. "We heard about her *years* ago. Little girl with snow-white hair, hiding out in the Ruin, eating bugs and stuff. Completely wild. Can't speak English or nothing. What'd you call it? Feral?"

Benny shook his head, but Chong said, "Yeah . . . that's ringing a faint bell." He closed his eyes for a moment. "Back in the Scouts. Mr. Feeney told us about her. We were, like, nine or something. It was that weekend we all camped out in Lashner's Field."

"I was sick," said Benny. "I had the flu, remember?"

"Riiight," said Chong slowly.

"What'd Feeney say about her?"

"Nothing much. He told a spooky story about people trapped in a farmhouse with zoms all around. Everyone died, but the ghost of the youngest daughter keeps haunting the hills, looking for her folks."

"Uh-uh," said Morgie, "that wasn't how it went. The people in the farmhouse kept going out, one by one, to try and get help, but no one ever came back until only the little girl was left. She's supposed to still be there."

"I heard she died," insisted Chong.

"Not according to Mr. Feeney," said Morgie.

"I remember that she was a ghost. Everybody died in the story I heard."

"Everybody dies in every story," said Morgie.

"If everybody died," said Benny as he turned the card over to look at the picture again, "then who told the story?"

They thought about it. "Maybe one of the trackers found the place and figured it out," suggested Chong. They considered it. There were several trackers in town, some of whom used to be cops or hunters before First Night.

"No," said Benny, shaking his head slowly. "No, if she died as a little girl, then why draw her as a teenager?"

Morgie nodded. "And why give her boobs?"

"Jeez, Morgie," said Chong. "Don't you think of *anything* else but boobs?"

"No," Morgie said, looking genuinely surprised. "Why would I?"

Benny turned the card over and stared at the back. In the lower left corner was the artist's name. "Rob Sacchetto."

"Hey," said Chong. "Isn't that the guy you tried to get a job with? The erosion artist. Has the blue house by the reservoir."

"Yeah."

"So go ask him. If he did this, then he must have talked with someone who saw her. I mean . . . if this is real."

"It's real." Benny shuffled through the rest of the cards. There were only three others that had been painted by Sacchetto. Charlie Matthias. The Motor City Hammer.

And Tom Imura.

"Are you two . . . ," Morgie began, but before he could finish, Benny was on his feet and heading toward the reservoir on the far side of town. He left the Zombie Cards behind—except for the one with the picture of the Lost Girl.

"What's his malfunction?" Morgie asked. "What, he fall in love with this chick, just because she's built?"

Chong said, "Do yourself a favor, Morg. Next time you're staring at a girl's boobs, look up. You'll be shocked to learn it, but there's going to be a face up there. Nose, mouth, eyes. And behind the eyes is an actual person."

"Yes, Confucius, I know. Girls are people. Wisdom of the ages. Nix is a girl and therefore a person. I *know* that."

"Really?" said Chong as he watched Benny vanish around a corner. "Maybe if you looked her in the eyes, *she'd* know that you know."

He got to his feet, shoved his hands down deep into his pockets, and headed home. Morgie watched him go, wondering what the hell had just happened.

THERE WAS A SIGN ON A POLE THAT READ **ROB SACCHETTO—EROSION ARTIST**. It hung from two lengths of rusted chain and creaked in the hot western wind. The outside of the house was painted with murals of lush rainforests filled with exotic birds and brightly colored frogs. Benny had barely glanced at the murals when he'd come to apply for a job, but now he lingered to look. The paintings were filled with life—monkeys, insects, flowering plants—but no people.

The artist opened the door on the second knock. He wore low-slung jeans that seemed to be held together by dried paint, and a plaid shirt with the sleeves cut off. His feet were bare, and he had a steaming cup of coffee hooked on one multicolored finger. He peered down at Benny.

"You're that kid," he said.

Benny nodded.

"I thought I told you that I couldn't use you."

"I'm not here about the job."

"Okay. Why are you . . . ?" the artist's voice trailed off as Benny held out the card. Sacchetto looked at the image and then at Benny.

"Who is she?" Benny asked.

Shutters dropped behind the artist's eyes. "It's just a card, kid. They're sold in every settlement in California."

"I've been out to the Rot and Ruin." When that didn't seem to do much, Benny added, "With my brother, Tom."

Nothing.

"Tom *Imura*."

The artist studied him, stalling by taking a long sip of his coffee.

"I need to know who she is," Benny said.

"Why?"

"Because I believe in her. Because she's real. My friends think she's dead or that she's just a ghost story. But I know she's real."

"Yeah? How do you know that she's real?"

"I just know."

Sacchetto drained his cup. "D'you drink coffee, kid?"

"Sure."

"I'll brew another pot. This might take a while." He wasn't smiling when he said it, but he stepped back to let Benny enter. The artist paused to look at something that caused his whole body to tense, and Benny turned to see the Motor City Hammer, crossing the street toward the livery stable. However, the Hammer was looking directly at Sacchetto, and he wore a peculiar smile on his ugly face.

The artist's house was clean but not neat. Sketches were thumbtacked to the walls; partially finished paintings stood on half a dozen easels. A wheeled wooden table held hand-mixed pots of paint. They passed through into a tiny kitchen. Sacchetto waved Benny to a chair while he went to fill the coffeepot. Every house in Mountainside had an elevated cistern that drew upon the reservoir and rainwater to feed the faucets and toilets. Because of some quirk of luck during the influx of First Night survivors, Mountainside had twenty-three plumbers and only one electrician. In terms of electricity they were a half step out of the Stone Age, but there was always water to flush the john and fill the kettle. Benny was cool with that.

"Tom Imura, huh," Sacchetto murmured. "I can see it now, but not when you were here the first time. I knew Tom had a little brother, but I always assumed he'd look more Asian."

Benny nodded. Both of Tom's parents were Japanese, so Tom had straight black hair, light brown skin, black eyes, and a face that showed only the expressions he wanted it to show. Benny's mother had been a green-eyed, pale-skinned redhead who looked like every one of her Irish ancestors. Benny got an even split of the genes. His hair was straight, but it was medium brown with red highlights. His eyes were a dark forest green. His skin was pale, but he took a good tan. However, where Tom's body was toned to a muscular leanness, Benny was merely lean.

"We're half brothers," he explained.

The artist digested that. "And he took you out into the Ruin?"

"Yes."

"Why?"

"I guess I'm his apprentice now. I'm fifteen."

"Did he take you to Sunset Hollow?"

"No, but he mentioned it. Or . . . someone mentioned it to us. I don't know what it is, though."

"If Tom didn't tell you, then it's not for me to do it," said Sacchetto, taking two clean mugs from the cupboard. Before Benny could press him on it, the artist said, "What did you see out there?"

"I don't know if I should talk about it."

"Kid, here's the deal. You tell me about the Ruin, about what you saw out there. About what Tom *showed* you, and I'll tell you about the Lost Girl."

Benny thought about it. The smell of brewing coffee filled the little kitchen. The artist leaned back against the sink, arms folded across his chest, and waited.

"Okay," said Benny, and he told the artist everything. It was the same story he told Nix. The artist was a good listener, interrupting only to clarify a point and to press him for more precise descriptions of the three bounty hunters who had been torturing the zoms. Sacchetto was on his second cup of coffee by the time Benny finished. The coffee in Benny's cup was untouched and cold.

When Benny was finished, the artist sat back in his chair and studied Benny with pursed lips.

"I think you're telling me the truth," he said.

"You *think*? Why would I lie about stuff like that?"

"Oh, hell, kid. People lie to me all the time. Even when they don't have a reason to. Folks that want an erosion portrait but don't have a photo of their loved one tend to exaggerate so much, the picture comes out looking like either Brad or Angelina."

"Who?"

"Doesn't matter. Point is, people lie a lot. Sometimes out of habit. Not many people are good at telling the truth. But what I meant just now was that nearly everybody who comes back from the Ruin, lies about what they've seen."

"What kind of people?"

"You see? That's the kind of question that makes me think you've actually *been* there. Most people would ask, 'What kind of lies?' You see the difference?"

Benny thought he did. "Tom says that people here in town want to believe their own version of the truth."

"Yes, they do. They don't want to know the truth and even when they say that they do, they don't ask the right questions."

"What do you mean?"

"There are a lot of very obvious questions about our world that nobody around here seems to want to ask."

"Like why we don't expand the town?" suggested Benny.

"Uh-huh."

"And . . . why don't we try and—what's the word?—*reclaim* what we lost. I know. Since we got back I've been thinking a lot about that."

"I'll bet you have. You're Tom's brother after all."

"Okay, now what about that? After what happened, I guess my opinion about Tom has changed a bit."

"But . . . ?"

"But I still don't understand why everyone thinks Tom is so tough. He's even on one of the Zombie Cards."

"You haven't seem him in action?"

"All I saw was him do was hog-tie one skinny zom."

"That's it?"

"Sure. He ran away from the three bounty hunters."

"'Ran away,'" echoed the artist, looking amused. "Tom Imura, running away." He suddenly threw his head back and laughed for a whole minute, his thin body shaking, tears gathering in the corners of his eyes. He slapped the tabletop over and over again until the cold coffee in Benny's cup jumped and spilled.

"Holy crap, kid." Sacchetto gasped when he could talk. "God! I haven't laughed that hard since Mayor Kirsch's outdoor shower blew away in the Santa Ana, leaving him standing stark naked with soap dripping off his—"

"What's so freaking funny?" interrupted Benny.

The artist held up his hands in a "sorry" gesture, palms out. "It's just that anyone who knows your brother, I mean, really *knows* him, is going to react the same way if you tell them that Tom Imura was afraid of anything."

"He ran away. . . ."

"He ran away because you were there, kid. Believe me, if he'd been alone . . ." He left the rest unsaid.

"You don't live with him," Benny said irritably. "You don't know what I know. You don't know what I've seen."

Sacchetto shrugged. "That pretty much goes both ways. You don't know what I know. Or what I've seen."

They sat there for half a minute, both of them re-evaluating things and trying to find a doorway back into the conversation.

Finally, the artist said, "The Lost Girl. My end of the bargain."

"The Lost Girl," Benny agreed. "Tell me that she's real."

"She's real."

Benny closed his eyes for a moment, then opened them and looked down at the card. "Tell me she's alive."

"*That* I can't say for sure," said Sacchetto, but when Benny looked up at him, his eyes filling with dread, the artist shook his head. "No, I mean that I can't say for sure how she is today, this minute. But she was alive and well a couple of months ago."

"How do you know?" demanded Benny.

"Because I saw her," said the artist.

"You . . . saw her?"

"Once, just for a minute. Maybe half a minute, but yeah, I saw her out in the Ruin, and I came back and painted her. Tom helped me remember a few details, but that card there . . . That's her to a tee."

"You were with Tom when you saw her?"

Sacchetto paused, his fingers beating a tattoo on the tabletop. "Look, I know I promised to tell you, and I will, but I think I'm only going to tell you some of it. The rest . . . Well, maybe you better hear that from your brother."

"From Tom? Why?"

The artist cleared his throat. "Because Tom's been hunting her for five years."

THE ARTIST POURED HIMSELF A THIRD CUP OF COFFEE, THOUGHT ABOUT IT, then got up and fetched a bottle of bourbon from a cupboard and poured a healthy shot into his cup. He didn't offer the bottle to Benny, who was fine with that. The stuff smelled like old socks.

"I grew up in Canada," Sacchetto said. "Toronto. I came to the States when I was fresh out of art school, and for a while I made money doing quick portraits of tourists on the boardwalk in Venice Beach. Then I took a couple of courses in forensic art, and landed a job working for the Los Angeles Police Department. You know, doing sketches of runaways, of suspects. That sort of stuff. I was always good at asking the right questions, so I could get inside the head of a witness to a crime or a family member who was looking for someone. And I never forget a face. I was in a police station on First Night. Lots of cops around me, lots of guns. It's how I survived."

Benny didn't know how this was going to relate to the Lost Girl, but the artist was in gear now, and he didn't want to interrupt the man's flow. He placed the card on the table between them, and sat back to listen.

Sacchetto sipped his spiked coffee, hissed, and plunged back in.

"You grew up after, kid, so all you know about is this world. The world *after*. And I know you've probably learned a lot about the world before the Fall in school or from hearing people talk. So you probably have a sense of it, but that's really not the same thing as having belonged to that world. You live here in town, with a slice of what's left of the population. What's our head count at the New Year's census? Eight thousand? When I was working on the boardwalk, I'd see three times that many people just sprawled in the sand, soaking up the sun. The freeways were packed with tens of thousands of cars, horns blaring, people yelling. I used to hate the crowd, hate the noise. But . . . man, once it was all gone—I've missed it every day since. The world is too quiet now."

Benny nodded, but he didn't agree. There was always something happening in town, always some noise or chatter. The only quiet he'd heard was out in the Ruin.

"When the dead rose . . . The noise changed from the sound of life in constant motion to the sound of the dying in panicked flight. I heard the first screams just as the sun was setting. A guy in the drunk tank died from a beating he'd gotten when he'd been mugged. I guess the cops didn't realize how hurt he was. They thought he was asleep on the bunk, didn't know he was dead. Then he woke up, if that's the right word. 'Resurrected' is closer, I guess. Or maybe there should have been new words for it. If there'd been time, if the world had lasted longer, I'm sure there would have been all sorts of new words, new slang. Thing is, the zoms—they weren't really 'back' from the dead, you know? They *were* the dead.

It's been fourteen years, and the idea still won't fit into my head." He closed his eyes for a moment, looking inward—or backward—at images that even his artist's imagination could not reconcile.

"The Lost Girl," Benny prompted gently.

"Right. That was later. Let me get to it how I need to get to it, because one thing leads to another, and if I tell it out of order, you might not understand." He took another sip of coffee. "The guy in the cell started biting the other drunks. Everybody was screaming. The cops thought they had a nutcase on their hands, so they did what they were trained to do: They unlocked the cell to try and break up the fight. But by then at least one or two of the other drunks were dead from bites to their throats or arteries. It was a mess—blood all over the walls and floor, grown men screaming, cops shouting. But I just stood there, staring. All of the colors, you know? The bright red. The pale white of bloodless skin. The gray lips and black eyes. The blue of the police uniforms. The blue-white arcs of electricity as they used Tasers. In a weird, sick way it was beautiful. Yeah, I can see the look in your eyes, and I know how crazy that sounds, but I'm an artist. I guess we're all a little crazy. I see things the way I see them. Besides, I was around death and dying all the time. I was around pain and loss all the time. This was so *real*, so immediate. Even working with the police, I'd never been there at the moment a crime was committed . . . and here it was. Murder and mayhem being played out in all the colors in my paint box. I was transfixed. I couldn't move. And then the dead drunks woke up, and they started biting the cops. After that . . . The colors blurred, and I don't remember much except that there was screaming and gunfire. The younger cops and all of the support staff—the people who weren't street cops—they went crazy. Screaming, running, crashing into one another.

"It made it easier for the dead to catch them, and the more people they bit, the more the situation went all to hell. A cop I knew—a woman named Terri—grabbed my sleeve and pulled me away a second before one of the zombies could take a bite out of me. She shoved me down a side hall—the hall that led to the parking lot. She told me to get into my car and get the motor running. Then she turned and went back down the hall to get some other people out." He sighed. "I never saw her again. All I heard was gunfire and the moans of the dead."

"Is that where it all started?" Benny asked.

The artist shrugged. "I don't think so. Over the years you talk to people, and you hear a hundred stories about how it all started. You know what I really think?"

Benny shook his head.

"I think that it doesn't matter one little bit. It happened. The dead rose, we fell. We lost the war and we lost the world. End of story. *How* it happened doesn't matter much to anyone anymore. We're living next door to the apocalypse, kid. It's right on the other side of that big fence. The Rot and Ruin is the *real* world. Our town isn't anything more than the last bits of mankind's dream, and we're stuck here until we die off."

"You always this depressing or is it that crap you poured in your coffee?"

Sacchetto tilted his head to one side and stared at Benny for a ten count before a slow smile formed on his mouth. "Subtlety's not your bag, is it, kid?"

"It's not that," said Benny. "It's just that I'm fifteen, and I have this crazy idea I might actually have a life in front of me. I don't see how it's going to do me much good to believe that the world is over and this is just an epilogue."

Sacchetto chuckled. "You're smarter than I thought you were. Maybe I should have given you the job."

"I don't want it anymore. I just want to know about the Lost Girl."

"And I'm wandering around everywhere but in the direction of the point, is that it?"

Benny gave an "if the shoe fits" kind of shrug.

"Okay, okay. Long story short, I got the hell out of Dodge."

"'Dodge'?"

"Out of LA. No one else came out of the police station . . . At least no one alive. After I sat in my car for ten minutes, I saw the desk sergeant come shambling out. His face was smeared with red, and he was holding something in his hands. I think it was a leg. He was taking bites out of it. I spewed my lunch out the side window, backed the hell up, spun the wheel, and burned half a block's worth of rubber getting out of there. I had three quarters of a tank of gas, and I was driving a small car, so I made it pretty far. To this day I couldn't tell you the route I took getting out of LA. The streets were already going crazy, but I beat the traffic jams that totally locked down the city. Someone told me later that thousands of people were trapped in their cars on blocked streets and that the dead just came up and . . . Well, it was like a buffet." He shook his head, sipped some coffee, and continued. "I passed under a wave of army helicopters flying in formation toward downtown. Had to be a hundred of them. Even with the windows closed and the sound of rotors, I could hear the gunfire as they opened up on the city. When my car ran out of gas, I was actually surprised. I was in shock. I never even looked at the gauge. I ran the tank dry and then started running. I got to a farmhouse and met up with some other people, other refugees. Fifteen of us at first. This was around midnight now. By dawn there were seven left. One of the refugees had a bite, you see, and we still weren't connecting the bites with whatever was going on. To us it still wasn't the 'dead' rising. We thought it was an infection that made people go crazy and act violent.

"A few people had cell phones, but everyone they called was just as confused as they were. All the lines to police or government were jammed or were down. People kept trying, though. We were all conditioned to believe that our little phones and PDAs would always keep us connected, that they'd always be a pathway to a solution. I guess you don't even know what those things are, but it doesn't matter. The batteries eventually ran down, and as you *do* know, help never came. Everybody was in the same mess.

"At dawn a bunch of hunters came through the area and began clearing out the zombies. We thought that it was over, that somehow the good guys had gotten ahead of it. We went the opposite way, thinking we were heading in the direction of safety, of order. We didn't get two miles before we hit a wall of them."

"Zoms?"

"Zoms. Maybe ten, fifteen thousand of them. God only knows where they came from. Some city or town . . . or maybe they started out as a few and the others followed with them, tracking movement the way the zoms will. Don't know, don't care. We kept running, kept trying to hide, but they smelled us—or heard us. They kept coming. We picked up a couple more survivors, and at one point we were back up to close on a hundred people. But, like I said, there were thousands of them. *Thousands*. They were in front of us, behind us, on both sides. They came at us from everywhere, and we died. I was in the center of our pack, and that was the only reason I survived. The dead kept dragging down the people on the edges of the pack, and with every few hundred yards, we lost another couple of people. Sure, we were faster, and one-on-one we were stronger, but we had no clear path to make a straight run for it. Then we went down into a valley near a vineyard.

"By now our group was down to twenty-five, give or take. We'd started arming ourselves. Rocks and tree branches. A few farm tools we found. A couple people had guns, but the ammunition had run out long ago. The valley had a stream running through it, and we splashed across. That helped. I think the dead lost the scent, or maybe it was the sound of the stream. Those of us who crossed where the water churned over some rocks—where it was noisy—we got across without being chased. Seven of us made it to safety that way. Me, four men, and a woman and her little daughter. The woman, though . . . She was pregnant. Two days away from her due date. Two of the men had to hold on to her arms to help her run. And I carried the little girl. We ran and ran, and even though the little girl was only two years old . . . After a thousand yards it felt like she weighed a hundred pounds." He stopped for a moment, and Benny saw a shadow was moving across his face. "I've never been a strong person, Ben. Not physically, and not . . . Well, let's just say that not everyone's as strong as your brother."

He looked suddenly gray and sick, and older than his fifty

years. He drained the cup and turned to stare longingly at the bottle of bourbon on the drain board, but he didn't get up to fetch it.

Benny watched the emotions that flowed over the man's face. The artist was one of those people who had no poker face at all. Everything he felt, everything he'd ever *seen,* was there to be read.

After another few moments Sacchetto continued his story. "Somehow—maybe it was fear or adrenaline or maybe we'd gone completely crazy—we kept running. Four or five miles on the other side of the vineyard, we found a cottage. Pretty little place tucked into the woods. We managed to get the pregnant woman into it, and we locked the door, closed the shutters, and pushed all the furniture against any opening where the dead could get in. There was food and water and a TV and a laptop. The owners were nowhere around. While the others helped the woman settle down on the couch, I turned on the TV, but all we got was a 'please stand by' message from the Emergency Broadcast System. So I turned on the computer and skimmed the news. The Internet was still up. Do you know about the Internet?"

"Yeah. They cram all that old-world stuff into our heads at school."

Sacchetto nodded. "Well, I was able to access news feeds from all over the world. By then it was everywhere. I mean, *everywhere.* Europe, Asia, Africa. Cities were in flames. Some areas had gone completely dark. The military was in the field, and the authorities were saying they were making headway, pushing back the dead, stopping their advance." He shrugged. "Maybe it was even true at the time. My cell phone was back at the police station, but I sent e-mails to everyone I knew. I didn't get very many replies. Those that did get back to me said that it wasn't happening where they were, but as the day went on, they stopped replying to my e-mails. The situation kept getting worse and worse, until it was spinning completely out of control. The news reports were all mixed up, too. Some of them said that the dead were moving fast, some said that they couldn't be killed, even with head shots. One reporter, a guy who was a really well-known news anchor from New York, reported that his own family had been slaughtered, and then he shot himself right on camera."

"God . . . ," Benny said breathlessly.

The artist snorted. "I was never much of a believer, kid, but if there ever was a God, then He wasn't on the clock that night. That's something you can debate at Sunday school. For my part, I don't see much evidence of any divine hand in what happened."

"What happened then?" asked Benny.

Sacchetto took a breath. "I stayed glued to the Internet all day, mostly watching news feeds of these huge battles in New York and Philadelphia, in Chicago and San Francisco. And overseas. London, Manchester, Paris. Everywhere. One field reporter, a woman who was braver and crazier than I ever was, got all the way into Washington DC when the Air Force tried to reclaim the city. Jets were laying down napalm, and I saw whole masses of zombies burning on the lawn in front of the White House. They were still walking toward the troops who were making a stand on the other side of the Mall, but they burned as they did so, dropping to the ground as their tendons melted. Crawling until the fire destroyed too much of their muscles, or maybe till it boiled their brains. Wave after wave of helicopters fired on them. The helicopters hovered ten feet above their heads and used machine guns. Miniguns, I think they're called. Firing hundreds of rounds per minute, tearing the zombies to pieces. I guess if you went by that footage, then it looked like we were winning. But I sat at that computer for more than twenty hours, and one by one the news feeds went offline. Then the power went out, and we got no news after that. The TV . . . It never came back on, so when we lost power, it was useless anyway."

Even though Sacchetto spoke of places Benny had never seen and technology that no longer existed, the images of carnage and desperation filled Benny's mind. When they were out in the Ruin, Tom had reminded him that there had been more than three hundred million people living in the United States on First Night. The thought of all those people, fighting and dying in just a few days . . . It made Benny feel sick and small.

"What about the pregnant lady?" he asked after a long silence.

"Yeah . . . well, that's the real story. That's the story you want to hear."

"What do you mean?"

"That woman . . . She gave birth that night. There was a daybed that we wheeled out into the living room, and made her as comfortable as possible, but we didn't know what we were doing. I sure as hell didn't. The others helped. I . . . Well, I just couldn't. You'd think someone who was around blood all the time—sketching crime scenes and all—you'd think I could take the blood and mess from her giving birth.

But I couldn't. I'm not proud, and I don't even understand that about myself . . . but there it is. I was still cruising the Net when I heard the baby cry. It was right about then—right after the baby started crying—that the first of the dead began pounding on the door."

"The baby . . . ?"

"It was a girl," Sacchetto said, but he looked away. "We didn't know the mother had been bitten."

"God!" Benny's mouth went dry, and when he tried to swallow, it felt like he had a throat full of broken glass. "The baby too? Was it a . . ." Benny couldn't make his mouth shape the word.

But Sacchetto shook his head. "No. I know there have been a lot of stories about infected mothers giving birth to babies who were, um, monsters. But that's not what happened." He cleared his throat. "Years later, when I told this story to Doc Gurijala, he said that maybe the disease, or whatever it was, either couldn't cross the placental wall or didn't have time to do it. The woman must have been bitten when we were breaking through the crowds of zombies. None of us noticed."

"What happened?"

"Well, the infection had already taken hold. We missed it because she was already sweating and moaning from the hard delivery, and we still didn't understand what we were up against. When they started cleaning her up, she just . . . died. She fell back against the bed and let out this long, sputtering exhale. It was horrible to hear. It was a series of clicks in the throat as that last breath came out of her. They call that sound a death rattle, but that's too ordinary a phrase for the sound that I heard. It sounded more like fingernails scraping on a hardwood floor, like her spirit was clawing at life, trying to stay in her body."

Benny felt the skin of his arms rise with ripples of goose flesh.

"By that time I'd seen hundreds of people die and had seen thousands of zombies . . . but that death was the worst," said the artist. "And after all these years it's still the worst. That poor woman had fought her way out of Los Angeles, had saved her daughter and struggled to survive long enough to bring her baby into the world, and when she'd succeeded—when she was *safe*—death just dragged her away."

He abruptly stood and walked over to the counter, snatched up the bottle, and stared at it. He set it down again, thumping the heavy glass against the countertop.

"That baby?" Benny asked tentatively. "Did she live? And . . . is she the girl on the card? Is she the Lost Girl?"

Sacchetto turned, surprised. "No. She was too young. She'd be only fourteen now."

"Then I don't understand. . . ."

"It was her sister," said the artist. "The little girl who was on the run with her mother. Lilah."

"Lilah," Benny echoed. The name was a cool breeze in the middle of the heat of Sacchetto's terrible story.

"She watched her sister being born, and she watched her mother die. Poor little kid. She was only two, so all the screaming and the blood must have hit her really hard. Before, while we were still running, while I was carrying her, she was talking. Some words, but mostly nonsense stuff. Kid stuff. After that last breath . . . the little girl screamed for five minutes. She screamed herself raw, and then she stopped talking."

"For how long?"

The artist looked away again.

"I don't know. The rest of that night is kind of a blur. The dead surrounded the place. I think they were drawn to the cottage because of the screams. And after . . . by the smell of blood."

"What happened to the mother?"

Sacchetto still didn't meet his eyes. "She woke up, of course. She woke up, and for an insane moment we thought that she was still alive, you know? That she hadn't died, that we were wrong about it." He laughed a short, ugly laugh. "She bit one of the men. He was bent forward, trying to talk to her, trying to *reach* her . . . and she craned her neck forward and bit him. Then we knew."

"What did you do?"

"What we had to do." He came slowly back to the table and sat down. "We still had our weapons. The sticks, the rocks, the empty guns. We . . ."

He could not say it, and Benny did not need it said. They sat together for a while, listening to the wind-up clock on the wall chip seconds off the day.

"Near dawn," the artist said at length, "one of the others said that he was going to try and make a break for it. He said that the creatures outside were slow and stupid. He was a big guy, he'd played football in high school and was in really good shape. He said that he was going to break through their lines and find some help. Everyone tried to talk him out of it, but not as hard as we could have. It was the only plan anyone had. In the end, we all went to the living room and banged on the doors and walls, yelling real loud. The zombies came shuffling from all sides of the house. I don't know how many. Fifty? A hundred? When the back was mostly clear, the young guy went out through the back door at a dead run. He was fast, too. I closed the door and looked through the crack and watched him in the light of the false dawn as he knocked the zombies away and rushed into the darkness."

"What happened to him?"

"What do you think?" Sacchetto snapped, then softened his tone. "There was nowhere to run to. We never saw him again."

"Oh."

"It was almost a full day later when another one of us tried it. A small guy who used to manage a Starbucks in Burbank. He made a torch out of a table leg and some sheets that he'd soaked in alcohol. He didn't run fast enough, though. And that myth about the zombies being afraid of fire? That's stupid. They can't think or feel. They're not *afraid* of anything. They surrounded him. Before he fell, the little guy must have set fire to a dozen of them. But the others got him."

Benny looked down at the card that lay on the table before him. "You said that seven of you made it to the cottage."

"Six adults, plus the little girl. And the baby made eight. The mother . . . died. So did the guy she bit. And you know what's really sad? I never learned either of their names. The little girl only knew her mother as 'Mama.' We couldn't even respect their deaths with their names. Maybe that doesn't seem important, but it mattered to us. To me."

"No," said Benny, remembering Tom reading the note to Harold Simmons. "I get it. It matters."

Sacchetto nodded. "So that left two of us. Me and last guy—a shoe salesman named George—played rock-paper-scissors to see who'd try next. Imagine that: two grown men playing a kids' game during the apocalypse to decide which one was probably going to live and which one was almost certainly going to die. It's comedy."

"But it's not funny," said Benny.

"No," said the artist. "No, it sure as hell isn't. Mostly because neither of us really thought we were going to live. We just didn't want to be the *next* to die."

"You won?"

"No," he said. "I lost. I was the one who had to try. George stayed back there with the two kids. I tore up a throw rug and wrapped strips of it around my arms, and put on a thick winter coat I found in the closet. When I told Tom all this, he joked that maybe I invented carpet coats. Whatever. I wound five scarves around my face. All I left free were my legs. I found a bag of golf clubs in a closet and took two metal putters, one for each hand. George went through the same ritual, banging on the front door. Zombies are as dumb as they are dangerous. They came lumbering around to the front of the house, and I went out the back. I heard the baby crying and George yelling, but I didn't look back. I ran. Kid . . . I ran for my life, and that's what chews me up every day and night since."

"I don't understand."

The artist gave him a bleak smile. "I ran for *my* life. Not theirs. Not for George or the little kid or the baby. I ran to save my own sorry ass. I ran and ran and ran. On good nights, when I can find a little scrap of self-respect, I tell myself that I ran so far because I couldn't find anyone alive, closer to the cottage, but that's not entirely true. At least, I don't know if it's true. I saw smoke a couple of times, and I heard gunfire. I could have gone there and maybe found some people who were still alive and fighting, but I was too scared. If there was gunfire, then they had to be firing at the zombies, and that scared me too much. I was crying and talking to myself as I ran, making up lies to convince myself that the little kids back in the house were safe, that the hunters or soldiers or whoever was firing the guns would find them in time. I ran and ran and ran."

He stopped and sighed again.

"At nights I slept in barns or in drainage ditches. I don't know how many days I ran. Too many, I guess. Then one morning I heard voices, and when I crept out of my hiding place, I saw a party of armed men, walking down the road. More than sixty of them, with a couple of soldiers and a few cops leading the way. I rushed out at them, screaming incoherently. They nearly shot me, but I managed to get out a few words in time. They gathered around me, gave me some food and water, and grilled me on where I'd been and what I'd seen. I don't think I made a whole lot of sense, but when I was finally able to get myself together enough to tell them about the cottage, I realized that I had no idea where it was. I wasn't familiar with this part of California, and I sure as hell hadn't paid attention to the crazy path I took. They had a map, and I tried to figure it out, but it was hopeless."

"What happened?"

He shook his head. "They never found the cottage. Not while I was with them, anyway. A party of about a dozen went to look for it, but they never came back. The main group pushed on, and after a week of fighting and running, we found a reservoir with a high chain-link fence and mountains behind it. It was defensible, and it became a rallying point for survivors."

"You mean here? That's how this town was started?"

"Yes. I helped reinforce the fence and dig earthworks and build shelters. I worked as hard as I could each day, every day. . . . And except for a couple of very short trips into the Ruin with Tom, I never left this town again. I don't think I ever will."

"What about the little girls? What about Lilah?"

Sacchetto sat back. "Well, kid, that's where I left the story of the Lost Girl, and it's where Tom entered it. You're going to have to get the rest from him."

Benny got up and fetched the coffeepot. He poured the artist a fresh cup and set the bottle of whiskey down next to it. The artist stared at the bottle for a while, then poured some into his coffee, sipped it, then got up and poured the coffee out in the sink.

"Thanks for telling me all this," said Benny. "Most people don't want to talk about First Night or what happened after. And those that do . . . They always make it sound like they were the heroes."

"Yeah, I sure as hell didn't do that."

"You didn't do anything wrong," said Benny.

The artist sneered. "I ran away and left an infant and a little girl in a house surrounded by the living dead. I sure as hell didn't do anything right."

"Could you have carried them out? Both of them?"

Sacchetto gave a single wretched shake of his head.

Benny smiled at him. "Then at least you tried to do what you could do," he said.

"Kid, I appreciate the effort, but that thought doesn't even get me through the night." He closed his eyes. "Not one single night."

18

"Talk to Tom," said the artist as he walked Benny to the door. "If he's willing to talk about it, then he can tell you the rest of it."

"I will."

"You never did tell me, though. . . . What's your interest? You don't know her. What's she to you?"

Benny was expecting the question but hoping it would slip by unasked. He shrugged. He took the card from his pocket and held it up so they could both look at the image. "It's hard to put into words. I was sorting through the new cards with my crew, and I saw this one. There was something about it, something about *her*. I . . ." He stopped, fishing for the right words, but he came up empty. He shrugged.

However, Sacchetto surprised him by nodding. "No, I get it, kid. She kind of has that effect on people."

Sacchetto opened the door to a bright spill of September sunlight. The light was clean and dry and seemed to belong to a totally different world than the one Sacchetto had talked about. They lingered in a moment of awkwardness, neither of them sure if this was the whole of their relationship or the first chapter of an acquaintanceship that might last for years.

"Sorry it didn't work out with the job," Sacchetto said with a crooked smile.

"Well, it's not like I'm *invested* in killing zombies. If you're hiring, I'm still avail—"

"No," Sacchetto interrupted, "I mean, I'm sorry your art kinda sucks. You're a nice kid. Easy to talk to. Easier to talk to than your brother."

"My art sucks?"

"You can draw," conceded the artist.

"I . . ."

"Just not very well."

"Um . . . thanks?"

"Would you rather I lie to you, kid?"

"Probably."

"Then you're Rembrandt, and having you around would make me feel inferior."

"Better."

They grinned at each other. The artist held out a paint-stained hand, and Benny shook it. "I hope you find her."

"I will," said Benny.

That got a strange look from the artist, but before Benny could say anything, a voice behind them said, "Well, well, what's that you got there?"

Benny knew the voice, and in the half second before he turned, he saw Sacchetto's face tighten with fear. Benny turned to see Charlie Pink-eye, standing on the street right behind him. Next to him, smiling a greasy little smile, was the Motor City Hammer.

"Whatcha holding there, young Benjamin?" said Charlie

with the slick civility he used when he was setting up a bad joke—or something worse.

Benny was suddenly aware of the card. It was small, but at that moment it felt as big as a poster. His hand trembled as if the card itself felt exposed and nervous.

The massive bounty hunter stepped closer, and his bulk blotted out the sun. It was weird. Benny *liked* Charlie and the Hammer. They were heroes to him. Or . . . had been. Since the Ruin, everything in his head was crooked, as if the furniture was the same but the room had changed. The way these men were smiling at him, the way shadows seemed to move behind their eyes . . . It made Benny want to gag. There was nowhere to turn, no way to escape the moment unless Benny actually took off running—but that was not any kind of option.

Charlie held out a hand for the card, but Benny's fingers pressed together to hold it more tightly. It was not a deliberate act of defiance; even in the immediacy of the moment he knew that much. It was more an act of . . .

Of what?

Of protection?

Maybe. He just knew that he did not want Charlie Pinkeye to have that card.

"It's just a card," Sacchetto said. "Like the ones I did of you and the Hammer. I did a couple new ones. You know, for extra ration bucks. It's nothing special."

"Nothing special?" said Charlie, his smile as steady and false as the painted grin on a doll. "Let's see, shall we?" Charlie reached for the card the same way Morgie had. Familiar, as if he had a right or an invitation born of a long-standing confidence. Benny was primed to react, and as the bounty hunter's fingers closed over a corner of the card, Benny whipped it away. Charlie grabbed nothing but air.

"No!" blurted Benny, and he took a reflexive step backward, turning to shield the card with his body.

The moment—every sound, every trembling leaf in the trees beside the house, even the wind itself—seemed to suddenly freeze in time. Charlie's eyes went wide. The Hammer and the artist wore identical expressions of complete surprise. Benny felt the blood in his veins turn to icy gutter water.

"Boy," said Charlie in a quiet voice that no longer held the lie of humor or civility, "I think you just made a mistake. I'll give you one second to make it right and then we can be friends again. Hand me that card, and you'd better smile and say 'sir' when you do."

Charlie did not make another grab, but the threat behind his words filled the whole street.

Benny didn't move. He held the card down by his hip and out of sight. He flicked a glance at Sacchetto, but the Hammer was up in the artist's face, and he had his hand resting on the top of the black pipe he carried as a club. There was no help there.

"Now," commanded Charlie. He held out a huge, callused hand, palm open and flat to receive the card. A stiff breeze filled with heat and blowing sand suddenly whipped out of the west. The card fluttered between Benny's fingers.

"Give him the card, Benny," urged Sacchetto.

"Listen to the man," agreed the Hammer, laying a hand on the artist's shoulder. The tips of his fingers dug wrinkled pits through the fabric of Sacchetto's shirt.

Charlie stretched his hand out until his fingers were an inch from Benny's face. The bounty hunter's skin smelled like gunpowder, urine, and tobacco.

"Boy," Charlie whispered.

Benny raised the card. He did it slowly, holding it between thumb and forefinger, and all four of them watched it flutter like the wing of a trapped and terrified butterfly.

"Give me the card," said Charlie in a voice as soft as the blowing wind.

"No," said Benny, and he opened his fingers. The hot breeze whipped it away.

The artist gasped. The Hammer cursed. Charlie Pink-eye snaked a hand after it, but the card tumbled away from his scrabbling fingers. Benny almost cried out as the small rectangle of stiff cardboard and printer's ink tumbled over and over, bobbing like a living thing on the wind. It struck the sign at the corner of the artist's property and dropped to the street where it skittered for a dozen yards before it came to a sudden stop as a booted toe stepped down on it, pinning it to the hard-packed dirt.

Benny, the artist, and the two bounty hunters had followed the card's progress with their eyes, and now—as one—they raised their eyes to look at the man who now stood in the street. The man bent and plucked the card from beneath his toe. He studied it for a moment, then blew dust and sand from its surface. He glanced over the card, then at the four people clustered together in front of the artist's door. He smiled and slid the card into his shirt pocket.

It was the first time Benny had ever been glad to see him.

"Tom," Benny said.

19

Tom Imura was dressed in faded blue jeans and a green travel-stained safari shirt with a lot of pockets. He wore old boots, an ancient Pittsburgh Pirates ball cap, and a smile that was every bit as friendly and inviting as a pit viper's. As he strolled slowly toward the front of the house, Charlie and the Hammer took small sideways steps to be clear of any obstructions. Both men wore knives on their belts. The Hammer had his black-pipe club, and Benny knew for certain that Charlie had a four-barreled derringer in his boot top.

"So," said Tom amiably, "what are we doing today?"

The question sounded as ordinary as Nix asking if Benny wanted to go swimming or Chong suggesting they entertain the trout down at the stream.

"Just having a chat, Tom," said the Hammer. "Ain't nothing."

"Happy to hear it, Marion."

Benny gasped. No one ever called the Hammer by his birth name. There was a story Morgie liked to tell about how when the Hammer turned fourteen, he killed his father with a screwdriver for giving him that name. And yet the Hammer didn't say a single word about it to Tom.

"You doing okay, Benny?" Tom asked.

Benny didn't trust his voice, so he gave a short jerk of a nod.

"Rob?" Tom asked with an uptick of his chin.

The artist said, "Just a friendly chat. The boys were just passing the time of day."

Tom stopped a yard away from Charlie. He shoved his hands into the back pockets of his jeans and looked up at the hard, blue dome of the sky.

"And it's a hot one, ain't it?" said Tom, squinting at a buzzard floating like a black kite, high in the sky. Without looking down he said, "I see they put the Lost Girl on a Zombie Card. How about that?"

"She ain't none of your business, Tom," said Charlie with quiet menace.

Tom nodded as if agreeing, but he said, "I seem to remember you telling folks that the Lost Girl was just a myth. Or was it that she was dead ten years ago and more?"

Charlie said nothing.

Tom finally lowered his eyes and turned toward Charlie. If there was anything to read in Tom's face, Benny wasn't able to see it.

"And then I see you getting all worked up over her picture on a kid's trading card. What am I supposed to think about that?"

"Think what you like, Tom," said Charlie.

"Yeah," added the Hammer with a laugh. "It's a free country."

The bounty hunters laughed, and Tom laughed with them, sharing a joke that clearly no one found funny. Benny shifted uncomfortably and threw an inquiring look at Sacchetto, who returned the look with a shake of his head.

"Charlie, you and Marion wouldn't be looking for the Lost Girl again, would you?"

"Can't look for someone who's dead," said the Hammer.

"Seems to me that we do that all the time," said Tom.

The Hammer colored, annoyed with himself for a foolish comment.

"The last time you were looking for her was after what happened up in the mountains. But you told me that it was all an accident. It made me wonder then, as it does now, if the Lost Girl might have seen something she shouldn't have. Or some*place* she shouldn't have . . ."

"There was nothing to see." Charlie growled. "Like I told you a dozen times."

Tom shrugged. "And yet you get all worked up over her card. Why is that? Are you afraid that now she's on a card, everyone will know that she really exists? That maybe someone will go looking for her? Maybe . . . bring her back to town? Ask her about life out there in the Rot and Ruin? Maybe ask her about her sister? Ask her about Gameland?"

Benny frowned. What was Gameland?

"Gameland burned down," said Charlie. "As you well know."

"Me? What do I know? As you said, Gameland burned down. Nothing left but cold ashes and a few bones. No way to tell who the bones belonged to."

Charlie said nothing.

"Wonder if anyone ever rebuilt it," said Tom. "Oh . . . not where it used to be. But somewhere else. Somewhere secret.

Somewhere that a wandering girl in the mountains might stumble upon." His voice was quiet, his tone mild, as if he and Charlie were passing the time of day, talking about the price of corn. But Benny could see clouds forming on Charlie's face, darkening his expression. Lightning flashed in the bright blue eye, and fire seemed to burn in the pink eye. Charlie took a step toward Tom.

"You keep making accusations like that, Tom, and we might have to have a talk."

Tom smiled. "We *are* having a talk, Charlie. And I haven't made a single accusation. I'm just wondering out loud about why a busy man like you would be afraid of what's on a paste-board card."

Charlie took another step, and now his bulk blocked the sun and cast Tom completely in shadows.

"Don't mess with me, Tom. You got lucky once. Luck don't hold long these days."

Tom's smile never wavered. He took a single sideway step and looked around Charlie Matthias. "Benny, it's past your time to come on home. We're supposed to be training today."

"Training?" said the Hammer. "You're teaching this pup the hunt?"

Tom turned his smiling face to him, but he didn't answer. Benny caught the quick sharp look that passed between the Hammer and Charlie.

Charlie edged another half step closer to Tom. He towered over Tom, but Benny's brother didn't back away and he didn't take his hands out of his back pockets.

"It's a risky business taking a young pup into the trade," said Charlie.

"He's of age," said Tom. "Got to earn his rations, like everyone else."

"Yeah . . . but he looks a little soft to me. The Ruin's a dangerous place."

"Benny's already been to the Ruin, Charlie. He did just fine."

Charlie's own smile returned as he looked at Benny. "You been out in the great zombie wonderland, kid?"

When Benny said nothing, Tom surprised him by saying, "Answer the man, Benny."

"Yes."

"Be polite, Benny," Tom chided.

"Yes . . . *sir*."

Charlie nodded approval. "You got him trained good as a hunting dog."

Benny held his ground. "He's training me to be a *hunter*," he said with a growl, "and we're going to go find the Lost Girl and bring her back to town. And there's nothing you can do about it."

He didn't know why he said it, and even as he said it he knew it wasn't true, but he wanted to wipe the smirk off of Charlie's face.

His words did just that. Charlie's eyes hardened to stone, and he opened his mouth to say something. Tom put a hand on Benny's shoulder. "We'll be moving on home, fellas."

He turned, pulling Benny gently, but before they went three steps, Charlie said something quietly to the Hammer, and they both laughed. It was a dark and ugly laugh, heavy and swollen with the promise of awful things. Benny tensed, wanting to turn, but Tom's hand was like iron on his shoulder.

"Hey, Tom!" called Charlie, and Tom slowed and half turned to look back. "Best tell the pup to be real careful out in the Ruin. Lots of things out there will take a bite out of fresh meat like him. Everything out there wants to kill you."

Tom stopped. He turned very slowly and looked at Charlie for several silent seconds, the smile still on his lips.

"That's true, Charlie. Everything wants to kill you."

Then he turned, patted Benny on the shoulder, and started walking. As Benny turned away from the tableau, he got a brief look at Charlie's face. Did the big man's smile flicker? Did his eyes show some emotion other than predatory confidence? Benny couldn't be sure.

He and Tom walked in silence all the way home.

When they reached the garden gate, Benny put his hand on the latch but didn't open it. He turned to his brother.

"Okay," Benny demanded, "what was *that* all about?"

"It's not about anything. Charlie and the Hammer like to turn dials on people. You can't let them get under your skin."

"What did you mean about the things the Lost Girl saw, about what she could tell people?"

"It's a bad world, Benny" was all Tom would say.

"Then . . . what's Gameland?"

It was clear Tom didn't want to answer, but eventually he said, "It's a place that shouldn't exist. It's an abomination."

Benny had never heard Tom use a word like "abomination," let alone load a word with as much contempt.

"It used to be an amusement park, a place where people would come for a day of innocent fun. It was closed down for a couple of years before First Night, but a few traders and bounty hunters found it and staked it out as theirs. Their version of it had nothing to do with family fun or innocence. Remember when I told you about how some of the bounty hunters have games where they put boys in pits with zoms?"

Benny nodded. He hadn't believed Tom at the time and

really hadn't given it much thought since. Now the idea of boys being tossed into pits with only a stick with which to defend themselves against zoms was almost overwhelmingly horrific.

"They used to do that kind of stuff at Gameland, and other stuff that's even worse. A lot worse. Bounty hunters, loners, and other people come from settlements all over this part of the state for these games. They bet on stuff like that. Z-Games they're called." He paused, and pain etched deep lines in his face. "When Nix was little and we had that really bad winter—you were six or seven—Charlie coerced Jessie Riley into going out to Gameland as a way of making enough ration dollars to feed her and Nix. Think about that, Benny. A grown woman, a *mother*, being forced to play 'haunted house'—a sick game where they make her go through a building filled with zoms and only a sawed-off baseball bat or a piece of pipe to defend herself."

"No," Benny said. It was a straight-up denial, a statement that such a thing could not be the truth. That it could never have been the truth.

"She'd had a little kid at home, Nix. Jessie was desperate. She couldn't let her daughter starve, and a parent will do *anything* to protect her child. Even if doing those things rips away a piece of her soul. I got her out of there," Tom said, "but she was never quite the same afterward."

"That's impossible. I mean . . . how can that be legal?"

"'Legal'?" Tom gave a bitter laugh. "There's no law past the fence line. What's done in the Ruin, stays in the Ruin. On the other hand . . . if it became commonly known what sort of things do actually happen out there, then I doubt anyone involved would be allowed in Mountainside. Or in any town. There may be no law beyond the fence, but letting criminals live next door . . . well, that's another matter. But," he said with a sigh, "so far no one's been able to adequately prove a connection between Gameland and any of the bounty hunters who live here."

Benny shook his head. The logic seemed twisted.

"A few years ago," Tom continued, "someone set fire to the place and burned it down, and the owners moved the Z-Games to a new location. They keep its location secret. Gamblers and such are taken there in shrouded wagons, so that they don't know where it is."

"Why?"

"Because whoever burned it down might want to do it again."

"Do you know who burned it?"

Tom didn't answer. Instead he considered the sky. It was still blue, but a moist haze was forming. "It's going to rain tonight. I don't want to waste the rest of the day talking about stuff like that."

"Like *what*? You're not telling me anything. Did the Lost Girl see something? And could she really say something against Charlie?"

"Ben, you're asking questions I don't know the answers to. *Could* she have seen something or know something? Maybe. Probably. What matters is that Charlie seems to think so. That's why he started the rumors that she was just a ghost story or that she died a long time ago. He can't find her, and he doesn't want anyone else looking."

"So he had nothing to do with her picture being on the card?"

"Not a chance. Having people think she was real and having a picture of her to help identify her if she was ever found . . . Those are the last things Charlie would want." Tom paused. "Charlie isn't a good person, kiddo, and he's not a forgiving one. Like most people of his kind, he's motivated by fear."

"Fear? What could Charlie be afraid of?"

Tom said, "The truth. A lot of people are afraid of that."

Benny nodded even though he didn't fully understand what Tom meant.

"Can I have my card back?"

Tom took the card from his shirt pocket and studied it for a moment, then handed the card to Benny. "I can't say I'm happy to find out that Rob sold this to the printers. I asked him not to. Stirring up trouble with Charlie isn't the smartest move."

Benny smoothed the card against his shirt front. "Why do you think Mr. Sacchetto painted the Lost Girl card after you asked him not to?"

"People do stupid things when they need money."

"He doesn't look broke."

"He's not, but for most people there's never enough money."

"Is this going to cause a lot of trouble?" Benny asked.

Tom looked back the way they'd come. "I hope not, but . . ." He let the rest of his sentence hang.

"Mr. Sacchetto said that you saw the Lost Girl a couple of

months ago, but he said I had to ask you to tell me about her."

The trees around them were filled with birdsong, and cicadas droned incessantly in the tall grass. Tom leaned his forearms on the fence and sighed.

"We haven't really talked much since we got back," he said. "I know that what we saw hit you pretty hard. I know that our relationship has changed a bit. As brothers, I mean."

After a slight pause, Benny nodded.

"So here's the problem, kiddo," said Tom, "and maybe you can help me sort it out. I'm not entirely sure who you are. I mean, you're not really a kid anymore, and you're not an adult. You're not the annoying brat I've been living with for the last fourteen years."

"Eat me," said Benny with a grin.

"Zombies wouldn't eat you. They have standards." Tom pushed himself off the fence. "So, you're going through all these changes, and I don't know who you'll be at the end of it."

"How's this all going to lead into you telling me about the Lost Girl?"

"That's the problem. Last time I checked, you thought Charlie Pink-eye was—and I quote—'*The Man.*' The Hammer too. But a few minutes ago I saw you holding your own against Charlie. That didn't look like a friendly chat, but if there's even the slightest chance you're going to share a single word of this with Charlie or the Hammer, then I can't and won't say a single word about Lilah. On the other hand, if I thought that I could trust you—completely and without reservation—then I might consider telling you the whole story."

"You can—," Benny began, but Tom stopped him with a raised finger.

"I don't want an answer right now, Benny. I want us to do our training session and then we'll have some dinner. We'll talk after."

"Why not now?"

"Because you want it too much now."

"Great time to go Zen on me."

Tom shrugged. "If I have to get to know who you are, you have to get to know who I am. Fair's fair." He opened the gate. "Let's go."

Benny stood outside the gate, drumming his fingers on the wooden top rail. He didn't understand Tom at the best of times, and for a few seconds he felt like he'd just missed the punchline of a joke. He looked down at the card, as if the Lost Girl could whisper some explanation to him.

"Honestly . . . is it just me or is Tom crazy?"

The Lost Girl's eyes held infinite answers, but he couldn't hear a word. He sighed, tucked the card into his pocket, and headed into the house.

Fifteen minutes later Tom tried to kill Benny with a sword.

BENNY TWISTED OUT OF THE WAY OF THE SWORD WITH MAYBE A MICRON to spare. He could feel the blade slice the air; he heard the swoosh of the wind. Benny threw himself to one side and tried to roll behind the picnic table, but Tom was as nimble as an ape. He leaped onto the tabletop, dropped quickly into a crouch, and as Benny came out of his roll and started to rise, Tom stopped him with the edge of his weapon across Benny's windpipe.

"You're dead."

Benny put a finger against the blunt edge of the wooden practice sword and pushed it away.

"You cheated."

Tom lowered his sword. "How do you figure that?"

"I dropped my sword," Benny said. "I told you to give me a second."

"Oh, please. Like anyone out in the Ruin is going to cut you any slack."

"Zoms don't carry swords."

"That's hardly the point."

"And, as far as I know, none of the other bounty hunters do either."

Tom picked up a towel and wiped sweat from his face. "Now you're lying to save face. You saw one of them use a sword when we were out in the—"

"Okay, okay, whatever. Let me catch my breath." Benny dropped his wooden sword and trudged over to the pitcher of iced tea and drank two cupfuls. "Besides," he said, turning back, "I'd rather learn how to use a gun."

"You already know how to shoot."

"Not like you." He almost said "not like Charlie," but caught himself. Last year Charlie had given a demonstration of pistol and rifle trick shooting at the harvest fair. Tom had watched the whole thing with narrowed eyes and a wooden face. Thinking back on that, Benny wondered if Tom was anywhere near as good as Charlie with a gun. He'd had never seen his brother shoot.

Tom didn't reply. He weighed the wooden *bokken* in his hand and cut a few slow-motion lines through the air.

"Will you teach me to shoot?"

"Eventually, sure," said Tom. "Though . . . you know enough now to stop one of the dead if you get into trouble. But I already told you that I prefer swords and knives. They're quieter and they—"

"Don't need to be reloaded," Benny interrupted. "Yeah, I remember. You've told me fifteen times. You also said that sometimes quiet doesn't matter."

"True, but there are a lot more times when it does." Tom hooked the tip of his sword under Benny's and flipped it up so that it tumbled over and over in the air. It came at Benny faster than expected, and he surprised himself by getting a hand up in time to catch it. Tom grinned. "At least your reflexes are good."

"Hooray for me."

Tom raised his sword in a formal two-hand grip and waited until Benny finished making faces and did the same. Tom moved to his right, beginning a slow sideway circle, always keeping his sword ready. Benny shifted to his left, matching him.

"Quiz time," said Tom.

"Do we have to?"

"No. You can quit and go shovel body parts into the pit. I'm easy."

Benny didn't voice the word that rose to his lips.

"Define '*kenjutsu*.'"

"It's Japanese for 'sword methods' or 'the way of the sword,'" Benny said in as bored a tone as he could manage. Tom darted forward a half step in a quick fake, and Benny stepped backward.

"What does 'samurai' mean?"

"'To serve,'" said Benny. This time he tried the same fake, but instead of retreating, Tom stepped in, parried his blade, and tapped him on the shoulder.

"Blood is now pouring out of a hole where your arm used to be."

"Yeah, yeah, and when I come back as a zom, I'm going to eat your brains."

Tom laughed and swung another cut, but Benny blocked it, and Benny blocked the next dozen attacks.

"You're taking it easy on me," Benny said.

"You have to work up to full speed."

"I can handle it."

"No, you can't."

"Yes, I can."

"No, you—Oh, hell." Tom moved forward and to one side, and just like that moment back in Harold Simmons's house, Benny saw his brother's body blur as Tom moved with incredible speed. His sword seemed to vanish, but then there was a loud *TOK!*, and Benny's *bokken* was flying out of his hands and the world was tilting. Somehow the grass was under his back, and Tom was kneeling on him with his sword pressed into the soft flesh beneath Benny's Adam's apple.

"Okay," Benny croaked. "Fair enough. I'm not ready. Get off my nads."

Tom raised his knee. "Sorry. Meant to pin your hip."

"You missed," Benny said in a tiny voice. "Ow."

"Really," Tom said. "Sorry."

He stepped away and let Benny climb to his feet.

"That was *cool*!"

Benny turned to see Morgie, Chong, and Nix grinning at him from the other side of the garden gate.

"Hit him again," said Morgie.

"Yeah," agreed Nix. She didn't smile as broadly as Morgie, and there was an edge to her voice.

"Kneel on his nuts some more," suggested Chong. "I don't think that's ever going to get old."

Benny wheeled on Tom. "Why are they here?"

"Suffering is easier to endure when shared," said Chong as he lifted the gate latch.

"What?"

"They're here for lessons," said Tom. "I invited them."

"Why? And remember that you can't defend yourself if I smother you in your sleep."

"Actually, I can. And I lock my bedroom door," Tom said over his shoulder as he knelt down by the ancient black canvas bag in which he kept his equipment. He removed three battered but serviceable *bokken*. "I figured you'd learn better in a class setting. You know . . . with your friends."

Benny looked at his friends. Nix was staring acid death at him. Morgie had his hands cupped around his groin, pretending to scream in pain. Chong smiled thinly at him and drew a finger slowly across his throat.

"'Friends'?" Benny echoed.

Three hours later the four of them stood on trembling legs. Sweat poured down their bodies. Their clothes were pasted to them, their hair hung in rat tails on their foreheads and the backs of their necks. Morgie could barely lift his wooden sword. Chong's face had lost its smile a while back. Benny was wondering if it was okay to wish for a coronary. Only Nix looked relatively alert. She was as flushed and sweaty as the others, but her hands didn't tremble as she raised her sword for the last drill.

Tom looked like he just got up from a long nap in a hammock under a shady tree.

"Okay," Tom said. "Pair up. We'll run through the same attack and defense we just did, but let's see if we can take it up a notch. Don't really try to hit one another, but make the attacks as real as you can safely manage."

Morgie pushed Chong out of the line, and they settled into stances. Chong was only slightly better than Morgie. He was faster, but Morgie was light on his feet for a stocky kid; he was at least twice as strong as Chong.

That left Nix and Benny as partners. Benny had avoided this all afternoon, but Nix seemed to find the pair-up faintly amusing. They squared off, raising their swords in the ritual salute and settling into their stances.

Tom called, "*Hajime!*" (Japanese for "Begin!"), and Benny lunged forward to deliver his attack. Nix slapped his sword aside and rapped him hard on the head. Benny saw stars.

"No," said Tom. "We're trying *not* to make contact."

"Oh," said Nix distractedly. "Right."

NIX AND BENNY SWUNG AND BLOCKED, STABBED AND EVADED AS THE afternoon sun baked their skin and boiled the sweat from their pores. When Tom finally found a sliver of compassion and ended the session, they dropped where they stood. Morgie lay like a beached starfish, arms and legs spread wide, mouth open. Chong crawled under the picnic table, curled into a fetal position, and appeared to pass out. Benny limped to the oak tree whose thick trunk anchored the whole yard, slid down with a thump, kicked off his shoes, and gasped like a trout.

"Here," Nix said, and Benny pried one eye open to see her standing there with two tall glasses of cold water. She held one out to him.

Benny hesitated.

"It's not poisoned," she said, "and I didn't spit in it."

"Thanks." He took the glass and drank half of it, then looked up again. Nix was still standing there. "Have a seat."

"You sure?"

"Yeah. Sit down before you fall down."

She lowered herself to the grass and sat cross-legged in the shade. Tom was in the house. The yard was still. Even the birds in the trees were too overheated to sing. There was a faint rumble of thunder way off to the west, but if there was a storm coming, then the clouds were still on the far side of the mountains.

They drank their water. Benny waved a fly away. The moment stretched.

"I'm sorry," they both said at the same time. They blinked at each other, and they almost smiled.

"You first." Again, both of them said it at the same moment.

Nix held up a hand. "Me first," she said, but then she took a few seconds to get the words out. "Look . . . I'm sorry for being such a *girl*."

"No—"

"Let me get it out," she interrupted, "or I won't be able to say it."

"But—"

"Please."

Benny gave in, nodded. Nix flicked a glance across the yard to where Morgie lay, apparently dead.

But when she spoke she didn't say what Benny expected. "Morgie told me about the card you found. The Lost Girl. He said that the second you looked at it, there were little red hearts floating in the air around your head."

"Morgie's an idiot." He said it as a joke, but in truth he wanted to go over and beat Morgie to death for opening his big, dumb mouth. Especially since the Lost Girl card was lying under his pillow at the moment, and he'd planned to leave it there when he went to bed tonight. His face was wet hot. He hoped she would think that it was still the postexercise flush, but he knew she was way too smart for that.

"Maybe," she said, "but is he wrong?"

"How could anyone fall in love with someone on a Zombie Card?" he said with a laugh, but he was at least a full second late in getting the answer out, and he knew it.

"So . . . you're not in love?" she said offhand, but Benny was already waiting for a snare, and he knew that this was it. That question had as much to do with Zombie Cards as their school textbooks on American history had to do with the world in which they lived. That question was a twisted path filled with thorns and bear traps, and he knew it.

Benny knew that he wasn't the smartest of his friends, and when it came to perception he wasn't usually the sharpest knife in the drawer. But he was a long way from stupid. He knew what was happening, and he knew that allowing it to go down that path would only do harm. Nix wanted him to say something about emotions, about love. She wanted him to open a door that would lead to a conversation that would really do neither of them any good. It was too soon to talk about why he hadn't taken her hand; too soon to talk about what he really felt about her or if he felt anything at all. He didn't know the answers to those questions himself, and he was afraid of what his mouth would say.

So, he turned to her and instead of saying anything, he simply looked at her. And let her look at him.

Heat lightning forked the sky above them.

"What?" she snapped, and then she heard the shrill sound of her own voice and the need threaded through it. Benny could see the awareness blossom in her eyes, and it was a shared experience, because she knew that he saw it. It was a sobering moment, and in a bizarre way Benny felt like it aged him. Matured him. Just a bit. Nix too; he was certain of it. Her green eyes lost some of their force, and her mouth softened for a second, as if her lips were going to tremble, and then her jaw tightened as she clamped her self-control into place. In an odd, distracted way Benny admired that. He loved that about her.

They sat there for a long time, their eyes shifting away and coming back, their mouths wanting to speak but uncertain what language was spoken in this strange new country.

"I—," he began, but again she cut him off.

"So help me God, Benny, if you say 'I'm sorry,' I'll kill you."

She meant it. Even her freckles seemed to glow with dangerous heat. But at the end of her anger, there was the whisper of a smile that lifted the corners of her lips. Benny wished right then that things were different for them, that they had been given the chance to meet at this age rather than growing up together. It would make so many things easier.

He cleared his throat. "So . . . where does that leave us, Nix?"

"Where do you want it to leave us?"

"I want us to be friends. Always."

"And are we friends?"

"You're one of my *best* friends. You and Chong—you're my family."

"Me and Chong? What about Morgie?"

Benny shrugged. "He's the family dog."

▪ ▪ ▪

Morgie raised his head at the sound of laughter. On the other side of the yard, in the shade of the big oak, Benny and Nix were howling with laughter.

"What the hell's so funny?" he asked irritably.

Chong peered weakly out from under the picnic table. He saw the two of them laughing together, but he also saw that they were sitting apart. He sighed.

"I don't like it," growled Morgie. "That monkeybanger's making a play for Nix."

"Morgie," Chong said.

"What?"

"Shut up."

But Morgie was persistent. "What? You're saying I don't have anything to worry about?"

Chong considered. "Knowing you, your personal habits, your general hygiene, and your raw intelligence, I think you have a lot to worry about."

"Hey!"

Chong grunted and closed his eyes.

Thunder rumbled again in the west.

After a while Nix took her journal out of her satchel, used a pocket knife to sharpen her pencil, and began writing. Benny watched her while pretending not to. He was particularly interested in the way her sweaty T-shirt molded to her when she stretched to grab the bag. And the way the sunlight brought out gold flecks in her green eyes. He banged his head against the rough bark of the tree. Twice. Hard.

What the hell is wrong with me? he wondered, and not for the first time.

Nix either didn't notice him watching or—even at fourteen and three-quarters—was too practiced at being a young woman to allow anything to show on her face. She bent over the book and wrote for nearly twenty minutes, only pausing long enough to whittle a new point at the end of each full page.

When she stopped again to reach for the knife, Benny said, "Why do you write in that thing?"

"I'm writing a book," she said, deftly shaving off a fleck of wood.

"About what? Love and bunnies? Do I get eaten by your attack bunnies?"

"Don't tempt me. No, it's not a novel. It's nonfiction." She blew on the sharpened pencil point. "About zombies."

Benny laughed. "What, you want to kill zoms? I thought you guys were doing this sword stuff for fun."

"I don't particularly want to kill zoms," she said. "But I do want to understand them."

"What's to understand?" Benny said, though even as he said it he knew it was a stupid thing to say. The real truth was, things had now changed between him and Nix, and he didn't know the territory. It had a new feel to it, a new language, and he felt immensely awkward. He tried it again. "I mean . . . why?"

Instead of answering directly, Nix said, "Do you want to live in Mountainside your whole life?"

"Got to live somewhere," he began, but he saw disappointment blossom in her eyes. Nix shook her head and bent over her book, pencil poised to pick up the thread of her argument. Before she'd finished half a paragraph, a ragged line of seagulls flew overhead, their stomachs as white as snow, their wings tipped with black. Nix nodded toward them. "They probably sleep on the coast, right by the ocean. According to the maps we're less than two hundred miles from the Pacific Ocean, but I've never seen it. No one our age has. The way things are going, no one will. It might as well be on another world."

"Why do you want to see it?"

"Why don't *you*?"

"I . . ." He knew he was on some dangerous ground here. There were all kinds of deadfalls and rabbit holes built into her question. He didn't know where she was going with this, but he was smart enough to know he was about to put his foot somewhere that would hurt him. "I never really thought about it," he said, and that was true enough. "Look, I kind of get your point. You're frustrated because this town's our world, it's all we have. Okay. That sucks and I don't like it either. But how are we going to change that by studying zoms?"

"Do you remember in history class when Mr. West-Mensch talked about war? He said that history shows that it's easier to conquer than to control. What was the line Chong likes so much?"

"'They won the war but lost the peace,'" Benny supplied. "But I forget which war Mr. West-Mensch was talking about."

"He might as well have been talking about this one. The last one. First Night was like a sneak attack, followed by a systematic invasion. Like the Germans in the early part of the Second World War. We lost because we were totally unprepared for the attack, and by the time we understood the nature of the attackers, it was too late to organize a counterattack."

"Are you quoting someone?"

"No. Why?"

"I don't know. . . . It just sounds pretty sophisticated."

"For a girl?" The challenge was making her freckles glow again.

"No," Benny said. "For someone younger than me. Or . . . even someone older than me."

She ignored the implied compliment and went back to her point. "Right now we hold our own. We're not losing the war anymore, because the enemy has reached the limits of how it can come at us. We build fences, and they can't dismantle fences. We know that anyone who dies will come back as a zom, and so we have all these precautions around the sick and dying. We have guns and weapons, we have carpet coats, cadaverine. We have the beginnings of a whole new science of warfare against the enemy."

"Okay. So?"

"So . . . we could take back whole sections of the country."

Benny nodded. He told her about his brief conversations on this topic with Tom and Rob Sacchetto. Neither of those conversations had gone very deep, though; and neither of them had the passion in their voices that he heard in Nix's.

"Out in the Pacific there are islands not that far off the coast. I read a book about them. Santa Cruz, San Miguel. Catalina. Some of them had only a few thousand people on them, and even if *all* of them are filled with zoms, we have enough people, enough weapons and know-how, to take them away from the zoms. Zoms can't swim; they can't use boats. We could take those islands. The book said that there's farmland on several of them."

"It would take years to do all that."

"We *have* years. We have nothing but time, Benny. Years and years and forever, because that's all we have left."

"How's all that better than what we have here? We have farmland that we don't have to fight for."

"Because out there on the islands, eventually there would be nothing left but people. Even if there was an outbreak where someone forgot to lock themselves in at night and zommed out, it wouldn't lead to another First Night. Not anywhere close. Everyone knows the basics of how to control a zom. Everyone. We played games about it when we were in first grade. We're a culture of zombie hunters, Benny, even if most of the people here don't want to accept it, or pretend otherwise."

Benny thought about that, tried to poke holes in it, but couldn't.

"If there was nothing left but people," Nix continued, "we wouldn't have to live in fear all the time. There wouldn't be any need for bounty hunters, either. It would be a real world again." She looked toward the east, as if she could see the fence line from Benny's backyard. "You see the fence as something keeping the zoms out. I don't. I see it as the thing that pens us in. We're trapped here. Trapped isn't 'alive.' Trapped isn't 'safe.' And it isn't 'free.'"

Benny looked at her, at the side of her face as she stared toward the unseen fence line. Nix was so pretty, so smart, so . . . everything. *Open your mouth you idiot,* he told himself. *Just tell her.*

"Nix," he said softly, but he had no idea what he would say next.

"What?" She still stared to the east, watching as more gulls came from that direction and flew over them toward the unseen coastline behind them.

"I *do* want to see the ocean."

Nix turned toward him.

He said, "The ocean, the islands to the west, or whatever's on the other side of the Rot and Ruin to the east. Maybe what's in another country. Whatever's there, I want to see it. I don't want to live my life in a chicken cage." He took a breath, fishing for the right way to say it. "You're right. If we don't get out of this town, we're going to die here. And I don't mean just us. You and me. The caged birds. I mean all of us. Mountainside was how Tom and the other adults survived First Night. But now it's—"

She finished it for him. "Now it's a coffin. No room, no air, no future."

"Yeah."

Even though his inner voice screamed at him to say more, he couldn't make his mouth form the words. He sat there, staring into her green eyes. After a long time Nix sighed. She touched his face. No more than a ghost-light brush of fingertips on his cheek.

"One of us is the stupidest person in the whole wide world, Benny Imura," she said. Then she rose and went inside to wash up.

THE CLOUDS SWEPT OVER THE MOUNTAINS AND ACROSS THE VALLEY, blotting out the sun. Morgie, Chong, and Nix stayed for roasted corn and hamburgers that Tom made on a stone grill in the yard, but as the first fat raindrops splatted down, they bolted for home. The wind picked up, and the Imura brothers ran to close the shutters and button up the house. By the time they were done, lightning was flashing continuously, throwing weird shadows across the lawn and stabbing in through the slats of the shutters.

"This is going to be a bad one," Tom said, sniffing the air.

Inside, they changed out of their workout clothes, washed, and shambled back into the kitchen in pajama bottoms and T-shirts. The temperature dropped like a rock, and Tom brewed a pot of strong black tea, flavored with fresh mint leaves. They drank it with honey-almond muffins Nix's mother had sent over.

"How come Mrs. Riley sends us stuff so often?" Benny asked, halfway through his third muffin.

Tom gave an enigmatic little shrug. "She thinks she owes me, and this is how she repays the debt."

"Does she owe you?"

"No. When a friend does a favor for a friend, it isn't with the expectation of repayment."

"What favor? Getting her out of Gameland?"

"Doesn't matter," Tom said. "And it was a long time ago. But I think it makes Jessie feel better to send us what she can."

Benny nodded, uncertain what to make of Tom's answer. He nibbled the muffin. "She's a pretty amazing baker."

"She's a pretty amazing woman," said Tom.

Benny straightened. "Really?" he said with a grin.

"You can wipe that smile off your face right now, because Jessie and I are just friends. She's one of the few people I really trust. And that is the end of that discussion."

Benny grinned all the way through the rest of his muffin. Thunder slammed against the house—hard enough to rattle the teacups.

Tom left the room and came back with his boots, rain slicker, and his sword. The real one, not the wooden training *bokken.* He set them by the back door.

"What's that for?"

"That last one sounded like a lightning strike. There are trees near the north wall of the fence."

"Sure, but there's a guard detail too."

"Sure, but it's always better to be prepared."

As Tom sat down he spotted the object that Benny had placed in the center of the table. The Zombie Card with the picture of the wild and beautiful Lost Girl.

"Ah," Tom said.

"Will you tell me about her?"

"Maybe. Will you answer my questions first?"

"About Charlie Matthias?"

"Yep."

Benny sighed. "I guess."

Tom stood up. "Good night, kiddo. Sleep tight."

"Hey!"

Tom said, "'I guess' doesn't sound like a show of trust. Either you *will* or you *won't*."

"You're going to go all Zen on me again?"

"Yes," Tom said. "I am. Now this time think it through and give me a straight answer."

"Yes," said Benny. "I'll answer any question you want to ask, as long as you tell me about Lilah."

"No reserves, no fake outs. Straight answers?"

"Yes. But I'm going to want the same."

"Fair enough," said Tom. "So I'll get right to it. Do you trust Charlie Pink-eye?"

"After what happened today? No, not much."

"How much is 'not much'?"

"I don't know, and that's the truth. I like Charlie . . . or I used to, but today he really freaked me out. For a minute there, he looked like he was going to *take* that card from me. By any means necessary."

"Do you think he would have hurt you?"

"To get the card?"

Tom nodded.

"That's a weird question, because it's only a card, you know? I mean . . . so what? It was only dumb luck that I even got it. It could have been Charlie's own nephew, Zak, who bought that pack. Or one of the other kids that Charlie doesn't know. It could have been Chong or Morgie. Or Nix."

"Yeah, things happen in strange ways sometimes," said

Tom. He sipped his tea. "When you let go of the card, was that an accident or did you toss it to keep it away from him?"

"I dropped it."

"Why? Why not show him the card? Why not give it to him?"

"It was mine."

Tom shook his head. "No. You were willing to let it blow away in the wind instead of letting Charlie have it. That wasn't about possession. So what was it about?"

"It's hard to explain," Benny said. "But when I first saw that card, when I saw *her*, I had this weird feeling that I knew her. Or . . . would know her. Does that make sense?"

"It's a dark and stormy night, kiddo. Mystical seems kind of appropriate." As if in agreement, another crack of thunder rattled the crockery in the cupboards and pulled groans from the timbers of the house. "Go on."

"I don't know. I felt like I needed to protect her."

"From Charlie?"

"From everyone."

Tom reached out and turned the card. The girl looked fierce, and the heap of zombie corpses behind her suggested that she was brutally tough. "She can take care of herself."

"You say that like you *know* her," Benny said. "I was square with you, now it's your turn. Tell me about the Lost Girl. Tell me everything."

"It's not a nice story, Ben," Tom said. "It's sad and it's scary and it's full of bad things."

Thunder punched the house over and over again.

"Like you said, this is the night for that kind of thing."

"Yeah," said Tom. "I guess it is."

And he told his tale.

"I FIRST SAW THE LOST GIRL FIVE YEARS AGO," TOM SAID. "ROB SACCHETTO told me his story, of course, but I didn't make the connection between the little girl he left in the cottage and the wild girl I saw in the Ruin. It's hard to believe they're the same person. Did Rob tell you about the search for the cottage?"

Benny nodded.

"There was more than one search. The first was made by the group that split off from the main rescue party that settled this town. That team never made it to the cottage. No one knows where they ended up. Maybe they gave up the search and found some other place to live or—more likely—they ran into trouble and died out there. It's odd. . . . People talk about First Night as if it was just that one night, but when the dead rose, it took weeks for civilization to fall. There were lots of fights. Big ones with the military and smaller ones with families defending their homes, or people grouping together to defend their neighborhoods. In the end, though, we kind of lost the fight more than the dead won it."

"What do you mean?"

"We let fear rule us and guide us, and that's never the way to win. Never. A long time ago a great man once said that 'we have nothing to fear but fear itself.' That was never truer than during First Night. It was fear that caused people to panic and abandon defenses. It was fear that made them squabble instead of working together. It was fear that inspired them to take actions they would never have taken if they'd given it a minute's more cool thought."

"Like what?"

"Like dropping bombs on the cities. Nukes and regular bombs. A lot of the big cities were destroyed; all the people killed by shock or radiation sickness. Sure, some of the zoms were killed too, but those hundreds of thousands of people who were killed by the bombs came back as zoms. I remember one of the last news reports from Chicago, in which a reporter screamed and wept and prayed as she described waves of radioactive zombies crawling out of the ruins of the city. They were so hot with radiation that they were killing humans long before they made physical contact." Tom shook his head. "It was fear that caused those bombs to be dropped."

"That's another thing they didn't tell us in school."

"They wouldn't," said Tom. "Trust me, though, fear is the code we live by here in town, and in the other towns scattered along this mountain range. I suspect that if there are other towns still surviving elsewhere in the country or the world, then fear is what they live by too."

"Not everyone's afraid, though. . . ."

"No. You're right. . . . There are some people who don't let fear rule their actions, and I suspect it'll be your generation that turns things around. Most of the people my age or older are lost in fear, and they'll never find their way back. But you and your friends, especially those young enough to not remember First Night . . . You're the ones who will choose whether to live in fear or not."

"Last week, when you said that people in town didn't trust anything out in the Ruin, that they think everything's diseased . . ."

Tom nodded. "You're on the right track. We—our town—could reclaim most of central California. Not Los Angeles, of course; that's lost for good. But we could retake hundreds of thousands of square miles of farmland. We could reclaim whole towns. Like that town where Harold Simmons lived. Don't you think three or four hundred armed people could retake that town?"

"We wouldn't need anywhere near that many. Fifty people in carpet coats, with rifles, axes, and swords could do it. It isn't a big town."

"Right. And there are a dozen towns within a day's walk from here. Hundreds just a few days away, with farmable land where we could grow more food than we could eat. No one would go hungry."

Benny looked at the muffin he held between his fingers, and it struck him that if Nix and her mother were as poor as everyone said they were, then just the ingredients for the muffins must have cut into their own rations. He set the muffin down.

His brother leaned his forearms on the table and said quietly, "Let me tell you a secret, Benny. The first secret you and I will share, okay?"

Benny nodded.

"I'll never let Jessie and Nix Riley go hungry. Haven't you noticed that we don't have meat on our table seven days a week, even though we can afford it?"

Another nod.

"That's so there's meat on their table. Nix doesn't know, and you have to swear to me that you'll never tell her."

Benny tried to say the words, "I swear," but his mouth was too dry to let the words out. Thunder punctuated his attempt, and Tom nodded, as if a deal had been struck.

When he could speak, Benny said, "I don't get it. How can the town let anyone go hungry? I mean, we have the rationing system and all. Isn't it supposed to provide—"

"Believe it or not, it was actually worse *before* First Night. There were hundreds of thousands of people without homes or food."

"What, just living on the streets?" Benny laughed.

"Exactly. Homeless. Whole families. In every city in the country. I'll bet they don't teach that in school, either. The zombie uprising didn't change everything."

Benny shook his head, unable to grasp the concept. "You know how Nix is always writing in her diary?"

"Sure."

"It's not a diary. She's collected everything she can about zoms. She has this idea about getting out of Mountainside." He told Tom about the Pacific Islands and Nix's practical dreams of reclaiming them and starting a new life without the constant threat of the living dead.

Tom listened very attentively to every word, nodding his approval. "Darn smart girl. You ever think of asking her out?"

"Don't go there, Tom."

"Oookay." Tom sipped his tea. "As far as Nix's idea . . . I did say that it would be your generation that would probably change things. A few of us—too very few of us, really—have been trying to make changes, to get the others to shake loose from the fear. Sadly, we haven't had much luck. Over the last dozen years, Mountainside has settled into a pattern, and the only thing more powerful than fear is routine. Once people are in a rut, it's sometimes the hardest thing in the world to get them out of it. They defend the routine, too. They say that it's a simpler life, less stressful and complicated, more predictable. Some of them are getting nostalgic about it, they mythologize it, as if we're living in the Old West, except with zombies instead of wild Indians."

"That's dumb," Benny said.

"It's fearful," Tom corrected, "but it's safe. At least they think it is. It allows them to think they know the whole size and shape of their world. Except for when you kids are talking, you almost never hear someone talk about the world that was. People don't ask one another where they're from. I mean, they kind of *know*, and certainly if you look around, Mountainside is a microcosm of global diversity. Doc Gurijala was born in northern India, Old Man Sanchez came here from Oaxaca in Mexico. The Mekong brothers are Vietnamese. Chong's Chinese, our dad was Japanese. And yet as far as you could tell from conversations around town, we're all 'from Mountainside.' End of story. The rest of the world no longer exists. Do you know why?"

"I think so," said Benny. "If they talk about where they're from, they have to talk about what happened. And . . . who they left behind."

"Right. Fear fueled by grief." Tom rubbed his face with his palms.

"What about the bounty hunters and . . . and what you

do? People have to talk about the outside world for that."

Tom nodded approval. "That's true, and it's a cultural quirk that surfaces once in a while, but once the closure is accomplished, then the client goes right back into their shell. There are plenty of people who were clients of mine in the past, who walk by me on the street without a flicker of recognition. Either they pretend to ignore me, so that they don't have to think about the service I provided for them, or they truly have forgotten it, as if a door closed in their minds. I can count the number of former clients on the fingers of one hand who will even talk to me about the closure job I did for them." He paused. "Jessie Riley is one of them."

Benny's teacup paused an inch from his lips. "What? Nix's mom was a client of yours?"

"Yes. Years ago."

"But . . . but Nix said that it was just her and her mom."

"Nowadays, sure. But everyone has family somewhere, Ben. Nix had a father and two older brothers."

"First Night?"

"First Night," Tom agreed.

"God! Does Nix even know?"

"That's hard to say. If Jessie told her, then either Nix has chosen *not* to say anything to her friends or she's blocked it out like everyone else does."

Benny shook his head. "Nix would have told me."

"Are you sure?"

"She would have told me. Especially after I told her . . ."

Benny's voice trailed off and Tom nodded. "After you told her about our trip to the Ruin?"

"Yes."

"It's up to her what she chooses to tell you, but as far as what I'm about to share, that's confidential. Family business. You can't tell her about this."

"But—"

"We never break a client's confidence. I need your word on this."

Benny finished his tea as he thought it through. He didn't want to agree, but he couldn't construct a single reason why not.

"Yeah," he said, "okay."

"Good. Now we get to what you want to hear, because the story of Nix's family is tied to the Lost Girl."

"Wait!" said Benny, "In the story the artist guy told me, there was a woman who had a baby. Was that baby Nix?"

Tom sat back and cocked his head to one side. "How long ago was First Night?"

"Almost fourteen years ago and . . . oh. Right. Nix will be fifteen in a couple of months. Can't be her."

"My brother, the math genius."

"Sorry."

"There is a connection, though, but it's not a blood link, not a family tie," Tom said. "I was doing the closure job for Jessie Riley. Rob had done erosion portraits of Mike Riley and the boys, Greg and Danny, and Jessie said that when she fled her house, she'd slammed the door behind her. Very few zoms can turn doorknobs, and most of them don't have the coordination to climb out of a window. So unless someone else opened the door, there was a good chance they'd still be there."

"How long ago was this?"

"About five years ago. Remember the first time I left you with Fran and Randy Kirsch? I left on a Sunday, as I remember, heading northeast. There were a lot more zoms roaming free back then, and the farther I went from Mountainside, the more of them I saw. Most of them were singles, walking along, following some movement—a deer, a rabbit, whatever—but there were groups of them, too. Biggest group I saw was about fifty, standing in the middle of an intersection. Probably they'd come down different roads and met at the intersection and had nowhere else to go. Sounds weird, doesn't it? But that's what happens if there's nothing for them to hunt and nothing to attract them. They just stop."

"What about the noms?"

"Good question and I don't have a good answer. They're different. The nomads keep wandering and never seem to stop, but they're rare. Maybe one out of every couple thousand will roam."

"I thought all zoms were the same," said Benny, unnerved by Tom's story.

"Not all of anything is the same. There are always differences, always changes."

"Zombie evolution?" Benny joked, but Tom shrugged.

"Maybe. We don't know."

"How can we not know?"

"Benny . . . it's not like anyone's made a formal scientific study of zombies. Get real. Who would do that? *How* would they do it? Mind you, I think they *should* do it, but as I already said, the people around here don't spend much active thought on what happens beyond the fence line. Any information on differences in zombies comes from the kind of people who go out into the Ruin. Bounty hunters, the way-station monks, the traders who go from town to town. A few others. And the loners."

"Loners?"

"There are people who live out in the Ruin. They're individuals who want to be alone and would rather deal with the threat of the zoms than rejoin society."

"Why?"

"That's hard to answer, because they're not a 'type,' if you know what I mean. Each one of them has their own reasons. I know some of them. A few are friends. Some never make contact with anyone with a pulse." He inhaled through his nose. "And a few of them are very bad people. I know of some that I wouldn't come within fifty yards of without a weapon in my hand."

"Why?"

"Because some of them will kill anyone they meet. Human or zom, they don't care. They've staked out a spot, and I guess it's their version of paradise, or maybe their corner of hell, and it's more than your life's worth to trespass."

"How can you tell what are the no-trespass zones?"

"Smart question. The borders are usually marked. Staked out, so to speak. It's very tribal. I know of a family, living high in the hills, who have driven a line of stakes into the ground all around their place and topped each stake with a head."

"Human heads or zoms?"

"After the crows have been at them, it's hard to say, but I wouldn't want to bet a torn ration dollar that they only kill zoms."

"Is that how the Lost Girl lives?"

Tom didn't answer immediately, but instead shifted back to his narrative. "I kept moving, following an old travel map that Jessie had marked for me. By nightfall on the third day, I reached the town where the Rileys lived. The place had been hit hard by First Night and what happened after. There was a big road—an interstate highway that ran past it—and it was choked with rusted vehicles. Zoms had been smashed by cars and trucks; run over by people trying to flee or by people who were trying to kill zoms. Even after all that time, you could see where cars skidded away from an impact with a zom and went off the road, or collided with other cars. I guess once a few accidents blocked the road, the cars behind them got jammed up and then the zoms must have closed in and attacked. It was strange, too, because there were clear signs that some of the zoms used stones and heavy sticks to smash through the windows."

"Zoms using tools?"

"Sounds weird, right? But I've seen it a couple of times. It's another one of the variations, and I can't explain it any more than I can explain why they don't rot away completely." Tom took a muffin and bit off a piece, chewed thoughtfully for a moment, then continued. "There were some military vehicles there, too, and I could tell there had been a huge battle. Everything had been chopped by heavy caliber rounds or blasted by grenades and rockets. Even with that there were very few bodies, of course, because the dead would have reanimated. That's why we didn't win the war. By the time the authorities realized that it was only damage to the motor cortex of the brain or to the brain stem that could permanently put them down, a lot of the combat units had been overwhelmed by zoms they'd hit with body shots. I saw a couple of those early fights, and I saw machine gunners emptying their weapons at the walking dead, chopping off arms and legs and tearing out huge chunks of hips and torsos, and the zoms just got back up and kept coming. Or they crawled toward the troops. I guess the soldiers permanently dropped half of the zoms they faced, but some of the dead got up three, four times, advancing a little closer each time until . . . well, you know. We lost. There were plenty of bones, though, skeletons from people that had been attacked by crowds of zombies and devoured, or from zoms that had been killed by head shots."

"What about walkers?" Benny asked, referring to mobile zombies.

"Most of them must have followed survivors out of town. But . . . there were still plenty of zoms in town. As I walked along the streets I could see some inside of stores or houses. I counted about twenty of them that had fallen into empty swimming pools and couldn't climb out. Plus there were a lot of them stuck inside of cars. A few banged against the glass as I passed, but they couldn't do anything to me . . . though I moved away fast, so the noise didn't attract the walkers. The worst, though, were zoms who were trapped under the wheels of cars, their legs or hips crushed, so that they were alive from the waist up but stuck there forever."

"God . . . ," Benny said. "Did you find the Rileys?"

"Sure. They were in their house, just like Jessie said they were. Front and back doors were closed. The family had owned a couple of big dogs—two German shepherds—and there'd been a terrible fight in the living room. The Rileys must have turned on the animals, and the dogs fought like dogs will.

They had old bites all over them. The father was missing his hands, and the oldest son, Danny, had almost no throat left. The dogs made a fight of it, but . . ." He left the rest unsaid. "Because of the damage, the zoms were very weak. I tied them up and quieted them without a fuss. I was in and out in twenty minutes."

"Did you have to read a letter? From Nix's mom?"

"Yes. She wrote a long letter. It was very . . ." Tom stopped, shook his head. "Jessie really loved her husband and sons. The letter was almost too hard to read, you know? By the time I was finished, I was telling myself that I was done, that I would never—*could* never—do that sort of thing again."

"But you still do."

"I still do."

"Do you like this stuff?"

Tom winced. "'Like'? Only a psychopath would *like* to do what I do."

"So why do it?"

"Because it needs being done. Someone has to—someone *will*—and if I don't, then the people who do won't necessarily bring any compassion to it. You've seen that. I've seen a whole lot of it. Way too much."

There was a burst of lightning and an immediate crack of thunder so loud that Benny jumped. Tom got up and peered through the slats in the shutters. "That was definitely a hit, but it was in town."

"Do you need to go out?"

"No," Tom said as he returned to the table. "Not unless I'm called. Where were we?"

"You finished the job at the Riley house."

"Right. I headed out of town as fast as I could. I was pretty upset—not quite the stoic your big brother has become, I guess—and I needed some time to sort things out, to make some decisions about my life. About our lives, really. I took a different route back, sticking more to the high ground, because there are fewer zoms up there."

"How come?"

"It's a gravity thing. Unless a zom is following prey, if it's walking, it'll follow the path of least resistance. They don't walk well, as you know. It's more of a stagger, like they're constantly falling forward and catching themselves with their next step. So if there's any kind of slant to the ground, they'll naturally follow it. In the Ruin we have to be careful in valleys and downlands. You're ten times more likely to see a zom on the lowlands than in the hills, so I went high, almost to the snow line. I camped out in a barn one night and in the cab of an eighteen-wheel truck the next. Funny thing . . . The truck had been hauling a load of microwave ovens. Scavengers had torn through the boxes; the road was littered with ovens someone had smashed. Definitely humans at work there, because zoms wouldn't be attracted to that kind of cargo."

"What are microwave ovens?"

"Ovens that run on electricity," Tom said. "Something I hope you'll actually get to use one day if people can shake off the superstitious nonsense they've associated with electricity. Now, listen close, because this is where the story takes a turn."

He and Benny both leaned forward, elbows on the table, hands curled around fresh cups of tea.

"That morning, after I left the truck, I found a dead zom in the middle of the road. Nothing too surprising about that, but it was the way it had been killed that intrigued me. Someone had come up on the zom from behind and slashed the back of one knee and the ankle of the other leg. Crude cuts, but effective. Took out the tendons and brought the zom down, and once it was down, they drove a knife into the back of its skull. As I said, this wasn't a skillful job, but it was smart. An hour later I found another one, and then another. By the end of that day, I'd found eighteen zoms killed the same way. Some of the kills were weeks old, a couple were very fresh, but the method was always the same. Tendon cuts from behind and then the knife in the back of the skull. After about the fifth or sixth kill, I was pretty sure I knew something about this particular zombie hunter. Everyone who works out in the Ruin, anyone who kills on a regular basis, develops a style. They find a method that works for them, a way to get the job done easiest and with the least amount of risk, and they stick to it. After all, it's not like the zoms can become aware of how hunters work, and change their tactics."

"So . . . who was doing this?"

"Ah," said Tom, "you just sailed past an obvious question."

"What?"

"Think about it."

Benny did, and then he got it. "Wait . . . you said that there weren't many zoms in the high country, but you found a whole bunch of dead ones. So, why were there so many up there?"

"Right. That had been worrying me all day. At first I thought there was a community up there that had been overrun. If that was the case, I could be walking into real trouble. But then something occurred to me. When I thought back to each of the zoms that this particular hunter had killed, I realized they were all very similar. They were all men. Adult men, all over thirty, all fairly big—or as big as a desiccated zom can be."

"Were they from a team or something? Or guys from an army base?"

"Good guesses, kiddo, but no. I went back to the most recent kills and followed their trails, backtracking them down to the lowlands. One was from a farm, the other from a service station. I climbed back into the hills and found another kill. A fairly fresh one, blood all over the place."

"Blood?" Benny said. "Zoms don't bleed."

"No, they don't," Tom agreed. "Now how about that?"

"This was a murdered person?"

"It was a dead person. 'Murder' is a relative term."

"Then I don't get it. I can see where you're going with this. These are kills the Lost Girl made, right? I mean, that's the surprise twist in your story."

"It's not a twist. You asked me to tell you about her, so there's no surprise. What I'm doing, little brother, is giving it to you as close as I can to the way I came into it. Laying out the evidence." Tom grinned. "Remember, I was in the police academy before First Night. I was studying to be a cop. Granted, I never spent time on the street, but I learned the basics of investigation and something about psychological profiling. When I bedded down that night, I looked at the evidence I had and made some basic deductions. Not assumptions, mind you. Do you know the difference?"

"One's based on evidence and the other's based on guesswork," Benny said. "We had the whole 'when you assume you make an ass out of you and me' speech in school."

"Okay, so make some deductions."

"Aside from the fact that this was the Lost Girl?"

"That's guesswork because I was telling her story."

"Okay. Well, describe the man she killed. The human, I mean."

"Not as big as the dead zoms, but sturdy."

"Was he a farmer or something?"

"No. From his weapons and equipment, it seemed pretty clear that he was a bounty hunter."

Benny sat back and thought about it, and Tom let him. The more he thought about it, the less he liked what he was thinking.

"She'd have been, what . . . eleven, twelve?"

"About that."

"And she was only killing men?"

"Yes." Tom was no longer smiling.

"Men who kind of fit a 'type'?"

"Yes."

Benny stared at Tom's hard, dark eyes for as long as he could. Thunder beat furiously on the walls.

"God," he said. "What did they do to her out there?"

But he already knew the answer, and it hurt his heart to know it. He thought of what Tom had said, of the fighting pits at Gameland, and tried to imagine a young girl down in the dark, armed with only a knife or a stick, the dead gray hands reaching for her. Even if she survived it, she would have scars cut deep into her mind. Benny and Tom sat together and listened to the storm punish the town.

"There's more to the story," said Tom. "A lot more."

But he never got to tell it. Not that night, anyway. A moment later there was a flash of lightning so long and bright that even through the shutters, it lit the whole kitchen to an unnatural whiteness, and immediately there was a crack of thunder that was the loudest sound Benny had ever heard.

And then the screaming began.

TOM WAS UP, AND HAD THE BACK DOOR OPEN BEFORE BENNY WAS EVEN out of his chair.

"What is it?" Benny asked.

Tom didn't answer. The wind whipped the door inward toward him, driving him back a step. Even over the roar of the storm, they could hear people yelling. There were more screams, and then a gunshot. A second later there were more shots.

"Stay here," Tom ordered. "Close and bar the door!"

"I want to go with you!"

"No!" Tom growled. He grabbed his rain slicker and pulled it on, looped the strap of his sword over his shoulder, and ran barefoot into the black downpour. Benny came out onto the back porch, but Tom was already gone, swallowed whole by the wind and blowing rain. In less than five seconds he was soaked to the skin. Lightning flashed again and again, each burst punctuated by a huge boom, and Benny wondered if this was what it must have been like during the battles on First Night. Darkness, screams, and the bang and flash of artillery. He moved backward into the house and forced the door shut. The locks were strong, but he realized that Tom had no keys. All his brother wore under his slicker was an undershirt and pajama bottoms. He hadn't even taken a gun.

Benny looked at the heavy piece of square-cut oak that stood beside the door. There were two iron sleeves bolted to the wall on either side of the frame. The bar slid through them and completely barricaded the entrance. Benny had seen Tom install it years ago, and the bolts went all the way through the wall into steel plates on the outside of the house.

"You'd have to knock down the whole wall to get through that," Tom had said.

Benny picked up the bar and hefted it. It was heavy and dense. Twenty zoms couldn't crack it. He fitted one end into the closest sleeve and began sliding it across the door.

Tom was out there with nothing but a sword. No shoes, no gun, no light. If a tree had fallen over and torn a hole in the fence, who knows how many zoms could be out there.

There were more shots, a whole barrage of them. Someone was yelling, but Benny couldn't make out any words. The hammering of the rain was too insistent.

He chewed his lip, torn by indecision.

On one hand, Tom had told him to bar the door. On the other, the door was already locked, and zoms couldn't pick a lock. All of the windows were shuttered, and the front door was as sturdy as this one. He was safe.

But what about Tom?

If there was a full scale invasion of the town, Tom might have to come running back here for shelter. It could come down to seconds. How long would it take Benny to get to the back door, push the heavy bar out of the sleeves, and unlock the locks? Ten seconds? Eight?

Too long.

He pulled the bar from the sleeve and set it back against the wall.

Tom's guns were locked up, and Tom wore the key on a chain around his neck. If he busted open the locker and this turned out to be nothing, Tom would fry him.

On the other hand . . .

Doubt was a hungry thing that chewed at him.

Something hit the wall outside. Hard and sharp. It wasn't rain. He listened, trying to remember exactly what he had heard, trying to listen the way Tom listened when they were out in the Ruin. Had it been an acorn blown out of the oak tree? No, they had a different, lighter sound. Whatever had hit the outside wall had hit fast and with a lot of power.

A bullet?

He was almost positive that's what it had been.

He crouched low and put his ear to the corner of the kitchen window. There were more screams and a whole bunch of gunshots. Then he heard footsteps on the back porch and a second later, the doorknob turned. Benny twisted around to see out the window, but all he could see was a flap of something glistening.

A slicker.

The doorknob turned again and again.

Tom!

Benny shot to his feet and threw open the locks. *God . . . please let Tom be okay,* he thought as he undid the four heavy dead bolts. Benny yanked the door open.

Tom staggered inside. Head bowed, his rain slicker torn and hanging in shreds, dark hair dripping with water.

Benny backed away.

It wasn't Tom.

It was Rob Sacchetto, the erosion artist.

He was a zombie.

26

THE CREATURE LIFTED ITS WHITE FACE TO BENNY AND OPENED ITS MOUTH. Blood ran over the artist's broken teeth and dripped onto the front of the slicker.

"Mr. Sacchetto . . . ?"

The zombie took a shambling step toward him, raising fingers that were bone white and looked strangely disjointed, as if all of the knuckles were broken. Benny was frozen in place. He had never known anyone who had become a zom—not since the disease had taken his mother from him. He and Chong and Nix had talked about it, wondered about it, even joked about it, but even to them, even in this world, it was slightly unreal. Zoms were out there, real life was here in town, and deep inside, in a flash of understanding, Benny realized he had been just as detached from the realities of the world as everyone else. Even with people talking about quieting a relative who'd died. Even with all of the incontrovertible evidence in his face every day, Benny realized he never quite equated zombies with people. Not even his trip into the Ruin had done that, not completely. But now, as this zombie—this *person*—reached for him, the horrible truth of it hit him with full force.

For a dreadful moment Benny was frozen to the spot and frozen into this state of awareness. The creature's eyes met his, and for a moment—for the strangest, twisted fragment of a moment—Benny could swear that there was some splinter of recognition, that some piece of Sacchetto looked out in blind panic through the eyes of the dead thing that he had become.

"Mr. Sacchetto," Benny said again, and this time his voice was full of cracks, ready to break.

The zom's mouth moved, trying to form words, and against all evidence and sense, Benny hoped that somehow the artist *was* in there. That he had been able, through some unimaginable way, to fight the transition from man to monster. But all that came from the dead throat was a low moan that possessed no meaning other than that of a hunger it could never understand and never assuage.

It nearly broke Benny's heart. To see the husk of the person and to know that what had made him human was . . . gone. Benny felt like his head would break if he tried to hold that truth inside.

The zom stepped toward Benny, reaching with its broken fingers, and still Benny was frozen into the moment, rooted to the rain-slick kitchen floor. It was only when the very tips of the zombie's cold fingers brushed his cheek that Benny came alive again.

He screamed.

It was terror and it was rage. The terror was for what was reaching for him—this dead and shambling thing; and the rage was for what had been taken from him—a friend, a person he knew.

Benny backpedaled away from those clutching fingers, his feet slipping and sliding on the floor until his back struck the edge of the doorway that led to the middle room. The impact galvanized him, and he spun off the frame and bolted toward the living room. He crashed into a small table and then flung it behind him, not bothering to look as he heard it crack against the zom's shins. The monster fell over it, and Benny heard the thump of kneecaps and elbows on the hardwood, but no cry of pain. Nothing normal like that.

He burst into the living room and dove for the bag of training equipment. The best weapons were in the kitchen—knives, hammers, a toolbox. He had the wooden swords. They would have to do. Benny pulled at the rough canvas, his fingers clumsily scrabbling at the zipper, pulling it down, half tearing one of his fingernails, cursing, not caring about the pain. The bag opened, and he reached inside just as Sacchetto lumbered into the living room. Benny flicked a glance at the front door. It was locked, and he knew that he would never get the locks opened before the creature could get him. It was the reverse of what he had imagined for Tom.

Fingers brushed his hair and tried to grab hold, but Benny threw himself over the couch, dragging the bag with him. The wooden swords spilled out with a clatter. He grabbed one and spun around on his knees as the zombie bent over the couch to grab at him.

Benny rammed the tip of the sword against the zom's chest. The impact had all of his fear behind it, and it was harder than he expected, sending shock waves up his arms. He almost dropped the sword.

The zombie swiped at his face, and Benny could feel a fingernail slice him across the cheek, from ear to nose.

He shifted his grip on the *bokken*, holding it like a quarter-staff, and used the span between his clenched fists to drive into the zom's shoulders, shoving it back and knocking it off balance. It was more powerful than he thought, and he realized that Sacchetto could only have been turned recently. Just before, or during, the storm. He wasn't decayed, hadn't lost his mass. Maybe hadn't even lost all of his mind. Maybe that was why he could turn the doorknob. What had Tom said?

Very few zoms can turn doorknobs, and most of them don't have the coordination to climb out of a window. Very few could. Not "none." Maybe it was the recent dead who could do this.

The realization gave him clarity, but not one shred of comfort. It meant that Sacchetto was even more dangerous. Stronger, faster, maybe smarter than the image of a zom that Benny had in his mind.

The zom lurched toward him again and began clambering over the couch.

Benny jumped to his feet and backed away, and as he did so, he almost unconsciously took the handle of the wooden sword into the proper two-hand grip. Fists apart for leverage, raising the sword, elbows slightly bent.

The zom reached for him, trying to grab his wrist.

"I'm sorry," Benny said.

And he brought the sword down on the top of the artist's head.

The creature did not stop.

Benny hit him again and again.

And again.

His arms rose and fell, rose and fell, slamming the hard wood down on the zombie's skull. Benny could hear screams as he struck. Not the zombie's. They were his own.

"STOP!"

Tom's shout cut through the air, and Benny froze in place, the wooden sword raised high, his hands slick with blood and brain matter. Benny turned his head to see Tom, standing in the doorway to the middle room. His brother was covered with blood and mud and rainwater; his steel *katana* was in one strong hand, a thick-bladed bayonet in the other.

"Benny," Tom said, "it's over. You won." Tom laid the bayonet on a table and stepped close. He reached up to take hold of the *bokken*. "You did it, kiddo. You killed the monster."

"'Monster'?" Benny said in a soft and distant voice. He looked down at the shattered, lumpy mass that was all that was left of Sacchetto. It no longer looked human. It no longer looked like a zom. All it was now was dead meat and broken bones and stuff that glistened and dripped. Benny let Tom take the sword from his hands. In truth he could barely feel his hands. They were icy, detached, alien. Those hands had just done things that *he* could never have done. Benny looked numbly at them; at the bloody hands of a killer.

Benny suddenly turned and threw up into a potted plant. Tea and muffins and burgers. He wished he could vomit up the last few moments of his life, to expel these memories and experiences.

Tom stood apart, a sword in each hand, panting.

"Are you hurt, Benny?" he asked. "Did he . . . ?"

"Bite me?" Benny wiped his mouth and shook his head. "No. He didn't."

Tom nodded slowly, but his eyes ranged up and down Benny, looking for injuries. The only injuries Benny had were a scratch on the cheek and a torn fingernail. However, Benny understood Tom's caution, and he wondered what Tom would have done if he *had* been bitten.

Finally, Tom put down the wooden sword and used a cloth to wipe the gore from his *katana*.

"What happened?" Benny asked thickly. "Was it lightning? A fallen tree?"

"The lightning hit the north watchtower. It collapsed and dumped Ramón Olivera over the fence. About a couple dozen zoms rushed at him when the tower fell. The two other guards must have been spooked by the storm. They panicked and opened the gate to try and rescue Ramón, and the zoms were all over them. Sally Parker—you know her, don't you? Lives next door to Morgie? Well . . . she was killed."

"No . . ."

"The other guards didn't hear the screams, because of the thunder, and before they knew what was happening there were twenty or thirty zoms in the streets. You'd think after all this time, after everything that's happened, people wouldn't panic. But they did. Every idiot who could pull a trigger started shooting. Three people were shot, and two others were bitten. I think the gunshot victims will all make it, but as for the others . . ."

He let it hang. Everyone knew there was nothing that could be done to stop the infection from a zombie bite. Depending on the strength of each person's immune system, they'd last a day or a week, but they were doomed. All victims would be taken to the Quiet House on the far side of town. They'd be given food and water and books. A priest or pastor or rabbi would come and sit with them. The doors would be locked, and everyone would wait. Chong said that bite victims often committed suicide and that a few were murdered by friends or family who didn't want to see them suffer. Benny didn't used to believe Chong. Now he knew his friend was probably right.

"Did they get all the zoms?"

"Yes," said Tom. "Captain Strunk and his crew made sure of that. And Ramón will be fine. He broke his leg, and he has some burns, but there was so much wreckage around him that the dead couldn't get to him."

"Was anyone else bitten?"

"No. The zoms never got farther than the red zone. Strunk has forty people with rifles at the north gate while the crew repairs the fence." He swore. "If I had a dime for every time I told the town council that we need a double line of fences . . ."

"Tom," Benny said. "Some zoms must have gotten past you."

"No. Not one."

"But . . . Mr. Sacchetto . . . Zoms got to *him*, and he lives all the way over by the reservoir."

Tom squatted down and rolled the dead artist over onto his back. He examined the man's hands and wrists, lifted his shirt to look underneath. Tom's lips were pursed and his eyes narrow and unreadable. Tom stood and walked quickly through the house, unlocked the back door, and stepped out onto the porch. Benny followed along and watched as Tom bent to examine the scuffed mud on the wood porch floor and the steps. The rain had washed most of it away, but there must have been enough left, because Tom made a disgusted sound and stared for a few seconds out into the darkness. Benny realized that the storm had eased, and there were no new screams, no additional gunshots.

Tom gently pushed Benny back inside and locked the door. Almost as an afterthought, he picked up the oak bar and slid it through the sleeves. Tom told Benny to wash the blood off his hands, and he gave him a bandage to wrap the finger with the torn nail. It hurt, but pain seemed to be such a small thing. All of this was done without words, and they walked back to the living room in silence and stood over the body. Benny could tell that Tom was working something out. His brother kept looking toward the back door and then down at Sacchetto.

"Damn," Tom said softly, "I hate it when I'm right."

Benny stood over Sacchetto, looking down at the body. He did not see the zombie. He saw the man who had painted the portrait of the Lost Girl. A man who had helped establish and build this town. A friend.

"What do you mean?" he asked Tom.

Tom studied his face for a moment and then nodded to himself, as if he'd just made a decision about whether it was safe to share his suspicions with Benny.

"Look at his fingers. Tell me what you see."

Benny didn't have to look. He'd already noticed how grotesquely crooked the artist's hands had been.

"Someone did that to him," Benny said. "While he was alive."

Tom nodded. "His ribs are bruised, too, and it looks like someone knocked some of his teeth out, broke a couple others. Someone tortured him to death, Benny. And when he reanimated as a zom, he was brought here."

"Brought here? Why would someone bring a zom here?" Benny demanded.

Tom looked at him with cold and dangerous eyes.

"Why, to kill us, of course."

"WHO WANTS TO *KILL* US?" BENNY SAID.

Tom didn't answer. Instead he asked, "Did you see anyone outside? Hear anyone?"

"No. Just the storm," Benny said, then paused. "Well . . . I did hear one thing. Something hit the side of the house. I think it was a bullet. You said that bullets could travel a long way, so I figured it was a stray shot from the fight. Then someone started jiggling the doorknob. I thought you were trying to get back in. You didn't take your keys with you, so I—"

Tom touched his shoulder. "It's okay. I understand why you opened the door, and it's my fault for not working out some kind of code. Like three knocks and then two."

"Or how about just yelling through the door?" Benny said.

His brother grinned. "Right. Sorry. This has me a little rattled. But go back to the doorknob. You said someone turned it?"

"A couple of times."

They looked down at the corpse. "I suppose Rob could have done it."

"With broken fingers?"

"Zoms don't feel pain, remember?"

"But . . . turning a doorknob? Zoms can't—"

"It's rare, but it's been known to happen. Usually you get that sort of thing in the first couple of minutes after reanimation, because the longer someone is a zom, the less coordinated they are. The brain continues to die."

"Has Mr. Sacchetto been dead that long?"

Tom knelt and put his fingertips against the artist's skin. "Mmm, hard to say. Hot day, cold rain. But I doubt he's been dead more than an hour or two. So, we're in a gray area."

"What's the alternative?"

"Well, if Rob didn't turn that doorknob, then someone else did. That same person, or *persons*, brought Rob over here. I'll maybe buy Rob having enough brain power left to jiggle a doorknob, but no way I'll buy that he turned zom and then walked all the way across town specifically to target us. Aside from the fact that zoms don't *do* that, there are hundreds of people living between us and the reservoir. No. This was as deliberate as if someone pointed a gun at us and pulled the trigger."

"But . . . *why*?"

Tom's lip curled into an almost feral grimace of anger. "'Why,' in this case, is the same as 'who.'"

"What do you mean?"

"I would have thought it was obvious, kiddo. Whoever did this doesn't want us to find the Lost Girl."

That was all Benny needed. The pieces fell into place.

"Charlie?" he asked incredulously.

"Charlie. And Marion Hammer."

"They weren't out at Mr. Sacchetto's house by accident,

were they? They must have found out that the new set of Zombie Cards came out. Zak Matthias bought a dozen packs. He must have gotten one of the Lost Girl cards, too, and showed it to his uncle."

"I'd bet on it."

"Zak was at the store when I found my card. Maybe he went home and told his uncle. But even so, why would Charlie care about Lilah? He doesn't even know her." He paused and stared at Tom. "Does he?"

"Yes, he does," said Tom. "And considering how tight Charlie is with Big Zak and your friend Zak Junior, Charlie probably has them primed to report back to him with *any* mention of the Lost Girl. Even something as apparently innocent as her picture on a Zombie Card. I can imagine it gave Charlie quite a start to learn that my little brother found a picture of Lilah in his Zombie Cards." He glanced down at the body, then cocked his head to listen. "The rain's almost stopped. Listen, Benny. I want to leave at first light, and I want you to go with me."

"Leave? For where?"

"For the Rot and Ruin, kiddo."

"But . . . why?"

"Because we have to save the Lost Girl from Charlie Pinkeye and the Motor City Hammer," said Tom. "And just pray that we're not already too late."

28

But the night was not done with the Imura brothers.

First they had to remove the artist's body from the house and turn it over to the town watch. Two men came with a horse-drawn cart to remove the body, accompanied by Captain Strunk, who looked haggard and worn from the night's activities. Once upon a time Strunk had been an acting teacher and director, but during the madness of First Night, he'd stepped up and organized the defense of a school that was attacked by zombies during a late rehearsal of a new play. The students held out for three weeks against the dead, always hoping that help would arrive. It never did, but eventually the zoms outside were drawn off by other distractions—people fleeing, animals trying to escape the small town in which the school was set. When there were fewer than a dozen of the dead in the schoolyard, Strunk dressed his kids in heavy coats and choir gowns; armed them with golf clubs, hockey sticks, and baseball bats from the gym; and led his makeshift army out of the danger zone. Of the thirty-seven kids and four other adults who left the building with him, twenty-eight kids and two adults were still alive and uninfected by the time they discovered another group of refugees who were bound for a fenced-in settlement in central California. Strunk helped organize the town's defenses and served as its first mayor, and now he commanded the fence patrols and the town watch. And although he and Tom agreed on many things, Strunk had no inclination to expand the town or reclaim the world. He was haunted by those kids he had not been able to save.

Strunk watched as the artist's body was loaded onto the cart by a cluster of deputies, and he listened to Tom's account of what happened. Mayor Kirsch came out of his house next door and joined them.

"And you think this was Charlie and the Hammer?" Strunk asked, running his fingers though his thick, curly gray hair.

"Yeah, Keith, I do."

Mayor Kirsch sighed. "I don't know, Tom. You've got nothing but circumstantial evidence, and pretty thin evidence at that. Guesswork isn't the same as proof."

"I know," said Tom. "But the pieces fit as far as I'm concerned."

"What do you expect me to do?" asked Strunk.

"How about arresting them?" said Benny.

"And charge them with what?"

"Murder. Torture. How much do they have to do before you'll do something?"

"Hush, Ben," cautioned Tom. To the others he said, "I know you can't do much based on my say-so, but I have to do something."

"Whoa now, Tom, let's not get ahead of ourselves," the mayor said quickly.

"Don't worry, Randy, I'm not going to do anything in town. Not without proof."

"We have to do something!" Benny said, and then realized he was yelling. He dropped his voice to an urgent whisper. "Tom, we *have* to do something. You said—"

"I know what I said, kiddo. Go inside and get washed up. Try to get some sleep."

"Sleep? *Sleep?* What are the chances that I'm ever going to be able to sleep again?"

"Try," said Tom.

"And what are you going to be doing?"

"Your brother asks a fair question, Tom," said Strunk. He had his thumbs hooked into a Western-style gun belt, and it made him look like a gunslinger that Benny had seen in a book about the old West. Benny realized that Strunk was willing to use force, or at least imply that he would, to keep Tom from taking the law into his own hands. Benny wanted to knock Strunk's teeth out. How could the man want to give Tom a hard time when Charlie Matthias was walking around free? When he opened his mouth to say something, he caught Tom's eye, and his brother gave him a small shake of the head.

Reluctantly Benny lapsed into silence.

To Strunk, Tom said, "I'm going to go over and take a look at Rob's place. I can do that alone or you can come with me. Rob was tortured, and I'm betting it was done there. Who knows what we'll find?"

"And then what?"

"Then tomorrow morning, at first light, Benny and I are going out into the Ruin to try and find that girl."

Mayor Kirsch snorted. "Every bounty hunter and way-station monk for five hundred miles has looked for the Lost Girl, and nobody's found her yet."

"I found her," said Tom. "Twice. And I can find her again."

The other men gaped at him. From their expressions it was clear they didn't want to believe him, but Benny knew that Tom never bragged. He had his faults, but lying wasn't one of them.

"Why would anybody care?" asked one of the deputies.

"Gameland," said Tom.

"That burned down."

Strunk sighed. "Tom thinks they rebuilt it and that they're dragging kids off to play in some kind of zombie games. He thinks the Lost Girl knows where it is."

The men looked at one another and shifted uncomfortably. Benny noticed that not one of them asked Tom to verify this, and no one asked where Gameland might be. They said nothing. Tom made a disgusted noise.

Strunk nodded. "Okay, Tom. Let's do it your way. Let's go over to poor Rob's house and see what we can see."

"I want to go too," said Benny.

"You need to sleep."

"We already covered that. Maybe—*maybe*—I'll sleep when I'm forty, but I just killed a zombie who used to be someone I know. If I close my eyes, he's going to be right there. I'd rather stay awake."

It wasn't said as a joke, and no one took it that way. All three men nodded their understanding.

"Okay, Ben," Tom said.

Before they left, Tom went inside, dressed in cowboy boots and jeans, strapped on a pistol belt, clipped his double-edged commando dagger inside his right boot, and slung his *katana* across his back.

"What the hell, Tom? The fight's over," said Mayor Kirsch.

Tom didn't dignify that with an answer.

They walked down the middle of the street—Tom on one side, Strunk on the other, with Benny in the middle. Tom had given him back the wooden sword.

"How about a real one?"

"How about no? You'd cut my head off, or your own. And besides, you already know you can do enough damage with this."

"How about a gun?" Benny asked hopefully.

"How about you stay home?"

"Okay, okay. Geez."

They walked on through the shadows. Now that the storm was over, the lamplighters had come out to relight the torches that served as streetlights. Captain Strunk took one of the torches to light their way through town. Mountainside was laid out on a broad, flat piece of ground. The mountains rose up impossibly sheer behind them, and the great fence line stretched in a rough three-sided box from cliff wall to cliff wall. Most of the oldest homes in town were little more than shotgun shacks that were a dozen feet wide and built like long, narrow rectangles with doors at both ends. There were several hundred motor homes, most of which had been dragged into town by teams of horses. Some, of course, had arrived before the EMP blew out the ignitions and electronics on the vehicles. Roughneck traders occasionally brought wagon trains of building supplies to town—along with clothing, books, tools, and other precious items recovered from abandoned farms and towns throughout that part of the

Ruin—and those materials had gone into the construction of some of the two-story houses. The Imura house was a tiny two-story that Tom had built himself.

The artist's house, one of the very first that had been built, was narrow. It would have been ugly except for the rainforest murals Sacchetto had painted on the exterior walls. As they stopped outside, Benny studied the art and felt a deep sadness spear through him. He'd only met the man twice, but he had liked him.

Tom must have sensed his feelings, because he put a brotherly hand on Benny's shoulder.

"Gate's open," Strunk said. "Rob *could* have walked out after he turned."

"And bright blue pigs might fly out of my ass," muttered Benny. Strunk shot him a stern look, and Tom turned aside to hide a grin.

"My point is that we shouldn't make assumptions," Strunk snapped.

Benny felt another joke coming on, but he restrained himself as Tom drew his gun—a Beretta nine millimeter—racked the slide, and stepped carefully through the open gate. Strunk drew his gun and followed, holding the torch high. Benny, feeling enormously underdressed for this party, took a firmer grip on his wooden sword and crept after them.

Tom walked beside the path rather than on it, and bent low to examine the mud, but he shook his head. "There are plenty of footprints here, but there was too much rain."

They moved to the top step, but the story was the same. Just meaningless smudges. Tom placed a finger on the front door and pushed lightly. It swung open, and as Strunk moved beside him, they could see that the lock was splintered.

"No zom did that," said Benny.

Even Strunk didn't argue.

Tom pushed the door all the way open, and Captain Strunk angled the torch to spill maximum firelight inside.

The house was a ruin. Even from outside they could see that the whole place had been trashed. They went in, careful not to step on anything that looked like a footprint. It was a mess. Every canvas had been slashed, all of the sketches had been torn from the walls and ripped to confetti, the pots of paint had been thrown against the walls or poured onto the floor.

"You still think this was zombies, Keith?" Tom asked quietly.

Strunk cursed continuously for more than a minute without repeating himself once. Benny was impressed, and he agreed with the captain's sentiments. Killing the artist had not been enough. The murderers had destroyed every last bit of the man's work. There was not one single piece of undamaged art in the whole place. And the carnage went beyond that. Every plate was broken, every bottle smashed, every piece of furniture kicked apart and broken into kindling.

"This is rage," Strunk said.

"Yes, it is," said Tom. "And it makes me wonder if maybe Rob didn't give them what they wanted."

"What is it they wanted, Tom?" Strunk asked.

Tom eased the hammer down and slid his gun into its holster. In the torch's yellow glow his face looked older, harsher.

"I told only a couple of people where I last saw the Lost Girl. Rob was one, and today Charlie saw Rob talking to Benny about the Lost Girl. I think they tried to torture the information out of him."

Benny stiffened and grabbed his brother's arm. "Wait! You said that there were only a *couple* of people you told about the Lost Girl. Who *else* did you tell?"

Tom's face went white, and his eyes snapped wide. "I'm a bloody fool!"

"What is it?" Strunk demanded.

"God, I hope I haven't gotten them killed!"

Tom shoved past Strunk and bolted from the house. Benny and the captain ran after him, but by the time they were on the top step, Tom was a block away and running full tilt for the poor side of town.

"Where's he going?" Strunk asked, grabbing Benny's shoulder.

Benny shook off the grab and ran after his brother without answering. He already knew where Tom was going. There was only one other person Tom trusted that much.

Jessie Riley.

As he ran, Benny repeated a single word over and over:

"Nix."

BENNY RAN AS FAST HE COULD, AND EVEN THOUGH TOM WAS FAR AHEAD, by the time they passed the stables, Benny had caught up. Captain Strunk was blocks behind. As they passed the long, flat Ration Office, they ran abreast, and it was side-by-side that they jumped the hedges on the left side of the Riley property. They skidded to a halt in the wet grass.

A boy sat on the top step of the tiny house. He was neatly dressed, and he held a small bunch of daffodils in one hand, the flowers lying in twisted tangles across his thighs.

Benny said, with total surprise, "Morgie?"

The boy did not move. His head was bowed forward, as if he dozed there on the porch step. Moonlight was breaking through the cloud cover, and in its wan glow, Morgie's face looked unnaturally pale.

"Careful, Benny," Tom warned. He drew his sword and looked up and down the street, but except for the flicker of torchlight, nothing moved. The only sound was the nervous nickering and blowing of horses in the stables.

Benny took a step forward. Morgie sat still, his arms crossed over his stomach, his knees pressed together. He looked like he was huddled there against the cold rain and had fallen asleep. Except that his clothes were dry.

"Morgie? Are you okay, man?"

Morgie did not raise his head or move in any way.

"C'mon . . . don't do this to me, Morg," urged Benny as he moved closer. He brought the *bokken* in front of him, taking it with both hands. "Give me something here, man."

Slowly, awkwardly, Morgie Mitchell raised his head, and what Benny saw tore a gasp from him. Morgie's face was as icy pale as the moon. His eyes were dark and uncomprehending, sunk into shadowy pits, his lips slack.

There was fresh blood on his lips. It glistened like oil in the moonlight.

"No . . ." Benny's breaths burned in his lungs, and he shook his head, denying the possibility of this.

Tom raised his sword over his shoulder, the steel glittering in the cold moonlight.

"Say something," Tom ordered, his voice hard.

Morgie's mouth worked, but no words came out. Tom's fingers tightened on the handle of his sword.

"Tom . . . don't," begged Benny.

"I'll do what I have to, Ben," said Tom between clenched teeth.

Benny took another step forward. Almost in reach. Morgie's dark eyes caught his movement, and turned to him.

"Morgie, you fat jerk, you freaking well *say* something!" Benny yelled. Behind him he heard Captain Strunk come huffing up.

"God!" he said, "Is that the Mitchell boy?"

"His name's Morgan," snapped Benny. "Morgie."

"Is . . . is he *turned*?" Strunk glanced at Tom, who gave a tight shake of his head. Not an answer to the question, but rather a command to be quiet.

Benny took one more step closer. Definitely in reach now. Tom hissed, but didn't move. His blade was poised to cut, and Benny knew how fast his brother was. If Morgie grabbed him, though, would it be fast enough?

"Morgie . . . you're freaking me out here. If this is one of your jokes, it's not funny."

Morgie's mouthed worked and worked.

"Morgie . . . *please*."

Morgie whispered, *"Nix!"*

Then he bent forward and toppled off the step. Strunk cried out in alarm, clawing at his pistol. Tom almost took the boy's head off, but checked his swing as Benny darted forward and caught his friend. Morgie was heavy, and he clamped cold fingers around Benny's arms and pulled himself closer until his mouth was right next to Benny's throat. Benny could feel the labored breathing on his neck.

"Benny get out of there!" Tom yelled. He grabbed Morgie's shoulder with one hand, keeping the sword raised with the other, ready for the killing blow. "Benny!"

"Kill it!" bellowed Strunk.

Benny wheeled on them with a snarl. "Shut up!" Then he turned back to Morgie and leaned close.

"Benny . . ." Morgie gasped weakly. "They took Nix."

"What? What happened?"

"Mrs. Riley . . . They wanted her to tell them . . . something . . .

but she wouldn't. They . . . beat her up. They made me stand and watch. Gun to my head. Nix tried to . . . stop them. Couldn't. She was hurt. Mrs. Riley . . ."

And then his eyes rolled up in his head, and he collapsed against Benny, his limbs going slack, his head lolling.

"Tom!" Benny said, trying to catch his friend, to keep him from tumbling to the ground. Tom and Strunk caught Morgie under the armpits and pulled him back. The handful of crushed flowers tumbled slowly to the ground, scattering petals. They laid him on the ground.

"Give me some light," Tom ordered, and Strunk brought the torch.

"Is he bitten?" Strunk asked. "Is he dead?"

Tom pressed two fingers into Morgie's throat. "No. He's alive, but he's hurt." He reached up to push the torchlight into place for a better view, and there it was. Although Morgie's clothing had not appeared to be wet from the rain, the back of his hair and shirt were soaked. Benny leaned over to take a look, and gagged. The back of Morgie's head was a tangle of matted, bloody hair, and the blood had run down his neck and soaked his back. Tom gently probed the wound, his expression lacking optimism.

"Is it bad?" Benny asked.

"It isn't good. I think he has a skull fracture, and he's going into shock. Keith, get me some help *now*."

Even though Strunk was the head of town security and was not used to taking orders from anyone except the mayor, he nodded and went off without an argument. He ran to the end of the block where there was an alarm bell, and began ringing it loudly, calling out for the town watch.

Tom waved Benny over and laid Morgie's head carefully onto his brother's lap. "Stay with him, Benny. I have to check inside."

They were both keenly aware there were lights on inside the Riley house, and no one had come out to investigate the voices and commotion on the lawn. Not even a bark from their dog, Pirate. Benny's heart was a cold stone that kept falling through the icy waters of a deep well.

"Tom, Morgie said . . ."

"I heard what he said." Tom sheathed his sword, drew his pistol, and thumbed back the hammer. As he turned toward the front door, Benny saw his brother's expression in the moonlight. It was equal parts rage and terror.

Benny sat on the muddy ground with Morgie's head in his lap. His friend's mouth moved once or twice, and even though Morgie made no sound, Benny knew what he was saying.

"Nix."

People were yelling now, boiling out of their houses with guns and axes and sharpened pitchforks. Some had oil lanterns, a few paused to light torches from the streetlight. Guards from the town watch came flying toward them on galloping horses that were covered in heavy carpet from flanks to withers.

"Where's Tom?" demanded Strunk as he raced back, his gun in his hand.

"He went inside," said Benny. There had been only silence from the house. No screams, no gunfire.

The silence was dreadful.

Two medics from the town watch took charge of Morgie,

gently pushing Benny away. Benny rose, and he realized that for the second time that day he was covered in the blood of someone he knew. He bent and snatched his *bokken* and headed up the stairs.

Captain Strunk got in his way. "What the hell do you think you're doing?

"Get out of my way." Benny wanted to hit him with the wooden sword. "I'm going in."

Strunk looked into Benny's eyes, and he must have seen something that changed his view of Benny Imura. Maybe he saw the shadow of Tom in Benny's eyes. Or maybe he saw a new version of Benny. But he nodded and said, "Okay . . . but with me. And stand out of the line of fire."

The other armed guards came up onto the porch, rifles and shotguns ready.

The front door was open. Candles were lit in the living room. The party moved inside, gun barrels seeking out each flickering shadow. The living room was a wreck. It was not as comprehensively destroyed as Sacchetto's had been, but most of the furniture was overturned, vases smashed, a guitar stomped to splinters, art torn from the walls. The floor was crisscrossed with muddy footprints. The Riley's dog, Pirate, a tiny mixed breed, was crouched under the overturned break-front, its eyes glazed with pain. There was a clear imprint of a muddy boot toe on its heaving side. The dog whimpered quietly, but did not move or bark. When Benny reached out to it, the dog gave his fingers a few frantic licks. Benny saw splashes of blood on the floor and a single bloody handprint on the wall outside of Nix's bedroom.

He cut straight across the debris-filled floor to her room.

It was empty, however. The mattress had been overturned; her collection of old dolls in pieces, their heads torn off. All of her clothing had been pulled out of the closet and slashed with knives. Even her sparse collection of Zombie Cards had been torn in half.

Nix was not there.

Deputy Gorman came up behind him and surveyed the room. "Looks like your friend Nix put up quite a fight," he said.

Benny swallowed and nodded. "She would."

"She a tough girl?"

"You have no idea."

"She'll need it," Gorman said as he turned away. "It looks like they took her."

Although he already guessed it, the words were like bullets striking his heart. As he turned to leave, he spotted the corner of a familiar book sticking out from the debris of her writing desk. Benny bent and picked it up. It was her diary. He pressed it to his chest.

"Nix," he whispered.

"In here," someone called, and Benny rushed out of Nix's room to see the guards clustered around the entrance to Jessie Riley's room. Benny pushed his way through the throng, but Strunk grabbed his shoulder.

"You don't want to go in there, kid."

"Let me go. Tom!" With a wrench he tore free of Strunk's grip and charged into the room. And stopped.

It was a small room. When he and Nix had been little, they'd played hide-and-seek in this house, and Nix's mom's room had always been too neat, too sparse to offer any good hiding places. Now it was a ruin. The cheap dresser had been kicked to pieces, and all of Mrs. Riley's clothes—pants and blouses, stockings and underwear—lay scattered on the floor, trampled by heavy feet and stained with blood.

Tom sat on one corner of the collapsed bed. His pistol lay on the floor next to him. Jessie Riley lay curled against him. Benny could see that her face—always a kind and pretty face—was an unrecognizable mass of bruises and torn flesh. One eye was puffed closed, the other with bright and glassy with shock. She clung to Tom, holding his chest and sleeve, as if they were all that tethered her to this world. Her knuckles were red and torn. Like Nix, she had fought back, and fought hard.

"Mrs. Riley," Benny said, but the woman showed no sign of having heard.

"Not now, Benny," Tom murmured. "She needs to sleep."

"Tom," said Benny, "will she be okay?"

Tom slowly raised his head, and from the lost and broken look in his eyes, Benny knew that nothing was ever going to be okay. That time had passed when men with brutal fists and empty hearts had invaded this home.

"We have medics, Tom," said the captain.

Tom shook his head. "Give me a sliver."

A sliver. A simple word, and yet to Benny, it was so ugly that it made him want to scream. The thing Tom wanted was a six-inch length of polished metal, flat on one end for pushing, sharp and narrow on the other for piercing. Everyone on the town watch had a holster full of them. Tom never carried one. He used the black-bladed dagger he kept in his boot. Benny had seen him do it, but Tom did not want to use that knife now. Not for this.

"Oh, no . . . ," Benny protested as Captain Strunk slid one out of a pack strapped to his gun belt and offered it to Tom.

Tom nodded, and then glanced at the door and back up at Strunk. Immediately the captain turned and ushered everyone outside, although they lingered in the hall. Benny stayed right where he was.

He said to Tom, "Maybe she'll get better, Tom. Maybe you're wrong."

"No," said Tom in a ragged voice. "She's already gone."

And Benny saw it then. The hands that clutched Tom were held in place only by the fingers caught in the folds of his shirt, but the knuckles were slack and the elbows sagged under their own empty weight. Tom hugged her closer to him, and as he did so, her dead hands fell away, opening like dying flowers on the edge of the bed. Tom held her with one hand and reached around behind her to place the tip of the sliver against the base of her skull.

Everyone who died came back as a zombie. No matter how, no matter who. Everyone.

"Go outside, Benny."

"I . . . can't."

"Benny . . . *please*!"

Benny backed away only as far as the doorway, but he could not make himself leave.

Tom closed his eyes, first lightly, as if asleep. And then he squeezed them shut with all of his might, as if lost in a terrible nightmare in which he was unable to scream. His lips curled back from his teeth, and his chest heaved—once, twice—and then there was a flash of silver.

Jessie Riley never returned from death. She had suffered enough and would be spared that last indignity.

Benny stood in the doorway for several minutes as Tom sat on the edge of the bed and rocked her back and forth in his arms. Tom did not weep, did not cry out. Instead he ate his pain, biting down on it hard enough to drive all of the poison deep into his soul. Benny understood that. Maybe there would be some other time when that rage could be allowed out. But not now, and not here.

Not with Nix out there somewhere.

After a long time, Tom lay Jessie down and tugged the sheets around her, so that she was completely covered. He got shakily to his feet and stood over her, head bowed, and Benny saw his brother's lips moving. Was it a prayer or a promise?

Benny said nothing. He knew that he was an outsider to this, an intruder into Tom's privacy . . . but he could not leave. He could not abandon his brother any more than Tom could abandon Nix's mother.

When Tom turned to him, his face was calm. Or at least it appeared to be calm. Benny wasn't sure if his brother's air of unshakeable poise was genuine or a mask he wore when he needed to fend off the rest of the world. Before now, that calm demeanor had annoyed Benny; now it unnerved him. It seemed so alien, so unnatural.

Tom passed Benny and went out into the living room, where the town watch was making a thorough examination of the crime scene. One of them, the short Navajo named Gorman, snapped his fingers. "Got something!"

Tom and Strunk hurried over, and Benny had to crane his neck to see past them. Gorman pushed aside some broken crockery, and there on the floor was an old battered coin. On one side was an exotic flower, on the other were the words: "*Chúc may mắn.*"

He handed it to Strunk, but Tom took it from him.

"It means 'good luck,'" said Tom.

"What language is that?" asked Gorman. "The Rileys are Irish. Is that Gaelic?"

"No," said Tom, "it's Vietnamese."

Strunk frowned. "Then . . . this *wasn't* Charlie and the Hammer?"

"It was the Mekong brothers," said Gorman.

Tom turned the coin over and over between his fingers. He didn't nod, didn't even grunt to show that he agreed with this assessment.

"Benny . . . let's go home and pack."

"Pack for where?" Strunk demanded. "I'll bring the bloody Mekong brothers in."

"Go right ahead," said Tom, "but in the meantime my brother and I are going to go after the people who actually *did* this."

"What are you talking about? We have proof right here."

Tom didn't bother to answer. He dropped the coin on the floor and walked toward the door.

Outside, they had to push through a crowd that was ten deep. Everyone had questions, but Tom's face was a stone. Benny shoved and pushed to stay at his brother's back. The medics had taken Morgie to the hospital.

When they were through they walked down the street. The sky above them had cleared, and there was a surprisingly cold wind. Benny waited until they were out of earshot.

"Tom . . . I'm sorry about Mrs. Riley."

If Tom heard him, he didn't reply.

"Are we going to find Nix?"

"We're going to try."

"They killed Mr. Sacchetto and Mrs. Riley to get information on the Lost Girl. Why hurt Morgie?"

"You saw him. He was dressed nice, carrying flowers. He was calling on Nix, and he showed up at the wrong time, poor kid."

"So why take Nix?"

Tom's bleak expression was answer enough. Nix would either be killed . . . or taken to Gameland.

One of the town watch guards caught up to them and reined his horse to a stop. "Tom," he said, "the gate guards said that Charlie and the Hammer left almost three hours ago."

"What about Nix?"

The guard answered, "It was just after all the excitement, you know? The Hammer had that big equipment bag of his—you know the long canvas one? It was slung over his back and looked heavy, but the guard didn't even think to ask what was in it. He assumed it was filled with guns and stuff. Bounty hunter's stuff. He figured Charlie and the Hammer had gotten a job because of what happened."

"Yeah," Tom said tightly. "What about the Mekong brothers?"

"They left a few minutes later. They both had their kit bags strapped over the saddle of that ugly donkey they have. The one they call Uncle Sam."

Tom had never thought much of the Mekong brothers' sense of humor.

"Thanks, Billy," Tom said.

"Are . . . you going out after them?"

"Yes. Benny and me."

Billy leaned out of the saddle. "Listen, it's not my place to tell you how to do your job, Tom, but if they are the ones who did this, they'll be expecting someone to follow. You follow too soon, and they'll kill you in the dark. You'll never see it coming. And torches at night out there in the mountains . . . Hell, they'll attract every zom for a hundred miles."

"Then we'll leave at first light."

"Wait," Benny interjected, "what about Nix?"

"Billy's right. We can't find her if we're dead."

They walked the rest of the way in silence. They did not sleep at all that night. They got cleaned up, ate a large high-protein meal of meat and eggs, and dressed for hiking. They packed only those supplies they needed to take, including several bottles of cadaverine and two tough but lightweight carpet coats. They took plenty of weapons—after all, this was no longer just a hunting trip. It was a rescue mission. And it was even more than that. The Imura brothers were going to war.

When they stepped out onto the porch an hour before first light, Benny turned and looked back at their house. A shiver ran up his spine and raised bumps on his arms, and he had a dark feeling that he would never see the house again, maybe never see the town of Mountainside again. The feeling lingered for a long moment and then passed, leaving him as abruptly as it had come. What remained in its place was a coldness of spirit that he had never felt before, and it had nothing to do with his house or this town. His world had changed again, and he knew it. This time it had not been the removal of veils from naive eyes. Benny knew that much for sure. No, this time he felt as if a piece of him had been carved out, forcibly taken, thrown away. Although he had not been tortured as Mr. Sacchetto had or beaten as Mrs. Riley and Morgie had, he had been hurt just as surely. He could feel it. It was a dead place on his soul, as insensate as scar tissue and as violently earned.

He turned away from the house and stood on the top step of the porch with Tom. Without speaking they adjusted the straps of their packs, patted their pockets for the necessary things they would need out in the Ruin, and made sure of their weapons. Benny had his wooden sword, and he had a sturdy hunting knife that Tom had told him to hang from his belt.

The last thing he'd packed was Nix's small leather notebook. He hadn't opened it yet. Nothing in there would be a clue to finding her, but having it felt like a talisman. He slipped it into his back pocket.

"Tom?" he asked.

"Yes?"

"Are you sure it's them? Charlie and the Hammer?"

"Yes."

"Not the Mekong brothers?"

"If they're involved at all, it's because Charlie's paying them. Or maybe Charlie planted that coin there to frame them. Maybe he thinks he can come back to Mountainside after he—"

"After he kills the Lost Girl?"

"Yes."

"He'd know that he couldn't come back as long as you're here," Benny said. "And me, I guess. We know about the Lost Girl, and we know about what he's done. Even if we can't prove anything to Captain Strunk and the others, we'd be able to cast suspicion on them, right?"

"Right."

"So . . . even if we didn't go out there, we'd always be in danger."

The moon was down, and Tom's face was almost invisible in the darkness. The street lamp torches were too far away for Benny to read his expression, but he could feel Tom searching his face, trying to read him.

"That's right, Benny."

"Then no matter what else happens, we have to face them."

"Yes."

"Can we . . . I mean, can *you* take them?"

"We'll see." Tom paused. "You don't think too much of me, do you?" Before Benny could answer, Tom pressed on. "Little brother, you may never have said it in so many words, but I know that you think I'm a coward. You think I ran away and left Mom to die back on First Night."

Benny didn't dare say a word.

"I did run, Benny. I ran like hell. I left Mom and I took you and I ran. Is that what you want me to say? Does it help that I said it?"

"I—"

"The world is bigger and harder to understand than you think, Benny. It was before First Night and it still is now. You have to keep your mind as wide-open as your eyes, because almost nothing is what it seems."

"What does that mean?"

Tom sighed. "It would take too long to explain it now, and we don't have the time. It'll be light in forty minutes, and I want to be outside the fence the moment it's bright enough to see. Are you ready?" Tom asked.

"Yes."

"Are you sure? I'll give you one chance, Ben. You can stay here, with the Kirsches or Chong's family . . . . Or you can go with me into the Ruin."

"I *have* to go."

Tom nodded. "I hope that means the same thing for you as it does for me. I'm not going to baby you. We're going to have to move light and fast, and we're not going out there for fun. This is going to be ugly work. Can you deal with that?"

"I was at the Rileys' too," said Benny, and that was enough answer for both of them.

"Okay."

"There are two of them now."

"Two?"

"Lost girls. Nix and Lilah. We have to save them both."

Tom put his hand on Benny's shoulder and gave it a single, solid squeeze. "Then let's go."

They started out walking toward the fence, but after a block they were running.

PART THREE

Lost Girls

"Man can live about forty days without food,
about three days without water,
about eight minutes without air,
but only for one second without hope."

—Author unknown

30

A TALL, SLIM FIGURE STOOD IN THEIR PATH, AND AS THE BROTHERS JOGGED past, he turned and fell into step between them. They ran down the length of Main Street and then cut over toward the Red Zone, the wide, flat area that lay between the town proper and the fence line.

"I heard," said Chong as he ran, and the shared awareness of what those two words meant carried them for a dozen yards. "I just came from the hospital. Morgie's in bad shape, but Doc Gurijala says he'll make it."

"Thank God," said Benny as he exhaled a knot of hot tension that had hung burning in his chest. "When you see him again, tell him we're going to get Nix back."

"I will. He's going to need to know that."

Despite the early hour—or perhaps because of everything that had happened—the streets were filled with people. The closer the brothers got to the Red Zone, the thicker the crowds. Eventually they had to slow to a walk. A lot of people stepped forward to offer condolences to Tom, and some school friends of Benny's asked about Morgie. Tom said very little and kept moving, his face set and grim. Those people with common sense stepped back and gave him room when they saw the look in his eyes.

The crowd thinned abruptly once they crossed over into the Red Zone, and for the first time in his life, Benny realized this: On some level he'd always known that people avoided the Red Zone, but he'd always assumed that it was because they were afraid of zoms. Now he realized that they stayed on the far side of the line because in town, and away from the fence, it was easier to pretend that there was no wasteland of zombies outside. This realization made him feel both sad and disgusted.

When they were out of earshot of the other townsfolk, Chong said, "Tom, my dad was talking to Captain Strunk and Deputy Gorman. I heard them arguing about the coin they found at Nix's house. The one Vin is always tossing and catching."

Vin Trang was one of the two men known as the Mekong brothers. The other man, who was not even related to Vin, was Joey Duk. Despite their clear Vietnamese heritage, both of them had grown up in Los Angeles. The closest they'd ever been to Vietnam was selling *phở* and *bánh cuốn* out of their food cart on the campus of UCLA before First Night.

"The captain said that Vin and Joey are the ones who attacked Nix and her mom. And probably that artist guy." Chong looked at Benny. "Did Morgie say anything?"

"No," Benny said. "All he said was that they took Nix. He didn't give any names."

Chong looked back at Tom. "Did . . . did Mrs. Riley say anything?"

Tom kept his eyes fixed on the fence as they walked through the Red Zone. "She only had the breath to say one thing." He paused for so long, the boys thought he wasn't going to finish, but then he said, "'Save my little girl. Save Nix.'"

"I can't believe this is happening." Chong wiped tears from his eyes. "My dad said that the Mekong brothers sometimes work with Charlie Matthias."

"I know," said Tom.

"Dad told Captain Strunk to have Leroy Williams look at the footprints you found. I think he was going to."

Tom nodded.

"What can he do?" Benny asked. He knew Williams as a farmer who had lost an arm in a car wreck while driving an SUV filled with refugees through the Ruin.

"Before First Night," Tom said, "Leroy was a robbery detective in San Diego. He'd have been captain of the guard here if it hadn't been for the arm."

They reached the blockhouse that was used as a guard station. A pair of horses were tied up outside, and Leroy Williams and Captain Strunk stood near them. A knot of fence guards and deputies from the town watch were clustered behind them.

Leroy, dressed in denim coveralls and a white cotton T-shirt, came to meet them. He offered Tom his left hand, and they shook.

"Sorry about Jessie, Tom," said Williams. He was a black man in his late sixties or early seventies. His dark skin was crisscrossed with terrible scars, but he had kind eyes. "This is a bad, bad business. Whole world gets wiped out, and people are still preying on one another. People just don't learn."

"No, they don't," agreed Tom bitterly.

Leroy glanced at Benny, sizing him up. "Maybe some of you kids will have better sense."

"We will," Benny said, although he wasn't as sure as he sounded.

"Leroy," Tom said, "Lou Chong here told me that you're going to look at the crime scene at Jessie's place."

"We just got back," said Strunk as he joined them.

"And . . . ?"

"Well," said Leroy, "the town watch pretty much walked over most of the footprints you found." He shot a disapproving look at Strunk, who stared at the dirt between his booted toes. "But I found some useful footprints in Nix's room . . . and Jessie's. I took five or six sets of boot prints and took them with me over to that piece of crap shack where Joey Duk lives. I found shoe prints in his laundry room that matched. He was there, Tom. Vin Tran too. No doubt about it."

"Don't try to sell me on that bull, Leroy," snapped Tom, but the big farmer held up a hand.

"Hush, son." Leroy stepped closer, dropping his voice, so that Benny and Chong had to bend forward to hear him. Strunk did, too. "The Mekong brothers weren't home, so I went over to the Matthias place. I asked Big Zak if I could look in Charlie's room, but Zak told me to . . . Well, I won't say what he suggested I do with myself. He said that Charlie was innocent of anything connected with what went on tonight, but I wasn't buying that because Big Zak don't open his mouth unless he wants to lie. He was also sweating and looking shifty. He tried to throw me off his porch. Me, an old cripple-man."

"What happened?" Benny asked.

"What you think happened, young 'un? I put my foot up his fool ass and threw him off his damn porch, then I went through the house and kicked Charlie's door off its hinges. Thought I was going to have some trouble with Big Zak's boy, but once he saw his dad lying in the rose bushes, Young Zak decided that he liked hiding in his closet better than messing in matters beyond his years."

"You find anything?" Tom asked. "Did you match the prints to Charlie's shoes?"

"No. Charlie's probably wearing those shoes right now, wherever he is. But that big ol' white boy wears size fourteen triple-Es. How many people in Mountainside got kickers that big?"

"It's circumstantial evidence," muttered Strunk, but Benny could tell that there was no emphasis left in the captain's voice. Benny realized that Strunk's resistance had nothing to do with his personal beliefs, and certainly not his intelligence. Strunk was a smart, caring man, but the truth was that it was easier to accept that the Mekong brothers had done the killings, because they only rented a room in Mountainside. They lived in a smaller and rougher town a hundred miles south. Charlie, on the other hand, lived *here*. If he was guilty, then Strunk would have to gather a posse and track him out into the Ruin. It was fear that was going to let Charlie Pink-eye and the Motor City Hammer get away with it.

Tom put his hand on the farmer's good shoulder. "Thanks, Leroy."

Pain and sadness showed on the big man's face. "I wish like hell I could go with you boys."

"I know, Leroy. But do me a favor."

"Call it."

"You can still shoot, can't you?"

"Only with a pistol, but, sure, I generally hit what I'm aiming at."

"Then if Charlie comes back here and we *don't* . . ." He let it hang.

"Oh, hell, son, you don't even have to ask. That pink-eyed gangster sets foot in this town again, he's dead."

"Wait a minute," interrupted Strunk. "Hold on . . ."

Leroy wheeled on him. Strunk's eyes came up to the middle of Leroy William's broad chest. "You have something to say, *Captain*?" He loaded that last word with enough acid to eat through sun-baked concrete.

"Yes, I do," Strunk said, not visibly deterred by the wall of pectoral muscles that seemed to stretch from horizon to horizon. "If Charlie Pink-eye or the Hammer comes back to Mountainside, then me and my men will arrest them. They'll be properly arraigned on suspicion of murder, kidnapping, and a few hundred other charges I'll figure out later, and they'll stand a proper and legal trial." Before anyone could reply, Strunk added, "Thing is, it'll probably be hard as hell to find a jury of twelve totally *impartial* townsfolk. Jessie Riley had a lot more friends in town than Charlie ever did. Besides . . . there are only two crimes that carry a death sentence anymore. Murder and kidnapping."

The meaning implied in his words hung burning like embers in the air. Tom and Leroy studied Strunk; Benny and Chong exchanged meaningful glances, eyebrows raised. Chong covertly drew a finger across his throat.

“No more talk,” said Tom. “We have a lot of miles to go, and they have a long lead.”

“So . . . let’s even things up,” said Strunk. He raised his hands and snapped his fingers, and immediately Deputy Gorman came toward them, leading the two horses by their reins. Benny could now see that both horses—an Appaloosa and a buckskin—were draped in coats made from tough, lightweight outdoor carpet. Strunk took the reins and handed one set to Tom and the other to Benny. Riding chaps made from durable carpet were hooked onto each saddle horn.

“The Appaloosa’s name is Chief; the buckskin is Apache. They’re fresh, fed, and fast,” he said. “Bring that girl home.”

Tom studied Strunk’s face for a long three-count, then nodded.

Dawn was a faint promise in the east. Two dozen guards with shotguns and torches met the brothers at the gate.

“My boys will go out as far as we can, Tom,” said Strunk. “We can help you get away, keep the zoms busy.”

“Thanks, Keith.” Then to Benny, Tom said, “You ready?”

“Yeah, but I feel like time’s flying.”

Tom gave him the first slice of smile he’d been able to dredge up all night. “They’re on foot.” He swung into the Appaloosa’s saddle. “Now we have a real chance.”

Benny scrambled up onto the buckskin’s saddle with less grace than his brother, with Chong pushing on his butt. He’d ridden before, but only ponies; this was a full-sized horse.

Strunk signaled to the gatekeepers to open up, and instantly all the guards ran out into the flat, open plain that stretched from the fence line to the foothills of the mountains.

There were at least fifty zoms in the fields, some standing still, others wandering endlessly back and forth. The guards broke left, and when they were a hundred yards from the gate, they began shooting into the air and waving torches. As if cued by some shared inner compulsion, the dead turned toward the noise and motion, their mouths dropping open. Even through the noise of the shotguns, Benny could hear the low, plaintive moans of endless hunger as the zoms began shuffling through the grass toward the guards.

"It's clear!" Leroy said in a fierce whisper. "Go! *Go!*"

Tom and Benny kicked their horses into canters, and once they were outside the gate, they turned to the south and kicked harder. The horses were young and strong, and they galloped away, bearing the brothers toward the narrow pass in the mountains that led to the great Rot and Ruin. Benny was a poor horseman, and pain lanced through his hips, stomach, and legs with each running step the horse took. But that pain was necessary, because they had to move fast. And really, he thought as he set his teeth against the discomfort and set his mind on the distant mountains, what did *his* pain matter? The pain Nix must be feeling had to be a million times worse. With that thought burning in his mind, he ignored his pain and kicked his horse into a faster gallop.

Chong climbed to the top of the tower and watched as Benny's horse dwindled to a small black dot against the bloodred dawn, then vanished altogether.

31

THEY RODE HARD ALL MORNING, PUSHING THE HORSES TO THE EDGE OF endurance. Several times the thunder of their hooves attracted zoms, but all horses shied away from zoms and were trained to alert their riders. Besides, the shuffling zoms could not catch up to the fast mounts, and even if they did, the carpet coats each horse wore kept the animals safe while Tom and Benny used their swords to chop the monsters down.

It was all terrifying to Benny, but the dread of what could be happening to Nix was far worse, and he ground his teeth together and kept pace with Tom.

At first, in the coolness of dawn, the horses could manage the grueling pace, but as the sun rose, the temperature soared, and the horses began blowing and wheezing. Foam flecked their mouths, and under the lightweight carpet coats, their flanks were streaked with sweat. Finally Tom slowed their pace to a walk and then dismounted. Chief, the big Appaloosa, almost visibly sighed in relief.

"What are you doing?" demanded Benny. "We have to keep going."

"If we keep this pace, we'll kill these animals and then

where will we be? We have to give them some water and then walk them for a while. Then they'll be ready for another run."

It was maddening to Benny, but he knew Tom was right. He slid from Apache's saddle, secretly grateful, because his legs felt like they were stretched out of shape. With every step it felt like there was sandpaper on the inside of his pants. Riding ponies around town was no kind of preparation for riding a big horse. His hips felt like his thighs had been forcibly unscrewed, and after all the awkward bouncing in the saddle, he was pretty sure there was no chance he'd ever father children. He tried not to squeak when he spoke.

They took a bowl from Tom's pack, filled it from one of the canteens, and let the horses drink. Then they walked on, the horses following along as the sun became an inferno overhead.

On foot it was easier to follow the trail, too. At first the footprints were easy to spot, since they ran in a line from the gate into the foothills, but the higher they climbed, the more obscure the prints became. At one point Tom dropped prostrate on the hard ground, and peered sideways at some marks that didn't look like they were anything at all—at least not to Benny. Tom kept frowning and squinting and grunting.

Benny stared at him, annoyed. He was exhausted from total lack of sleep, and flies were threatening to pick him up and carry him off. And every time the wind blew through the trees, he swore he could hear Nix calling out to him.

"Are you actually doing anything down there?" Benny asked.

"No," Tom muttered. "I'm just screwing around to piss you off."

Benny gave that a minute, then said, "Sorry."

Tom said, "I'm looking at the footprints to see if there's a clear direction."

Footprints? Benny thought. All he could see was dried mud and bare patches of rock. He looked from the ground, off into the direction they had been following; a twisted course through empty foothills that wandered south by southeast. The heavy rains of the previous night had soaked all of the ground, and Tom had been able to follow the foot trails leading from Mountainside. But as the morning wore on, Tom became less certain.

Tom got to his feet and slapped dust from his clothes. Even after the rains, the top dirt had dried to powder in a matter of hours.

"What's wrong?" Benny asked.

"Here's the problem," Tom said. "The rain last night was really heavy, and it came down too fast for the soil to absorb it all, which means that there was runoff. This pass was probably like a small river for a while, with all the water coming down these slopes. Whoever passed this way came through just after the storm, but while there was still some runoff, and that runoff smeared the boot prints pretty thoroughly."

"What's that mean for us?"

Tom took a hefty swig of his canteen. "This isn't just an accident, either. Charlie's one slick, sneaky son of a gun. So far he's doubled back on his trail three times, used brush to try and wipe out his tracks, crossed water, and now has deliberately gone out of his way to cross hardpan, because this kind of terrain doesn't hold a print very long or very well."

"So are we catching up or chasing our butts out here?"

"Little of both." Tom was smiling when he said it.

"So you didn't lose the trail?"

"Sure, I lost it. Several times . . . but every time he shakes us off his trail, it's just where you think it'll be again. Charlie has no respect for anyone's intelligence other than his own. He must think Captain Strunk is after him."

"Isn't the captain smart?"

"Huh? Oh, sure. . . . But Strunk's not a tracker. Charlie's confusing the trail for someone who doesn't know the same tricks. Maybe he'd play it differently if he knew another bounty hunter was tracking him."

"Are you sure he doesn't?" Benny said, and for a moment Tom's smile flickered.

Tom looked at his brother for a second, pursed his lips, and then turned in a slow circle, re-examining the trails. "We have three possible routes through these hills that are safe. And by that I mean that the zoms have been pretty well cleared out. This pass has become a kind of trade route, and the armed guards the traders use usually go through here and chop down any of the dead they find. They're quiet about it, too, so as not to draw more zoms into the area. Follow me?"

Benny nodded.

"So the footprints we're seeing here are almost certainly human. Question is whether these are older prints that were mostly, but not entirely, erased by runoff, or prints left by men moving fast but not carrying heavy loads. The last of the runoff blurred the edges and in this area here, the topsoil is thinner, because we're coming to some rocky areas."

"Okay, but if people came through here recently, then it *has* to be Charlie and the Hammer, right?"

Tom didn't answer right away. "What bothers me most about it is that I'm not seeing small footprints."

"Nix's?"

He nodded. "We saw her prints earlier, but I haven't seen one in the last hour. Not one."

"What if one of them's carrying her?"

Tom considered. "If the ground was softer, we could make that call, because one of the male footprints would be deeper. You might be right, but I'm not sure, because the footprints I'm seeing here look like they're from several different pairs of shoes."

"More than Charlie and the Hammer?"

"Yes."

"The Mekong brothers?"

"Could be them, which means we're hunting four men rather than two." Tom started to say something else, but stopped himself. Benny caught it, though.

"What?"

"There are a couple of other options, Benny, and we have to be ready for them."

"What are they?"

"The option I like is that Nix somehow escaped. If that's the case, her trail could have split off at any time. If she's free, let's hope she continues to head for high ground instead of trying to go back to town."

"Because there aren't as many zoms high up, right?"

"That, and higher up, there's always the chance of finding food and shelter. There are some monks out here. If she runs into one of them, she'll be fine. They'll take care of her and get word to me."

"What's the other option? The one you *don't* like."

Tom met his eyes. "There are a lot of places out here to hide a body, Benny."

There was nothing Benny wanted to say to that. On some superstitious level, he felt that to respond to it would be to increase the chances that it might be possible, and he could not allow that thought to take hold in either his heart or head. Nix's notebook was still in his back pocket, and he touched it like it was a talisman, to ward off any evil possibility.

His throat was so dry that his voice was a dusty croak. "So what do we do now? What *can* we do?"

"If I was Charlie and I wanted to lay low . . . I'd either head for the trader's compound on the eastern slopes, or . . ." He frowned.

"Or what?"

"Gameland."

"Do you have any idea where the new location is?"

"No. But there's an old fire access road that we can use to cut across country to a spot where they'd have to pass no matter where they're going. It's a pass through to areas that have more or less been cleared of zoms, and it's the route all travelers take."

As they walked, Tom said, "I never finished my story about how I found the Lost Girl. We'll talk about it more at length later, but just in case we have to try and find Gameland, there are some things you should know. After finding the human that Lilah had killed, I was able to pick up her trail. It took about four days, but I finally tracked her to one of the mountains not too far from here. There was a ranger station up on stilts, built high on the mountain, and I climbed that and used my binoculars to scan the whole area. I guess I was up there for two or three hours when I saw her. She walked out from under some trees and stood in a clearing for a couple of minutes, eating an ear of raw corn. She was dressed like she was on the Zombie Card. Not the one you have, but the earlier one."

"Earlier one? What do you mean? I have nearly the whole set. . . ."

Tom shook his head. "You don't understand, Benny, but the Zombie Cards weren't intended for kids to collect. That came later, when the printers wanted to make some extra ration bucks. No, the original purpose of them was so that bounty hunters could carry pictures of the dead that had been reliably sighted, so that people could reach out to arrange for closure." Still holding Chief's reins, Tom reached into his pack, pulled out a soft leather pouch, and handed it to Benny.

Benny opened the pouch and removed a thick stack of the cards. He began riffling through them. "I never saw most of these. And . . . they're different." The cards didn't have the Zombie Cards logo or the sensationalist writing on the back. The images were more like the standard erosion portraits that people put up on the walls near the Red Zone. On the backs were names, probable locations, and some brief biographical information. In the lower left corner was a price—the amount of ration dollars to be paid for a confirmed closure; and in the lower right corner on some of them was a date starting with either an *S*, *L*, *SU*, or Q.

"*S* for 'spotted,' *L* is for 'living,' but most people use it to designate 'loners.' Q for 'quieted,'" Tom said. "*SU* means 'status unknown.' Lilah's card is in there."

Benny shuffled through until he found the card marked

with both *L* and *SU*. The picture was that of an eleven-year-old girl with wild snow-white hair, wearing ratty jeans and a bulky UCLA men's sweatshirt. She carried the same long spear she'd held in the more recent card. The Lost Girl. Benny turned the card over and silently read the back.

> **This apparently uninfected girl was spotted in the mountains by Tom Imura. If found, please contact Tom in Mountainside, or pass word to "George Goldman" via the way-station networks. She may answer to the name Lilah or Annie. Approach with caution, she is considered dangerous and may suffer from post traumatic stress disorder.**

"Who's George?"

"Remember the story Sacchetto told you?"

"Right! George was the guy who stayed behind with the girls. . . . But I assumed he'd died."

"After I spotted the girl, I climbed down from the guard station as fast as I could, but she was gone by the time I reached the clearing. I looked for a few more days, but found nothing. I don't know whether she somehow spotted me and cleared out or just moved on. Next time I went out, I ran into George Goldman at the way station where we met Brother David. He was a nice guy, but he was just about used up and maybe more than a little crazy."

"Didn't he stay with the girls? Lilah and the baby?"

"Yes," said Tom. "George was with them for years. They

stayed at the cottage, surrounded by zombies, for almost two years. At first they had plenty of food, and George made sure the girls ate most of it. When it was about to run out completely, George made a very tough decision and went out. He locked the children in the bathroom, made sure they had the last of the food and some water. Then he imitated what Rob had done: He wrapped himself in torn strips of carpet, took the heaviest golf club he could find, and snuck out of the house. He was nearly killed a dozen times that night *and* the following day, but he managed to get to another farmhouse.

"The people who lived there were dead, and he had to fight his way through a few of them, but once he did, George was able to gather up a lot of food. He packed as much as he could into two big suitcases on wheels and pulled them down the road, back to the cottage. Getting through the zoms around the cottage was very hard, and it took him nearly a full day of trying one trick and then another, of running and hiding and sneaking around, before he was able to manage it. That became the pattern of their lives. About twice a month, George would go out, foraging for food, raiding all the places where people once lived, hoping to find help, hoping to find someone else alive. He didn't see another living soul for years. Imagine that." Tom shook his head. "Eventually George cleared out most of the zoms in the immediate area, and that allowed him a little more freedom. He would go foraging and bring back a wheelbarrow filled with books, clothes, toys—anything he could find to make the lives of the girls easier. He taught them how to read, schooled them the best he could. He wasn't a teacher, wasn't a scholar. He was a simple, middle-aged guy; an average and ordinary man."

"He doesn't sound ordinary," Benny said. "He sounds like a hero."

Tom smiled. "Yes, he does. I've heard a lot of survival stories about First Night and the times that followed, and even though a lot of people died, a lot of heroes were born. Often it was the most unlikely of people who found within themselves a spark of something greater. It was probably always there, but most people are never tested, and they go through their whole lives without ever knowing that when things are at their worst, they are at their best. George Goldman was one of those, and I doubt he would ever accept that anyone would think that he was a hero."

"What happened to him?"

"As Lilah got older, he taught her how to take down zoms. She's small and fast, so George taught her to come up behind them and cut their leg tendons to drop them, then spike them when they're down. George worked it out for her, teaching her and practicing with her until she was faster than he was. He said that she had a natural talent for it."

"That's half cool and half sad," Benny said. "Maybe more than half sad."

"Yes, but it meant that she survived."

"What about the baby?"

Tom's face tightened. "This is where we get into the darkest part of the story. George had named the baby Annie, after his own sister who had been living in Philadelphia when the dead rose. He taught Annie the same way he taught Lilah, and the little girl grew up to be a lot like her sister. Strong, smart, and vicious when she had to be."

They stopped for a few minutes to let the horses drink

from a stream. Normally Tom would have steered well clear of the running water, but now they were forced to follow the trail. Even though the forest was quiet, Tom's eyes never stopped roving over the terrain as they continued their hunt. The horses' ears constantly shifted around, and both of them pranced nervously. Chief, though bigger, was more skittish, and he kept jerking his head up to look off into the woods, although each time the movement he tracked was a rabbit or a bird. Apache looked around slowly, but his whole body rippled with tension.

"Let's keep moving," he said. "Another ten minutes, and we'll be able to ride again."

Benny nodded, although again he touched Nix's book in his pocket to ward off bad luck.

Tom picked up the thread of his story. "It was about eight years after First Night when George first found a living person. It was a man walking through the woods near where we are now. The man was dressed like a hunter and smelled like a corpse, and George nearly attacked him, thinking he was a zom."

"The guy was wearing cadaverine?"

Tom nodded. "George followed him and watched him make a kill with a pistol, and then he knew the man was alive. For George it was like getting hit by a thunderbolt. He started yelling and ran down the hill toward the man, crying and babbling because he thought that the presence of this man meant that the long nightmare was over. The man spun and fired a shot at George, almost hitting him, but George hid behind a tree and yelled, telling him that he wasn't a ghoul."

Benny grunted at the word "ghoul." It was what some of the older people called the zoms.

"The hunter, realizing that George wasn't one of the dead, told him it was safe to come out. George ran to him and hugged him and shook his hand and—as he put it to me—'acted like a total damn fool.' The hunter was pleasant and kind. He gave George some food and told him that there was a whole town full of people not too far away, who were alive and thriving, and there were other towns all up and down this part of California. He offered to take him back to his own camp, saying he was part of a group of a dozen men who were clearing the zoms out of this region in order to allow people to reclaim it and rebuild."

"But I thought—?"

"Wait, hear the rest of it. George told them about the two little girls, and the hunter got excited, saying that it was God's own miracle that two children had survived for so long. He encouraged George to take him to where the girls were, so they could all go to the camp where it was completely safe. George agreed, of course. After all, this was the answer to years and years of prayers. They hurried through the woods to a farmhouse where George had been living with the girls for the last year. At first, the girls were terrified of the man. Lilah hadn't seen another living adult since she was two, and Annie had never seen one. Lilah almost attacked the man, but George restrained her and took her weapons away. It took a long time to cajole and convince the girls that it was safe, and all the time the hunter sat on the floor and smiled and waited patiently, making sure to do nothing threatening."

"He sounds like a good guy," said Benny.

"Does he? Yes . . . I suppose that from this part of the story he does. Anyway, the hunter told George to gather up anything valuable and go with him to his camp. George brought the wheelbarrow filled with food, books, and other things that were useful or precious to them. It took four hours to follow the winding country roads to the camp, which had been set up in a big cornfield. The men in the camp all looked very hard, and everyone had weapons—and that much was okay, because of the nature of the world and what they were doing—but he didn't like the way they smiled at him and his wheelbarrow or the way they looked at the girls. Even though he was delighted to see so many people, George began to get suspicious."

"Wait. Were these guys bounty hunters?"

"Yes."

"What happened?" Benny asked with a sinking feeling.

"Things went wrong pretty much right away. The hunter made some remark about the girls looking tough, and when George explained they had both hunted and killed zoms, the hunter really perked up. He said that the girls were worth their weight in gold for 'the games,' and when George turned to him to ask what that remark meant, someone hit him from behind. George woke up hours later, but the cornfield was empty and everyone was gone. He had no weapons or food and no idea what had happened to the girls. He searched every inch of that field and the woods beyond, but the girls were gone.

"He found horse tracks and footprints, but the best he could determine was that when the camp broke up, the men went in different directions. He said he went a little insane, and I can't blame him. His whole life had been built around protecting those girls, and at the moment when he thought that they were really and truly saved from the monsters, it was *people* who took them away. It turned his whole world inside out. George staggered away and finally found a deserted house where he found some old cans of food. At first light he started searching for the girls. It became his obsession, and it consumed every waking second of every day."

"What happened to the girls?"

"George looked everywhere, and along the way he met more and more people. He met the way-station monks and told them what had happened, and they started spreading the word. He started to hear rumors. One set of rumors talked about a place called Gameland that a bunch of bounty hunters and travelers had built in the mountains. The things people said about that place really tore George apart. When he described the girls and the men who had taken them, a lot of people suddenly stopped talking to him. Their fear of the men who ran Gameland was greater even than their compassion for a couple of lost children. Soon people were actively shunning George. Only the monks tried to help him, and some of those who went out to try to find the girls went missing."

"And you don't think it was zoms who got them?"

"Do you?"

Benny shook his head.

"By the time I ran into George, he was worn out. I told him that I'd spotted one girl, and when I described her, he said that it was Lilah. He begged me to say that I'd also seen Annie, but I didn't. . . . And when I found the spot where I'd seen the girl standing, there was only one set of prints."

"What happened to Annie?"

"I don't know for sure. Some of the travelers I met were more willing to talk to me than they were to George. A few of them told me that there was an old rumor about a couple of girls who had been taken to Gameland and that something bad had happened and only one little girl escaped."

"No . . . ," Benny said softly. "Were Charlie and the Hammer involved?"

"George gave me pretty good descriptions of several of the men in the camp. He wasn't clear about which one hit him or who actually took the girls, but Charlie and the Hammer were definitely there."

Benny nodded. The respect he once had for Charlie had transformed into a murderous hatred.

"What happened to George?"

"I don't know. Brother David said there was a rumor that George had hanged himself, but I don't believe that. George might be dead, and he might have hanged, but I don't believe for a minute that he would have killed himself. Not as long as Lilah was still out there."

"Somebody killed him?"

"Murder is easy out here."

They walked on. The horses were looking better, less haggard, and Benny hoped that they'd be able to ride them again and make up the distance he felt they were losing with every minute they stayed on foot. "If we find Lilah . . . what do we do?"

"Try to get her to come to Mountainside with us. The kid needs a life, needs people."

Benny took the card out of his pocket and stared at it, trying to imagine that wild creature going to school, being *normal.* His mind wouldn't fit around the concept.

"Come on," Tom said tersely. "The horses are rested enough. Let's ride. . . . Let's see if we can catch those animals."

Both horses were spitting foam again by the time they reached the top of the mountain; then the ground leveled out, and they found the fire access road. Like all roads in the Ruin, it was badly overgrown, but Benny could see footprints, wheel ruts, and dried horse dung that looked recent.

"Is this the route the traders take?"

"Yes. This is the same area where I first saw the Lost Girl," Tom said. "This is where I found the first couple of zoms that Lilah killed. I told you they were all similar in size and look."

"Yeah," Benny said. "Like she was hunting one person over and over again. Hard to believe that a little girl could do that."

"What, kill a full-grown man? All it takes is stealth and the right weapons."

"No," said Benny. "It's hard to believe that a little girl could kill *anyone*. I mean, sure, zoms . . . but how does a kid get to the point where they want to take a life?"

"Fair question, Ben, but let me ask you one in turn. If Charlie Pink-eye was in front of you, right now this minute, would you want to kill him?"

Benny nodded. "In a heartbeat."

"You're sure?"

"After what he did?"

"Even if we get Nix back unharmed?"

"No question about it, Tom."

Tom studied him for a while before he said, "Couple things about that. I hear you when you say you'd kill Charlie, and for the most part I believe you, but there's a little hesitation in your voice. If I'd have asked the same question last night, you'd have said yes without the slightest hesitation, because the hurt was immediate. It was right there in your face. But this is hours later. The blood cools, and the more distance you put between the heat of passion and any act of commission makes something like killing much harder to do. When people talk about killing in cold blood, they're referring to something someone does even after they've calmed down and had time to think. If it takes us a month to find Charlie, you might not want him dead at all. You might want to see him put on trial, you might want to see the system work instead of getting blood on your own hands."

"Okay, okay, I get the idea. You said there was a couple of things. What's the other?"

"Why do *you* want Charlie dead?"

"Is that a real question?"

"Sure. I mean, he didn't physically hurt you. He didn't kill anyone in your family. He didn't kill Nix, at least as far as we know. . . . And I don't think he has, even now."

"He . . . ," Benny began, but faltered. "Because of Mr. Sacchetto and Nix's mom. Because of what he might be doing to Nix. What kind of question is that?"

"So, you want to kill him for revenge?"

Benny didn't answer. Apache blew loudly, scaring some robins from the grass.

"Will that bring Rob Sacchetto or Jessie Riley back from the dead? Will it fix Morgie's head or guarantee that we'll find Nix safe and unharmed?"

"No, but—"

"So, why do you want Charlie dead? What good will it do?"

"Why do *you* want him dead?" Benny snapped, frustrated by Tom's questions.

"We're not discussing me," said Tom. "We can, but we're not right now."

Benny said, "Charlie's hurting people that I care about, and last night we agreed that Charlie's going to come after us. To shut us up or whatever. He knows that we know, and he knows that we're not going to let it go, even if the court clears him."

"Right," said Tom. "Charlie's smart enough to have figured that out. So . . . you want to kill him to prevent him from killing you?"

"Us, not just me. But, yeah. That makes sense, man. Doesn't it?"

"Sadly, yes, it does."

"Why sadly?"

"Because it's the way things still seem to be among us humans. Like Leroy Williams said, we never seem to learn."

"What's the alternative? Do nothing and let Charlie kill us?"

"No. I'm a pacifist by inclination, but I have my limits. And on top of that I'm not a martyr."

"So, you intend to kill Charlie?"

Tom's eyes were black ice. "Yes."

"So why are you grilling me on this stuff, Tom?"

"Because the things that happened yesterday just kicked you into the same world as the Lost Girl. There's some logic to it, even some justice in it, but the more you walk in that world, the more damage it's going to do. And I don't think there's a way for us to turn back. Not anymore."

"What do you mean?"

"The bodies that I found. The girl wasn't just trying to kill a certain person or a certain type of person. She was trying to punish the image of that person that existed in her mind. Something had been done to her that was so bad, so tragic, that it changed her—maybe forever. Revenge isn't really enough of a word to explain what she's feeling and why she's doing what she's doing. It's more like an infection of the spirit, and it distorts everything she sees and everything she does."

"So," Benny said, sorting through it, "she's trying to kill the *idea* of this guy? That she's trying to kill the infection by killing what caused it?"

Tom cut a sharp look at Benny.

"What?" asked Benny.

"That may have been the smartest thing you ever said, kiddo. It shows that you have insight. Yes, that's exactly what Lilah is doing."

"So . . . who's the guy she's trying to kill?"

"Maybe one of the bounty hunters killed Annie, or maybe she died in the Z-Games and Lilah's fixated on the image of the man who put her into one of the pits. Finding that out is one of the reasons I want to find her."

Benny digested this as they came out from under the shade of the trees into a gorgeous field in which wildflowers ran rampant and proclaimed their freedom in shouts of colors. The sky was a distant blue, and massive white clouds sailed across it. The image was so lovely that Benny's mind saw but discounted the abandoned cars that were covered with weeds and probably filled with old bones.

"It's hard to imagine that there is so much hurt and harm out here, isn't it?" said Tom softly.

All Benny could do was nod. He took the Lost Girl card out of his pocket and stared at it. Such a beautiful, proud, tragic face. "Lilah," he murmured, but the breeze through the tall grass answered him in Nix's voice.

They reached the creek and turned north; riding in silence for several miles till Tom swung out of the saddle and squatted down by a rusted metal footbridge. Benny watched his brother's face as he examined a series of overlapping footprints and turned his head to see which direction their prey went.

33

THEY CAME DOWN ANOTHER SLOPE AND THERE, NESTLED BETWEEN A LONG tumble of boulders left over from a glacier thousands of years ago, was a stream that glimmered like a blue ribbon through the forest. They dismounted and led the horses as they followed a crooked path that kept trees between them and whoever might be down there—bounty hunters or zoms. Chief clearly did not want to go that way and tugged on the reins; Apache looked equally nervous.

Tom picked up some loose bits of dirt and leaf debris and threw it into the air, watching where the wind took it. "Wind's blowing toward us. If we stay on this side of the creek, we should be okay. But we'll need to keep our voices low."

The path along the creek had once been a scenic country road, and it was wide enough for them to walk side-by-side, leading the horses.

"Tom?"

"Yeah."

"We're going to find her, aren't we?"

"Lilah? I—"

"No," Benny said, "Nix. We're going to find her, right?"

"We're going to try."

"That's not good enough, man. We've *got* to find her. She's lost everything. Everyone. We can't . . . abandon her."

"We won't."

"Swear it."

Tom looked at him.

"Swear that no matter what happens, we'll find her. That we'll never stop looking for her."

In another place, under other circumstances, what Tom did next might have seemed silly or corny, but out here in the Rot and Ruin it had a strange sense of grandeur, perhaps of nobility. Tom placed his hand over his heart.

"I swear to you, my brother, that we will find Nix Riley. I swear that we will never stop looking for her."

Benny nodded.

They walked on, entering the thickest part of the forest that ran alongside the creek. Under the roof of leaves the air was cooler, but it was as damp as a cave. There were so many songbirds singing in the branches that it was impossible to pick out a particular voice.

Half a mile in, Tom knelt and ran his fingers over the damp grass. "Got you, you bastard!"

"What is it?"

"Footprints. Big, have to be Charlie's. Grass hasn't even had time to unbend all the way."

"How long?"

"Half an hour. We're close now, kiddo. Time to move quick and quiet."

"The horses make a lot of noise."

"I know, but it's what we have, so we'll need to be twice as vigilant."

They remounted, and Tom led the way down the grassy lane. The soft green of the grass as it ran along the glistening blue water, and the constant birdsong all around them, gave the moment a fairy tale feeling that Benny found hard to shake. It was unreal, even surreal in its gentle, unhurried beauty. So at odds with everything that was real in their immediate world of hurt and harm and hurry.

"Tom? About Gameland. Do you know for sure that they rebuilt it?"

"Not firsthand, but from people whose word I believe. People who said that Lilah's been there. Even if we don't find it today, I'll keep looking for it."

"Why? No one in town even cares about it. They won't do anything about it."

"I know. But I care." Tom sighed. "We lost the world, Benny. That should have taught us something about the value of human life. Gameland shouldn't be allowed to exist. It needs to be taken down."

"They rebuilt it once, wouldn't they do it again?"

"Maybe. And if they did, then someone should always be ready to burn it down again."

"Who?" Benny asked. "You?"

Benny was suddenly aware that too much of his skepticism about his brother's abilities showed through in his tone. He immediately regretted his words. They were part of an old reflex, and he didn't actually hate Tom anymore. In fact, after everything that had happened last night, on top of what they had experienced together that first time in the Ruin, Benny was seeing Tom in a different light.

But the words were said, and Benny didn't know how to unsay them.

Tom squinted into the sun. Small muscles bunched and flexed at the corners of his jaws. "Some of the travelers and traders I've talked to say that certain bounty hunters that they declined to name have been gathering kids—girls and boys—to take to Gameland."

"Kids from where? I haven't heard about any kids from town going missing."

"There are other towns, Benny. And there are kids living with some of the way-station monks. Some of the loners have kids, too. None of these kids would be missed, not by the people in Mountainside. The bounty hunters prey on them because of that, and there's nobody out here to protect them. No one to stand up for them or speak for them. It's a bad, bad world out here."

"All of it?" Benny asked. "Is that all there is? Fear back in town and evil out here?"

"I hope not."

The path rounded a bend and then moved sharply away from the water and eventually left the shelter of the trees to run through a series of low, rocky hills. Without the canopy of cool leaves, the heat returned like a curse. Even through his shirt, Benny's shoulders and back felt charbroiled. His forearms glowed with sunburn, and sweat boiled from his pores and evaporated at once without any perceptible cooling of his skin.

Tom studied the landscape and slowed to a stop, looking concerned.

"What is it?"

"Something doesn't make sense," Tom whispered. He pointed to where their path curved around between two walls of rock. The red-rusted span of a train bridge arched over the path.

"There's a spot down there that everyone avoids. It's thick with zoms, one of the natural lowland points where the nomad zoms gather. Last time I came this way, there were a few hundred of them."

"*Hundred?*"

"Yep, some of them had probably been there since First Night. Others just kind of wandered in."

"Pulled by gravity, right? Following any downsloping path."

"Exactly. There's a crossroads down there. A highway intersects with two farm roads and this road we're on. Big intersection."

"So . . . why don't we just go around?"

"We can, but the trail we're following goes straight along this road." He pointed to visible footprints in the soft clay beside the road.

"That doesn't make sense. Why would Charlie go right into a nest of zoms? Isn't he supposed to know the Ruin as well as you?"

"He knows it better than me. He spends more time out here."

"Okay, look . . . I may only be your little brother, and I know I'm not a bounty hunter and all that, but doesn't this have 'trap' written all over it in bright red paint?"

Tom almost smiled. "You think?"

"So you *know* it's a trap?"

"Benny, this whole thing is a trap. Everything Charlie's done since he attacked Rob Sacchetto has been a trap."

Tom stopped and suddenly pointed to the trail of footprints that led off around the bend. The prints were mostly those of a man with big feet. Charlie. However, at one point, another set of prints suddenly appeared beside his. Small bare feet.

"Nix?" Benny asked.

Tom put a finger to his lips and whispered, "It looks like Charlie was carrying her and set her down here. See? Their prints go all the way around the bend. Right toward the crossroads."

"Maybe they don't know how close we are," Benny suggested. He looked for confirmation in Tom's face, but didn't see any. Benny started to draw his knife, but Tom shook his head.

"Wait until you need to," Tom cautioned. "Steel reflects sunlight, and that'll attract zoms as much as movement. Now, I need you to stay steady, kiddo. Once we round this bend, it's going to get weird. Maybe it's a trap, maybe not; but even if it isn't, this is one of the most dangerous spots out here. You'll see why."

"Great pep talk, coach."

Tom grinned.

Moving very slowly, careful not to make a sound, they rounded the bend in the road, hugging close to the wall and staying in the shade of the rocks. Apache and Chief were trained for this, and they moved only when and where they were steered.

Around the bend, the view opened up, and Benny saw the roads that wandered from all directions over hills down to the crossroads.

"God!" Benny gasped, but immediately clamped a hand over his mouth.

It was neither the beauty of the vista of endless mountains nor the tens of thousands of silent cars crowding the road that tore a gasp from him. The crossroads and the fields surrounding it were crowded with the living dead. There were at least a thousand of them. Benny stared, searching for movement, waiting for the sea of monsters to turn and begin shambling toward them. But they did not. The zombies just stood there in one crowded mass. Others, alone or in small groups, stood along the roads or in the fields. All still, all silent.

The horses now showed their training, and in the actual presence of the dead, they made no sound, but Apache's trembling terror vibrated through his entire body and up into Benny's.

Benny tried to understand what he was seeing. He didn't believe that all of them had just wandered here because the roads sloped down and they followed the unrelenting pull of gravity. There were too many for that. Maybe they chased some people down here and after the kills, they had nowhere to go and nothing to distract them. Some of the zoms were probably the people from the cars, who had been killed there and reanimated with no direction or purpose. The tough grass covered them to the waist, and some of them were completely wrapped in ivy and twists of wisteria and trumpet vines. There were soldiers, nurses, kids his own age, ordinary people, old people, many of them showing signs of the terrible bites that had killed them. Just standing there in the midday sunlight. It was such a strange sight—all these dead standing there like statues.

No . . . that wasn't it. They were like gravestones, using their own flesh to mark where they had died and where they would spend eternity. Not buried in a box but trapped in decaying tissue that could move, that *would* hunt and attack, but that, in the absence of something to attract it, would remain in place forever. The thought was as horrible as it was sad. Suddenly, Benny could feel something deep inside of him begin to undergo a process of change. His fear, which had been as big as the whole Rot and Ruin, seemed to shrink. Not completely, but enough so that he was consciously aware of it. He thought he understood why.

On their first trip into the Ruin, Tom had said that fear makes you smart, but Benny understood now that his brother had been talking about caution rather than fear. These zoms, every last one of them—even the smallest child—would kill him if they could, but not one of them *meant* him harm. Meaning, intention, *will* . . . None of that was part of their makeup. There was no more malice there than in a lightning strike or bacteria on a rusted nail, and as he sat there, he felt his terror of them give way to an awareness of them as something merely dangerous. The intense hatred of the dead he had once harbored was gone completely; burned out of him in Harold Simmons's house. Only the fear had remained, and now that, too, was wavering in its intensity.

Charlie, on the other hand, was something still to be feared. Charlie was far more dangerous than any single zombie on the planet because his malice *was* deliberate.

Understanding the difference between these two types of

dangers—unthinking and deliberate—felt like a huge revelation, and Benny wanted to tell Tom about this, but he said nothing. Now was definitely not the time.

Tom turned sharply in his saddle, staring behind them. Benny saw a few of the zoms catch the movement and raise their withered faces.

"What?"

"Something's burning," Tom said, and that fast, Benny caught it, too. A sulfur stink that he knew very well. He'd smelled it a hundred times at the pit on the days when they set off dynamite to drop a layer of shale and loose rock down on the ashes and partly burned bones.

"Fuse!" Benny shouted. Or . . . thought he did. Anything he might actually have said was erased by an immense blast that tore half a million pounds of sandstone from the cliff walls. Fiery clouds of jagged debris burst from both walls, exploding into the pass from ground level and above. Apache screamed and reared and then bolted away from the tons of rock that smashed down all around them.

Benny kept screaming as the horse galloped at full speed, away from the collapsing walls . . . right toward the sea of zombies. Every single one of them turned toward him, a thousand black mouths opened, two thousand wax white hands reached for him as he raced without control toward them.

34

THERE ARE MOMENTS THAT DEFINE A PERSON'S WHOLE LIFE. MOMENTS IN which everything they are and everything they may possibly become balance on a single decision. Life and death, hope and despair, victory and failure teeter precariously on the decision made at that moment. These are moments ungoverned by happenstance, untroubled by luck. These are the moments in which a person earns the right to live, or not.

Benny Imura's horse galloped toward death as certainly as if the path was marked with signs. If he did nothing, his crazed and panicked horse would crash into the sea of zombies, and Benny would die. If he tried to slow Apache down, the zoms would surround him and drag him out of the saddle. If he dismounted and ran, they would close around him and he would be lost. There was only one possible choice left, and it was as improbable as it was insane. The Benny Imura who had gone reluctantly out with his brother ten days ago could not have made that choice. The Benny Imura who had faced the reanimated corpse of the artist Sacchetto but had not yet faced the other horrors that last night had forced upon him would not have made that choice.

As Apache bore him toward the hungry mouths, Benny's lips spoke a single word. It was not a cry for help. It was not his brother's name. It was not a prayer. In his mind there was only one thing larger than his own death, only one thing more powerful than his fear of the living dead.

He screamed, "Nix!"

And he drew his wooden sword, kicked Apache's flanks as hard as he could, and charged into the monsters.

35

THE HORSE RESPONDED TO THE KICK AND TO THE CONTROL THAT POWERED that kick. Within three galloping steps his flight straightened from wobbling panic to determined attack. Benny screamed as Apache's broad chest slammed into the front rank of the zombies. Benny's right arm rose and fell, rose and fell, slamming the brutal edge of the hardwood sword down onto faces and hands and necks and shoulders. The dead reached for him, but he kicked with both feet, and struck and struck and struck. Apache, covered in his carpet coat, felt only the muffled pain of bites that could not tear through the carpet and did no harm. Instead it drove him into a towering fury. He reared up and lashed out with steel-shod hooves. Jaws shattered, skulls cracked, and then they were through the front rank and racing toward the line of stalled cars. The zoms turned and followed, and those in front of them shambled toward the horse.

Benny wheeled Apache around and tugged back on the reins to encourage him to rear up again and again. The hooves were backed with all the power and terror in the half-ton animal, and withered bodies crumpled before him. Benny's carpet chaps protected his legs, but he wasn't wearing his carpet coat. If he fell, or if the creatures grabbed a wrist, then only the last bits of the cadaverine would protect him. At the speed with which things were happening, they did not seem to have the time to react to the presence of the noxious chemical, and if any of them were repelled by it, Benny could not tell.

"Go! Go!" Benny yelled, and Apache surged forward toward another line of the dead. Beyond that was open ground. The sword rose and fell, and Benny felt the shock tremble up his arm, but he used the pain to fuel his rage. He drew his hunting knife with his left hand and used it to stab and slash as the hands tried to drag him down, screaming inarticulate bellows that filled the air. But the blade hit bone, and the impact wrenched it from his hand, and he lost the knife.

They slammed through the second line, and one hand snagged in his pants cuff and nearly tore him from the saddle. Benny slewed halfway around and slashed backward at the clutching hand, feeling the forearm bones break as he struck down.

Where the hell is Tom? When the walls had exploded, Benny had lost all sight of his brother, and he risked a single backward glance and saw nothing but brown smoke that obscured the entire cliff wall.

Panic flared for a moment in his chest, threatening to dampen the fires of his anger, but as the white hands reached for him again, his fury swelled, and he raised the sword and brought it down, again and again.

Something flashed blue and bright. The creek! It had wound around the far side of the cliffs and here it was, running within a hundred yards of the crowded road. Benny jerked the reins to one side and kicked again, and the horse cried out in an almost human voice. The muscles in its thick haunches bunched, and the animal leaped forward, smashing aside more of the dead. Benny flattened himself against Apache's neck, and together they raced across the field toward the water. There were dips and small valleys hidden by the tall grass, and Benny realized that it was a longer, harder run that he thought, and there were at least fifty zoms between him and the safety of the fast blue water.

He caught movement to one side and saw a man—a man, not a zombie—entering the treeline on the far side of the field.

The Motor City Hammer.

It had to be the Hammer who'd set off the dynamite. A second sooner, and the blast would have dropped half the mountain on Benny. And on Tom.

Tom.

Benny knew he was trapped on this side of the cliff wall. There was no way back, and he didn't dare race for the treeline. If the Hammer was there, then so was Charlie. Maybe the Mekong brothers, too, and they all had guns. Nix was there, too, but she might as well be on the far side of the moon for all that Benny could do about it right now. His—and *her*—only hope lay in his survival. And the only route to safety lay on the far side of Coldwater Creek. Zoms don't have the coordination to wade through fast water. That's what Tom had told him.

A zom lurched into his path, and Apache had no time to swerve, so he ran the creature down. Brittle bones made a sickening sound as the horse crushed them into the grass.

Two others, a fireman and a man wearing only boxer shorts, closed in on him, blocking their way. Benny steered with his knees, and the horse angled just slightly to the left as Benny slashed down to the right, hitting the fireman on the side of the head and knocking him into the other man. They fell in a tangle of pale limbs.

As they crested the last of a series of rolling hills, Benny felt his blood freeze. The valley beyond was shallow, no more than a dozen feet deep at the end of a long, gradual slope. The horse could easily make the run, but the valley was thick with the living dead. Zoms that Benny hadn't even seen. Maybe a hundred of them, and half of them were children.

Children.

The kids were dressed in school uniforms, and there was a male zom in the middle of them who still wore the rags of a school bus driver. He looked like a shepherd in the midst of a flock of grotesque sheep. Some of the children's faces were wrinkled and blackened. Had their school bus crashed and burned? Benny gagged at the thought, and again his resolve wavered. Sweat weakened his grip on the sword. He knew that these creatures were dead, that they were reanimated echoes who wore the disguise of the people they had once been, but Tom's words rang in his mind.

They used to be people.

How could he strike them? How could he *hurt* them?

Children, women, old people. Lost souls.

Apache pounded down the slope; the blue water beckoned.

Something burned through the air an inch from his nose, and for a moment he had the crazy notion that it was a bee or wasp. Then, almost like an afterthought, the crack of a gun-shot echoed across the plain.

And then he heard a girl scream.

"BENNY!"

Benny turned toward the sound and saw a tiny figure break from the trees and run out into the field. She was too far away to be sure, but Benny *was* sure.

"Nix!" he yelled.

Nix jumped over a fallen tree, stopped, snatched up a thick branch, and as one of the men leaped over the tree after her, she swung so hard that Benny could hear the *crack* all the way across the field. But then three more men ran after her, and she fled and then was out of sight behind a cluster of trees. A fifth man stepped to the top of a small ridge and aimed something at Benny that glinted with blue fire in the sunlight. Without realizing that he was going to do it, Benny ducked down, and he felt the bullet sear the air just above the back of his neck. The sharp bang of the shot chased the bullet through the empty air. There was another shot, and another. Something plucked at his pack, and he waited, listening inside his body for the pain, but there was nothing. Fifty feet away a zom spun and fell, a black hole punched through its stomach, but even as the horse raced past, the zombie was struggling back to its feet.

The water was there, the crowd of dead school children spread out before him.

Which would kill him, he wondered. The zombies or the bullets of the bounty hunters?

"BENNY!" Nix's voice carried as clear as a bell over the hills. He turned to see her running toward him with five men only yards behind her. "RUN!"

He was running. Thirty yards now. Twenty.

He heard Nix scream once more, and when he turned again, he saw that the largest of the men had grabbed her, snatching her up as if she were a toddler. The five men immediately turned and ran back toward the trees as a wave of zoms shambled after them.

"NO!" Benny yelled, reaching one hand impotently toward the retreating figures.

And then something flashed past him and slammed into the wall of zoms. Benny saw silver fire dancing in the sunlight, and the zoms fell away, coming apart in desiccated sections, arms and heads flying away from the screaming thing that plowed through them.

"Benny!" Tom bellowed. "Follow me!"

It was impossible, but there he was. Covered in blood and dust, his sword glittering like flowing mercury, Chief's eyes rolling with insane fear as Tom smashed aside the living dead and splashed into the blue water.

Benny's horse leaped over the last of the dead, his hooves caving in the head of the bus driver, and then they were in the water. The cold current struck them, and Apache neighed and blew, and Benny gasped as icy water bit his ribs and chest. Forty or more of the zoms followed them into the water, but the powerful current plucked them up and swept them away.

Benny turned and looked toward the treeline. There was no sign of Nix, but for a moment—perhaps it was his imagination or the shimmer of the heat or even a wandering zom—but Benny thought he saw another small figure moving across the field toward the treeline, heading in the same direction that the men had taken Nix. She ran fast, bent low, and she carried something in her hands that glinted like steel. Benny blinked sweat out of his eyes, and when he looked again, the small running figure was gone.

The treeline was an unbroken line of oaks and maples, with no sign of human life. The field was covered with the living dead—thousands upon thousands of them—and that way was as blocked and useless as the collapsed pass through the cliff. Their horses clambered up onto the far bank.

They were safe.

But Nix was gone.

And they could not follow.

36

BITTER, EXHAUSTED, AND ANGRY, THEY MOVED AWAY FROM THE CREEK as fast as their horses could go, heading into the hills, seeking the safety of the high ground. When they were safe in a thick copse of trees, and when Tom was convinced that there were no zoms nearby, they slid from the saddles and collapsed onto the thick grass. For several long minutes they lay there, unable to move, gasping like beached fish, running with sweat, barely able to think. Apache and Chief stood nearby, their legs trembling with tension and fear.

"Are you okay?" Tom asked when he had the breath.

"No." Benny groaned.

Tom turned his head so sharply that it looked like it was unscrewing from his shoulders. "Where are you hurt? Are you bit—?"

"No . . . it's not me. It's Nix!"

"At least we know she's alive, Benny. That's something. Hold on to that."

"They also know we're coming."

Tom managed to sit up. He was bleeding from a dozen small cuts, but he assured Benny they were from the sharp fragments of stone that pelted him when the cliffs blew. He crawled over and pulled the canteen from his saddle, drank deeply, and then handed it to Benny. "They knew long before now," he said. "You can't rig charges like that and bring down that much stone without taking time to set it up. No, kiddo. . . . They knew we were onto them, and they set a very smart trap."

The water opened up Benny's parched throat, but he coughed and gagged on it.

"You sure you're okay?" Tom asked, peering curiously at him, his eyes darting to Benny's arms and legs. "You're positive you didn't—"

"I'm not bit," snapped Benny. "I want to go find Nix."

"We will," Tom promised. "But the horses are a step away from dead. Unless you want to chase them on foot, we *have* to rest."

"How long?"

"At least an hour. Two would be better."

"Two hours!"

"Shhh . . . keep your voice down. Listen to me, Ben," Tom said, and his face was tight. "If we rest for two hours, we can catch up with them in maybe two more hours. If we don't rest, it'll take all day, if we catch up at all. This is a situation where slow is faster."

Benny glared at him, but then he growled and turned away. He knew that Tom was right, but every second they sat there felt like it was one less second for Nix. Seconds burned away into minutes, and it took centuries for enough minutes to gather into an hour, and then two. By the time Tom said that they were ready to go, Benny was a half tick away from screaming insanity.

"How come Charlie and the others didn't just hide behind rocks and shoot us?"

Tom busied himself by putting the carpet coats back onto the horses.

"Tom?"

"I guess they didn't like their chances in a shoot-out," Tom said.

"Are you kidding? Six or seven against one?"

All Tom gave as a reply was a shrug, and Benny stared at his brother. What the hell did that mean?

"Besides," Tom said as he tightened the last of the straps, "the dynamite was a big bang, big enough to draw most of the dead toward the pass, which meant that it drew them away from the forest. If we'd been killed, they would never have risked shooting at us. It was a stupid risk even if he'd hit us, because it drew some of the zoms toward them. I expect Charlie's going to be pretty upset with the shooter."

"It wasn't the Hammer?"

"No. Too skinny. Probably one of the Mekong brothers. Whoever it is, though, I want to have a chat with him."

"A 'chat'?" Benny said, grinning for the first time in hours.

"A meaningful chat," Tom agreed. "C'mon, mount up. We'll stay under the trees for a while. This side of the creek is all farms, so we can cut through and then cross the water a couple of miles upstream. If we're lucky, we'll hit the highway and cross that before they can reach it, and then we can see about laying our own trap. The highway's the tough part, and I want to have time to figure it out, so let's make tracks."

"Good," Benny said, reaching for the saddle horn and pulling himself up.

"This is probably the last leg of this chase, Ben," said Tom. "I know what we just went through was rough, but there's a big difference between fighting zoms and fighting people. When we find Nix, I'll try to draw Charlie and the others off, and I want you to grab Nix and make a run for it. Don't worry about where you go, I'll find you. If you can, get to the water and wade as far south as you can before you come out on the bank. Try to leave no trail."

"How will you find us then?"

"Don't worry, kiddo. I've got a whole lot of sneaky I haven't even used yet." He gave Benny a reassuring smile as he swung back into the saddle. "Let's go."

They headed northeast, following a series of farm roads that were almost completely reclaimed by the relentless forest. As they rode, Tom pulled a bottle of cadaverine from his pocket, dabbed some onto his clothes, and then handed the bottle to Benny. Apache nickered irritably from the stench. Benny considered the bottle for a moment.

"Tom . . . do you think this is why we got away?"

"It helped. It made the zoms hesitate. Remember, they won't bite something that already smells dead."

"I don't understand that," Benny said as he sprinkled some of the foul-smelling liquid onto his jeans.

"No one does. It's another of the mysteries associated with the living dead. Just be glad it works. Hey—not so much. Save some for later. We only have two bottles."

Benny put the cap back on and tossed the bottle to Tom, but the cap was still loose, and as Tom caught the bottle, the liquid splashed out and splattered his shirt.

"Oh, crap, man," Benny cried. "Sorry!"

Wincing at the odor rising from his clothes, Tom fitted the cap back on. "Well . . . that ought to about do it. I could probably square dance with a zom and not get bitten right now." He leaned over and handed the bottle back to Benny. "There's still half a bottle left. Keep it. I'll hold on to the other."

"What if we run out?"

"Let's hope we don't."

The last of the farm roads ended by a curve in the creek, and they splashed across, moving slow to keep the noise down, each of them scanning the terrain. Everything was still. They came up from the stream bed and found a highway that was entirely blocked by cars. Four lanes and both shoulders, stretching away around a bend in the road a mile to their right and off into the misty horizon to their left. An army helicopter that Tom identified as a UH-60 Black Hawk lay crashed in the meadow that ran along the road, the huge propeller blades broken and twisted and hung with creeper vines. Benny wondered how the chopper had come to crash. Had one of the crew been infected? Were they airlifting victims and took the wrong kind? Or had they run out of fuel and were too far from home? Maybe it had been caught by the EMP. There was no way to know, and no matter what had brought the powerful machine down, it stood as a monument to a war in which technology and sophistication had served no purpose, had ultimately accomplished nothing.

They rode their horses to the outside edge of the shoulder and stopped. The animals did not like the endless line of cars, although Benny didn't see any zoms hiding among the dead machines.

Bones, however . . . There were plenty of those. Skeletons—long since picked clean by zoms, scavengers, and the elements—were scattered everywhere. Thousands upon thousands of skulls and rib cages, leg and arm bones, bleached white by the merciless California sun. The cars themselves were slammed and smashed together. Some had burned, some were skewed sideways or overturned. A few had rolled off the highway and lay half hidden in the tall grass beside the road. Benny could see that the windows of all the cars were broken. Some had been smashed out by people escaping—or trying to—and some were smashed in by fresh zoms who still had enough of a functioning brain to pick up stones. There were plenty of stones. The roadbed was edged with countless white plum-sized rocks, placed for drainage, Benny knew, but used as weapons.

Benny nudged a cracked thigh bone with his toe. "Tom, how come there are so many bones? Didn't most people turn into zoms?"

"Most did, sure, but there were still hundreds of thousands, maybe millions who died fighting. Died in ways that kept them from rising. Broken necks, crushed skulls, bullets in the brain. Arms and legs torn off. It's not like back in town where we bury the dead. Here . . . Those that truly die just rot away until bones are all that's left."

Hundreds of the cars were pocked with bullet holes, and it was clear that at one point the helicopter had fired on the stalled vehicles. Tom saw where Benny was looking, and he pointed out a black shape rising from the side door of the crashed Black Hawk.

"They used their minigun. It's a 7.62 mm, multibarrel

machine gun that could fire three thousand rounds per minute."

"Wasn't enough," Benny said.

"No," Tom agreed.

On the far side of the line of vehicles was a vast meadow of tall grass and wild wheat that stretched into green and brown forever. Scattered here and there were hundreds of young trees—scrub pines, oaks, poplars, maples—rising above the sea of waving grass. The trees made it impossible to tell if the meadow was free of zoms, an assessment further spoiled by the constant breeze that made everything sway and shift.

A bird cawed, and Benny turned to see a threadbare crow perched on the broken vane of the downed helicopter.

"Which way do we go?"

"That's the problem," said Tom. "We need to cut across this road if we're going to catch them before they reach their camp. God knows how many of their cronies they have there. If we cut the road here and then cross that big meadow, we can get ahead of them. On horseback . . . Yeah, we can get ahead of them." He nodded toward the northeast corner of the big meadow where a mountain rose, green and gray. "Charlie's camp is on the other side of that mountain. There's half a dozen trails—man-made and game trails. I'm pretty sure I know which one they'd take. You know, the second time I saw Lilah was right over there. Halfway up the mountain. Rob Sacchetto and I were out here together. I wanted him to do sketches of some zoms I thought might be related to folks in town. We were up on the catwalk of that old ranger station, and I had a big high-powered telescope with me this time. I'd picked up Lilah's trail that morning, and I left him there and went through the woods. I found her, and it took me half the day to first convince her that I didn't want to hurt her and the rest of the afternoon convincing her that she didn't want to hurt me."

"You talked with her?"

"I talked. She didn't say much, and just when I thought that she was going to open up, something spooked her and she vanished. God only knows where she went, because I lost her trail."

"You found her twice around here," Benny said. "She must live near here."

"Maybe. She might have moved on since then. But let's deal with first things first. We have to get the horses across this road."

"But how?" Benny walked up and down the row of cars. There were some spots where he could squeeze through, and certainly he and Tom could climb over the vehicles . . . but he did not see one spot where a horse could pass. "Can we go around?"

"We'd lose half a day." There was an overturned panel truck jammed at a right-angle to a big car that was riddled with bullet holes. "Escalade" was written on the fender in tarnished silver letters.

In the cleft formed by the two vehicles, there was a shaded spot big enough for the Imura brothers and their horses. They dismounted, and Tom looped the reins around the rear axle of the truck. "Stay here. I'm going to find us a way through. Keep your eyes and ears open. Watch for zoms, but more importantly, watch for Charlie Pink-eye and his crew."

But Tom hadn't gone a dozen steps before he suddenly stopped and crouched.

"Benny!" he hissed, and Benny ran over to see what Tom had found. On the blacktop, drying in the hot sun, was a small puddle of water. It was no larger than a dinner plate, but it was clear from the faded edges that it had been bigger and was shrinking in the heat. Tom touched it, sniffed his fingers.

"It's not rainwater. Last night's rain had a bit of a saltwater smell. This doesn't smell at all. I think this is filtered drinking water."

Benny could see it now—someone stopping in the sweltering afternoon to gulp down some water, letting the cold liquid splash on his throat and chest and fall to the ground. Tom stood and held his own canteen out at about six feet, tilted it, and let a little fall. The splash pattern was just about the same, even to how far the rebounding drops fell from the main impact point.

"Tall man. Charlie or the Hammer," said Tom. "The Mekong brothers are both short."

Benny was impressed, and he looked around for other evidence and immediately saw something that snapped wide his eyes. "Tom!"

On the ground ten feet away, there was half of a wet footprint, drying quickly under the sun's glare. Not a man's foot. This print was made by a small, delicate foot that wore no shoe.

"Nix," Benny said.

"Has to be," Tom confirmed, but he looked uneasily from the print back to the puddle.

"What's wrong?"

"Distance is too far. If she stepped in the water, there should be a print closer to the puddle." He quickly paced it off, shortening his stride to approximate that of a girl who stood barely five-two. "This is wrong. Even if she stepped in the puddle with only one foot, the distance is too far. The wet print should be here." He tapped a spot on the blacktop with his toe.

"What's that mean?"

Tom suddenly grabbed him by the sleeve and pulled him back into the shadows of the overturned truck.

"No one else but Charlie and his crew comes out this way, so I think it means that they somehow managed to get ahead of us. Charlie knows these hills better than me. He must have a pass or route that I don't know about."

"You mean . . . we missed them?"

"We have to get the horses through these cars. We're falling behind again, and I don't know how many more breaks we're going to get."

"Breaks? What breaks have we gotten so far?"

"Stay here," Tom ordered, and he ran out in a low crouch, moving fast along the line of cars until he disappeared around some wreckage. He was gone for almost three minutes, during which Benny was ready to drag Apache and Chief up and over the vehicles. Tom returned but said nothing, and took off running in the opposite direction, heading down the line of cars. Benny watched him run, saw him stop every few hundred feet and use his arms to measure a gap, saw his shoulders sag a little more each time the gap wasn't wide enough to allow a horse to squeeze through. He went almost half a mile, then turned in defeat and ran back. His face was set, jaw clamped hard around his disappointment.

"Nothing?"

"No. We're going to have to do this the hard way. Rig towlines and use the horses to pull one of the cars enough to make a gap. Horses are half dead as it is." He swore under his breath.

He went past Benny and looked at the puddle and Nix's single footprint. Both had almost entirely evaporated. Benny saw something register on Tom's face as he calculated the time that must have passed since the bounty hunters had come through here, based on the rate of evaporation. Benny couldn't do the same calculation, but he didn't have to. Tom snapped erect, and in a blur he drew his pistol.

At that same moment, Benny heard a strange sound behind and above him, and he turned and looked up as something weirdly disconnected to their present circumstances sailed through the hot air and landed on the blacktop just outside their shelter of wrecked vehicles. The thing looked like a great red snake but with many stubby legs; or like a gigantic centipede. It struck the ground and lay there, twisting and hissing and smoking. Benny stood with his mouth open, unable to process it. This was something from summer celebrations, from garden parties and New Year's Eve.

"Firecrackers," he said in a strangely conversational voice. Benny turned to see the look of concern on Tom's face turn to a mask of absolute horror. He slammed his pistol into his holster and whipped out his sword.

As the first of the firecrackers began to explode, Benny's

surprise evaporated, and he caught up with everything. The puddle, the carefully placed footprint. They weren't accidents, they weren't clues. They were put there deliberately. To stall them, to draw their focus.

The firecrackers banged and banged, and the echoes bounced off every car and rolled out into the field of tall grass and the forest behind them. The barrage of bangs was so incredibly loud in the still air. Loud enough to wake the dead. Or at least call them.

Almost at once Benny saw movement in the trees and in the tall grass. Dark, slow shapes detached themselves from crevices between smashed cars or tottered out from the dappled depths of the woods. Behind Benny, the horses screamed.

They'd walked into another trap.

37

The last firecracker popped and a semi-silence fell. All Benny could hear were the slow, scuffling steps of the zoms. The closest was still a quarter mile away, but they were coming from all directions. The path back to the creek was totally blocked.

"Tom Imura!" called a voice, and Benny and Tom turned to see Vin Trang step out of the tall grass on the far side of the road. He stood in the one spot that was farthest from the living dead, although a few turned stiffly toward him. Vin held a pistol in one hand and several thick strings of firecrackers in the other.

Tom's lip curled, but when he spoke he sounded almost casual. "Where's the girl, Vin?"

"Girl?" Vin laughed. "What girl?"

"Let's not play games."

There was a hissing sound to their left, and they saw a second string of firecrackers come arching out of the woods behind them. It landed on the blacktop and began popping. The zoms that were coming out of the cars began to moan.

"Tom," Benny whispered.

"I know," said Tom without moving his lips. He pitched his voice louder. "The girl!"

"She's dead!" Vin yelled back. "Zoms got her."

Benny almost cried out, but Tom gave him a fierce single shake of his head. "I'm looking at her footprint, Vin. Hasn't even had time to dry yet."

"What can I tell you?"

"Nice trap. Who thought of it?"

"I did."

"You couldn't zipper your pants without instructions, Vin. This has Charlie Pink-eye all over it."

Vin barked out a short laugh. "What's the girl to you? I thought you had the hots for Jessie. Granted, that little girlie has some potential, but she ain't her mama yet."

Benny ground his teeth and started to say something, but Tom touched him, gave him another shake of the head. He bent close and whispered. "Don't let him get inside your head."

"I want to tear his—"

"Me too, kiddo. But let me play this my way. You keep your eye on the zoms. Let me know when they get to within a hundred feet. That's our red zone."

Tom yelled, "Were you at Jessie's last night, Vin? Isn't that where you took the girl?"

"Jessie's? I never been to Jessie's place—although I wouldn't mind paying a call. But Charlie's the one with a sweet spot for Jessie."

"You're saying you weren't at her place last night? That's funny, Vin, 'cause Captain Strunk found your lucky charm there last night."

"My lucky . . . ? What are you talking about? I lost that weeks ago."

"You lost it at Jessie's."

"I was never *at* Jessie's."

"Then how come Captain Strunk found it on the floor?"

"Four hundred feet," Benny whispered.

Another string of firecrackers began popping behind them, and Vin yelled something in Vietnamese. No more firecrackers came flying out of the woods.

Under his breath Tom said, "He just told Joey Duk to cut it out for a minute. I think I rattled him a little."

"What was Strunk doing at Jessie's place?" yelled Vin. "And what do you mean that he *found* my coin on the floor?"

"Mighty bad luck for you to drop your lucky coin at a crime scene, Vin."

"Crime scene? But . . . hey, man . . . What crime? Joey and I don't *do* crimes in town. You know that."

"Tell that to the town watch. They want your head on a pole, Vin. Joey's too."

"For *what*?" Vin demanded, and Benny thought he sounded genuinely outraged.

"For what you did to Jessie Riley."

Silence. Then, "You're jerking us around, Tom. We didn't do anything to Jessie."

"Evidence says different."

"Well, then *ask* Jessie. She'll tell you."

Tom's face wore a twisted smile. Hard and predatory. "Jessie's dead, Vin. You and your 'brother' beat her so bad that she died."

The ensuing silence was broken only by the low moans of the dead.

"Three hundred yards," said Benny.

"You're trying some kind of sick con on me, Tom," protested Vin.

"Not much in the mood for games, Vin. Jessie died in my arms, and your coin was on the floor. You're a wanted man, Vin. You and Joey. Do you know what the people in town will do to you if they catch you? *When* they catch you?"

"No way, man . . . no way in hell." Vin's voice was filled with doubt now. And fear. "You gotta believe me here, Tom."

"Why should I believe you about anything? You're trying to feed me and my brother to the zoms. That doesn't build a good case for innocence."

"Almost two hundred feet, Tom."

The closest zoms were a mix of ordinary people in everyday clothes and soldiers in the burned remains of their uniforms. One wore the black slicker and helmet of a firefighter.

"That's your brother?" Vin called. "That's little Benny. Oh . . . hell, man."

"Yeah, you're really racking up the points, Vin. Beating on women, kidnapping little girls, and now you're thinking about murdering a teenager. Yeah, you're innocent, Vin. You're a real saint."

"You got it wrong, Tom. This stuff out here . . . This is just business. You, me, Joey—we're pros. We know the risks, we know how it works out in the Ruin. No rules, no slack. It's all part of the job."

"Is murder part of the job?"

"Out here? Hell, you know it is."

"Tom," Benny said urgently. Tom turned and saw more zoms emerging from the forest. The terrified horses nickered and tossed their heads, pulling at the tethers that held them to the axle.

"Okay, Vin, but how's the girl fit into all of this?"

"She's Charlie's niece. Or cousin. Something like that. He said so."

"And you *believed* him?"

No answer. Even Benny knew that Vin probably didn't believe that story, but like most people, Vin Trang was not in the habit of calling Charlie Matthias a liar.

"Didn't you think it was strange that he should take his niece away from her mom by force and in the middle of the night?"

No answer.

"The coin, Vin . . . what about the coin?"

"Someone must have put it there."

"Why?"

"To frame me."

Tom smiled and winked at Benny. "And why would they do that, Vin? Who would want to go those lengths to throw suspicion on you?"

It was a long and ugly silence. The zoms were almost at the hundred-foot line. Benny counted sixteen of them in the first wave. Cold sweat ran down his face and back, and pooled like slush at the base of his spine. He had his *bokken* in his hands, but the hard wood felt like a toothpick against what was coming for them.

"Charlie wouldn't do that," Vin protested. "He'd know that we'd clear our names once we got back."

"You mean *if* you got back. You said it yourself, Vin. No rules out here in the Ruin."

"Hundred feet," Benny said, and edged backward, raising the sword in both hands. "We have to go!"

"Vin," called Tom. "I have to get Benny out of here. You let us walk, and I promise to help you with Captain Strunk and the court."

"How do I know you'll keep your word?" Vin said after a pause.

"Because you know what my word's worth," said Tom.

The moans of the dead were as loud as the shouting men. Tom whirled and saw that the firefighter and one other zom were out in front of the pack. With a snarl he leaped toward them, and the silver blade of his *katana* flashed in the sunlight. Tom backpedaled as the zoms fell one way and their heads crunched and rolled the other.

"Clock's ticking on that offer, Vin."

"I could just let the zoms have you and take my chances with the court. Joey and I never broke no laws in town. We have a clean record."

"Tell that to the court when Strunk gives them the only piece of evidence found at the scene. They'll hang you just to have someone to vent on."

The fourteen remaining zoms were now only fifty feet away. Tom stared at them and then at the horses. "Damn it!" he said with a growl, and with a flick of his wrist, he cut the reins that held the horses to the overturned truck. With his free hand he slapped their rumps and yelled at them. Chief needed no urging and was already racing away. Apache ran a few steps, then stopped and looked back at Benny. He was just starting to turn to come back when a zom made a grab for him. Apache reared up and kicked the corpse in the face, then with a whinny of protest he wheeled around and galloped after Chief. They headed for the trees, but Benny saw that the woods were filled with the hungry dead. Even with the carpet coats, how could the horses hope to survive?

And how could he and Tom survive without them?

"Benny!" Tom snapped. "Climb!" He pushed Benny toward the Escalade, and Benny scrambled up onto the hood and then turned and scaled the mangled front of the panel truck. Tom pivoted in place and hacked at the zoms who were closing in on them now. Hands and parts of arms and heads flew, but there were far too many of them. Tom slammed his sword into its sheath and jumped onto the Escalade, just as the living dead reached for him. He kicked backward and then Benny was there, reaching down a hand to pull his brother to safety.

They crouched on the overturned truck, completely exposed. On the far side of the road, Vin Trang stood with his pistol raised.

Tom slowly straightened, and in a movement so smooth that it looked like flowing water, Tom pulled his pistol and pointed it at Vin. The range was too great for accurate handgun shooting, but Tom's hand was rock steady. Even from that distance Benny could see that Vin's whole arm trembled.

"If you take a shot, Vin," Tom warned, "you'd better pray you kill me with the first round."

Vin tried to meet Tom's stare, tried to man it out, but after a few seconds he lowered his gun.

"Where's Charlie taking the girl, Vin?" Tom asked.

But Vin shook his head. His will was broken enough to refuse to fight, but his fear of Charlie was greater than his fear of Tom. Still shaking his head, he backed away and then turned and ran full-tilt into the deep grass. Benny could hear him yelling in Vietnamese to Joey, and soon Joey Duk broke from the woods and ran in Vin's wake.

"Shouldn't we follow?" Benny asked, but he didn't need an answer. Between them and the fleeing Mekong brothers were at least a hundred zoms. And more came shuffling out of the woods. Not just hundreds but thousands.

All around the truck, white hands reached up toward them. They were safe only as long as they stood in the center of the truck's overturned side. But they couldn't stay there forever. Tom looked up and down the row.

"What do we do?" Benny whispered, although in truth there was no longer any reason for silence. Every zom in the region knew where they were. For once Tom did not have a ready answer. His face was almost as pale as the monsters that reached and moaned for their flesh.

"We have no choice," Tom said. "We have to run down the tops of the cars, as far and as fast as we can. We have to get to a point where the zoms are thin on the ground and then make a break for the meadow. I think I know where Vin and Joey are going. Charlie's camp is up on that mountain." He pointed to a craggy lump of granite in the distance.

Benny looked at the row of cars. Some of them were compact cars that were so low to the ground that even standing on the roof, they'd be within grabbing range.

"We'll never make it," he said.

Tom shook his head. "We have to try, Ben. No other choice. You go first. It'll be easier if I'm behind you, in case you get into trouble. Run fast; plan your jumps to land in the widest, flattest places; and keep moving." He drew his sword. "I'll be right behind you."

A cold hand closed around his ankle, and Benny screamed and kicked his foot loose. It was all the incentive he needed. He looked down the row. Past the Escalade there was a mix of sedans and SUVs. They looked like a miniature mountain range. There were zoms on both sides of the outer row of cars, but fewer on the inner rows. He pointed this out to Tom, who nodded.

"Good call, kiddo. Now, go, go, GO!"

Benny took two running steps and jumped over a sea of reaching hands. He heard and felt the dry rasp of desiccated fingers brushing against his ankles and shoes. He landed with a thump on the hood of the Escalade, barely remembering to bend his knees to absorb the shock. Zoms lunged over the hood at him, but Benny swatted their hands away with a fierce slash of his *bokken* and ran up the windshield, along the roof, and then jumped onto a burned-out shell of a Subaru. Then onto a boxy Scion that was high enough to keep the hands away from him, but the next three cars were compacts. He ran and slashed, ran and slashed, feeling the shock as his sword connected with dried tendon and brittle bone. One zom rose up in front of him, its mouth open to reveal two rows of broken and jagged teeth. Benny swung the *bokken*, and the mouth disintegrated into white chips of bone. He had a lingering image of empty black eyes glaring at him as the zombie fell away into the hands of its fellow inmates of the living hell to which they belonged.

He heard Tom's feet pounding behind him and the occasional clean whoosh of the *katana* as it did its deadly work.

Then three things happened all at the same time that changed everything in Benny's life, then and forever.

First, out of the corner of his eye, he saw two shapes break from the cover of the fields to his left. One was huge and burly, with skin as pale as any zom and one eye that burned with red fire. Charlie Pink-eye. And the other was slim and sun-freckled, with masses of red curls and bare feet that slapped the ground, heedless of rocks and nettles.

"NIX!" Benny yelled and at the same time she screamed his name.

"BENNY!" she cried. "IT'S A TRAP!"

It was such an absurd thing to say, because he already *knew* that this was a trap.

The second thing that happened proved to him how little he knew about the evil and devious twists of Charlie Pink-eye's mind, because the Motor City Hammer rose up out of the side window of an overturned police cruiser and pointed a shotgun at him. Two other men—bounty hunters Benny recognized as Turk and Skins Harris; friends of Charlie's—stood up from behind cars farther down the road. They also had shotguns.

Nix's voice was one long continuous scream that blended with Benny's as he twisted out of the way as the Hammer pulled the trigger. Benny dove for the second lane of cars, leaping across a gap that was filled with the undead. He made a jump he would never have believed possible for him, landing on the hood of a Ford pickup truck, tucking, rolling, falling into the back bed, and twisting around to look at where he'd been.

The third thing that happened in that same splintered

second was the sight of Tom twisting away in a spray of blood. The echo of the shotgun was as loud as thunder, but Benny's scream was louder as Tom pitched off of the roof of the car and fell out of sight, right into the hands of the living dead.

"TOM!"

Benny got to his feet as a zombie crawled over the tailgate of the truck, and he swung the *bokken* with so much force that it tore the creature's head half off. Benny was still screaming Tom's name.

"BENNY!"

He whirled, and there was Nix, running over the tops of the cars on the next lane. Her clothes were torn, and there was blood on her face. Benny jumped over the gap just as she reached him, and for a moment everything stopped as he pulled her into his arms. They hugged with such force that it crushed the breath from both of them.

The sound of the Hammer racking the pump of the shotgun snapped them both back to their senses, and they spun and ran back the way Benny had come, dipping and dodging as they ran up windshields and leaped from hood to trunk.

"Get them!" bellowed Charlie, and the Hammer fired shot after shot. Turk and Skins began firing, and even though they were too far away for accuracy, the buckshot they fired filled the air with broken glass and metal splinters. The Hammer was closer, and his next shot exploded car windows all around them. But Benny and Nix were running toward the setting sun, and the Hammer was firing into the glare. There were several sharper cracks as Charlie emptied his pistol at them, but Benny pulled Nix down behind a tall flower delivery van. Bullets pinged and whanged, but none of the shots found them.

"We have to go back for Tom!" Nix said.

Benny looked back to the spot where Tom had fallen. There were at least fifty zoms clustered there, and his heart plummeted in his chest.

"He's gone," he said in a desolated voice.

"Benny," she said, tears boiling from her eyes, "I'm so sorry."

The truck canted slightly to one side, and Benny peered around to see five zoms awkwardly climbing up the side. "We have to go. *Now!*"

She looked and saw and nodded. Although it broke their hearts to do it, they turned and ran down the long line of cars. Charlie and the Hammer kept firing, but soon they had to turn their guns on the zoms who staggered toward them. Benny and Nix ran and jumped, climbed and dodged. The sun was a great glaring eye that stared accusingly at Benny, condemning him for failing his brother, for running . . . as his brother had once run. But he could *not* go back. Not with Nix here. He had to save her . . . and it was already too late to save Tom.

Pain was sewn through the fabric of his heart and stitched deep into his sides as they ran and ran and ran.

38

Benny had no idea how long they ran. A mile, maybe two. His legs felt like lead and his chest burned, but he held onto Nix's hand on every jump and never once let her fall. With every step, his heart lifted with the knowledge that Nix was alive and safe. And then it fell as he thought of Tom.

"Look!" Nix said, pulling him to a stop on the roof of a Chevy Suburban. She pointed to a path that wound like a snake and vanished into the tall grass. "It's empty."

She was right. The last of the zoms were hundreds of yards behind them. In their panic they'd far outrun the immediate threat.

"What about Charlie?" Benny stood on his toes and looked back the way they'd come, but the bounty hunters were nowhere to be seen.

"I don't know," she said. "But let's get off these cars."

They jumped down to the ground and froze there for a moment, checking forward and backward for any sign of movement or for zombies standing still, whose appetites would be triggered by their own movement. They saw nothing but empty cars, carrion birds, the waving grass, and the bones of a thousand dead people.

Benny dragged a forearm across his eyes, although he didn't know if he was wiping away sweat or tears.

"Let's go," he whispered. "Move slowly. Follow me, do what I do, move when I move, stop when I stop."

They were Tom's words on his lips, and it hurt him to say them, but he knew that he had to draw on everything his brother had showed him if he and Nix were going to survive.

Together, still holding hands, they moved slowly from the shelter of the endless line of cars. Benny waited for the wind to stir the grass and tall stalks of wild wheat, and when they bent to the left, he moved that way. When the wind stopped, so did he. When the grasses stood back up again, he moved to the right. Stop and start, taking his time. Doing it right. It took them five minutes to move from the highway to the path and then they were inside the tall grass. The shadows of early twilight cast the trail in shades of purple, and in that velvet gloom Benny and Nix vanished entirely.

They lost track of how long or how far they ran. Benny took every upward sloping road, remembering what Tom said about there being fewer zombies in the high mountain passes. They passed burned-out houses and houses where zombies stood in the yard, but when Nix and Benny saw them, they slipped into the deepest foliage and moved without a sound. Terror made them cautious, and with each encounter, they refined the skills of not being seen and not being hunted.

By the time the last of the day's light was melting into shadows, Benny realized that it had been more than an hour since the last time they'd see a zom.

"How did you get away from them?" he asked Nix.

"I kicked one of the other bounty hunters in the groin and ran."

Benny grinned at her. "You are one tough chick."

"Call me a chick again and I'll show you how tough I am." It was meant as a joke, but it was weak. Even so, Benny gave her a big grin, and they headed higher up the mountain slope.

Then Nix grabbed his arm and pointed to something. Benny looked up. Just ahead was a building on stilts that rose a hundred feet above a steep rocky slope. Sunlight still touched its eaves. They raced to the foot of the ladder.

"Can you climb?" he asked. Nix didn't have the breath to answer, but she nodded and they grabbed the rusted rungs and began to ascend. After the long uphill run it was torture to scale the ladder. Their muscles burned and their limbs trembled, but they never stopped, never faltered.

The ladder rose to a narrow catwalk that surrounded the boxy wooden structure of the ranger outpost. The catwalk was red with rust and littered with old birds nests and animal droppings. The windows were white with dust and grime, and Benny couldn't see in. He pulled his *bokken* out of his belt,

"Stay here," he told Nix, and she crouched down at the top of the ladder. She had no weapon, and Benny thought that her eyes looked terrified and maybe a little crazy. He couldn't blame her. How could she *not* be whacked out after everything she'd been through?

With the *bokken* poised to thrust or strike, he moved slowly and quietly along the catwalk. Darkness was closing its hands around them, and the last golden touch of sunlight was melting from the peaked roof of the tower. The walls and windows were pitted from weather, and none of it looked safe, and here and there were smudges that might have been old mud. Or it might have been something else.

At the corner he paused and looked around the edge, but the catwalk was empty and the door to the station stood ajar.

Was that a good thing or a bad thing? He didn't know.

He crept forward, breathing shallowly, sweat running down his hot face.

Three soft steps took him to the door, and he paused, drew a breath, and then kicked the door open. The ancient hinges squealed, as if they were in pain, and the door swung inward and stopped, jammed against something soft that crunched like leaves. Benny waited for an attack, for movement. Saw nothing.

He moved inside and looked quickly around . . . and then lowered his sword.

Except for leaves and branches from some creature that had long ago made a nest in the corner behind the door, and a few rotting sticks of furniture, the place was empty. There was a door set in the back wall with a sign marked RESTROOM, and Benny moved to it and gingerly opened it. The light was so bad that he couldn't see a thing, so he took a match from his pocket and scraped the sulfur on the doorframe. In the sudden glow, Benny saw that the tiny cubicle held only a toilet and sink, but the water had long ago evaporated, and the corners were filled with trash and rags.

Benny froze. He held the flickering match out to take a second, longer look at the pile of rags. It was crammed into the corner between the wall and the toilet. Leaves and other debris covered it, and the chitinous carcasses of dead bugs were littered around.

The match flame gleamed dully from the barrel of a pistol that lay on the floor in a tangle of old twigs.

No . . . not twigs. Bones.

He set his sword down and used his thumb and forefinger to lift a bit of the fabric, and as he did, he understood what this was. The rags were the remnants of clothes—a brown uniform trimmed with gold cord. An old flat-brimmed hat lay under the remains. A tarnished badge was pinned to the crown. Benny had never met one, but he'd seen pictures of forest rangers in books. This was the ranger. Had he been bitten and crawled in here to die? No . . . that made no sense. He'd have turned. Then Benny considered the pistol, and he understood. The man had been bitten, and he'd come in here to do what was necessary to keep himself from becoming a monster. Even though Benny knew this sort of thing had probably happened hundreds of thousands of times around the world, seeing it here, firsthand, made it almost unbearably sad.

Benny's match was burning down, but he had enough light left to poke among the rags and find the ranger's name tag.

M. Horwitz.

"I'm sorry," Benny said.

Was this the same ranger station where Tom and Mr. Sacchetto had come with their telescope? If so, there was no sign of it, and Benny guessed there were probably several similar towers scattered throughout the mountains.

He straightened and stepped out of the bathroom and then hurried through the station and around the corner to where Nix still crouched. Despite the heat she was shivering, and Benny felt a knife of panic stab him. He'd learned about shock in the Scouts, and he knew it could be as dangerous as a bullet.

"Come on," he said, holding out his hands. Nix hesitated for a moment, her eyes unfocused, as if she didn't quite recognize him. She reached for him, and he pulled her against his chest. Nix wrapped strong arms around him and clung to him, and after only a sliver of a second, he wrapped his arms around her shoulders and back, and squeezed her with all his strength.

Together, still holding onto each other and moving in an awkward ballet, they stumbled back to the door and shambled inside. Benny kicked the door closed and leaned back against it, sliding down to the floor, taking Nix with him.

She whispered a single, heartbroken and heartbreaking word.

"Mom!"

Benny clutched her to him, sharing his heat with her.

"I know," he said. It was all he had to say, all she needed to hear. That he knew, that he understood, was as necessary to her as it was terrible, and she disintegrated into tears that burned against his face and throat. Benny held her, and his grief for her, for her mother, for Mr. Sacchetto . . . and for Tom was a vast and unbearable ache that filled every inch of him.

They held each other and wept as the night closed its fist around their tiny shelter, and the world below them seethed with killers both living and dead.

PART FOUR
FAMILY BUSINESS

"Fear is only as deep as the mind allows."

—JAPANESE PROVERB

39

Benny opened his eyes and realized that he'd been asleep . . . and that he was alone. The ranger station was in absolute darkness. Benny tensed, reaching for his sword, but his fingers found nothing. He remembered then that he'd left the *bokken* in the bathroom.

"Nix . . . ?" he whispered.

Nothing.

Very slowly he shifted onto his knees and then climbed to his feet, staying low, listening for some sound. His shirt collar was still damp from her tears, so he knew he couldn't have been asleep for long. Half an hour maybe?

He went outside. Nix was at the corner of the rail, her arms crossed tightly over her chest, her hair blowing in the breeze. There was a sliver of moon and a splash of stars, and the light outlined her face and glistened on the tears that ran like mercury down her cheeks. He stood next to her, leaning his arms on the rail and looking out at the vastness of the sky. The starlight glimmered on the canopy of leaves, and the ocean of trees seemed to stretch away forever.

"Have you heard anything?" he whispered as they sat

down on the edge of the catwalk, their feet hanging over into the lake of darkness.

"No."

"Good. I think we're safe," he said, then added lamely, "Up here, I mean."

She nodded. A mockingbird sang its schizophrenic melodies from a nearby tree.

Benny said, "When there's light we'll have to try and find our way back to town."

Nix just shook her head, and the denial had so many possible meanings that Benny left his questions unasked.

"Morgie," she said. "Is he . . . ?"

"No, he's okay. Or will be. They hit him pretty hard in the head, but they say he's going to make it."

Benny saw Nix steeling herself for the next question, and he was pretty sure he knew what it was going to be.

"My mom," she began, and he quietly curled his fingers around the lip of the catwalk's metal floor. "They said that she was . . . They said that she'd . . ." Nix stopped and shook her head, trying it another way. "They wanted to leave a present for Tom. That's what they called it. A 'present.'"

"It wasn't like that," Benny said. "We got there pretty quick. Your mom was still . . . your mom. Tom held her all the way up to the last, and she held onto him. It was . . . I don't know. I've never seen anything like it. But then she was . . . gone. It didn't look like she was in pain when it happened. She just went to sleep."

"Sleep," Nix said in a soft echo. "And . . . after? Did she . . . I mean, did they let her . . . God, Benny, don't make me *say* it!"

"No," he soothed. "No. She never returned. There wasn't time. Tom did what was necessary."

"Tom?"

"Yes. With a sliver. He did it fast and quick. She never knew. And he held her afterward."

Nix made no comment, but he could *feel* her pain. She sat and stared into the darkness of her own thoughts as the wheel of night turned above them.

"Why did they come after you, Nix?"

She turned to him in the dark. "It was because of that card. The Zombie Card with the girl on it."

"I don't get it."

"Zak Matthias got one too. I ran into him yesterday. He was on his way home from the store with his Zombie Cards, and I asked to see them. He was kind of weird about it, but he showed them to me. When I saw the card for the Lost Girl, I told him that I'd seen that picture before. He seemed really interested and asked where, and I told him that my mom was friends with Mr. Sacchetto, the erosion artist. He came over to the house with Tom a few times, and they talked about the Lost Girl."

"You never told me about that."

She shrugged. "Why would I? It didn't seem to involve us. Just my mom and her friends talking. But when I told Zak, he kept asking me about it. What did my mom know about the Lost Girl? What had Tom and Mr. Sacchetto told her? Did I know where the Lost Girl was?" A tear rolled down her face, and she brushed it away. "I thought he was just interested because of the picture. The girl's so pretty, you know? Like something out of a book. A faerie princess or something like that. Zak was smiling the whole time and . . . I don't know . . . He's good-looking, and he was being nice to me and . . ."

"And I'd blown you off?"

Nix shot him a sharp look, but her face softened and she looked away. "I don't know. Maybe."

"What did you tell him?"

She was a long time answering, and twice her face screwed up as she fought to control the pain in her soul. "I . . . I told him everything I knew. It wasn't a lot. I didn't really pay much attention when Mom and the others were talking about her. I told Zak that Mom knew a lot about her." She shook her head in confusion. "I don't *know*, Benny. Zak was being so nice. . . . I don't know what I said."

"It's okay, Nix."

She wheeled on him. "Okay? No, it's not okay! Don't you get it? I told Zak that my mom knew about the Lost Girl, and I think that's why Charlie came to the house. *It's because of what I said!*"

She hissed the last words at him in a voice that boiled with pain and self-hatred.

"My mom's dead because of me!"

"No, she's not," Benny said with a growl. He took her by the arms. She was strong. She tried to break away and stand up, but he held her. "Listen to me, Nix! Your mom's dead, because Charlie Matthias is a freak and a murderer and a . . . a . . ." He couldn't find a word vile enough to describe that monster's nature.

Tears streamed down Nix's face, but her teeth were set and bared. "Charlie knew you had the same card. All the time he was at the house, Charlie kept saying they should have just *taken* the card from you. He was furious with you. He said that you sassed him and that if Tom hadn't come along, he'd have shown you manners. Manners . . . That's a word he used at our house. He said that we all needed to show him some manners."

Benny let go of her arms, and Nix leaned back away from him. "Why come after your mom, though? There have to be several of those cards in print now, even rare Chase Cards like that. In all the towns. He can't kill everyone who has one."

"No . . . it wasn't just the card. It was what he thought Mom knew about the girl. Where to find her. And . . . I think maybe Mom *did* know something. I think Tom might have told her where he thought the Lost Girl was." She cut him a look. "Did Tom tell you anything about my mom and Gameland?"

Benny nodded.

"Mom had nightmares about that place. About fighting zoms to make money for us to live on. God—the things she had to do just because of me!"

"Whoa, don't think like that, Nix. That's going to make you crazy, and it's not true. Your mom did what she thought was right. She did what she had to do. She did it because she loved you. Only a mother would have the guts or even care enough to do what she did. You can't let it chew you up."

Nix wiped more tears from her eyes and nodded, but Benny knew this was something that would take her years to work through. He hoped they would have those years.

"A few months ago Mom told me that Charlie had rebuilt Gameland. I guess Tom told her. Her nightmares were a lot worse after that, and she kept on me all the time not to ever be alone with Charlie or the Hammer. And . . . and . . . last night, Charlie told her that they were taking me there. It hurt Mom worse than the beating they gave her. Mom freaked out and smashed him over the head with a rolling pin. I wished she'd killed him, but he turned on her like an animal." Nix stopped, and Benny did not encourage her to tell any more of that part of the story.

The night birds kept up their continuous chorus.

"Then they hit me so hard that I guess I blacked out, and when I woke up we were already out here in the Ruin. They told me that they were taking me to Gameland."

"Then it's somewhere close?"

"I don't think so. I overheard the Hammer telling one of the other bounty hunters that they were heading to Charlie's camp up in the mountains and would turn east to Gameland in the morning."

"I'm glad you escaped, Nix. I was going crazy thinking about you with those maniacs."

"Charlie wouldn't let them hurt me too much. He said that I had to be 'fresh' for the Z-Games."

"The stuff they're doing," Benny said, "in town last night, out here, at Gameland . . . It's worse than what the zoms do."

"I know," she said. "Zoms are driven by some disease, but, really, they're mindless and soulless. These men *have* souls and minds, and yet they still do this stuff. Not once, but over and over again."

There was a sound off in the distance that sounded like a scream. Not a human throat, though. Was it Apache or Chief? Or just the call of some night-hunting bird?

Benny shifted to sit a little closer to Nix. "Tom said that

he'd heard rumors about them grabbing kids from places where they wouldn't be missed. Kids for Gameland. Did anyone say anything about that?"

"Yes. One of the men said that they'd rounded up a bunch of kids and that they were waiting at the camp."

"Do you know where this camp is?"

"No . . . but it can't be far."

Benny chewed on that. "If Tom was . . . I mean . . . Maybe Tom would know what to do. He might be able to find the camp and get those kids out."

Nix looked at him. "God! I wish there was some way that we could do it."

"Us? Fat chance. We don't have weapons, training, or anything, and there are about a million zoms out there."

"So what are you saying? We don't do anything? We just let those kids be taken to that place?"

Benny shook his head. "That's not it, Nix. . . . It's just that we *can't* do anything. I mean, be realistic."

"Realistic? Yeah, and you're always living in the real world, Benny Imura."

"What's that supposed to mean?"

"You're in love with a girl you saw on a Zombie Card, and you're asking me to be realistic." She shook her head, and they lapsed into a tense silence.

"I'm not in love with anyone, Nix. Besides, I don't even know Lilah. Don't be crazy," Benny said.

Nix merely grunted.

"Benny," she said after a while. "A couple of years ago, when Mom thought I was asleep, I heard her beg Tom to kill Charlie. She wanted Tom to find him out here in the Ruin and kill him. . . . But he *didn't* do it, Benny! He should have done it . . . but he didn't."

"I know. But . . . I think he might have burned Gameland down."

"So what? The problem isn't the place, Benny, it's the people. Tom didn't stop them. I think he was afraid of Charlie."

Benny shook his head. "You don't understand. Tom wasn't who I thought he was. I was completely wrong about him. He wasn't afraid of—"

But Nix was on the attack and cut him off. "You never liked Tom, so don't start defending him now. You always said he was weak. He was supposed to be so tough, and yet he wouldn't even do what my mom wanted. He *couldn't* . . . and look what happened. Mom's *dead*." She pounded her fists on the metal rail, and the echo bounced off the night-black trees. Benny heard the echo and quickly grabbed her wrist.

"Don't," he said. "Not out here. The noise . . ."

She wheeled on him. "Are you afraid too?" she mocked.

"Yes," he said. "I am. There are zoms out there, Nix. Zoms and *them*. Sound carries."

But her hurt and anger still needed a target. "You're just as bad as Tom. You and Morgie and Chong. You worship Charlie and the other bounty hunters. You think he's *cool*." She injected that word with so much venom that Benny knew he would never allow himself to speak it again. It sounded hollow and immature and stupid.

"Not anymore," he said.

"Oh, sure. Now that it's too late to do anything, you act all wise and noble. Please."

Her voice was drenched with bile, and it was getting louder. Benny tried to read her face by starlight, but all he saw were harsh lines.

"And about Tom . . . I'm not sure what I feel about him anymore. I mean, I miss him. A lot. More than I thought I would." He shook his head. "Ever since he first took me out to the Ruin, everything's different. I don't understand him. I don't know if I ever did."

She shoved him hard in the chest. "Who cares? He didn't save my mom and he could have."

"Nix, I know you're hurt. I wish I could fix it, I swear to God. I wish I could make it all different, make what happened not true. If I could . . . I'd give anything. I'd die to make it right for you and for your mom."

She started to say something, but he touched her arm.

"If you need to lash out at me, if you need to do anything to me—say anything, throw me off this tower—if it will help even a little, then do it. I don't care what happens to me anymore. I got what I wanted."

"What's that?" she demanded.

"You," he said. "I got you back safe. The monsters didn't get you."

Nix stared at him, unable to speak even though she tried.

Benny tugged the worn leather diary out of his back pocket and pressed it into her hands. "I found this on the floor in your room. I kept it. I . . . haven't opened it, haven't read it. I kept it, because as long as I had it, I knew I'd find you again."

Nix took the diary, and in the pale light from stars and

moon, she ran her fingers across the cover and along the binding. When she raised her eyes to look at Benny, her eyes were wet with new tears.

"Benny, I—," she began, but before she could say anything more, he bent forward and kissed her. It was the wrong time, the wrong place, the wrong circumstances. There was nothing right in their whole world.

Except that kiss.

NIX FELL ASLEEP WITH HER HEAD IN HIS LAP. BENNY STAYED AWAKE for another couple of hours, stroking her hair and staring into the infinite star field that stretched above him. After that first scalding kiss, there had been others. And then there had been more tears as the full reality of her loss hit Nix. These tears were quieter, though. They weren't the tears of shock and denial. They'd already been through that storm. These were the deep, heartbroken tears of acceptance.

Their lives had changed. Their worlds had changed. As he sat there stroking Nix's hair, Benny had the weird feeling that if he turned around, he would be able to see yesterday and the day before that, all the way back to the point where he had decided to apprentice with Tom. It had been at that moment that his footfalls had diverged from the sane and predictable course of his life. He wished he could call out to the Benny of ten days ago and shout a warning not to come this way. Take the job at the pit, work for the German locksmith, get a tower job with Chong. Anything but this.

As he thought about it, Benny felt sickness creeping into his mind, making ugly questions form like tumors.

Would all of this have happened if I hadn't taken that damn job with Tom?

And worse yet . . .

Would any of it have happened?

On a deep level he knew that these thoughts were stupid and wrong. Charlie and the Hammer would have still come after Tom and Sacchetto and Nix's mom.

Wouldn't they?

He also knew that the guilt he felt was no different than the guilt Nix felt for having told Zak about her mother knowing Lilah. Things said and done innocently should never be used as weapons. There was guilt here, he finally decided, but it all belonged to Charlie.

Just thinking that name made fires ignite in the pit of his stomach.

For the first time in his life he wished that Tom was here to help him make sense of it. Tom. Benny had hated him most of his life and had just started to like him—even if he didn't quite understand him—and now the zoms had gotten him.

The sudden realization that Tom was not only dead but was probably a zom was like a punch in the face. Benny closed his eyes and found that old, old memory of Mom in her white dress with red sleeves, handing him to Tom, screaming at Tom to run, and Tom running away, leaving her behind. Tom the zombie hunter. Tom the coward.

Tom the zombie. Would there be a new Zombie Card? Two weeks ago Benny might have thought that was funny. Or appropriate.

Now the horror of it was bigger than the night that loomed around him. He remembered the argument they'd had when Tom had showed him the old man and the girl in the waitress uniform.

"It's not the same. These are zoms, man. They kill people. They eat people."

Tom had said, "They used to be people."

Now Tom was one of them. He tried not to think of what Tom's last few seconds had been like. The Hammer's shotgun blast had caught him; Benny had seen the blood fly. Had the blast killed him? That would have been a kindness. The alternative was beyond horrible. Falling down into the mass of them, covered in blood. White hands clawing at his skin, rotting gray teeth biting into him, tearing at him . . .

Tom did not deserve that. Benny was unsure if Tom was a coward or had ever *been* a coward. He doubted his own memories of First Night, or, at least, of what those old memories meant. No matter what, though, Tom did not deserve what had happened to him.

He shivered and Nix stirred restlessly.

Looking at her dragged his mind into another room of thought. That kiss. With *Nix?* Nix, of all people. It was absurd, impossible. They'd already come to that hurdle back in town, and they hadn't been able to climb it together. It was dangerous and wrong to fall in love with a friend. It complicated things. He and Chong had once sworn that they would never ever fall for a girl they knew. A bold claim in a town as small as Mountainside. Now . . . Nix Riley lay asleep on his lap, and he swore he could still feel the warmth of her lips on his.

He tugged the battered and sweat-stained Zombie Card from his shirt pocket and looked at the Lost Girl. A dagger of guilt stabbed him beneath the breastbone, and he quickly glanced down at Nix. He could see her eyes move under her closed lids and knew that she was dreaming. A soft cry escaped her parted lips, and it was filled with jagged pieces of emotion. Hurt and loss, despair and terror, but also rage and defiance.

Benny brushed a strand of hair away from her cheek.

His stomach churned with confusion and conflict. Even now, even after that incredible kiss he and Nix had shared, when he looked at the picture of the Lost Girl, he felt an almost physical impact. The desire to find and protect Lilah was every bit as strong now as it was when he'd first turned over her card on the porch at Lafferty's General Store, and that made as little sense to him now as it did then. He didn't *know* this girl. Even Sacchetto and Tom hadn't really known her. Even if she was still out here somewhere, she was nothing and no one to him. And yet . . .

And yet.

He studied the card for a long time, even as exhaustion dragged on his eyelids. Nix groaned again in the private hell of her troubled sleep. Benny looked from Nix to the Lost Girl and back to Nix.

"I'm sorry," he said.

Then he stretched out his other hand, and for the second time, he opened his fingers and let the wind take the card. It blew high into the air, tumbling over and over again, its pasteboard face flashing with silver starlight, and then it dropped into the darkness below.

Benny bent and kissed Nix's cheek. He leaned back against the wall and stared at the night and drifted off into a sea of stars.

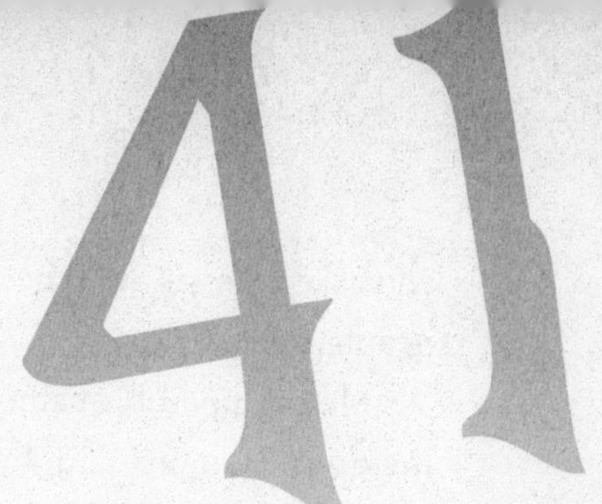

"NOW AIN'T THIS JUST ADORABLE."

Benny and Nix jerked awake at the sound of the voice, blinking in the harsh dawn light, struggling to disentangle themselves from each other and understand where on Earth they were.

Two men stood on the metal catwalk that ran around the outside of the deserted ranger station. Both men had guns holstered on their hips, shotguns slung over their shoulders, and ugly smiles on their mouths.

Skins and Turk.

"Ain't nothing like young love," said Turk.

"Warms the cockles of my heart," agreed Skins.

Benny instinctively spread his arms, like a barrier between the bounty hunters and Nix.

"Charlie's going to like this," said Skins. "He was pretty smoked about the little witch skipping out like that."

"Leave us alone," Benny said with a growl.

"Yeah." Turk laughed. "That's gonna happen. We spent the whole damn night searching these freaking woods and then climbed this big mother of a tower, just to go away 'cause you asked. Yessir, we'll be on our way, so sorry to bother your beauty sleep."

Skins tapped his palm on his thigh, like he was calling in the dogs. "C'mon . . . get your butts over here."

Benny and Nix slowly got to their feet, but they made no move toward the bounty hunters. Turk went into the ranger station and came out with the *bokken*. "Look," he said. "Kid has a toy sword."

He raised it over his head and brought it down in a powerful two-hand swing onto the metal rail. The hard wood rebounded from the hit, but did not break. Turk cursed and turned it sideways and slammed the flat of the blade onto the rail, and with a sharp crack the sword snapped in half. The long end went spinning off into the canopy of trees far below. Turk laughed and tossed the broken handle onto the catwalk.

"They have anything else in there?" Skins asked.

"Nah."

"Then let's haul it," snapped Skins to Benny and Nix. "C'mon, kids, Charlie is going to have a lot of stuff to *talk* to you two about. Should be a pretty interesting chat."

"A heart-to-heart." Turk laughed.

"A meaningful discussion," agreed Skins.

"Let us go," said Nix. "You can do that. You can just tell Charlie that you didn't find us."

Skins looked genuinely confused. "Now why on Earth would we want to do that?"

Benny took a step forward. "Do you know what Charlie did last night?"

"None of my business."

"You're *with* him. You're helping him do this stuff."

Skins looked bored. "Is this where you try to appeal to my better nature, kid?"

Behind him Turk cracked up. "Good luck with that."

"Please . . . ," Benny said. "We didn't do anything to you."

"Who cares?"

"I won't let you take her—"

Skins suddenly backhanded Benny across the face. It was so fast and hard that Benny was falling before he realized that he'd been hit. He hit the railing with the small of his back and might have gone over if Nix hadn't grabbed him and hauled him away. Benny sank to his knees and spit blood and a piece of tooth onto the catwalk.

"Leave him alone!" Nix yelled.

The bounty hunter snatched a handful of Nix's hair, tore her away from Benny, and slammed her against the station wall.

"Shut up, girlie. You don't tell us what to do."

Benny came off the deck in a surge and drove his fist into Skins' ribs. It was a good try, but he was still dizzy from the blow he'd taken, and his fist merely skittered along the big man's side. Skins pivoted and drove a heavy punch into Benny's back, nailing him squarely between the shoulder blades and knocking him flat onto his chest.

"Try that crap again, kid, and I'll cut pieces off of you."

It was all Benny could do to breathe. When he'd landed, his breastbone had struck the broken *bokken* handle, and it felt like the hard wood had punched a hole through his chest.

"Benny!" Nix cried, but when she tried to bend to help him, Turk grabbed her by the sleeve and pulled her away. The action caused her shirt to ride high and expose most of her midriff. Both of the bounty hunters whistled and laughed and made comments that were as vulgar as they were threatening. Nix did not give in or give up. She fought them, kicking out as hard as she could, slapping at Turk's face, raking her nails on his arms, pounding her fists on his chest and cheeks. Her attack was so sudden and fierce that for a moment the bounty hunter reeled back, letting go of her to use both hands to block his face. Nix tried to kick him in the groin, but Turk turned his hip and swatted hard enough her across the face to spin her into the wall again. She hit hard and slid down to her knees.

"Filthy little whore!" Turk growled. His lip and right ear were already swelling.

But even then Nix would not stop. As Benny watched she launched herself from her knees and drove into Turk's legs, knocking him back against the rail. She made a sound like a hunting cat, a snarl that started low in her gut and rose up, filtered through rage and humiliation and the certain knowledge of what the future held. Her scream scared the birds from the trees and echoed off the mountain slope. Turk kept backing away from her, startled and confused by this child who had been frightened and cowering all last night and who was now attacking him with insane strength and speed.

"Slap some sense into that little hellcat," demanded Skins. "Screw it . . . let me do it."

Skins stepped over Benny and reached to take a handful of Nix's hair, just as Turk caught one of her wrists and then another. Skins drew a knife with his free hand. "I've had enough of your crap, girlie girl. You don't need both eyes to fight in the zombie pits."

That was all Benny could take. Even though he could barely breathe, he dug one hand under his chest and grabbed the broken *bokken* handle, then jammed the other hand hard against the catwalk and heaved himself to his knees.

"Leave her alone!" he screamed and with all of the fury and fear that flowed through him, he drove the jagged end of the *bokken* into Skins's back. When the sword had snapped, it left a hardwood stump that was as sharp as a real blade, and Benny threw his weight behind the thrust. The jagged point bit deep into the soft spot above the bounty hunter's belt, and Benny buried it to the hilt. Blood ran hot and red over his fist, and Skins whirled and clubbed him down. Benny fell, raising his arms to ward off the next blow, but Skins stood there, gasping like a fish out of water, eyes bugged wide in unbelieving surprise.

Nix stamped down hard on Turk's foot and tore her wrists free of his grip, then shoved him in the chest as hard as she could, hoping to knock him over the rail. Turk was so busy staring at Skins that he was caught off guard, and staggered back all the way to the rail by the ladder, but he did not go over.

Instead, he caught his balance at the last second. Skins dropped heavily to his knees, the impact causing the metal catwalk to ring like a bell. His eyes rolled up, and he fell forward onto his face with a meaty crunch.

"You're dead." Turk snarled at Benny. He grabbed his pistol and whipped it from the holster, thumbing back the hammer in a smooth and practiced move. "I'll friggin' kill you both for—"

That was all he got out. It was all he would ever say again.

He looked down at his chest, at the bizarre thing that suddenly sprouted from between the ribs on the left side. Benny and Nix stared as well. The whole front of Turk's shirt exploded with red as three gleaming inches of sharpened steel extruded from the bounty hunter's chest. He tried to say something, but there was no air left in his lungs, no power left in his voice.

Behind him there was a blur of movement and a grunt of effort. The blade vanished, pulled back into the wound and then out of Turk's body. Benny watched as the person behind him cocked a leg, placed a foot on the bounty hunter's body, and shoved him forward, so that he landed face-down, inches from Skins.

The figure stood there in the harsh morning sunlight. Tattered jeans and hand-sewn leather moccasins, a shirt that had once been bright with a wildflower pattern, with a leather pouch slung across her body on a thin strap. Hair the color of newly fallen snow swirled around her tanned face, and she stared at them with cunning hazel eyes. In her tanned hands she held a spear crudely made from a long piece of quarter-inch black pipe wrapped in leather and topped with the blade from a Marine Corps bayonet.

The Lost Girl.

"WHO ARE YOU?" NIX ASKED, BUT AT THE SAME TIME BENNY SPOKE her name.

"Lilah!"

The girl stiffened, and the bloody spear swung around in his direction. Her hazel eyes narrowed into dangerous slits.

Benny held up his hands. "No, wait . . . I'm Benny Imura."

She showed no sign of recognition.

"I'm Tom Imura's brother."

The girl said nothing.

"My brother, Tom . . . He knew George!"

If he had struck her across the face, he could not have changed her expression more quickly. The suspicion vanished to be replaced by shock.

"G—George?"

She spoke the name, as if her throat was dusty from disuse, and Benny realized that in a very real way it probably was. Almost immediately her suspicions returned, and the tip of the spear rose another inch, level with his eye.

"Where?" she demanded. "George."

Nix glanced at Benny, putting things together very quickly. "Is this *her*?" she whispered.

"George!" the Lost Girl prompted with a shake of her spear. Her voice was still a husky whisper, and Benny remembered that horrible story that Rob Sacchetto had told him of how Lilah had started screaming when the men in that little cottage had been forced to kill her mother after she'd reanimated as a zombie.

She screamed herself raw, and then she stopped talking. Those screams must have damaged her vocal chords for good, leaving her with a voice like a graveyard whisper.

God.

"I . . . don't know where he is," Benny said quickly. "My brother knew him. He helped George look for you."

"Look? For . . . me?" It was clearly hard for the girl to form sentences. It was a skill that she'd lost over time. Benny could not imagine going for years without speaking to anyone. In some odd way that was as bad as living out here in the zombie wasteland.

"When the bounty hunters took you and your sister from George, he started looking for you." Benny risked taking a slight step toward her, despite the threat of the deadly spear. "He never stopped, Lilah. George never stopped looking for you. And for Annie."

At the mention of her sister's name, Lilah's eyes filled with tears, but her mouth tightened into a bitter line.

"Lilah, listen to me. The men who hurt you, the men who hurt Annie and George . . ."

"Benny," Nix said softly. "Don't . . ."

"Those same men hurt Nix's mother." He turned his head for a second to indicate Nix. "They hurt her . . . and she died."

Lilah held her ground, eyes boring into his.

"And they killed my brother." Benny licked his lips. "Those men took the people we all loved. They took from each of us." As Benny said it, he realized that he did love Tom. As troubled and confused as their relationship had once been, Benny felt an ache that went all the way to the core of his heart. "They hurt all of us, Lilah. Do you understand? All of *us*." He leaned on that last word and saw how it worked on her, changing her eyes and the line of her mouth. The spear tip wavered ever so slightly.

"Us," he repeated. "You . . . Nix . . . me. Us."

Benny waited for a moment, his heart pounding in his chest, and then took another step forward. The tip of the spear was inches from his face now. Moving very slowly, hands open, eyes fixed on Lilah's, he reached up and touched the point where the Marine Corps bayonet was attached to the shaft of the spear. He pushed it aside, and the Lost Girl allowed it.

After a moment she stepped back and lowered the weapon.

"Us," she said.

"Us," agreed Benny.

After a moment Nix said, "Us."

Abruptly the Lost Girl stiffened and looked over the rail. Benny and Nix looked as well, but if there was something to see, they didn't see it. Lilah, however, did.

"Go," she snapped. "Now. Now!"

Without waiting to see if they followed, she spun around and climbed down the ladder as quickly and smoothly as a monkey. Nix followed, but Benny lingered for a moment, looking at the man he'd killed.

"Benny!" Nix called.

"Wait. Give me a second," he said. "I have work to do."

He took the weapons from the dead men, stripping off Turk's gun belt and buckling it around his narrow waist. The gun was heavy, but the weight was comforting. He left the shotguns. They were big and clumsy, and he had never fired one before. Now didn't seem like the time to fool around with unfamiliar weapons. However, he took Skins's knife. It was not as good as Tom's double-bladed dagger or the hunting knife Benny had lost back at the field, but it would do.

Benny knelt beside the corpse for a second, the naked blade in his hand.

"This is probably cutting you a break," he muttered, "but we may need this place again."

With that he plunged the tip of the blade into the back of the man's neck, right below the skull. Quieting him. He pulled the blade free, lips curled in disgust, and then repeated the process with Turk. Then he wiped the blade clean on Turk's shirt, slid the knife into the sheath on the gun belt, and climbed down to catch up with Nix and Lilah. His mind churned with what he had just done. Closure, of a kind, although it felt more like taking out the garbage than giving peace to the dead. Either way it was necessary work.

All part of the family business.

Benny and Nix followed the Lost Girl into the woods that surrounded the ranger station. She led them thirty yards up a crooked path that had been carved by rain runoff, making sure to step on rocks or fallen logs, leaving no footprints at all. Nix noticed that first and pointed it out to Benny, and they imitated her careful ways, though it meant that they went more slowly and with far less grace than the lithe Lilah.

Lilah suddenly stopped with her head cocked to listen.

"Hide!" she hissed with quiet urgency, and immediately she appeared to vanish into a tangle of wild roses. Nix pulled Benny down behind an ancient rhododendron, and they huddled together, trying to make themselves as small as rabbits.

"What is it?" Benny whispered, but Nix jabbed him in the ribs and pointed.

They had a good view of the open space at the base of the tower and the various game trails that crisscrossed in front of it. At first Benny didn't see anything, but then the tall grass in the clearing shifted and a man stepped very cautiously out of hiding.

Charlie Matthias.

Nix gave a sharp inward hiss and grabbed Benny's arm

with such force that he thought she'd break the bones. Her fingernails dug into his flesh, and from that point of contact he could feel a shudder of disgust and murderous fury wash through her. Here was the man who had killed her mother. With his other hand Benny reached for the pistol at his hip, but Lilah appeared out of nowhere and touched his arm. When he looked at her, she shook her head and nodded to the other side of the clearing. Three more men stepped into the sunlight. The Hammer and the Mekong brothers. All of them carried guns.

The men walked to the foot of the ranger tower, casting cautious looks at the surrounding woods and checking the ground for footprints. When they passed the spot where Lilah had led Nix and Benny into the woods, the men saw nothing to attract their attention.

At the base of the ladder, the Hammer cupped his hands around his mouth and gave a short, sharp whistle that sounded like a woodland bird. He waited for a few seconds, then made the call again. He turned to Charlie and shook his head.

"Go on up and see what's what," Charlie growled to Vin. His voice carried easily in the clear morning air.

"Yeah, maybe I'll find my lucky coin," Vin said as he turned toward the ladder, but Charlie grabbed him by the shoulder and spun him around.

"You have something to say, boy, you say it to my face."

Vin looked up at Charlie, and for a moment Benny thought that the smaller man was going to try something. He was holding his shotgun; he could have stepped back and brought the gun up into Charlie's face. One act of courage or pride, and the devil would be on his way down. Nix gripped Benny's wrist and gave it a pump, as if that would somehow encourage Vin to do the right thing.

In the end, however, Vin did the cowardly thing. He mumbled something and lowered both his eyes and his gun.

"Go about your business, then," Charlie said flatly. "Git your skinny butt up that ladder and see what those two morons are doing,"

Vin shot a quick look at Joey Duk, but he didn't let Charlie see his expression. He slung his shotgun across his back and began climbing as the other men trained their weapons on the catwalk. Vin went up carefully and slowly, and when his head and shoulders were just above the level of the platform, he froze. Benny could hear his curses floating through the trees.

"What is it?" demanded Charlie.

"You better get up here, boss."

With a growl, Charlie and the Hammer climbed to the catwalk while Joey remained at ground level to guard the ladder. Benny had to crab sideways a few yards to see the three men as they stood there, examining the bodies of their fallen comrades.

It was then that the reality of what he'd done hit Benny.

I killed a man.

Not a zombie . . . but a real, living human being.

He listened inside for his conscience to scream about the wrongness of it, but all he heard echoing through his internal darkness was the sound of Morgie's trembling voice back at Nix's house, and the sound of Tom's voice as he held Jessie Riley. And the sound of Nix's awful sobs last night. If his conscience had something to say about what he'd done, it didn't dare say it loud enough to be heard. And some other part of him wished that he'd driven that wooden spike into the big man with the pale skin and the one red eye, who stood with his fists on his hips thirty yards away. If only Tom had taught him how to shoot. But then, he reflected, he knew enough about handguns to understand that thirty yards was a long way for any kind of accuracy. Even if he emptied the entire magazine at the catwalk, he might not hit anyone and would, in turn, draw deadlier fire from their long guns. Charlie had a rifle slung on his back.

He bent close to Nix and Lilah, and mouthed the words: "Stay or go?"

Lilah made a palms-down gesture. Stay.

Charlie went to the rail of the catwalk and looked out over the mountain slope and the surrounding forest. He swept his eyes slowly from one side to the other, and for one chilling moment his gaze rested on the spot where Benny and the girls crouched. Could that evil red eye see them? Then the big man's gaze swept past.

The Hammer came and stood beside him. "This is a complete waste of time, Charlie. We need to get them kids and get ours asses over the hill."

"I don't like leaving it like this," growled Charlie. "Unfinished business is sloppy."

"Yeah, well, wasting time is wasting money," retorted the Hammer. "We already got us a round dozen for the games."

"What if the Imura pup gets back to town?"

The Hammer laughed at the idea. "There's an army of zoms between him and safe, Charlie. Best-case scenario for him is that he falls and breaks his neck before they get him."

"Worse-case scenario is that I pick up his trail," said Charlie.

"Truer words, brother," said the Hammer, slapping him on the back. "Truer words."

"Okay, let's roll. Houston John and Bull should be getting in tonight, and I want to be on the move at first light."

Charlie turned away, and they began climbing down, leaving the bodies of their friends behind, as if they weren't even worth the effort to bury. The men reached the ground and faded back into the tall grass. From their direction, Benny figured they were going back to the highway or to some spot near it, where their own trail would take them to their camp.

Benny turned to Nix and opened his mouth to speak, but Lilah put a finger to her lips and held it there for a long minute. Then she rose slowly from her crouch and searched the clearing and the woods beyond it. Finally the tension left her shoulders, and she turned to Benny and Nix.

"Thank you," he said to Lilah.

The Lost Girl looked momentarily confused, as if she didn't know how to respond to that.

Nix said, "How did you know that we needed help?"

Lilah's mouth worked as she tried to sort out how to answer, testing and tasting different words. For the second time Benny wondered how long it had been since she'd spoken with another human being.

"Follow," she began, then changed the word. "Follow-*ing*. Men. Following men?" She ended it as a question, hoping they understood.

"You were following the men?" Nix asked.

"Yes," she said. "Following *the* men. I was. Since, um . . . dark morning."

"Since dawn?"

"Dawn," Lilah agreed, smiling a little. "I was following the men since dawn."

"Why were you following them?" Benny asked.

Lilah thought about it. "You."

"Us?"

"Saw you. Last night. Saw you run from *them*. Walkers. Men. Heard shots. Followed. Heard you last night. Crying. Talking."

Benny cut a quick look at Nix, who avoided his eyes. Had this feral girl heard them kissing? Benny thought about it, then dismissed it. The kisses were hot, but they weren't loud. On the other hand, he mused, she could have stood on this very spot and *watched* them kiss. As he thought it, he realized that Nix had already reached that conclusion, hence her avoiding his eyes.

"Lilah . . . last night, when you heard us talking. Did you hear everything we said?"

She considered, shrugged . . . then nodded.

"Did you understand?"

That small smile flickered over her lips again. "I . . . understand. Just not . . ." She waved a hand back and forth between them.

"You're just not used to talking," Nix said. "Not used to conversation?"

"Conversation." Lilah repeated the word slowly, enjoying it.

Benny said, "We have to get out of here. We have to get

back to town. Do you know about town, about Mountainside? Where we live?"

"Know. Some. Not much."

"Can you take us there?" Nix asked.

"Can," Lilah said. "Won't."

Benny frowned. "You won't? How come?"

"Eat," she said, and when they didn't react, she looked irritated and mimed the action of picking up food and eating it. "Eat."

"Yes," Benny said, "I understand that we have to eat, but we also have to get home."

As soon as he said it, the reality of that word—"home"—hung in the air, filled with ugly images and new meanings.

"Home to what?" Nix asked, turning sharply to him. "Home to *who*?"

"I . . . ," he began, but clearly he had no idea of where to go with that thought. She was completely right. Home to who? Her mother was dead. So was Tom. Both of them had empty houses back in Mountainside. Empty houses and wrecked lives.

"Eat," Lilah said. "Eat first. Eat and think."

"Eat where? Here?"

Lilah shook her head. "Follow."

Without another word, Lilah turned and headed into the woods along a path that whipped and turned, snakelike as it cut around the shoulders of the mountain. Nix tried to talk to Lilah as they walked, but the Lost Girl shook her head and moved way out front, apparently liking to be in her own head when out in the wild.

Soon they heard the gurgle of water, and several times they glimpsed streams that cut downland toward Coldwater Creek. Seeing the streams was comforting, because Benny knew that he could use them to find the creek and from there, maybe find his way back to Mountainside. But just thinking of the creek reminded him of Tom.

Nix must have noticed a look on his face and asked him what was wrong.

"Thinking about Tom," Benny said.

She nodded. "I know. I'm sorry for what I said about him. Mom . . . Mom really cared for him. I think maybe she was a little bit in love with him."

"I think it went both ways, Nix." He gave a short, self-deprecating laugh. "I used to think I was a reasonably intelligent person. Not like Chong—"

"No one is," Nix said with a smile.

"And not like you."

She said nothing.

"But I'm not completely dense."

"Okay, but what's your point?"

"I . . . I never told anyone about this," Benny began, and then he told her about his memory of First Night, and of his mother in her white dress and red sleeves and screaming mouth. Of Tom taking him and running away. "It's the first thing I remember," Benny concluded, "and it's how I used to see Tom."

"As . . . what?" she asked, although Benny thought she'd already guessed where he was going with this.

"As a coward. I think he ran away."

"Maybe," she said. "Maybe your mom told him to get you to safety."

"She did. Tom told me that much, and I believe him, but he didn't go back for her. He didn't do *anything* to help her. All he did was run."

Nix was quiet as they climbed over some rocks. Lilah was almost a hundred yards up the trail and didn't show any sign of slowing down to let them catch up.

"Is she what you expected to find?" Nix asked, one eyebrow arched.

"Not even a little," Benny said. "She's pretty weird."

"She'd have to be," said Nix.

"Living out here? Fighting zoms and dodging guys like Charlie every day? Yeah, if it was me, I'd have gone buggy a long time ago."

Nix dropped down on the far side of the rocks and waited for Benny to scramble down. They moved along up the trail, side by side.

"The thing is," Benny said, "what if I was wrong about Tom all this time?"

"What makes you ask now?"

"Stuff that's happened. Seeing how he was out in the Ruin the first time he took me out here. He was smart and skillful. He knew things and could do things that I never knew about."

"That's true of most people until you get to know them," she said. "And sometimes even after you think you know them really well."

He nodded. "Then there's the way people talk about him. They act like he was all Joe Tough. I think the Hammer and Charlie were even a little scared of him outside of Mr. Sacchetto's house. Well . . . maybe the Hammer was scared, and Charlie was just cautious, but *why*? Tom wasn't big, and he wasn't strong like those two guys."

"My mom said she saw him fight once, but she would never tell me under what circumstances."

Benny guessed that Mrs. Riley had probably been referring to the time Tom rescued her from Gameland.

"Yeah, and I saw him face down Vin Trang and Joey Duk while all those zoms were closing in on us. Tom was figuring it out. Maybe he was stressed, but I kept looking for him to be afraid, because that's what I expected to see when the chips were down."

"But . . . ?"

"But all he did was fight. He died fighting."

"There's another thing," Nix said, her eyes sad. "Charlie and the Hammer went over to Mr. Sacchetto's and killed him. They broke into our house. But . . . they didn't attack Tom directly."

Benny sighed and trudged along beside her for a while, lost in a sick depression. "It sucks," he said eventually. "Tom died, thinking that his brother, the only relative he had left on Earth, thought he was a piece of crap coward." He shook his head. "But I stopped thinking that the first time he took me out here. I'd give a lot to change things between us."

Nix took his hand and squeezed it. There was a whole world full of things they both wished they could change.

THEY FOLLOWED LILAH THROUGH A FOREST OF ANCIENT OAKS THAT WAS SO lush that the canopy of leaves cast everything below into a twilight darkness. Morning mist clung to the mossy ground, and the trunks of the trees rose, like ghosts in the humid gloom. After only a few steps into this nightmare landscape, the wind settled and died, leaving behind a dreadful stillness.

It was Nix who first heard the moans of the dead.

"Wait!" she hissed, dropping into a crouch. "Zoms!"

Benny pulled the big hunting knife he'd taken from the dead bounty hunter.

The moan was a wordless cry of hunger that drifted to them through the pillars of oak trees, like the plaintive call of a wandering ghost.

"Where is it?" Nix whispered.

"There," said Benny, pointing. "I think it's coming from over there."

Lilah bent and ran quickly in that direction, her feet making no sound on the mossy ground, her body bent, spear ready.

"Um . . . Benny?" said Nix. "She's running *toward* the zombies."

Fifty yards up the trail, Lilah stopped and waved to them.

"And she wants us to follow."

"Oh crap."

"Well," said Nix, "she's your object of obsession."

"Very funny."

Reluctantly and slowly, they followed.

The closer they got, the louder was the moan of the zombie. It was different from other zom voices that Benny had heard, although he couldn't yet put his finger on what was different. Whatever it was, it made the hairs on his arms and the back of his neck stand up.

They reached Lilah, and together they crept around a bend in the path. A zombie stood right in front of them. He had once been a great brute of a man, and even withered and dead he had a massive chest and broad shoulders, and hands that looked big enough to snap Benny in half. He was wearing a mechanic's coveralls, and there was a line of gaping black bullet holes across his chest and stomach.

Nix yelped in fear. Benny cried out and brought up his knife, ready to make a fight of it. He crowded Nix backward, willing to sacrifice himself for her.

The moan of the zombie changed to a growl of immediate need, and his wrinkled lips curled away from rotted yellow teeth.

The forest around them erupted into a chorus of other hungry moans as an army of the undead began to howl for their flesh. Benny and Nix turned and saw that there were, indeed, hundreds of zombies—men and women, children and adults—and they were everywhere. Lilah had taken them the wrong way. Instead of leading them to safety, she'd stumbled into a terrible trap.

Lilah stood inches from the massive zombie. She turned to Benny and Nix . . . and laughed.

"What . . . ?" Nix said, blinking as if it was her eyes and not her mind that needed clearing.

"You bitch!" Benny snarled. "You betrayed us!"

THE MOANS OF THE DEAD FILLED THE ENTIRE FOREST.

Benny and Nix stood back-to-back. Without realizing it they had already passed dozens of the zoms as they followed Lilah into the woods, and looking back they could see them standing there, dead eyes turned their way.

Lilah put her hand on the center of the big zombie's chest.

The Lost Girl was still laughing. The big zombie tried to grab her, tried to bite her. But it couldn't do either.

"What . . . ?" Benny said softly. His mind was struggling to understand this moment.

And then he saw it.

The zombie was tied to the tree. A length of sturdy rope was wrapped around its waist, and shorter lengths anchored each hand. It could move its hands a few inches, but that's all.

Benny turned and saw that the zombie by the next closest tree was similarly bound. And the next.

"They're all . . . tied up," said Nix, turning in a slow circle.

It was true.

The forest was filled with hundreds upon hundreds of

zombies, and every one of them was tied to a tree. In some places three or four were tied to the trunks of massive oaks.

"I . . . don't understand," said Nix, but Benny did. He suddenly remembered something Tom had told him about Charlie rounding up zoms and tying them to trees, so that he could find them more easily if he got a bounty.

He knew where they were.

The Hungry Forest.

Nix wheeled on Lilah. "You think this is *funny*?"

Lilah's eyes twinkled. "Yes. Very funny. Your faces!" She laughed, and the sound of it drew another series of long moans from the dead.

"What *is* this place?" Nix demanded.

Benny told her. Lilah listened and nodded, and Nix looked horrified. Lilah pointed out a few trees where the ropes had been cut and the zoms taken.

"God . . . ," Nix said, "Charlie's *harvesting* them."

"Sometimes," Lilah said, "I come here. Cut some loose. Let them go."

"Why?"

"I do it when I think Charlie is coming."

"An ambush. Sweet," Benny said with a grin. "Sick and twisted . . . but sweet. Oh, and . . . sorry for calling you a bitch."

She shrugged. "Been called worse. Don't care much."

Nix could not take her eyes off of the legions of living dead. "How many of them are in here?"

Lilah considered, shrugged. "Three thousand. More."

"It's horrible."

Lilah shrugged again and turned to Benny. "You think it's horrible?"

"I'm not sure what I think about it," he said.

To Nix, Lilah said, "Two times I came here and let them go. Cut all ropes."

"Why?"

"To free them. They followed me to the field. By the water."

"Geez," Benny said, "those were the zoms we ran into by Coldwater Creek. You let them *go*?"

Lilah nodded. "Sometimes . . . seeing them. Tied. Makes me sad. I untie and lead them away."

"You lead them? How do you do that without getting chomped?" Benny asked.

She looked at him as if he was a moron. "They're slow. I'm not slow." Then she pinched the skin of her forearm. "They follow flesh."

Benny swallowed hard, trying to imagine a horde of zombies, shambling along after this beautiful and crazy Lost Girl.

Lilah looked up through a small opening in the canopy of leaves at the position of the sun. "Time to go."

With that, she turned and walked deeper into the Hungry Forest. Each zombie she passed craned its neck and tried to bite her, but the Lost Girl did not appear to notice. Or care.

Benny and Nix lingered a moment longer, caught up in all of the different ways in which this place was wrong. Whether the zoms were tied to the trees or taken for bounties or freed to wander, the horror of it was overwhelming.

The zombies closest to them moaned incessantly, biting the air, as if aching to feed on just the smell of living flesh.

"Your girlfriend is deranged," said Nix.

"She's not my girlfriend, thank you very much. And I believe Tom said the expression was 'touched by God.'"

"She's touched all right. Come on, this place is way beyond creepy. Let's get out of here, Benny," Nix said. "Right now."

"With you on that," he agreed, but as they hurried along the path to catch up, Benny kept looking back, compelled to lock this image in his mind. There was something about it that was starting to shove ideas around in his head. Weird and wicked ideas.

Nix caught the look on his face. "What is it?"

"Nothing," he lied. The thoughts running through his head were not thoughts he wanted to share with her. Not yet.

THEY CAME TO A SHELTERED CLEARING BY A ROCK CLIFF, THROUGH WHICH a million years of erosion had cut a waterfall that fed all the streams that ran down to Coldwater Creek. It was a strange place. The woods were overgrown with vines and scrub pines, the ground was covered with a thick carpet of pine needles. At the base of the cliff was a pool of threshing water that looked as clear as glass. However, all around the clearing, there were dead animals in various stages of decomposition. The stink was ungodly, and the air was thick with flies.

Nix gagged, and Benny dug the bottle of mint paste from his pocket, showing her how to dab it below her nose to kill the smell. As he did so, he marveled at the restraint with which she'd managed to put up with his smell since last night. He realized that his clothes were probably still ripe with the stench of cadaverine.

Lilah stood at the point where the path reached the clearing.

"Here," she said, pointing to the waterfall.

"What, through there?" Benny asked.

She nodded, then pointed to the open ground in front of them. "Feet where my feet go."

Benny didn't immediately understand what she meant, and when she set off across the clearing in a weird zigzag pattern, he started walking straight toward the cool water. Lilah turned abruptly. "Stop!"

She hurried back, following the same twisted route.

"Stupid?" she asked harshly, then knelt in front of him and dug her fingers under the covering of pine needles and lifted a section of ground that proved to be a very thin, woven screen with needles and other debris cleverly sewn onto it. Beneath the screen was a hole that was filled with the pointed ends of wickedly sharp sticks.

"Oh my God!" Benny said.

Nix gestured to the clearing. "Is the whole clearing like that?"

"Yes," said Lilah in her graveyard whisper of a voice. "So, watch my feet. Where I walk only. Yes?"

"Absolutely," agreed Benny weakly.

In single file they followed Lilah around the clearing toward the cliff wall. There was no way anyone could have picked out a safe route through without knowing exactly where to step. Benny was impressed.

Along the wall was a screen of bushy pine trees, and it wasn't until they'd all reached them that Benny and Nix could see that there was a narrow path behind them, which led to a depression behind the waterfall. The water cascaded out and away from the wall, and there was a cave mouth five feet high and seven feet wide. The whole mouth of the cave was covered with multiple sheets of heavy industrial plastic that Lilah had scavenged from somewhere. She pushed through, and they followed her into a short, damp chamber. Another set of plastic was hung ten feet in, and behind that was a thick layer of heavy drapes. Benny was blown away by how smart this was. The plastic kept the water out and the drapes kept light in, and together they muffled the roar of the waterfall. Lilah went in first and Benny followed, with Nix holding the drapes open to allow diffused light in. Lilah apparently didn't need it, because she went into the darkest depths of the cave, and soon there was the scrape and smell of a sulfur match. Lilah lit an oil lantern, and a comfortable yellow glow expanded out to fill the huge inner chamber.

Benny and Nix were speechless. The cave was a treasure trove. There was a comfortable chair and a small table, a wire rack of dishes, barrels filled with canned food, some old toys, and books. Thousands and thousands of books. Technical manuals and novels, anthologies of short stories and collections of poetry, biographies of great thinkers and joke books, magazines and comic books. There were stacks of books on every surface, heaped against the walls. Even in the town library, Benny had never seen so many books. Nix looked dazed, her mouth open in a silent "oh."

Lilah looked from them to the books and back again. "I read," she said simply.

Then Benny noticed the second thing that Lilah had been collecting. There was a table made from boards stretched across stacks of heavy encyclopedias, and the table bent under the weight of weapons. Handguns and boxes of bullets, knives and clubs, spears and axes. Enough weapons to start—and win—a war. Benny realized Lilah was doing exactly that—fighting a war. He walked over to the table, aware the Lilah was watching him, and saw that a how-to manual for making bullet reloads was open and looked well-thumbed. There were coffee cans filled with lead pellets and gunpowder, and a bullet mold with castings for various calibers. Several men in town had similar setups.

"This is amazing," he said.

She shrugged. It was commonplace to her. It was her day-to-day life.

Lilah folded some blankets and set them on the floor, then indicated that they could sit down while she started a fire in a small stone cooking pit. Benny noticed that the smoke funneled upward instead of filling the cave, and he bent forward to see that there was a hole in the ceiling. No daylight showed through, so he figured it didn't rise straight up, but instead filtered out through various fissures in the rock. He thought that Tom would approve.

Benny watched Lilah as she busied herself with what probably passed for her daily routine. Her first concern was security, and she checked the hang of the drapes to prevent any trace of light from showing through. Even a pinpoint of firelight would be visible for miles in the absolute darkness of these mountains at night. Then Lilah strung two lines across the entrance. The first was a length of twine on which dozens of empty tin cans and pieces of broken metal were strung. When it was in place, it lay against the drapes. If anyone moved the cloth, the metal would kick up a jangling din, loud enough to wake her. The second line was a length of silver wire she positioned at mid-shin level. It was virtually invisible in the gloom, but once someone passed the drapes, they would trip over it. Between the noise and this delaying trick, whoever broke in would not be sneaking up on a sleeping girl, but would be sprawled on the ground while a practiced killer hunted *them* in the dark.

"Did you ever have to use that trip wire?" he asked. He and Nix and their friends had learned all about simple booby traps in the Scouts. They were great for slowing down a zombie attack.

Lilah tested the tension on the trip wire, plucking it like a guitar string, so that it hummed. "Once," she said. "It worked."

"Zom or human?" asked Nix.

Lilah shrugged. "What does it matter?"

Once the entrance was rigged, she unbuckled her gun belt and placed it next to the pallet she used as a bed. She put the spear into an old umbrella stand in which there were various clubs, baseball bats, hockey sticks, and a long-handled axe.

"Lilah," said Nix. "This place—all these things—it's incredible. You brought all of this here by yourself?"

Lilah poured water into a cooking pot and began adding bits of meat and vegetables. "By myself. Who else?"

"How many of these books have you read?"

"All." She smiled for the first time since they'd started walking. She leaned over and began stirring the mixture in the pot. "I . . . read, um, better than talk. Sorry."

"Sorry?" said Benny enthusiastically. "Lilah, you're amazing! Isn't she amazing, Nix?"

Benny, caught up in the moment, turned to Nix, but her expression was a few hundred degrees colder than his. Benny's common sense took a giant step back for an emergency re-evaluation of everything that had happened in the last few seconds. Lilah, lit by the soft glow of the cook fire, was bending over and smiling. The inadequate rags of her shirt were doing even less of their job. Benny, who, to his credit, hadn't even been *aware* of all this, was suddenly very aware—and aware of the fact that Nix was watching both of them. The common sense part of him slapped his forehead and prayed for an earthquake or a timely invasion by a horde of zoms. Benny tried to salvage the moment by stretching his last question into a longer one. ". . . to have read so many books."

As lame attempts go, this one was barely able to limp.

The grin he gave Nix was intended to be earnest, scholarly, and totally oblivious to the miles of cleavage Lilah was showing. Nix's smile was chilly enough to kill houseplants.

And Chong fries Morgie for being thick, Benny thought, feeling the edges of his smile begin to crack.

To Lilah, Nix said, "George taught you to read?"

Lilah, who was unpracticed enough with people to misread the moment, nodded and sat back. "Yes. We had to read. All the time. 'Knowledge is power,'" she recited in a voice that was clearly an attempt to imitate George's.

They nodded. Benny took the opportunity to ask her some questions. "Lilah, have you been alone all this time? I mean . . . since Gameland?"

She nodded. "Alone."

"How did you survive?" asked Nix.

Lilah turned cold eyes on her. "What I see," she said, "I kill."

"God," said Nix.

Benny said, "What about the way-station monks? Do they help you at all?"

"Monks . . . We don't talk. They have their, um, things. I have mine."

"Tom said he saw you twice."

"Tom," she said, and shook her head.

"He looked like me. But he was older. Darker hair, darker skin. Tall. Carried a sword."

The Lost Girl brightened and smiled in a way that Benny thought it showed she not only knew who Tom was but maybe betrayed something more than simple recognition.

"Sword man," Lilah said. "Very, um, pretty." She looked at Nix for approval. "Pretty?"

"Handsome," Nix said. "Hot."

Lilah liked that word. "Hot." She turned to Benny. "But . . . dead?"

He nodded. "The Hammer shot him, and he fell into a bunch of zoms."

Her smiled vanished. "Then he's a walker."

Benny couldn't bear to think about that and changed the subject. "Lilah, Tom said that you could tell people where the new Gameland is."

"What people?"

"People in our town. In Mountainside."

She shrugged. "Why?"

"I think he was hoping to have Charlie arrested. Do you understand what that means? Arrested?"

"Read about. Old world stuff. Not our world."

"No," said Nix bitterly. She touched Lilah's arm. "Tell us, though. What happened after they took you and Annie away from George?"

"George," she said in a small, sad voice that was an echo

of the child she had once been and would never be again. She sorted through her conflicted emotions and jumbled thoughts. "They hit George. Killed him, I thought. But . . . not?"

"No," said Benny. "He was hurt, but he lived. As soon as he woke up, he started looking for you and your sister. He met Tom, and they looked together. They couldn't find you. I guess George didn't know where to look. How far is Gameland from here?"

"Far. Three days fast walk. Two mountains from here," said Lilah. "Have to know how to, um . . . *find* it. Hard to find."

"George never found it. All he heard were rumors of what goes on there. It tore him up."

It took Lilah a second to understand that last comment, then she nodded. "George loved us. Loved him. He is . . . dead?"

"I think so. A monk told Tom that George hung himself."

Lilah barked out a harsh laugh and shook her head. "No," she said decisively.

"Tom didn't believe it, either."

They sat for a minute in silence.

"He was murdered," Nix said eventually. "Do think it was Charlie?"

"Or one of his creeps," said Benny. Lilah's lip curled, but she said nothing.

"Lilah . . . tell us about Annie."

"Annie." Lilah's eyes were as hard as knife steel, but they glistened wetly. "They took us. Lots of girls at Gameland. Boys too. They . . . make us *fight*." She loaded that last word with enough venom to kill a hundred men.

"Did they make *you* fight?" Nix asked, and Benny winced, not wanting to hear the answer.

But Lilah shook her head. "Tried. Many times they tried. Fought them instead. Bit. Kicked. Thumbs to eyes. George taught me. Taught Annie." She made a fist so tight, her knuckles creaked, and the lights in her eyes looked both dangerous and a little crazy. "Be tough, George said. Be tough and live. George always said that."

"George was right," Benny said. "I wish I'd met him. He sounds like a pretty great guy."

Lilah gave Benny a slow up-and-down appraisal, perhaps re-evaluating him. Or maybe seeing him for the first time and *getting* who he was. She nodded, although Benny wasn't sure if that was an agreement with what he'd said or a confirmation of some unspoken thought.

"So you fought?" Nix said, perhaps a little more sharply than was absolutely necessary.

Lilah's eyes lingered on Benny as she said, "Yes."

"What did *they* do?" Nix asked, and this time there was more compassion in her voice.

"They beat me." Lilah shrugged as if that was nothing, as if measured against all that she had endured, it was a small thing. Nix paled and Benny shivered. "Beat me a lot. No food."

Nix cursed.

Lilah gave another shrug. "Made me tougher. Made me mad. Mad enough."

"And Annie?"

"She . . . ran."

They looked at her and saw a tear break from the corner

of one hazel eye and roll down her tanned cheek. It glistened like a diamond in the lantern light.

"Ran?"

"Fought and ran. Stormy night, lots of rain. Annie ran, the ugly man chased her. Hammer. He chased. Annie tripped. Slipped on mud. She fell. Badly. Hit her head on a stone."

"No . . ."

"I couldn't do . . . anything." Lilah shook her head in denial of the memory. "They left her there. Like trash out in the rain. Like she was nothing. I was already out of there, escaped two days before, but came back. Sneaky, quiet. To get Annie. But . . . when I found her, Annie was gone. Already gone. Then she . . . came back."

"Oh God, no . . ."

"Tried to bite."

More tears fell from Lilah's eyes. It was all that Lilah would say on the subject. Nix asked her what she'd done with her sister, but Lilah just shook her head. Benny matched this against what Tom had told him, of the man Lilah has been trying to kill over and over again. The Motor City Hammer. All these long, frustrating years, Lilah had been killing the image of the Hammer in the hopes that one day she'd get him within range to take revenge for what had been done to her and her little sister.

"I'm sorry," said Nix.

Lilah turned to her, eyes cold, voice frosty. "Sorry? Does that bring Annie back?"

"Well, no, but I—"

"Save words like 'sorry.' Save for the dead. Living don't need them."

She snatched up her spoon and forcefully stirred the stew, slopping some bits into the fire. Benny reached out and took Nix's hand.

"How can the world be this cruel?" Nix asked quietly.

There was no chance that Benny could answer that question, but there was something about the warmth and reality of the hand he held in his that made an argument that cruelty wasn't the only force at work in their world.

Nix said, "Lilah, will you come back to town with us?"

The Lost Girl looked up. "Why?"

"So you'll be safe," said Nix.

"Safe now."

"It's safer in town," Nix said, but Lilah laughed.

"Charlie and the Hammer killed your mother in your town." She pointed to Benny. "Killed his brother out here. Nowhere is safe."

Before Benny or Nix could reply to that, Lilah added, "Out here—*I kill*. Walkers, bad men. I kill and I live. I'm safe here."

That put an end to the conversation until after the stew was cooked. She dished out food, and Benny had to use real effort to maintain a straight face, because the one thing this wild girl could *not* do was cook. The stew tasted like hot sewage. He noticed that Nix was pretending to enjoy it while not actually eating much.

"Lilah," Benny said, "Charlie Pink-eye's camp is up here, right? On the other side of the mountain?"

Lilah nodded.

"Nix, you heard him," Benny said. "He has kids up there, right?"

"Yes," Nix said with a shudder. "They're taking them to

Gameland. It's where they were going to take me."

"Gameland," Lilah said, and she bared her teeth like a hunting cat. Her fist knotted around her fork until the tendons in her hand were as taut as fiddle strings. "Annie."

"Gameland," repeated Nix in a sick, flat voice.

"Charlie and the Hammer have destroyed all of our families. They're worse than any zom out here in the Ruin. They're worse than a world of zoms. At least the zoms don't know that what they're doing is wrong. Charlie and the Hammer do. They're evil."

"Evil," Lilah said, and the Nix echoed the word.

"Where are you going with this, Benny?" Nix asked.

He set down his dish and leaned his elbows on his knees. "Look," he said, "I'm nobody's idea of a hero, but I don't think I want to go back to town just yet. In fact, I don't think I *can* go back to town, knowing that those other kids are up there."

"What are you suggesting?" asked Nix. "That we march into his camp and ask him to release those kids?"

"I don't know, but we have to do *something*," said Benny. He jumped to his feet in agitation and began walking back and forth as he spoke. "I can't just go on with my life, knowing that they're out there and that they're going to just go on destroying other families and other lives without anyone even *trying* to stop them. Tom said that before First Night, people wouldn't do anything. They'd let families live on the street and starve. I *can't*. That's not the kind of world I want to live in."

"But the camp," said Lilah. "Too many men."

"How many?"

She thought about it. "Maybe twelve. Maybe twenty."

"Too many of them, but—," began Nix.

"Not enough of us," said Lilah, finishing the thought.

Benny suddenly straightened. "Wait, wait . . . Let me think for a second. Lilah, you said it. There's not enough of us. Right . . . riiiight . . ." He trailed off and looked at the rocky ceiling, as if he could see out of the cave and through the mountain and all the way to Charlie's camp. An idea was forming in his head. But the idea was insane and stupid. It was absurd and impossible.

"What is it?" asked Nix.

"Hm?" he said distractedly.

"Why are you smiling?"

He hadn't realized that he was, and he certainly had no reason to smile. The idea that had started to take form in his head wasn't funny. It was suicidal.

"Okay," he said, his eyes brighter than the lamplight. "I have an idea, but you won't like it."

"Tell," insisted the Lost Girl.

"For this to work," said Benny, "we'll need to create a diversion and then get the kids out."

"What kind of diversion? The guys are used to being out here. They're always on guard. Whatever we do, they'll see it coming."

Benny Imura gave the girls a very strange, very dark grin. "No," he said, "I can guarantee you they won't see *this* coming."

And he told them what that was.

Lilah and Nix stared at Benny in total silence for more than two minutes. The stew in the pot began to bubble and burn; the waterfall roared softly in the background. Somewhere deep in the cave, water dripped with the constant rhythm of a metronome. Benny stood there and waited out the silence.

"You are crazy," said Lilah.

"Probably," said Benny.

"Are you serious?" asked Nix.

"As a heart attack," said Benny.

Lilah took the burning stew off the fire and set it on the rocks. She leaned toward Nix. "Is he . . . damaged?" She touched her head to indicate where the suspected damage might lie. Nix held one hand up and seesawed it back and forth.

"Opinions vary," she said.

"It *could* work," said Benny.

"We could die, Benny," Nix said.

"We could," admitted Benny. "Maybe we will."

"Maybe not," said Lilah, and they both looked at her. A crooked smile had worked its way onto her lips, and she appeared to be re-evaluating his plan.

"Maybe not," repeated Benny.

Nix ran her fingers through the red tangles of her hair. "Maybe not," she agreed eventually, although with far less conviction.

The shadows made the cave seem as vast as outer space.

"You do understand that this plan is crazy," Nix said.

"Yes," said Lilah, tapping her skull again. "Very crazy."

"No doubt." Benny nodded. "But it's also *justice*."

Nix snorted. "Justice is dead."

Benny broke out into another twisted grin. "It sure as hell is."

The Lost Girl turned to him, and her smile was every bit as big and bright and dark as his.

It took Nix another few seconds, but then the crazy sense of it took hold in the cracks that had been torn in her heart by Charlie Pink-eye and the Motor City Hammer. Then she too smiled.

Anyone seeing those three teenagers smiling the kinds of smiles they wore would run in terror.

Benny was counting on it.

48

ONCE THE IDEA WAS OUT, THEY TACKLED IT AND WRESTLED IT AND BANGED it into a weird shape. It became immediately clear that they had to move fast and start at once. Lilah's trove of weapons and equipment provided them with everything they needed. As they sorted through the supplies, Lilah never took her eyes off Benny, and he was uncomfortably aware of it. Just as he was aware that Nix never took her eyes off Lilah, and Benny wondered if Nix was trying to telepathically transmit some message. If so, Lilah was either immune to the nuclear radiation of Nix's thoughts, or didn't care. Or maybe having lived alone for so long—and all through puberty—she had no clear understanding of what she was feeling, what signals she was sending, and the complexities of social interaction. Benny wished Chong was here to explain it to him.

When they were done gathering the equipment, Lilah led them out of the cave and through her maze of booby traps, then back directly into the forest. She moved fast, selecting paths that were secret as well as efficient. They struggled to keep up as they crossed running water, climbed rocky outcrops, crawled through thorny thickets, and ran along game trails through dappled sunlight. The day felt like the hottest of the whole summer, and sweat poured out of them, but none of them cared. Having a purpose put iron in their limbs; knowing there was a chance to get revenge against Charlie ignited fires in their chests that burned hotter than the sun.

The bounty hunters' camp was on the far side of the mountain, and it took them almost two hours to reach it. Lilah guided them to a rocky promontory that was overgrown with white sage. They flattened out on the edge of the narrow cliff and pulled foliage over themselves. The camp looked strangely exposed, with paths leading up through forestland to a plateau as flat as a tabletop. Three traders wagons were positioned to block each path, their sides reinforced with sheet metal. The teams of horses were corralled in the center of the camp, each of them wearing a carpet coat, even in the afternoon heat. Without saying a word, Lilah slowly pointed out each guard and the other men wandering around the camp.

Nix cursed very quietly under her breath. There were twenty-three men in the camp. She glanced at Benny, but he kept his jaw set, so she didn't see the new fear that was making his heart jump around in his chest. The resolve he'd had back in the cave—one part bravery, one part need for revenge, and a couple parts craziness—felt suddenly brittle.

He had not expected there to be so many. Then his roving eyes found the pen where they were holding the kids. It was a pen, too, the kind used for keeping pigs. Two guards stood watch over the captives, and through the shimmering heat haze, it took Benny a couple of tries to count them all. There weren't a dozen kids. There were nineteen of them. Other bounty hunters must have joined the camp in the last few hours, which would account for the higher number of guards and captives.

Nineteen kids. Five boys, fourteen girls. The oldest looked to be twelve, the youngest about eight. They were all hunkered down, tied together by ropes that were attached to metal rings in the leather collars each of them wore.

Any doubts Benny had when he'd first looked down at the camp withered and died at the sight of those kids huddled like animals in the pen. If Nix hadn't escaped, she'd be collared and penned with the rest. He knew that Lilah had already been through that hell.

He saw Charlie Pink-eye walk across the center of the camp, and Benny pointed a finger at him, tracking the big bounty hunter, as if he was looking down the barrel of a hunting rifle. If wishes were bullets, Charlie would be sprawled dead in the dirt.

Careful not to make the slightest sound, they crawled back from the edge of the plateau and huddled together under a willow.

"Harder," Lilah said. "More than I thought."

"More kids, too. Nineteen."

Benny cleared a space on the ground and, taking a small stick, began drawing a map of the camp. The others helped, making additions and corrections. Benny asked Lilah to mark where the landmarks were: Coldwater Creek, the blocked highway, the ranger station, and other places that had factored into recent events. Benny studied the map for a long time in silence. He rolled over onto his back and marked the position of the sun. In the Scouts, Mr. Feeney had taught them how to tell the time of day by using the sun, and Benny had a rough guess as to when it would set.

"Okay, we have about five hours until twilight," he whispered.

"Less," said Lilah, and jerked a thumb over her shoulder. They looked to where she was pointing and saw a line of heavy clouds.

"Rain?" asked Nix. "Will that help or hurt us?"

"Rain is bad," said Lilah. "Can't hear, can't see."

"Neither can they," said Benny. "If it rains, we deal with it. We'll find a way to make it work for us."

Lilah took a last look over the edge. "Need go. Much . . . to . . ." She stopped, and Benny could see her working something out, then she said, very slowly, "I need to go, now. I have much to do." She almost blushed. "I don't . . . think . . . the same way I read. It is . . . harder to put thoughts . . . into sentences."

"You're doing better than I would have if I lived alone all this time," said Nix. "And you're doing better than Benny does now."

"Hey!" said Benny, but he was grinning.

"It's strange," said Lilah. "I never thought I would . . . *want* to talk. To people. I just talk to Annie and George. In my head."

For the first time since they'd met the Lost Girl, Benny felt that a window had opened into who she was. It was only open a crack, but he thought he caught a glimpse of the stark loneliness and sadness that defined her interior life, just as the weapons and quick actions defined her exterior world.

"Lilah," he said, "when this is all over . . ."

"Yes?"

"I'd like to go on knowing you. I'd like us to be friends." He cut a look at Nix, who was listening intently. "You, me, Nix. And our other friends. Morgie Mitchell and Lou Chong."

"'Friends,'" Lilah echoed, as if it was a word she'd never encountered in any of her reading. "Why?"

Benny opened his mouth to speak, but it was Nix who answered. "Because after all of this, after everything that's happened to us, Lilah . . . We're already family."

It wasn't exactly what Benny was going to say, but what she said was right. He nodded. The Lost Girl considered it for a while, then said, "Let's talk about that tomorrow."

"Okay," said Nix, "I'd like—"

"If there is one." She turned away and checked her weapons as she prepared to depart.

"Lilah," said Benny, "are you sure you can do this?"

Instead of a smile or some reassuring comment, Lilah simply said, "Have to try." Then she paused and looked Benny straight in the eye. "Why?"

"Why . . . *what*?"

"You could go back. To your town. You and Nix. These people"—she waved a hand in the direction of the kids in the pen—"aren't yours. So . . . why?"

Benny didn't have a ready answer for that. There had not been time to explore his own feelings about everything that had happened or was still happening. He would liked to have made a bold speech about honor and dignity, or fired off a remark of the kind that would be quoted by future generations. All he managed was: "If we don't do something to stop this, who will?"

Lilah considered him, her hazel eyes seeming to open

doors into his thoughts. She must have seen something that she liked, or perhaps it was the simple honesty of his words, because she nodded gravely.

"Have to try," she said.

"Have to try," Benny said, nodding. "For Tom, for Nix's mom . . . for Annie."

Lilah closed her eyes for a moment, nodding silently to herself. Then, without another word, she turned and slipped like a promise into the shadows under the trees.

Benny and Nix climbed down from the plateau and found a dark and sheltered spot under a row of thick pines. Their part would not start for hours.

Overhead a lone buzzard drifted on the thermals.

Benny held his hand out to Nix, and she came and sat next to him. They drank from Benny's canteen and ate some of the dried meat Lilah had given them. It was only marginally less disgusting than her stew, but they were hungry and eating gave them something to do. They said nothing for almost an hour. Benny spent much of that time reviewing the plan and looking for holes. There were plenty to be found. In fact, there were more ways the plan could go wrong than go right.

"Life's weird," Benny said.

"Thank you, Captain Obvious."

"No . . . It's just that two weeks ago the worst thing I had to worry about was finding a job before they cut my rations. All summer long the bunch of us—you, me, Chong, and Morgie—all we did was goof off, hang out, and laugh. We used to laugh a lot, Nix. Life used to be fun."

She nodded sadly.

"I have to believe," Benny continued, "that we'll get through this. Not just this stuff tonight, but all of it."

"Get through it for what reason? Nothing seems to matter anymore."

"That's just it, Nix. I can't let myself believe that nothing matters. *You* matter. We matter. We both need to believe that we'll get past this. That we'll be able to laugh again. That we'll want to."

She shook her head. "I don't know. I can't imagine that right now."

He had no comeback to that. Her argument was too strong, and his was based only on wishful thinking and a threadbare piece of optimism.

They sat together and listened to the forest.

"Benny?" Nix asked quietly after a while.

"Yeah?"

"Last night . . . when you kissed me . . . ?"

His throat went instantly dry. "Yeah?"

"Why did you do it? I mean, was it because I was so upset and you didn't know how else to help me? Or was it because you really wanted to?"

"I—"

"You don't have to answer if you don't want to."

He took a breath. "I kissed you because I wanted to," he said.

She nodded. "Last night, when you thought I was sleeping . . . I saw you looking at her card."

Benny plucked a stem of grass and ran it slowly between his fingers. It felt like cool silk. "Did you?" he asked.

"I saw you throw it away, too."

"Did you?" he asked again softly.

"Yes, Benny . . . I did."

She didn't say anything else, didn't speak another word for a long time. She leaned her head on his shoulder, and they sat there and waited for the day to burn away.

By late afternoon the sun was completely covered by a sheet of thick gray clouds. The temperature fell, but the humidity thickened the air to a hot soup. Benny drowsed against the trunk of one of the pines, and in his dreams he heard a sound that was like the roar of Lilah's waterfall. The sound started small and far away, and Benny's dreaming mind made it *be* the noise of the waterfall, which was a perfect backdrop for his dream of running through the woods, being chased by Charlie and the Hammer, both of who were now zoms but who also somehow managed to keep their personalities. They yelled to him in mocking voices, calling him "Little Benny" and promising to do terrible things to him. In his dream Benny ran as fast as the wind, and somehow the surrounding landscape barely moved, as if he was almost running in place. The zombie bounty hunters shuffled along behind him, almost close enough to grab him.

The roaring sound grew steadily louder, and Benny thought that maybe he was making some distance, that he was nearing the waterfall, but when he looked around, all he saw was the plateau on which the bounty hunters had their camp. Something brushed him, and he turned to see that

Nix was running next to him. She was screaming, but Benny could not hear her voice. The roar of the waterfall kept getting louder and louder. And it was deeper in tone now, more of a loud drone than the splash of water.

"Benny!" Nix called his name, but it didn't match the shape her mouth made.

The roar was huge.

"BENNY!"

With a start, Benny realized that Nix's voice was not coming from the girl running beside him, and just as quickly he understood that he was dreaming and that the real-world Nix was yelling at him. He snapped his eyes open. The camp and the zombies vanished. The roar, however, was still there. Deep and loud, and getting louder.

"Benny!" Nix yelled.

"What . . . what is it?"

"You have to come and look!"

Nix grabbed his hands and fairly hauled him to his feet and then pulled him out from under the shelter of the trees. Not toward the promontory that looked down on the camp. Instead, she pulled him toward the trail that led back into the woods. She was running, and her grip was so tight and insistent that Benny ran too.

"What is it? What's that sound?"

"You have to come *see*!"

They raced along the path to a clearing, and there, Nix stopped and pointed. She need not have bothered, because Benny saw it. His eyes bugged wide, and his mouth fell open as he stared up at the roaring thing.

It was silver and white, with vast wings that lifted it high above the mountains. Benny raised his hand, as if he could touch it. The thing appeared to move slowly, but that was an illusion. It was just so far away. Higher than the tallest of the surrounding mountains, skimming just below the ceiling of gray storm clouds. In another hour there wouldn't have been enough light to see it. If the storm had started, it would have been both invisible and unheard.

But they stood there, holding hands, staring up as it roared above them, soaring with alien majesty from one horizon to the other. Coming from the west, heading east; far, far above the Rot and Ruin.

"I don't understand," he said.

Nix just shook her head.

"Where did it come from?"

"From the east."

"No, it's heading east," he said, but Nix shook her head.

"It came from the east and turned around. I saw it and ran to get you."

They watched it go, diminishing in size from a giant to a gnat and then to nothing, taking its roar with it. When it was gone, there was at least five minutes of silence before the birds began to sing again. They stood in the clearing for ten minutes more, hoping it would come back. *Willing* it to come back.

Benny said, "Nix . . . did we just see that? I mean, tell me we actually saw that."

Nix's green eyes were filled with magic, and her smile was bright enough to hold back the storm. "It's real, Benny. We saw it."

"But *how*? It doesn't make sense."

She shook her head, and they stared off to the east. The thing they had just seen belonged to another age, to the days before First Night. They knew about them from the history books, but neither had ever seen one. Never expected to. They kept looking into the distance.

But the slow, lumbering jumbo jet did not return.

THEY DID NOT KNOW HOW TO TALK ABOUT WHAT THEY HAD JUST SEEN. It was strange and wonderful, but it seemed more like a dream than a part of what they were about to do.

"I wish I could tell Tom," Benny said.

"I wish I could tell Mom," said Nix, then she said, "Benny, if we get out of this—"

"*When* we get out of this," he corrected.

She gave only a tiny nod to acknowledge that possibility. "After this is over," she said, "we need to find out about that jet."

"Sure, I mean we let everyone know—"

"No," she said firmly. "*We* have to find out about it. Lilah was right. We don't have a home anymore. We've been—I don't know how to say it. Cut loose? We're no longer connected to anything, and certainly not to Mountainside."

"There's Morgie and Chong."

She shrugged. "If you want, we can go back for them, Benny. But then I want to follow that plane."

"Where? All we know is that it went east."

"It came from the east and turned around and went back.

Why? Was it exploring to see what was out here? Or was it sending a message."

"What message?"

"'Follow me'?" she suggested. "I don't believe in much anymore, Benny . . . but I believe that was a sign."

"And if it's not?"

"Then I'll find that out. One way or another, Benny, my life is over in Mountainside."

He thought about it and looked up at the cloud-covered eastern sky. "Yeah," he said after some long thought. "Maybe."

"That's what I'm going to do, Benny. If I'm alive tomorrow, then I'm going east."

"We don't know that there's anything out there but three hundred million zoms."

"Sure. Three hundred million zoms and enough people to repair, fuel, and fly an airplane. A jet. That says something. That says a lot."

The storm clouds pulsed with lightning.

"If you're going east," he said, "then so am I."

They sealed the deal with a kiss.

Two hours later the storm roiled and boiled above them, and Benny knew that this one was going to be every bit as bad as the one that had pounded the town two nights ago.

God, he thought, *was it only two nights ago?*

In less than two hours the clouds went from white to slate gray to bruised purple to midnight black, and fierce winds from the lowlands snatched up leaves and branches and desert dust and used them like artillery. The rain had not yet started to fall, but the humidity made Benny and Nix feel like they were underwater as they climbed down from the promontory and began sneaking toward the camp. Lilah was nowhere to be seen, nor had they had a sign of her in hours. Had she succeeded or had Benny sent her to her death with his harebrained plan?

The wind howled through the trees, like a host of banshees. Benny had never heard anything like it, and despite everything, there was some weird little part of him that liked it. It wasn't "cool"—He'd cut off his leg before he used that word again. No, it was, in its own raw and primal way, magnificent. Nature screaming in anger, and Benny could not help but believe that it was screaming in anger against all that had been done by the men in this camp. Maybe some of those whistling shrieks were in support of what three kids—a red-haired beauty of a sun-freckled girl, a wild hazel-eyed man-killer, and a moody and battered boy who had no right trying to be a hero—were trying to do.

As they crawled through the foliage, Benny kept grinning. Nix looked at him and shook her head. *That's okay*, he thought, *she already thinks I'm crazy*.

Charlie Matthias whipped open the flap of his tent, and the wind nearly knocked him over. He tilted into the gale and grabbed a sapling for support. All around him debris was flying. A cooking pot sailed past him, and he was pelted by acorns and pinecones. Using one massive hand to shield his eyes, he roared orders to his men to secure their gear.

He pointed at the pigpen, where the kids huddled in terror. "Joey! Get over there and see to the merchandise!"

On the far side of the camp, Joey Duk climbed out of his

tent and bent into the wild rain to comply. He climbed over the rail of the pen and pushed through the kids. All of their collar ropes were bundled together in one central point, and that was wound around the trunk of a small tree, but the tree was whipping back and forth with each gust. Joey lashed the lines tighter and shifted the central line lower to make use of the thicker base of the tree.

Benny and Nix watched from thirty feet away. They were in shadows and hidden behind a cracked boulder. Benny pointed to the tent Joey had come out of. Every time the wind blew, the flap opened, and they could see part of Vin Trang's face.

"That's it," Benny said in an urgent whisper. "That's how we're going to create part one of our diversion." He quickly told Nix what he had in mind.

"How are you going to get past Vin?"

"I'll think of something."

"Okay, but we also have to get Charlie and the Hammer away from the pen," said Nix, her mouth right against his ear, so that he could hear through the storm.

He nodded. The storm was complicating things. Half an hour ago most of the men were in their tents; now everybody was running around. He grumbled about it, but Nix shook her head. "Maybe Vin will come out of his tent too."

"Yeah. Maybe."

"Where's Lilah? Shouldn't she be back by now?"

"Give her time," said Benny, but in truth he was starting to worry. Lilah *should* have been back twenty minutes ago. He began to get a sinking feeling about whether she would be coming back at all.

The wind began to slacken, and they looked up to see that the dense black cloud cover was now a swirling gray blue.

"Oh come *on,* man," Benny said despairingly. "Can you try and cut us one frigging break? I mean, really . . . just *one*?"

A fat raindrop splatted him right in the eye.

Just the one.

Benny quietly cursed as he wiped his eye clear. He and Nix turned and looked at the camp. The bounty hunters were laughing now, bending to pick up their scattered possessions, making rude jokes about Mother Nature. The kids in the pen cringed together. Benny leaned as far forward as he could, almost coming out of the shadows, trying to get a handle on their next move.

On the outside edge of the huddle, the oldest of them, a girl of about twelve, knelt with her arms around the shoulders of the smallest. Her face was streaked with tears, but she spoke soothing words to the others, keeping up a steady patter, reassuring them, calming them. Then she raised her head and looked straight into Benny's eyes. From her kneeling position she had an angle between the rocks that the others in the camp did not have. Only she could see Benny as he crouched behind the cracked boulder. Her eyes widened, and she opened her mouth to say something to the others, but Benny quickly put a finger to his lips and shook his head.

The girl closed her mouth. Benny held up a finger and mouthed the words: "Be ready!"

He could see her lips move as she read his words. She

gave a quick nod, and then the girl did something that she probably never thought she'd do again in this life: She smiled.

A second later the rain began to fall.

Five seconds later the vault of the heavens opened up and dumped an ocean on the mountain.

"Perfect," Benny said. He said it aloud, at normal level, but it didn't matter. The rain was falling so hard that not even Nix heard him, and she was standing right next to him.

51

Benny pulled Nix closer and spoke quickly in her ear.

"We can't wait any longer," he yelled. "I don't think Lilah's coming back."

"Don't say that."

"Okay . . . but she's not here now, so we're on our own. I have an idea. Here's what I need you to do. . . ."

The rain was hard and steady, but the sky above was still not as dark as Benny would have liked. He had no idea how long this downpour would last. If it didn't last until Lilah got here, then this was very likely going to be the shortest rescue attempt in history.

"Be careful!" Nix said.

"You be *more* careful," he said.

They smiled at each other, then Benny pulled her to him and they kissed. They had no time for this, but Benny took the time. If it was going to be their last kiss, then it was going to be one of history's best. There were no words, no "I love you"s shared back and forth. It was not a good-bye kiss, either. After that kiss, as Benny released Nix and they both staggered back from that moment, Benny knew that he damn well wanted to live.

He turned and left without another word.

Benny faded back into the forest and circled the camp, running fast, slipping now and then in the mud. Any sounds he made were lost to the roar of the falling rain. He was soaked to the skin, and his clothing and weapons felt heavy, but he held an image in his mind as he ran. Those kids huddled together, and the oldest girl's smiling face filled with hope. Filled with the belief that despite all of the evidence to the contrary, someone in this world still cared what happened to her and the other children. When Benny fell, that image was what picked him up. When his lungs began to burn from the effort of slogging through the mud, that image put steel into his legs and fire in his muscles. When the fear threatened to take the heart out of him, that image made him keep going, step after trembling step.

He reached the last of the paths that led into the camp and skidded to a muddy stop between a pair of dead trees. There was a guard. A big man with a yellow rain slicker and a shotgun, the big double barrels pointed at the ground to keep them from filling with water. Benny had only two chances, and he'd thought long and hard about them this afternoon while waiting for this moment. He could try and sneak past the man or he could attack him.

He liked the first idea better, because it seemed to have a future attached to it. But the reality was that if he left the guard in place, then Lilah would probably be spotted when she returned. No, Benny decided, this was the moment to stop acting like a kid and start acting like a man. He crept forward to the trunk of the larger of the two dead trees. Old branches littered the ground, and Benny had to be careful where he stepped. If the branch was old enough, then breaking it would sound like a gunshot. They might not hear that from the camp, but this man certainly would.

The man stepped closer to the cliff wall, to try and keep the rain from pounding his head, and began fishing in his pockets. He brought out a pipe and some matches and leaned into a cleft to light it, turning completely away for a few seconds. Benny used those seconds. He bent and picked up one of the dead branches—a length of gnarled hardwood nearly as long as his *bokken*. He held it like the wooden sword as he crept catfooted through the mud, and he was nearly within striking range when the man turned, his pipe lit, smoke funneling out from under his hood.

He saw Benny.

The man was fast. He dropped the pipe and swung the shotgun up, the deadly weapon sliding easily on its wet shoulder sling at the same moment as Benny jumped forward and hit the guy across the face as hard as he could. The old branch was brittle, and it shattered into a hundred soggy splinters as it broke over the man's cheek and nose.

The blow slammed the guard back against the cliff wall. The strike from the stick did not knock him out. Hitting his head on the wall, however, did.

The crack of bone on rock was lost as thunder boomed overhead, but Benny saw the shiver that ran through the man's whole body. He dropped to his knees and fell face forward into the mud, an inch from Benny's toes.

Benny looked dumbly at the fallen man for a moment, then dropped the broken remains of the stick onto his back. He gagged at the thought of what he had just done, but even while his chest was still hitching, he drew his knife, positioned the tip of the blade in the correct spot at the base of the skull, and pushed. When he straightened, the world seemed too loud and too bright for a moment, and he took a couple of dizzy steps away from the corpse.

"One down," he mumbled, his voice thick, his heart hammering. "Only twenty-two to go. We can start the victory party now."

He took a breath to steady his nerves, turned, and ran as fast as he could through the rain.

Nix wormed her way to the outside of a tent that was at the very edge of the camp. The tent's occupant had crawled out when the rain had started, and had run to another point in the camp. Nix listened at the side of the canvas long enough to assure herself that there was no one else in the tent.

She drew her knife.

"Come on, Benny," she whispered. "Please . . ."

Benny reached the far edge of the camp and slipped inside without anyone noticing. He could see groups of the bounty hunters, standing together under tarps strung between trees. Benny remembered that trees could attract lightning strikes, but he didn't think his good luck extended to a timely bolt from the heavens that would fry all these creeps.

He kept to the shadows, moved to the rear of the tent, and squatted down. There was no light from inside and no movement. If Vin Trang was still in there, then he was being very quiet. Benny fished in the mud for a stone and lobbed it in a slow overhand, so that it hit the far side of the tent.

Nothing. No movement. No head poking outside to see what had made the noise.

Benny grinned and moved from his spot, keeping the tent between him and the rest of the camp. When he reached the flap, he tossed another wet rock inside.

Still nothing.

Benny drew a breath and slipped inside the tent. It was pitch-dark, and Benny wasted several seconds feeling around for what he wanted, finding only socks, a dog-eared book, some toiletries. Nothing of use.

He had to risk a light.

"Crap," he whispered as he fished in his pockets for his tin of matches. He rattled them and then dried his fingers hastily on Vin's bedroll. Then he opened the tin and removed one of the three remaining matches.

He closed his eyes and took a breath. Then he struck the match on the knurled end of the tin. The match flared at once, and the light filled the whole tent. There were two bedrolls and a lot of junk scattered around. Two shotguns lay on one bedroll. For a moment Benny didn't think he would find what he was looking for, and without it the whole plan was going to come crashing down. Then he saw that the thin pillow of one of the bedrolls rested on a small leather satchel.

He found what he was looking for in the satchel.

"Perfect . . . ," he said breathlessly.

"Hey!"

Benny heard the cry and recognized the voice at once. Joey Duk.

The flaps were closed, so Joey could not have seen him, but the glow from the match made the whole tent glow.

Outside, there were shouts and the slopping sound of feet running toward the tent. There was no time to do anything but act. Benny dropped the burning match on the bedroll, slung the satchel over his shoulder, and drew his knife.

The match ignited the bed linen, and fire spread with frightening speed. Benny used his knife to slash at the rear wall of the tent. Even in his haste he did it the smart way—cutting the bottom of the wall, right where the lacing was wrapped around the aluminum frame—and then he pushed the canvas up and slithered out like a snake. The canvas fell back into place, so that the back of the tent appeared undamaged.

The shouts were almost on top of him as he shimmied on his belly through the mud and slid over the edge of the plateau. He froze and tried to melt into the landscape, as if he was just another lump in the big, wet, muddy mountain.

The shouts increased in volume, and he risked a quick backward look.

The tent was ablaze.

Vin Trang and Joey Duk stood staring at the blaze. Other bounty hunters ran from all parts of the camp, some shouting, some laughing. Nobody was firing a gun. No one seemed to be looking out into the woods or down the slopes. Vin turned to Joey and yelled something very loud in Vietnamese, then shoved his friend violently in the chest. Joey went staggering back, slipped in the mud, and fell hard on his ass. The others burst out in uproarious laughter. Vin, not content with knocking Joey down, snarled like a cat and jumped atop Joey, then started hammering at him while behind them the tent burned.

This was even better than Benny could hope for. Vin

obviously thought Joey had left something burning in the tent and was pummeling him for having lost all of his possessions.

"There is a God," Benny said to himself as he slipped away into the shadows, "and apparently He has a warped sense of humor."

He moved off into the darkness and circled halfway around the camp. Even with the heavy downpour, he could still hear the shouts and laughter. He had a sudden flare of panic. Had Nix heard it too? Would she think this was the diversion that Benny had planned? If so, she was going to start too soon!

He ran faster.

Then his foot came down wrong in a puddle that was deeper than it looked, and Benny pitched forward, sliding face-first through the mud. His hands opened, and he watched in absolute horror as the little tin of matches went sailing into the rain and out of sight.

"NO!" he shouted.

It was small a blessing that no one heard him. It almost didn't matter, because without those matches, he and Nix were probably going to die.

Nix cut open the side of the tent and crawled quickly inside. The pen was just outside, and she knelt, knife in hand, and peered out into the rain. The twelve-year-old girl had the other kids clustered together, and they were as calm as they could be under the circumstances. She must have told them about what she'd seen, because they were not wailing. Each of them stared into the storm with huge eyes that were filled with tears and hope.

One of the guards walked past, and Nix watched as he went several paces down the center path of the camp and stretched his head to try and catch what was going on over at Vin Trang's tent. She'd hoped he would have gone all the way over, but he stayed relatively close to his post.

"Here goes," Nix whispered to herself and then crept out of the tent and crabbed sideways in a low crouch, until her shoulder bumped up against the pen rail. The kids gasped, but Nix shushed them. She reached through the wood slats of the pen and touched several of them, assuring them of her reality. Nix slid along the pen rail to the back corner and watched the guard. He was still craning to listen through the hammering of the rain.

Nix straightened and then climbed quickly and quietly over the rail. She dropped down in the mud and then huddled next to the crowd of kids. In the gloom and with all the mud, she blended in. When the guard cut a quick look over his shoulder, all he saw were children hunkered down in a bunch. He grunted to himself and turned back to watch the fun. Vin and Joey were beating the hell out of each other, and everyone was yelling and cheering them on.

Nix showed her knife to the oldest girl. The girl's eyes went wide, but she understood. Nix gritted her teeth and attacked the bundle of ropes, and in less than a minute the whole bundle of ropes was cut.

Nix pulled the twelve-year-old girl close. "Go over the rail and down the slope. There's a path down there. Follow it all the way down to the creek. Don't leave the path and don't stop. You understand?"

"Yes! But, who are you?"

"Doesn't matter," Nix snapped. "Just run!"

The girl scrambled over the edge of the pen and reached out to pull the first of the children over.

Then something big and dark moved out of the rain, and they all looked up in horror.

Charlie Pink-eye stood there above them. He held a pistol in one hand, and the barrel was pointing straight at Nix's face.

52

"Well, I'll be a one-eyed skunk," yelled Charlie Pink-eye so loud that Benny could hear him through the rain, the laughter, and the noise of the fistfight. All of the men who were clustered around the burning tent stopped and turned to see their boss standing by the pig pen, pointing a gun at the red-haired girl who had escaped the day before. They laughed as if this was some new form of entertainment, and the whole mass of them broke into a run to go share in the fun. Vin pushed Joey away from him, and the pair, bruised and bloody, got to their feet and staggered along as well.

Benny came out of hiding and ran low and fast to the shadowy cleft between two of the wagons. There was a big bonfire that had been sheltered from the rain by a thick stand of tall pines. He craned his neck to see what was happening.

"Move one muscle, little darlin'," said Charlie, "and I'll cut my losses and leave you for zom meat. Don't think I won't."

Benny's heart froze in his chest at those words. He climbed onto the side of the wagon for a better view. Despite the rain, his mouth went dry at what he saw. Nix, covered in mud, stood inside the pen, and Charlie stood on the other side of the rail, his pistol held in one rock-steady hand. Stark terror and raw hatred commingled on Nix's face, transforming her beauty into a mask equally as feral as Lilah's, but in some indefinable way, more savage. Perhaps it was because Lilah had never been civilized, and any thought she felt was immediately and unthinkingly displayed on her face, whereas Nix had always been controlled and self-aware. What Benny saw now was her unguarded, naked emotion.

Two of the men climbed over the fence and closed in on Nix from either side. It was clear they did not consider her a major threat, but they were nonetheless cautious of the big-bladed hunting knife she held. Charlie used the barrel of his gun to gesture to the knife Nix held clutched in her fist. "Drop that pig sticker, little darlin'."

Nix did not drop the knife. She clutched it to her chest, cutting desperate looks to her left and right for some way out.

Charlie swung the barrel of the pistol away from her and aimed it at the twelve-year-old. "Drop the knife, girl, or I'll put a hole in this little cutie."

The girl, seeing her death, straightened and held her head high. Then she spat into the mud at Charlie's feet.

Charlie thumbed the hammer back.

Nix dropped the knife. It struck point-first into the mud and stopped there, standing straight out from the ground like King Arthur's sword. Nix looked down at it with regret. One of the men laid a heavy hand on her shoulder.

Benny darted through the shadows until he could see the big bonfire on the other side of the wagon. Working quickly, he opened the satchel and removed a few items that he hoped he'd live long enough to use, and then he tossed the bag with a slow underhand pitch, straight into the fire. It struck the center of the blaze and kicked up a huge tower of sparks, but when the men in the crowd turned to see what had happened, Benny was already back into the darkest corner of shadows, totally invisible.

"What the hell was that?" demanded Charlie.

"Nothing, boss," said one of the bounty hunters. "Log shifted in the fire."

Nix took that moment. She suddenly bent forward and grabbed the handle of her knife. She pivoted as fast as she could, and Benny saw a flash of steel and then the guard to her left suddenly bent double and let loose with a terrible cry of pain. The other one had been looking at the bonfire and turned at the sound, but Nix spun toward him and then he was falling, the knife buried in his chest.

Charlie bellowed in surprise and fury, and swung the gun back toward Nix and pulled the trigger.

His shot sounded like an entire barrage of artillery, because at the same second that he pulled the trigger, all of the firecrackers in Joey Duk's satchel exploded. The sudden sound made Charlie jump, and his shot tore through Nix's hair rather than her head.

The night was filled with a thousand sharp cracks, and all of the men ducked and dove for cover, thinking they were under armed attack. They whirled and fired in every direction, filling the air with louder bangs as shotguns and heavy pistols spat fire and hot lead. A dozen bullets ripped jagged holes in the sheet-metal sides of the wagon beside which Benny crouched, and he bent and rolled beneath the wagon, feeling the shudder as the barrage continued to tear at wood and metal.

Nix tore her knife free, rushed at the pen rail, and tried to leap over it, blade high, to stab Charlie, but the big man swatted her out of the air. The blow caught her on the shoulder, and it was so shockingly powerful that Nix went flying. She hit the ground and slid five feet. Her knife went spinning out of her hands.

Benny saw this from where he lay, and the sight of Nix falling made something snap in his mind. He rolled out from under the wagon and ran around behind it, circling the camp at a dead run to come up on Charlie from the shadows.

The bounty hunters were still firing, and someone's shotgun pellets struck the flanks of a massive Clydesdale in the corral. The huge draft horse screamed and reared up, throwing all of its two thousand pounds of muscle and bone against a tethering line that snapped like cotton twine. The Clydesdale's flailing hooves struck another horse, and soon the whole pack of draft animals were screaming and kicking and tearing loose. They charged across the camp, spooked by pain and the continual popping of the firecrackers, scattering bounty hunters who dove for sudden cover. One man was caught in a moment of indecision, shifting right and left half a dozen times before his last moment of choice ran out. The herd of horses ran him down and ground him into the mud. Benny saw the Hammer trying to make a grab for them, but one of the animals rammed him and sent him flying into Joey Duk's burning tent. The Hammer landed hard, but instantly began screaming and thrashing as he rolled out of the fire. The mud and the rain put out the flames, but he lay there, smoking and dazed.

The twelve-year-old was pushing the children over the

rail. She was the last one over, and they raced together into the darkened woods, but as they fled, Benny realized he was on the very path that Nix had told them to take. He tried to dodge behind a tree, but the whole pack of kids saw him at once . . . and screamed.

Charlie whirled, thinking that one of his men had circled to block the kids.

He stared straight into Benny Imura's eyes, saw all nineteen of his captives fleeing past him into the shadows.

Charlie Pink-eye's face darkened with a brutal rage, and he raised his pistol.

And Benny Imura raised his own.

"LIFE JUST KEEPS GETTING MORE AND MORE FUN," GROWLED CHARLIE Matthias.

"BENNY!" Nix screamed, but the Hammer moved behind her and wrapped an iron arm around her throat. The other bounty hunters laughed, knowing that a bad night was suddenly about to become more entertaining.

"If you think getting shot is fun," Benny said, "then you're going to die happy."

Charlie laughed. "Boy, maybe your brother might have pulled off that kind of banter, but it doesn't carry the same pop if your voice cracks while you're talking trash."

The gun was heavy, but Benny forced his hand to stay firm. Charlie appeared to be unimpressed. The rain was thinning, and the last of the firecrackers banged and then went silent. Benny licked his lips, tasting mud and cold sweat.

"If you're going to pull that trigger, pup, do it while you still have some balls."

"I'll pull it," said Benny, stepping forward in what he hoped was an aggressive move. Charlie merely looked amused. "But I want to know something first."

Charlie grinned and looked around at the other bounty

hunters. Most of them were trying to round up the horses, but a handful had stood to watch the fun. Now they were pointing guns at Benny too. "Kid wants to have a fireside chat, boys. Ain't that cute?"

"Maybe he wants to know how to grow a set!" yelled one man.

"Maybe he wants to join," suggested Vin Trang.

"Maybe he wants to cry about what happened to Tom," offered the Hammer, who was scuffed and blackened, but did not look much worse for wear. He gave Benny a truly murderous look, and Benny knew that if the Hammer got his hands on him, he'd make him pay very dearly for what had just happened.

Benny could have taken his shot when Charlie was turned away, but he kept hoping that Lilah would show up. One more diversion was all he needed to rescue Nix. But all he heard in the woods behind him was the diminishing splat of raindrops on leaves and the moan of the wind through the trees.

Showing no trace of concern that a gun was pointed at him, Charlie turned back to Benny. "Sure, kid. . . . You got some burning question you want to ask, then ol' Charlie'd be happy to oblige. Charlie's everybody's friend."

The bounty hunters all laughed at that.

"Why do you do this?" Benny demanded. "I mean, how can you live with yourself after everything you've done?"

The big bounty hunter chuckled. "Grow up, boy. You think I'm evil? Sure, you want to hang that word on me, because I use muscle to take what I want, but you don't have a clue about how the world works. It's the same now as it was before First Night. Anyone says different is a fool or a liar."

He took a step closer, and Benny reflexively backed away. Charlie looked pleased, and he bent forward and leered at Benny.

"You look at me and you see the Big Bad Wolf. You think I'm some kind of monster. Well, there's a lot worse than ol' Charlie out here in the Ruin, and I ain't talkin' about zoms. You got no idea what *evil* is."

"I'm looking at it."

"Hell, boy, I ain't evil. I'm just the guy that's in power. I'm a conqueror, like all them great kings and generals in history. You want to call me evil because of Gameland? You think that's the height of evil? Boy, there are people who conquered half the world, slaughtered whole populations, wiped cultures off the face of the planet, and you know what history calls them? Heroes! Kings, presidents, champions, explorers. You think America was settled by white men because the Indians *invited* us here? No, we *took* this land because we were stronger, and that's how every page of human history is written. It's just our nature. We're a predator species, top of the food chain. Survival of the fittest is written in our blood, it's stenciled on every gene of our DNA. The strong *take* and the strong *make*, and the weak are there only to help them do it. End of story."

"You're wrong." The gun was getting impossibly heavy. Benny's whole arm trembled.

"I can see it in your eyes, boy, you know I'm right. You're so wrapped up in wanting to be a hero your ownself that you can't admit it." He took another step, and Benny yielded ground again. It was that or pull the trigger, and he couldn't make himself do it. Not yet. Charlie said, "I know they teach you pups history in school. They teach you about the old world, about the heroes who built this great nation, blah, blah, blah. But do you think any general anywhere ever won a war without taking exactly what he wanted, whenever he wanted? Or without letting his men have what they needed, whenever they needed it? All through history the winners ran rampant when they conquered a city or a country, and it was one big party—just as it should be. If a man is going to put his life on the line, then he deserves some benefits. It's only fair."

"What are you talking about? You're not some general fighting an invading army. You're not freeing anyone. You're not fighting *for* anything!"

Charlie's face darkened. "Oh I'm not, am I? Well, learn a little of your own history then. I was there when we found Mountainside. Me, Charlie Matthias. I helped *build* that stinking town. I scouted the first trade route through the Ruin. I brought the first wagons of supplies from the cities to help reinforce the fence. I was the one who raided the hospital and brought back half a ton of medical supplies. Most of the men who protect the traders and city scavengers now work for me or were trained by me. And I brought more survivors, including a couple hundred whole families out of the Ruin to Mountainside. I've saved more people than you ever met, my young pup. So don't tell me I haven't been fighting for anything."

He took one more step, and this time Benny was too flummoxed to step back.

"Benny!" yelled Nix. "Don't listen to him. He's just trying to confuse you." She would have said more, but the Hammer flexed the massive muscles in his arm, and his biceps choked Nix to silence. Benny licked his lips.

Charlie said, "Once upon a time I met a group of travelers in these mountains, who were half dead and running from a pack of zoms. A group that included a skinny Japanese kid and his baby brother . . . and I showed them the path to Mountainside. So, boy, you want to get your facts right before you tell me that I ain't been fighting the good fight. A hundred years from now, when they write the history of First Night and the years that followed, they'll put my name down as the greatest hero of the zombie war. Me, Charlie Matthias."

Benny did not want to believe Charlie, but he knew the big man was telling the truth. At least the truth as he knew it.

"Maybe you did all that," Benny said, using his left hand now to support his trembling right. "But it still doesn't give you the right to do the other things you're doing."

"Don't it? Being 'right' is all about living up to a set of laws, and there are no laws out here in the Ruin. Even your worm-meat brother told you that much. The laws of places like Mountainside end at the gate, because nobody there has the guts to step past those fences and *establish* the law outside. Nobody but me, and since I'm the top dog out here, I get to make whatever laws I want."

"I'm not talking about laws," said Benny through gritted teeth. The moaning of the wind in the forest behind him was louder. Was the storm going to build back up again? "I'm talking about right and wrong."

Charlie laughed. "You're going to stand here with a gun in my face, ready to kill me, and you're going to lecture me on right and wrong? Who appointed you judge, jury, and executioner? You pass a burning bush on the way here and get some new Commandments? I think the old ones kind of dried up and blew away when the first of the dead rose up and started eating people. Call me crazy, but I think that was a game changer. When dead ain't even dead no more, then as far as I'm concerned, no other previous rules apply. So that means 'right' is whatever I decide it is."

"No—," Benny began, but Charlie made his move. He stuck his left hand out to the side, and Benny's reflexes reacted before he could control them and his eyes flicked toward the movement. With lightning speed, Charlie used his right to slap the pistol out of Benny's hand. With one step he was chest to chest with Benny, and his face was a mask of naked fury. He grabbed Benny's shirt with one hand and hauled him to his toe-tips and knocked his head to one side with a powerful slap of his hard open palm and then backhanded him, so that his head whipped all the way to the other side. The shock to Benny's cheek was nothing compared to the double jolt to his neck, and Benny's knees buckled.

"Benny!" Nix cried, but all that escaped the stricture around her throat was a desperate croak.

Charlie Pink-eye shoved Benny away in disgust. "You're a worthless little piece of crap, kid. You talk big when you're holding a gun, but you don't even have the stones *or* the smarts to pull the trigger when you have the chance. That's why people like you don't run the world. It's people like me—people who aren't afraid to make the hard choices and take the tough actions—who get things done and who deserve to say what's what. Power is the only thing that matters, pup, and the sad news is that you just don't have enough of it."

"Kiss my ass!" Benny snarled, and he launched himself at Charlie. His training with Tom hadn't lasted long enough for him to learn the subtleties of combat. He didn't know many tricks, wouldn't have qualified for any belt. All he had was his rage. He barreled into Charlie so hard that the big man was actually forced backward two steps. Benny came in low and fast, driving his shoulder into Charlie's thighs, hoping to knock him down. If he could get him down, maybe he could stomp on him, break an ankle or a knee. Or Charlie's face.

But Charlie didn't go down. He dug his heels into the mud to stop Benny's rush and then he clubbed Benny aside with a forearm shot to the side of the head. Benny saw it coming and ducked enough to miss most of the force, but there was still enough power there to drive him to one knee. With a growl of anger, Benny tried to hook a punch into Charlie's crotch, but Charlie turned into it, and Benny's fist collided with the big man's hip bone. Pain exploded in Benny's hand.

"Nice try, pup," Charlie said. "Points for having *some* stones. More than I thought. Not enough, though."

He grabbed Benny by the hair, jerked him to his feet, and then buried an uppercut so hard into Benny's stomach that his whole body was lifted off the ground. His entire abdomen seemed to be folded around Charlie's massive fist, and the impact drove all of the air out of the world. Benny fell, eyes bulging, face purpling, gasping, capable only of making high-pitched squeaks as he fought to take in even a mouthful of air.

He heard Nix calling his name, screaming as she fought against the Hammer.

He heard the laughter of Charlie and the other bounty hunters.

He heard his own inhuman squeaks.

He heard Charlie say, "Digger, Sting . . . You boys do me

a favor and drag his sorry butt into the pen and tie him up. Don't be nice about it. Hammer, show the girl some manners and then tie her up with the others. The rest of you, go find those other kids and let's get this camp together. This whole thing's been a total clusterfu—"

And something came hurtling out of the dark and slammed into the back of the man called Digger as he bent to grab Benny. He gurgled out a single low cry and fell face forward onto the ground. Benny stared at the man, at the knife that was buried nearly to the hilt between his shoulder blades. The handle was black and ribbed, and the inch of blade that showed was equally black and double-edged.

Benny felt his brain twist around backward. He *knew* that knife!

Then a scream cut through the air as something massive leaped over the dying man's body and crashed full force into the knot of bounty hunters. The horse was not one of the bulky draft horses that had broken free from the camp.

It was Apache!

And riding the big buckskin was a bloody man, whose clothing hung in rags, whose eyes were dark and wild, and who slashed at the bounty hunters with a glittering sword.

Tom!

"*TOM!*" Benny yelled, not knowing if what he was seeing was real or if he had just gone completely crazy. How was it even possible?

Apache reared up and kicked one bounty hunter in the chest, and the man flew backward, as if he'd taken a double load of buckshot. Another man rushed the horse from the side and tried to pull Tom from the saddle. Tom's sword flashed downward, and the man fell shrieking beneath the horse's hooves.

"Christ!" bellowed Charlie. "That's Tom Imura. Kill him!"

He brought his gun up, but Benny came up out of the mud and once more drove his shoulder into the big man. Charlie wasn't ready for it this time, and the impact knocked them both to the ground. Charlie's shot punched a hole through the shoulder of Texas Jon McGoran. As the bullet slammed Texas Jon backward, his fingers jerked the trigger of his pump shotgun, and the spray caught Wild Bill Fairchild full in the face.

Benny had no chance against Charlie in any kind of a fight, but he could at least keep him from shooting Tom, so Benny lunged at Charlie's arm and bit his wrist. Charlie howled in pain, dropped the gun, but then used that hand to punch Benny in the face. Benny felt his nose crack. He kneed Charlie in the thigh twice and then flung himself away from a second and more powerful punch that would have easily broken his neck.

He scrambled to his feet and spun around looking for Nix. She was twenty feet away, and the Hammer was holding her like a shield as Tom advanced on him. The rain faded to a drizzle and then stopped, although thunder rumbled through the heavens and lightning flashed in the west.

"Drop that sword, Tom, or I'll snap this little girl's neck," the Hammer promised. He meant it, too. He had his whole arm looped around her throat and held her so that her feet were inches above the ground.

The other bounty hunters were recovering from the initial shock of seeing Tom Imura, returning from the dead as a living, breathing, fighting man. They pulled their guns and pointed them at him.

Tom reined Apache to a stop. The buckskin still wore the remnants of his carpet coat, although it looked like it had been gnawed on by every zom from here to the state line.

"You don't want to do that, Marion," said Tom in a voice that was surprisingly calm. "Put the girl down."

"Kiss my hairy butt, Tom. You drop that sword or so help me, I'll pull her head clean off."

Tom flicked his wrist so that the blood that streaked the sword was whipped off. It splashed Joey Duk across the face.

"Benny," Tom said, "are you okay?"

Benny got to his feet, his head spinning from the punch to the nose. "Yeah," he said breathlessly.

"That's going to cost you." Charlie growled as he also got to his feet. His gun was muddy and useless, but he didn't need one. Tom was surrounded by nearly twenty bounty hunters.

Tom slowly raised his sword until the tip of the blade was pointed directly at the Motor City Hammer. "I'm going to give you one last chance, Marion. Let Nix go."

The Hammer laughed, and so did the other men. "Or what?" He sneered. "You're outnumbered and outgunned, Tom. What the hell do you think *you're* gonna do?"

"Me?" Tom looked faintly amused. "Hell, I'm not going to do anything. But you *will* let her go."

"Says who?"

"Says me!" A voice snarled out of the darkness, and there was a heavy whoosh as a long metal pole cut through the air, and a flash of silver as a wickedly sharp bayonet blade cut through the back of the Motor City Hammer's left leg. His Achilles tendon parted with an explosion of blood, and he screamed—as high and shrill as a little girl—and fell. He literally threw Nix from him, and she staggered toward Benny, who rushed to catch her.

Everyone turned as a pale figure jumped forward into the firelight, her snow-white hair swirling as she landed and pivoted and slashed again with her spear. The air was suddenly filled with a new rainfall, but these drops were a red so dark that it was almost black. The Hammer clamped both of his hands around his throat. His eyes went wide and were instantly filled with the dreadful certainty that no matter who won this night's conflict—Charlie Pink-eye or Tom Imura—he, Marion Hammer, would own no piece of either victory or defeat, and that he would play no part in whatever future was being written here. He tried to speak, to say something, to articulate the terror and need in his heart, but that bull throat of his was no longer constructed for speech.

He toppled slowly forward, like a great building finally yielding to years of corruption and decay, and then he fell into the mud.

The Lost Girl stood over him, her hazel eyes as cold as all the hatred and loss in the world, and then she spat on the unmoving back of the man who had chased her sister into the rain and then left her body in the mud, as if it was garbage.

"God," Nix breathed, massaging her bruised throat.

Charlie Matthias stared at his fallen friend, his mouth open, disbelief painted on his features. Benny could only imagine what was going on in the big man's mind. Benny had heard all of the stories of Charlie and the Hammer. He'd sat in Lafferty's General Store on far too many afternoons and listened as they recounted their adventures. Always *their* adventures. Always together, a pair of devils, drawing power from each other, enabling and supporting each other. The right and left fist of violence out here in the great Rot and Ruin.

And now the Hammer was dead.

In a few minutes he would reanimate as a zom. As one of *them*, as one of the things that Charlie and the Hammer hated and humiliated and debased for fun and profit.

As Benny watched, Charlie's face changed. His eyes went from wide shock to narrow slits filled with lethal intent, and his mouth tightened into a grimace of bloodlust.

"I'm going to rip you apart, girl," he said. "I should have done it five years ago, and now I'm going to make sure it's done and done right. By God you are going to scream all the way to hell!"

Lilah raised her spear, and the bounty hunters raised their guns. Benny and Nix stepped up to flank her, the three of them ready to make a stand against Charlie Pink-eye.

Tom stepped between Charlie and them.

"A long time ago I gave you a chance," said Tom. "Your goons here don't know it, but I had you down and bleeding when you tried to invade Sunset Hollow. Your life was in my hands, Charlie, and you begged me—*begged* me—to give you another chance. You swore to me that you'd change, that things would be different. I didn't know then that you were the one who was behind everything bad that goes on out here. That *you* started Gameland and that *you* were the one who kept it going. Back then I thought you were just a hired gun, working for someone else. Now I know different, Charlie. Now I know the truth, and every day for the rest of my life I'm going to feel sick, knowing that I let you live when I should have just switched you off. I thought I was doing the right thing. I thought I was being merciful. Never kill a helpless enemy." Benny saw Tom's face darken with self-loathing. "I've got five years of blood on my hands, Charlie. How many lives is that? How many men, women, and children whose futures were ruined? How many people tortured or murdered?"

Charlie was not impressed. "Yeah, you suckered me once and got the upper hand, big friggin' deal. You think that makes you tougher than me? You think that makes you *anything*? You ain't nothing but a sad footnote in an old history book, Tom. You're not a cop and you're not a samurai. You're not even a good bounty hunter. You don't have the guts for it. You're nothing but a fool and a coward."

Benny stepped forward and punched Charlie in the face. He put every ounce of outrage and almost fourteen years worth of inner conflict into that punch, and it caught Charlie on the point of the jaw and spun him halfway around.

"My brother is not a coward!" he bellowed.

Time seemed to grind to a halt.

Charlie turned slowly back to face them. There was a purple knot forming on his jaw, but if the punch had done him any real harm, then it didn't show on his face. His eyes danced with humor, and he wore an ugly butcher's smile.

"You throw a good punch for a little pup," he said. "How's the hand?"

Benny said nothing. In fact, he had to clamp his mouth shut, because he was pretty sure that he had just broken his hand. Every one of the thousands of nerve endings in his fist was sending white hot flashes of pain to his brain, and his knuckles were swelling like balloons. He tried to block out the pain, tried not to let his eyes fill with tears. He concentrated on hating Charlie and tried to figure out a way to save Nix. The rain started falling again, and the wind was moaning louder than ever in the trees.

Charlie pointed to him. "I'm going to save you for last. After I kick your brother's ass, I'm going to take the Lost Girl and see how she does in a zombie pit *without* any weapons. That goes for your redheaded friend, too. Think that'll be fun? Afterward, I'm going to feed you to the zoms, one finger at a time."

Nix made a lunge at Charlie, but Tom grabbed her shoulder and held her back.

"No, sweetie," he murmured, "this animal is mine."

Charlie gave him "a come and get it" gesture with both hands, then called to his men. "What kind of drugs are you taking, Tom? You're frigging well *surrounded* and outnumbered. We're not going to duke it out. This isn't a fair fight. You're just going to die. I don't know how you escaped them zoms back on the highway, but you should never have come back here. Not alone."

"No," Tom agreed, "it isn't a fair fight. And just so you know . . . I'm not alone."

Charlie looked momentarily perplexed. A few of the bounty hunters exchanged looks and then everyone turned slowly around. The rain was falling steadily now, but the moaning in the forest had nothing to do with the wind.

The entire camp was surrounded by hundreds of the living dead.

Tom Imura looked at Lilah, and they both smiled.

The zoms shambled into the camp, and the moan they let loose was an unrelenting cry of hunger that now had the promise of being satisfied. The bounty hunters screamed and backed away, colliding with one another. Everyone who had a gun began firing.

"Benny!" cried Nix, and shoved him out of the way as a zom lurched toward him. She ducked under the zombie's arms and kicked it savagely in the knee, but as it toppled, she shoved it into the arms of one of the bounty hunters. The man shrieked as the crippled zom bore him to the ground and clamped its rotting teeth onto his shoulder.

Lilah used the butt end of her spear to jab several of the zoms in the chest, knocking them away as she retreated. "With me!" she called, and Benny and Nix clustered next to her. Neither of them had a weapon. "Gun!" Lilah barked, but Benny looked around, expecting to see someone trying to shoot him. Nix, however, caught Lilah's meaning and reached for the pistol in the Lost Girl's holster. It was an automatic, and Nix racked the slide and took the gun in a firm two-handed shooter's grip as the three of them kept backing toward the wagons.

Benny saw one of the zoms—it was the huge man in the

tattered overalls of a mechanic—grab a bounty hunter by the throat and drive him back against a tree. The ropes that had once held the mechanic to the tree in the Hungry Forest still dangled from his wrists. Other shapes moved through the shadows behind him. Ropes dangled from withered necks and emaciated waists, and firelight sparkled in their dead, black eyes.

Benny felt a mix of savage pride and relief—it had been an insane plan, and it had taken longer than Benny had expected—but it was working. He should have trusted that Lilah would get it done.

But . . . *Tom*! Nothing in his plan explained how his brother had returned from apparent death and had come here to save them. And it was clear from what Tom had said, and from the knowing look he'd shared with Lilah, that he had known that the zoms were closing in on the camp. How had he known? Had he met the Lost Girl and, after all of his attempts, finally spoken with her? Here, on this night of storms and blood?

Benny turned to find his brother, and there Tom was, right in the thick of it. Several zoms separated him from Charlie. Several bounty hunters tried to rush Tom at the same time that half a dozen zoms closed in on him, and it was in that moment that Benny finally saw, and *understood*, the kind of man Tom Imura was.

His whole body was a blur of coordinated movement. Big Jim Starr, one of Charlie's fiercest men, grabbed Tom by the shoulder and spun him around, but Tom turned into the pull, and his left hand shot out with whiplike speed. Big Jim clutched a ruin of a throat and fell away, but before he even had time to fall, Tom slashed up and wide, then left and across, and two zoms seemed to fly apart. Joker Brills pulled a pistol and snapped off a shot, but Tom had seen him go for his gun and was moving before the barrel was properly aimed. Gun and gun arm flew into the air, and Tom pivoted and cut the legs from another zom, then rose and slashed Axeman Santiago across the chest in a double cut that left a deep red *X* across his torso. Tom whirled and cut, whirled and cut, and his attackers—both the living and the dead—fell before him. Benny could see Charlie watching all of this from the far side of the clearing, and there was a slack expression, somewhere between shock and awe, on his heavy features.

Then a powerful hand clamped onto Benny's leg, and he was falling. As he went down he twisted around and saw the Motor City Hammer, staring at him with black and lifeless eyes as he pulled Benny toward his bloody mouth.

Benny screamed and kicked him in the face, over and over again, but the Hammer was beyond feeling pain. Then Nix stamped down on the Hammer's wrist and put the barrel of the pistol hard against the zom's forehead and pulled the trigger. The Hammer's head jerked back, and he collapsed down, dead forever this time.

"Thanks!" Benny gasped as Nix hauled him to his feet.

"Here!" Lilah said. She knelt by the Hammer's side and pulled from his belt the heavy metal club he always carried. She tossed it to Benny, who caught it with his swollen hand.

He yelped and cursed, but he managed to close his fist around it. *Maybe it's only sprained,* he told himself, then he had no more time to think about it as Vin Trang rushed at him with a butcher knife in his fist. Joey Duk made a grab for Nix, and four zoms staggered toward Lilah.

"You and your brother are a pain in my—," Vin began, but Benny didn't want to hear it. He used the pipe to batter aside the knife and then rang the club off of Vin's forehead. Vin's eyes lost focus, and Benny closed the deal with an overhand swing that put Vin down. Benny didn't know or care if he'd killed the man or not. He needed to help Nix and Lilah, but as he turned, he saw Nix moving backward and firing with each step. Her bullets punched into Joey Duk with such force that it made him look like a puppet, dancing on the strings of a demented puppeteer. The last shot caught him high and he pitched backward into the arms of three zoms—a nun and two men in business suits. The man collapsed under the zoms, screaming as they began to feast.

Nix stared at the fallen man, then down at the gun she held.

"God . . . ," she murmured, her voice sounding lost, and for a moment Benny thought that killing Joey had somehow broken her. But then a zom reached for her, and Nix calmly, coldly, turned and shot it between the eyes.

Another body fell past Benny, and he turned to see Lilah dispatch the last of the four zoms who had rushed her. Her face ran with rainwater, and she was grinning. *Grinning.*

That is one spooky girl, Benny thought. From all that Lilah had been through, she was "lost" in more ways than one. He wondered if there was any roadmap that would lead her toward some kind of normal life. Or was she too far out in the wilderness of her own experience for that?

"Benny!"

Tom's voice shook him back to the moment, and he saw his brother running toward him. The last of the bounty hunters were trying to make a stand by the bonfire, and a wall of zoms was closing in on them.

"The east path!" Tom yelled, pointing with his bloody sword, and Benny turned toward the path the children had taken. It was the only path clear of the dead. Lilah had said it was the best one for their escape, because it was elevated—part of an ancient rock wall that had long ago collapsed, and unlike all of the other paths, it didn't directly connect with the forest. It had been their planned escape route, but in all of the turmoil, Benny had become confused.

"RUN!" Tom yelled, and even as he said it, Apache came tearing out of the shadows and galloped at full speed along the path, sensing the direction of safety. Benny began backing up, but he was still looking at the camp. There were more than a thousand zoms closing in now, and only eight bounty hunters. After all they'd done, after all the harm they had caused, Benny felt a flicker of compassion for them, and he knew that this was the same thing Tom must have felt when he'd spared Charlie's life years ago. Back in Sunset Hollow, whatever that was.

But there was no saving these men. Lilah and Nix knew it, because they ran along the path without a flicker of hesitation. Tom knew it, though when he caught up with Benny, he too turned and looked back for a moment.

"We can't save them," Tom said.

"No," whispered Benny, but his reply was lost in the rain.

"Go catch up with the girls," Tom said. "I'll hold this trail until you're well clear. Leave Apache for me, because when I leave, I'll be in a hurry."

Benny ran down the road and whistled for the horse, and Apache stopped, turned reluctantly, and trotted back to him. Benny tied the reins in a loose pull knot to a stunted tree.

"Tom, how did you . . . I mean . . . How are you *alive*?"

Tom flashed him a grin. "Remember when you threw that bottle of cadaverine to me with the cap loose, and I spilled it all over myself? I think you saved my life. After I fell, I landed right in the middle of them, but they didn't go for me. Not right away. The cadaverine gave me a couple of seconds, and I rolled under a car. I was stuck there for hours. I didn't know where you were . . . or if you were alive."

"Geez. How bad are you hurt? I saw a lot of blood. . . ."

"I took some buckshot pellets. It'll be fun getting them out, but it could have been a lot worse."

The gunshots and screams were intensifying.

"Family reunion later, kiddo. Haul ass."

Benny did just that. He turned and followed Nix and the Lost Girl out of the camp, leaving the dying to the dead.

But as he rounded the bend in the path, Benny skidded to a stop. Nix and Lilah stood on either side the road, and fifty yards beyond them was the twelve-year-old girl and the other children. Standing like a monster from some old fairy tale—covered with mud and blood, fierce and terrible—was Charlie Pink-eye.

He held the pistol at arm's length, but his gun hand was no longer steady. He was breathing hard, and his red eye leaked tears of blood. There were deep gashes on his cheeks, and his shirt was torn open to reveal a body that was crammed with muscles and crisscrossed by scar tissue.

"Damn you all to hell," he said in a low hiss. "You took everything I had away from me. You *led* those monsters here! You turned against your own *kind*."

Benny's lips curled back, but Nix got her words out first. "You're not *our* kind, you freak. You killed my mother! You're not even human."

She pointed her pistol at Charlie and fired, but he read her intent and ducked to one side, and the shot went wide by five inches. The slide locked back with a hollow click, the magazine empty. Growling with frustration, Nix threw the pistol at Charlie and caught him on the shoulder, but he only winced. Lilah tried to gut him with her spear, but the big man moved so fast that only the tip of the blade grazed him. Even so, it drew a hot red line across his abdomen, and he howled in pain. He used one fist to club the spear down, so that the point dug into the mud, and with his other fist he punched Lilah in the stomach. She collapsed to her knees and threw up into the weeds. Nix made a grab for Lilah's spear, but Charlie backhanded her to the edge of the path, so that she stood wobbling on the edge of a sheer drop, her arms pinwheeling for balance.

And then Benny moved. He ran to Nix and grabbed her wrist and pulled her away from the ledge and then he rushed at Charlie. He still had the Hammer's club, and Benny swung it hard at Charlie's head. The bounty hunter was actually starting to smile at the obviousness of the attack, but Benny was tired of being obvious, tired of being beaten up, clubbed down, tossed aside like something that, in the grand scheme of things, just plain didn't matter. He turned the swing into a fake, checked the hit, and used his left hand to punch Charlie in the nose. It wasn't a very powerful blow, but it doesn't require power to break a nose. Charlie's head rocked back as his nose flattened and blood flew from his nostrils.

And that's when Benny hit him with the pipe.

He grabbed the weapon with both hands and swung it in a sideways arc that fourteen years ago would have sent a baseball into the bleachers in any major league park in the country. The swing had everything Benny had to give: rage and hate, hurt and fear, passion and confusion. And it also had love and grief. For Nix and her mother. For Lilah and her sister, Annie. For the twelve-year-old girl and the kids who huddled around her. For George Goldman, the quiet hero. For Tom and the heartbreak he felt over Jessie Riley. For people named and unknown who had fallen victim to this man. This abomination.

He hit Charlie Matthias only once.

And once was enough.

The big man took a single wandering sideways step, all sense and control knocked out of his head by the blow. He staggered past Nix, who was crouched down holding Lilah against her. He swung around in a sloppy turn, fighting for balance that was no longer his to own, and then his next step came down three inches past the edge of the path. Below his big foot was a drop that plunged a hundred yards into darkness. Charlie Matthias shot Benny one last, momentary glance of desperation and fear.

Benny would like to have seen guilt there or some last

minute awareness and acceptance of the wrongness of all that he had done. That would have been nice. That would have been closure.

All he saw in Charlie's eyes was hatred.

Then Charlie fell.

With the rain, with the last few pops of gunfire from the camp, and with the moans of the hungry dead, they never heard him land. Benny stood on the edge of the trail, and for all that he could see or hear, he might as well have been on the edge of the world. He held the Hammer's club out at arm's length, opened his hand, and let the weapon fall. There would be a need for weapons, he knew that; but there would be other weapons. This one, like the man it had killed, was unclean.

He turned to the others and sank to his knees by Nix and Lilah. They both stared past him to the edge of the road, their eyes wide. Benny rested his head on Nix's shoulder, and she gathered him to her. Lilah wrapped her arms around them both. Then there were other arms—the twelve-year-old girl and the children.

Tom Imura sat on Apache's back and stared at the huddled mass. He'd heard the single gunshot behind him and had come as fast as he could. He read the scene and understood what he was seeing.

He heard Benny and Lilah and Nix and the others as they wept.

Tom bowed his head and he too wept.

EPILOGUE

SUNSET HOLLOW

THEY WALKED IN SILENCE, SIDE BY SIDE, HEADING SOUTHEAST. MILES FELL away behind them. They passed another gas station, where Tom greeted another monk. They didn't linger, though. The day was burning away.

Benny's hand was still wrapped in tape. One of his knuckles was cracked and his wrist was sprained, but in the two weeks since the fight at the camp, he'd healed quickly. Tom looked like an Egyptian mummy. Doc Gurijala had pulled forty-one shotgun pellets out of him, and there were at least ten that he couldn't reach without doing more harm than good. Tom told him to leave them.

Lilah was healing, too, although more slowly. When Charlie had punched her in the stomach, he'd clipped her rib cage and broken three bones. She was staying with Lou Chong's family. They had the room, and Chong's aunt was a nurse. If Lilah was impressed by the town and all it had to offer, she didn't show it. And getting her to part with her spear nearly caused a minor war at the Chong residence.

Benny was surprised to see that Nix and Lilah were bonding, and the two girls spent hours sitting apart from Benny and Chong, heads bowed together, talking. Nix never told him what they talked about.

One night, while walking back from Chong's, Benny said, "I'm trying to see things from her perspective. She must not know where she belongs."

"She belongs with us," said Nix.

"Even if we leave? Wouldn't she be better off staying here with the Chongs or the Kirsches?"

Nix shook her head. "Would they understand what she's been through, Benny?"

"Do we? Nix . . . we don't even really *know* her."

She shrugged and brushed a curly strand of red hair from her face. "Maybe not. But we know her better than anyone else."

They went home. Nix slept in Benny's room; Benny camped out on the couch. The couch was uncomfortable, but he really didn't care.

Morgie came to see them, but he was weak and fragile. Even with a head injury, he was able to see how things were between Benny and Nix. Benny braced himself for Morgie to be angry, but he too had been changed by what had happened. He nodded thoughtfully, and went home.

It all seemed like a thousand years ago. Gameland was still out there, and now they knew where. However, if Benny thought that hearing Lilah's story would change the people in town or spark them to action, he was disappointed. They were shocked, they were sympathetic . . . but they said that it was too far away. That it wasn't their concern. That it was too dangerous to mount a raid on it. After a couple of days they even stopped talking about it.

"It's just like everything beyond the fence," Benny complained. "They act like it's all happening on a different planet."

"To them it is," said Nix. "My mom told them about the first Gameland, and they didn't do anything then, either."

Nothing would be done, and that was the ugliest truth.

But when he said this to Tom, his brother's eyes became distant, and he changed the subject. Each day, however, he spent at least an hour in his workroom making bullets, and he had maps pinned to the walls.

Benny, Nix, and Tom spent every evening talking about things. Not about the fight or the dreadful things each of them had been forced to do. No. They talked about the jumbo jet. Tom had seen it too. He'd watched it fly out of the east and then turn slowly over the mountains and fly back.

"What do you think is out there?" Benny asked Nix one night after Tom went to bed. "Out where the jet went?"

"I don't know. It won't be my islands," she said. "It'll be something . . . different. Something that isn't *here*."

"*Here* isn't that bad. Not now that Charlie's gone."

Her green eyes were full of shadows. "'Here,' Benny, they accept that Gameland exists and won't do anything about it." She shook her head. "Here isn't enough, Benny. Not for me. Not anymore."

Later, when Benny told Tom that Nix wanted to go find where the jet came from, Benny had expected Tom to scoff at the idea. Tom hadn't. Next morning there was a stack of maps on the kitchen table. There was one for every state.

On the fifteenth day since the camp, Tom told Benny that he had one more closure job he had to do. "I want you to go with me."

Benny sighed.

"I don't know if I can," he said.

Tom sat down with him at the table. "Please," he said. "Just this last one, and then I'm done. I . . . can't do it alone."

Benny studied his brother for a long time and then nodded.

"Okay," he said. "But after this, I'm done, too."

Nix went with them, but only for the first part of the trip. She was harder than before, less apt to smile, which Benny understood. Much of her softness was gone, and Benny hoped that with time it would return. The toughness, he knew, would remain. Nix spent hours writing in her book of zombie lore. She practiced with Benny every day with the wooden swords. When she trained, her beautiful face was set and grim, and Benny was sure that each time she swung the sword, she wasn't seeing him. She was seeing the faces of the men who would have put her into a pit with zoms.

"Give her time," Tom said one day after practice.

"I plan on it," said Benny, and Tom smiled. "All the time she needs."

They left Mountainside on a gray morning in late September. Tom led the way, often walking alone as a way of dealing with his own sadness and loss. Benny and Nix followed behind, vigilant of the world around them and the threats it offered, but feeling safe and strong in each other's company. Even if neither of them was ready to say so.

They found the way station where Brother David and the two young women lived. Over lunch Benny and Tom and Nix told their story. The monk and the girls exchanged long looks, their faces sometimes sad at the news of pain and death, and sometimes hopeful as they considered a future without Charlie Pink-eye and the Motor City Hammer.

"Nix," Benny said, "do you mind staying here?"

"No," she said. "Tom told me that you have a job to do."

"He told you?"

She gave him a funny look. Deep and penetrating. "He told me everything, Benny. I understand about what he does . . . what you do. About the family business. About the need for closure."

Benny touched her face. "Nix, I—"

"Benny Imura," she said with a rare flicker of a smile on her mouth, "if you are going to say something like 'I love you' and you choose here, in a way station out in the Rot and Ruin to do it, so help me, I will kick your ass."

There was a fragile quality about her smile and a glimmer of the old Nix woven into the complexity of this new Nix. He loved both versions, but he valued his butt and had no doubts that she could kick it completely and with great enthusiasm.

"As if I would say something so stupid," he said.

She cocked an eyebrow at him.

"Can I at least ask for a kiss without being stomped and humiliated?"

He could, and she proved it.

Benny and Tom left at noon. They walked for several hours, rarely talking. The sun broke through the clouds as they cut through a grove of trees that were heavy with apples. Tom picked a few, and they ate them and still said almost nothing until they reached the wrought-iron gate of a community that was embowered by a high red-brick wall. A sign over the gate read: SUNSET HOLLOW.

Outside of the gate there was trash and old bones and a few burned shells of cars. The outer walls were pocked with bullet scars. To the right of the gate someone had used white paint to write: "This Area Cleared. Keep Gates Closed. Keep Out." Below that were the initials TI.

Benny pointed. "You wrote that?"

"Years ago," Tom said.

The gates were closed, and a thick chain had been threaded through the bars and locked with a heavy padlock. The chain and the lock looked new and gleamed with oil.

"What is this place?" Benny asked.

Tom tucked his hands into his back pockets and looked up at the sign. "This is what they used to call a gated community. The gates were supposed to keep unwanted people out and keep the people inside safe."

"Did it work? I mean . . . during First Night?"

"No."

"Did all the people die?"

"Most of them. A few got away."

"Why is it locked?"

"For the same reason as always," Tom said. He blew out his cheeks and dug into his right front jeans pocket for a key. He showed it to Benny and then opened the lock, pushed the gates open, and then restrung the chain and clicked the lock closed with the keyhole on the inside now.

They walked along the road. The houses were all weather damaged, and the streets were pasted with the dusty remnants of fourteen years of falling leaves. Every garden was overgrown, but there were no zombies in them. Some of the doors had crosses nailed to them, around which hung withered garlands of flowers.

"Your job's here?" Benny asked.

"Yes," said Tom. His voice was soft and distant.

"Is it like the other one? Like Harold Simmons?"

"Sort of."

"That was . . . hard," said Benny.

"Yes, it was."

"Tom . . . I never wanted this. I mean, we all played games. Y'know, Kill the Zoms. Stuff like that. But . . . this isn't how I imagined it."

"Kiddo, if you were capable of imagining *this* without having seen it, I'd be scared for you. Maybe scared *of* you."

Benny shook his head. "Doing this over and over again would drive me crazy. How do you do it?"

Tom turned to him as if that was the question he'd been waiting for all day. "It keeps me sane," he said. "Do you understand?"

Benny thought about it for a long moment. Birds sang in the trees and the cicadas buzzed continually. "Is it because you knew what the world was before?"

Tom nodded.

"Is it because if you didn't do it . . . then maybe no one would?"

Tom nodded again.

"It must be lonely."

"It is." Tom glanced at him. "But I always hoped you'd want to join me. To help me do what I do."

"I . . . don't know if I can."

"That's always going to be your choice. If you can, you can. If you can't, then believe me, I'll understand. It takes a lot out of you to do this. And it takes a lot out of you to know that the bounty hunters are out there, doing what they do."

"How come none of them ever came here?"

"They did. Once."

"What happened?"

Tom shrugged.

"What happened?" Benny asked again.

"I was here when they came. Pure chance."

Benny looked at him. "You . . . killed them," he said. "Didn't you?"

Tom walked a dozen steps before he said, "Not all of them." A half dozen steps later he added, "I let one of them go."

"That was Charlie, wasn't it? That's what he was talking about."

"Yes."

"Why did you let him go?"

"To spread the word," Tom said. "To let the other bounty hunters know that this place was off-limits."

"And they listened? The bounty hunters?"

Tom smiled. It wasn't boastful or malicious. It was a thin, cold knife-blade of a smile that was there and gone. "Sometimes you have to go to some pretty extreme lengths to make a point and to make it stick. Otherwise you find yourself having to make the same point over and over again."

Benny stared at him. "How many were there?"

"Ten."

"And you let one go."

"Yes."

"And you killed nine of them?"

"Yes." The late afternoon sunlight slanting through the trees threw dappled light on the road and painted the sides of all of the houses to their left with purple shadows. A red fox and three kits scampered across the street ahead of them. "I let the wrong one go."

"How could you have known? With one of the other guys, even Vin or Joey . . . It might not have been any different."

"Maybe. But I don't get to play that game. I made a choice, and a lot of people suffered because of it."

"Tom . . . when you made that choice, you'd already beaten Charlie, right?"

"Yes. He was hurt and disarmed."

"Then you did the right thing, I think. You can't know the future. You believed him when he said that he'd change his ways, right?"

Tom nodded.

Benny said, "I would have done the same thing, Tom, because I don't ever want to live in a world where something like mercy . . . or maybe it's compassion . . . is the *wrong* choice. Just 'cause Charlie said you were wrong to let him live, it doesn't make him right."

Tom didn't answer, but he nodded and gave his brother a small, sad smile. They stood there, taking each other's measure perhaps for the very first time. Taking each other's measure and getting the right values.

Tom pointed, and Benny turned toward the front door of a house with peach trees growing wild in the yard. "This is it."

"There's a zombie in there?"

"Yes," Tom said. "There are two."

"We have to tie them up?"

"No. That's already been done. Years ago. Nearly every house here has a dead person in it. Some have already been quieted, the rest wait for family members to reach out and want it done."

"I know this sounds gross, but why don't you just go house to house and do it to every one of them? You know . . . *quiet* them. Release them."

"Because a lot of the people here have family living in our town. It takes a while, but people usually get to the point where they want someone to go and do this the way I do it rather than as part of a general sweep. With respect, with words read to their dead family, and then let the dead rest in their own homes. Closure isn't closure until someone's ready to close the door. Do you understand what I mean?"

Benny nodded.

"Do you have a picture of the . . . um . . . people in there? So we know who they are? So we can make sure."

"There are pictures inside. Besides . . . I know the names of everyone in Sunset Hollow. I come here a lot. I was the one who went house to house and tied the dead up. Some monks helped, but I knew everyone here." Tom walked to the front door. "Are you ready?"

Benny looked at Tom and then at the door.

"You want me to do this, don't you?"

Tom looked sad. "I want *us* to do it."

"If I do my part . . . then I'll be like you. I'll be doing this kind of thing."

"Yes."

"Forever?"

"I don't know, Benny. I told you that I think I'm done with this too. But I don't know if that's true. Besides, we don't know the future, remember?"

"What if I can't?"

"If you can't, I'll do it. Then we go to the way station for tonight and head home in the morning. After that . . . maybe you and Nix and I will talk about going east. That jet had to land somewhere."

"Tom, I know I've asked this already, but why don't people from town come out to places like this and just take them back? We're so much stronger than the zoms. This place is protected. Why don't we take *everything* back?"

Tom shook his head. "I ask myself that every day. They think they're safe in town."

"That's not true. Ask Mr. Sacchetto. Ask Nix's mom. It's stupid."

"Yes," Tom said, "it surely is."

He turned the doorknob and opened the door. "Are you coming?"

Benny came as far as the front step. "It's not safe in there, either, is it?"

"It's not safe anywhere, Benny. Not unless your generation makes it safe. My generation gave up trying."

They were both aware in that moment they were having a different discussion than the words they exchanged.

The brothers went into the house.

Tom led the way down a hall and into a spacious living room that had once been light and airy. Now it was pale and filled with dust. The wallpaper had faded, and there were animal tracks on the floor. There was a cold fireplace and a mantel filled with picture frames. The pictures were of a family. Mother and father. A smiling son in a uniform. A baby in a blue blanket. Two women who might have been twin sisters. Brothers and cousins and grandparents. Everyone was smiling. Benny stood looking at the pictures for a long time and then reached up and took one down. A wedding picture.

"Where are they?" he asked softly.

"In here," said Tom.

Still holding the picture, Benny followed Tom through a dining room and into a kitchen. The windows were open and the yard was filled with trees. Two straight-backed chairs sat in front of the window and in the chairs were two withered zombies. Both of them turned their heads toward the sound of footsteps. Their jaws were tied shut with silken cord. The man was dressed in the tatters of an old blue police uniform; the woman wore a tailored frilly white party dress whose sleeves were dark with blood that had dried years ago. Benny came around front and looked from them to the wedding picture and back again.

"It's hard to tell."

"Not when you get used to it," said Tom. "The shape of the ears, the height of the cheekbones, the angle of the jaw, the distance between the nose and upper lip. Those things won't change even after years."

"I don't know if I can do this," Benny said again.

"That's up to you." Tom took his knife from his boot. "I'll quiet one, and you can quiet the other. If you're ready. If you can."

Tom went to stand behind the man. He gently pushed the zombie's head forward and placed the tip of the knife at the base of his skull, doing everything slowly, reminding Benny of how it had to be done.

"Aren't you going to say anything?" said Benny.

"I've already said it," said Tom. "A thousand times. I waited, because I knew that you might want to say something."

"I didn't know them," said Benny. "Not like I thought. . . ."

A tear fell from Tom's eye onto the back of the struggling zombie's neck.

He plunged the blade and the struggles stopped. Just like that.

Tom hung his head for a moment as a sob broke in his chest. "I'm sorry," he said, and then, "Be at peace."

He sniffed and held the knife out to Benny.

"I can't!" Benny said, backing away. "Jesus Christ, I *can't*!"

Tom stood there, tears rolling down his cheeks, holding the knife out. He didn't say a word.

"God . . . please don't make me do this," said Benny.

Tom shook his head.

"Please, Tom."

Tom lowered the knife.

The female zombie threw her weight against the cords and uttered a shrill moan that was like a dagger in Benny's mind. He covered his ears and turned away. He dropped into a crouch, face tucked into the corner between the back door and the wall, shaking his head.

Tom stood where he was.

It took Benny a long, long time. He stopped shaking his head and leaned his forehead against the wood. The zombie in the chair kept moaning. Benny turned and dropped onto his knees. He dragged a forearm under his nose and sniffed.

"She'll be like that forever, won't she?"

Tom said nothing.

"Yes," said Benny, answering his own question. "Yes."

He climbed slowly to his feet.

"Okay," he said, and held out his hand. His hand and arm trembled. Tom's trembled too as he handed over the knife.

Benny stood behind the zombie, and it took six or seven tries before he could bring himself to touch her. Eventually he managed it. Tom guided him, touching the spot where the knife had to go. Benny put the tip of the knife in place.

"When you do it," said Tom, "do it quick."

"Can they feel pain?"

"I don't know. But you can. I can. Do it quick."

Benny closed his eyes and the old image was there. The white blouse, the red sleeves. Not red cloth. Blood. It had been blood. He took a ragged breath and said, "I love you, Mom."

He did it quick.

And it was over.

He dropped the knife, and Tom gathered him up, and they sank down to their knees together on the kitchen floor, crying so loud that it threatened to break the world. In the chairs the two dead people sat slumped, their heads tilted toward each other, their withered mouths silent.

The sun was tumbling behind the edge of the mountain by the time they left the house. Together they'd dug graves in the backyard. Tom locked up the house and then relocked the chain on the front gate. Side by side they walked back the way they came.

"On First Night," Benny began, "all those years ago. I remember Mom with red sleeves. I remember her screaming. I remember you taking me and running. I looked back and saw Dad behind her."

"Yes," said Tom. "All of that happened."

"The red sleeves . . . she'd already been bitten. By Dad. Hadn't she?"

Tom's voice was a ghost. "Yes. She'd seen what happened when Dad got bitten. She was smart, she understood. She wanted us safe. Maybe she could already feel the change inside. The hunger. I don't know. But she begged me to take you, to save you. To run." He buried his face in his hands, and his whole body trembled with that terrible memory and all the years of grief.

"I . . . You saved me."

Tom said nothing.

"And all these years you knew that I hated you. That I thought you were a coward. Why didn't you ever *tell* me?"

Tom raised his head and dragged a forearm across his eyes. "By the time you were old enough to be told, you already believed your version of it. Tell me, Ben, if I had told you the truth, would you have believed me? If we had never come out here, would you have believed me?"

Benny slowly shook his head.

"So I waited."

"God . . . that must have been hard."

Tom shrugged. "I knew that one day we'd come here. But when we got here . . . you knew, didn't you? When did you figure it out?"

Benny sniffed and wiped his eyes. "Since . . . since we got back from Harold Simmons's house. When I was sitting on the back porch all that time. I figured it out. I just didn't want it to be the truth. I didn't ever want to come here."

Tom nodded. "Neither did I. But you do understand that we *had* to, right?"

"Yes," whispered Benny. "Because we needed closure, too."

Benny still held the knife. He'd cleaned the blade, but he gripped the ribbed handle with a tight fist.

"Can I keep this?" Benny asked, holding out the knife.

"Why?" his brother asked.

Benny's eyes were puffy from crying, but they were dry. "I guess I'll need it," he said.

Tom stopped and studied him for a long time. His smile was sad, but his eyes were filled with love. And with pride. He removed the boot sheath and handed it to Benny, who clipped it inside his own boot.

"Come on," he said. "Let's go back to the way station. Nix will be waiting."

"I don't think Mountainside is home anymore. Not for me, and definitely not for Nix."

"We could go east," said Tom. "Find out what's on the other side of the Ruin."

"The jet," Benny said.

"The jet," Tom agreed.

Benny Imura looked back at the wrought-iron gates and at the words painted outside. He nodded to himself.

Together they walked through the gathering twilight back to the way station where Nix would be waiting for them. They walked side by side in the vast silence of the Rot and Ruin.

THE
BOUNTY HUNTERS
No
113
TOM IMURA
Tom, a resident of Mountainside, is a first-
class bounty hunter who prefers to be called
a "closure specialist." He's known through-
out the Rot & Ruin for his quiet manner and
lightning fast sword.
FAMOUS ZOMS
No
66
THE
BRIDE OF COLDWATER
SPRING
Have you seen a woman in a bloodstained
wedding dress roaming the downlands?
Beware—that's the infamous Bride of Cold-
water Spring, one of the most active and
dangerous zoms in the Ruin. The Bride is
known to have taken down six bounty hunters
and more than a dozen way-station monks.

CHASE CARD
No 3
THE LOST GIRL
Legends persist about a beautiful girl living wild and alone in the Rot & Ruin. Many have tried to find her, but none have. And some never returned. Who is . . . the Lost Girl?

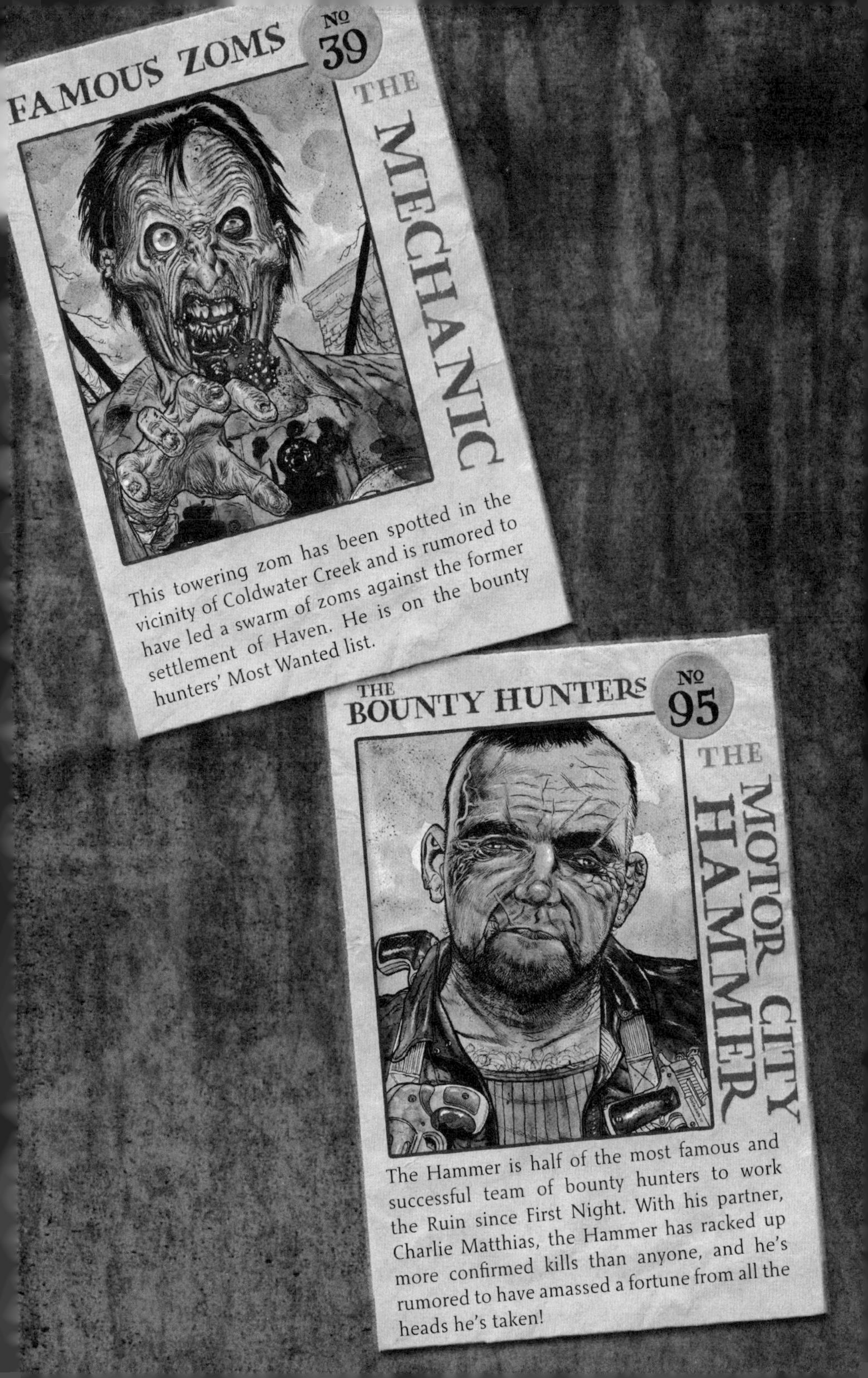

FAMOUS ZOMS

No 39

THE MECHANIC

This towering zom has been spotted in the vicinity of Coldwater Creek and is rumored to have led a swarm of zoms against the former settlement of Haven. He is on the bounty hunters' Most Wanted list.

The Hammer is half of the most famous and successful team of bounty hunters to work the Ruin since First Night. With his partner, Charlie Matthias, the Hammer has racked up more confirmed kills than anyone, and he's rumored to have amassed a fortune from all the heads he's taken!

DON'T MISS THE NEXT EXCITING CHAPTER IN THE WORLD AFTER FIRST NIGHT!

SIX MONTHS HAVE PASSED SINCE THE TERRIFYING BATTLE with Charlie Pink-eye and the Motor City Hammer in the zombie-infested mountains of the Rot and Ruin. It's also been six months since Benny Imura and Nix Riley saw something in the air that changed their lives. Now, after months of rigorous training with Benny's zombie-hunter brother, Tom, Benny and Nix are ready to leave their home forever and search for a better future. Lilah the Lost Girl and Benny's best friend, Lou Chong, are going with them. Sounds easy. Sounds wonderful. Except that everything that can go wrong does. In the great Rot and Ruin everything wants to kill you. Everything. . . . And not everyone in Benny's small band of travelers will make it out alive.

BENNY IMURA WAS APPALLED TO LEARN THAT THE APOCALYPSE CAME WITH HOMEWORK.

"Why do we have to study this stuff?" he demanded. "We already know what happened. People started turning into zoms, the zoms ate just about everyone, everyone who dies becomes a zom, so the moral of this tale is: Try not to die."

Across the kitchen table, his brother, Tom, stared at him with narrowed eyes. "Are you deliberately trying to be an idiot, or is it a natural gift?"

"I'm serious. We know what happened."

"Really? Then how come you spent most of last summer complaining that no one my age tells anyone your age the truth about the living dead?"

"Telling us is one thing. Essays and pop quizzes are a whole different thing."

"Because heaven forbid you should have to remember anything we told you."

Benny raised his eyebrows mysteriously and tapped his temple. "I have it all right here in the vast storehouse of knowledge that is me."

"Okay, boy genius, then what started the plague?"

"Easy one," Benny said. "Nobody knows."

"What are the leading theories?"

Benny jabbed his fork into a big piece of buttered yam, shoved it into his mouth, and chewed noisily as he spoke. It was a move calculated to annoy Tom in three separate ways. Tom hated when he spoke with his mouth full. He hated it when Benny chewed with his mouth open. And it would muffle most of what he said, which meant that Tom had to pay even more attention to the yam-packed mouth from which the muffled words came.

"Radiation, virus, bioweapon, toxic waste, solar flares, act of God."

He rattled it off so there was no break between the words. Also annoying, and worth at least another point on Benny's personal Annoy-O-Meter.

Tom sipped his tea and said nothing, but he gave Benny the *look*.

Benny sighed and swallowed. "Okay," he said, "at first people thought it was radiation from a satellite."

"Space probe," corrected Tom.

"Whatever. But that doesn't make sense, because one satellite—"

"Space probe."

"—wouldn't carry enough radioactive material to spread over the entire world."

"We think."

"Sure," conceded Benny, "but in science class they told us even if one of the old nuclear power plants did a whatchama-callit, there—"

"Meltdown."

"—wouldn't be enough radiation to cover the entire planet even though it has more radioactive materials than a satellite."

Tom sighed. Benny smiled.

"What conclusion can you draw from that?"

"The world wasn't destroyed by radioactive alien space zombies."

"*Probably* wasn't destroyed by radioactive alien space zombies," Tom corrected. "How about a virus?"

Benny cut a piece of chicken and ate it. Tom was a great cook, and this was one of his better meals. Yams, broiled chicken with mushrooms and almonds, and rich green kale. A loaf of steaming bread made from the last of the winter wheat sat near where Benny could plunder it.

"Chong's dad says that a virus needs a living host, and zoms aren't alive. He said that maybe bacteria or a fungus was sustaining the virus."

"Do you know what a bacterium is?"

"Sure . . . it's a bug thingy that makes you sick."

"God, I love it when you display the depth of your knowledge. It makes me proud to be your brother."

"Kiss my—"

"Language."

They grinned at each other.

It had been nearly seven months since Benny's lifelong hatred and distrust of Tom had transformed into affection and respect. That process had started last summer, shortly after Benny's fifteenth birthday. On some level Benny knew that he loved Tom, but since Tom was his brother and this was still the real world, the chances of Benny ever using that *L* word were somewhere between "no way" and "get out of my way I'm going to throw up."

Not that Benny was afraid of the *L* word when it came to someone better suited for it, namely the fiercely red-haired queen of freckles, Nix Riley. Benny would like very much to toss that word up for her to consider, but he had yet to do so. Shortly after the big fight, when Benny had tentatively tried to bring up the subject, Nix had threatened bodily harm if he said that word. Benny had zipped his mouth shut, understanding completely why the moment had been so inappropriate.

Charlie Pink-eye Matthias and the Motor City Hammer had murdered Nix's mother, and the insane events of the days that followed hadn't allowed Nix to properly react. Or grieve.

Those days had been the weirdest mix of absolute horror, black despair, and soaring happiness. The emotions he'd felt didn't seem to even belong in the same world, let alone the same person.

Benny gave Nix her time for grief, and he grieved too. Mrs. Riley had been a great lady. Sweet, funny, kind, and always a little sad. Like everyone else in Mountainside, Jessie Riley had suffered terrible losses during First Night. Her husband, her two sons.

"Everyone lost someone," Chong often reminded him. Even though they'd been toddlers, Benny and Chong were the only ones among their friends to remember that night. Chong said that it was all a blur of screams and shouts, but Benny remembered it with a peculiar clarity. His mother handing him through a first-floor window to Tom—who was a twenty-year-old cadet at the police academy—and then the pale, shambling thing that had been Dad coming out of the shadows and pulling Mom away. Then Tom running away, his terrified heartbeat hammering like a drum inside the chest to which he held a squirming, screaming Benny.

Until last year Benny had remembered that First Night in a twisted way. All his life he had believed that Tom had simply run away. That he had not tried to help Mom. That he was a coward.

Now Benny knew different. Now he knew what kind of torment Tom had suffered to save him. He also knew that when Mom had handed him through the window to Tom, she had already been bitten. She was already lost. Tom had done the only thing he could have done. He ran, and in running had given value to Mom's sacrifice, and that had saved them both.

Now Benny was fifteen and a half, and First Night was a million years ago.

This world was no longer that world. On First Night the old world had died. As the dead rose, the living perished. Cities were incinerated by the military in a futile attempt to stop the growing armies of the dead. The electromagnetic pulses from the nukes fried all electronics. The machines went silent, and soon, so did the whole country. Now everything east of the small town of Mountainside was the great Rot and Ruin. A few other towns littered the foothills of the Sierra Nevada north and south of Benny's home, but the rest of the old world had been consumed.

Or . . . had it?

During that adventure in the mountains east of town, Benny and Nix had seen something that to them was as inexplicable and potentially world-changing as the zombie plague had been. Flying high, high above them had been a thing Benny had only ever read about in old books.

A jet.

A sleek jumbo jet that flew out of the east, banked in a slow circle around the mountains, and then headed back the way it had come. Now Benny and Nix were counting down the days until they left Mountainside to find where the jet had come from. The calendar pinned to the wall by the back door had black Xs over the first ten days of this month. There were seven unmarked days, and then a big red circle around the following Saturday. April 17, one week from today. The words ROAD TRIP were written in block letters below the date.

Tom thought that the jet was flying in the general direction of Yosemite National Park, which was due east of the town. Benny and Nix had begged Tom for this trip for months, but as the day approached, Benny wasn't so sure he still wanted to go. It was just that Nix was absolutely determined.

"Earth to Benny Imura."

Benny blinked and heard as an after-echo the sound of Tom snapping his fingers.

"Huh?"

"Jeez . . . what planet were you orbiting?"

"Oh . . . just kind of drifted there."

"Nix or the jet?"

"Little of both."

"Must have been more about the jet," Tom said. "There was less drool."

"You are very nearly funny," said Benny. He looked down at his plate and was mildly surprised that it was empty.

"Yes," said Tom, "you were eating on autopilot. It was fascinating to watch."

There was a knock on the door. Benny shot to his feet and crossed the kitchen to the back door. He was smiling as he undid the locks.

"That's got to be Nix," he said as he pulled it open. "Hey, sweetie . . ."

Morgie Mitchell and Lou Chong stood on the back porch.

"Um," said Chong, "hello to you, too, sugar lumps."